Junkyard Leopard

Oliver Brackenbury

Copyright © 2015 Oliver Brackenbury

All rights reserved.

ISBN: 1-62827-989-3
ISBN-13: 978-1-62827-989-4

This book is a work of fiction. Names, characters, places, and incidents are products of this author's imagination or are used fictitiously. Any resemblance to actual events or locales or persons living or dead is entirely coincidental.

Published by Bad Day Books, an imprint of
Assent Publishing

DEDICATION

To HSBC.

Your laundering $800 million worth of drug money for cartels and terrorists—while not having any of your management or employees go to jail—was very inspiring.

1. ATTN

*B*ING

Burnished bronze elevator doors opened to reveal two slim men in Brooks Brothers latest. Each looking down at their phones, the pair stepped out in unison to enter the small reception area of Byrne Investments. Despite it being a large firm, the two Germans hired to design the forty-second floor offices took an approach of quality over quantity. Small rooms containing expertly chosen decorations, luxurious carpeting, and carefully placed lighting that had a way of flattering your features, no matter which angle you were facing, filled the floor.

The reception area fit the aesthetic perfectly. Two Wassily chairs still bearing their production run numbers in stark white against black, #006 and #007, were set at forty-five degree angles to a white marble coffee table bearing the Byrne Investments logo along its surface in Yves Klein Blue.

Not that the two businessmen were interested in any of this. The one on the right was reading an article on the *Economist* website about the end of the long tail in music sales while the other was seeing what *Gawker* had to say about an errant nipple finding freedom at the Golden Globes the previous evening. He sniffed at the all-too-obvious headline as the front desk clerk, Evan, buzzed them through the frosted glass doors that opened into the rest of Byrne

Investments.

Neither man interacted with Evan in the slightest, but he was okay with that. Evan was still new to this job, an odd mix of secretary and security guard his company had only recently begun offering to higher-end clients. The idea of two roles in one person greatly appealed to the designers Byrne Investments hired, so here he sat in front of a brand new tablet, a stun gun on one hip, and a company phone on the other.

Pushing back the fringe of a haircut he wasn't sure about, Evan sighed while contemplating going home tonight to the other half of a relationship he was only marginally more confident in. He'd said yes to her moving in just two days ago and today she was bringing over gym bags filled with her thrift store treasures, clothes that had been interesting to him at first.

BA-DEE-DEEP

A text from her. Was he was still as excited as she was about their relationship moving to the next level? Being at work bought him a few minutes but he knew she'd want an answer soon or insecurity would set in, a surefire prelude to interrogating him about his feelings. Somewhat ironically, one of the reasons Evan was becoming less certain about the relationship had to do with how she so often reinforced his negative stereotypes about women. He didn't like that she did that.

Shit. Daydreaming about the problem of the text meant using up valuable reply composition time. Maybe an emoji? No, too juvenile and open to interpretation. A nice, safe "Yeah!" would work but then he'd come home tonight to see her stuff in his bedroom and it would only get harder to admit he'd not so much liked the idea of her moving in as the idea of a girl liking him enough to want to do so. "Yes," he'd said to that feeling. "Yes, I like that you are into me that much," would have been the truly honest thing to say to her.

Christ. That was at least four minutes of daydreaming about the problem and still no text reply.

BA-DEE-DEEP

Crap. Evan didn't log the visitors into the system, he was so distracted by the text.

BING

"Hey, remember when serial killers were a thing?"

Evan looked up from his laptop into the expensively landscaped teeth of Gerald Byrne himself, the CEO and top man at this office. Evan wasn't sure how to reply and he felt sheepish for not noticing the elevator. Luckily for him, Gerald didn't need anyone else to talk in order to enjoy a conversation.

"It's like..." Gerald thought out loud. "Ever since this whole shitty century got rolling, it's all been about terrorism or random shootings. Like, was there a memo sent out to the crazies? Attention madmen! From now on, it's all just one big explosion of violence. Don't create a nice narrative with spaced out, individual killings. Don't establish a theme, don't build a pattern. Just get a gun, a blank look on your face, and then show up to kill as many people as you can for as vague a reason as possible."

Gerald added to this little bit of performance by adjusting his ivory cufflinks while approximating a thoughtful expression.

"I know how it sounds, but I'm just being honest about how news is only entertainment."

As with most things that Gerald tried to put out there as slightly edgy or profound, it was as dull and uninspired as the look in Evan's eyes when he stared up at a man who was very much his master.

BA-DEE-DEEP

BA-DEE-DEEP

BA-DEE-DEEP

"Huh, sounds like you've got someone who really wants your attention there!"

Evan nodded in reply. A quick glance revealed three innocent questions about what goes where in the apartment, none of them the question she actually wanted an answer to.

"It's alright, go ahead and answer whomever it is. I know it's against the rules, but really." Gerald made an exaggerated look around the tiny lobby. "It's not like we've got a crowd here and you're hardly going to miss someone coming in."

Gerald finished with a conspiratorial wink as if he'd given Evan permission to flip off one of the wealthy drug dealers from Guinea-Bissau who came there twice a year to get their money laundered. A sterling silver bracelet on his left wrist gleamed from underneath the cuff as Gerald glanced at his phone, before Aiden Patent Oxfords by Salvatore Ferragamo carried the young CEO briskly past Evan and into the office.

As this happened, a whiff of some expensive cologne Evan couldn't name or afford wafted off Gerald and caught the young secre-curity guard—a terrible job title but the one Avalanche Security had given him—right up each nostril. It was actually kind of nice, making Evan feel like he had his nose in a glass holding some warm, well-distilled brandy.

BA-DEE-DEEP

BING

Anxious about the whole text reply countdown and all that was attached to it, Evan chose to look at his phone instead of the elevator door. He managed to type, *I think we need to talk*, and was going to press send before being interrupted by the impact of an eight-pound sledgehammer colliding with his temple.

The young man was catapulted out of his chair and onto the carpet. His survival instinct took a similarly swift path, going straight past fight, past flight, and arriving at a state not unlike that of an airline pilot who discovers none of the controls are working anymore.

Horrified to still be alive, Evan was unable to process the soft thump of the sledgehammer dropping to the floor.

An ankle swathed in leopard-print tights crossed his flickering, unfocused vision. Merciful unconsciousness swept over Evan as his own stun gun was set to maximum, then jammed into the freshly exposed portion of his frontal lobe.

The last, lingering wafts of Gerald's cologne were gently swept away by sickly sweet smoke.

2. Mary

Couch. TV. Cereal.
Underwear. Mary. Tuesday night.

Mary's mother would have walked in and told her to stop acting like a woman-child. That was just one of the reasons Mary had recently left home despite not being entirely sure what her long-term plans were. Living in the moment was more her style. Right now, that moment involved shoveling multi-grain Cheerios past her lips while staring at her old television, its slowly dying screen struggling to bring the world into Mary's studio apartment.

A thick, deeply creased pile of denim clothing sat in a pile only a few steps from the front door. Only a step or two closer sat two steel-toed work boots, shucked off after a vigorous day at the junkyard, waiting to be put back on in the morning.

Mary didn't feel like she "got" art, but she knew what she liked and sometimes she brought something home from work to use in the apartment. Once in a while she even made stuff, like the coffee table her feet were currently resting on. Three standing crankshafts formed the legs while the surface was made of seven flattened copper discs, six welded in a ring around the seventh to form a vaguely floral pattern. Heavy gears at the base helped keep the table steady.

"Pfffft, seen it," and *CLICK*, off went the television. Bringing her bowl to the kitchen, Mary noticed the stub of a loyalty card poking out of her discarded work clothes. Warm water fell over her hands as she washed the bowl, clashing with a cold shiver of embarrassment that zipped up and down her body. The card was from one of those coffee places the other guys at Mary's work wouldn't have gone into before she introduced them to it, a trendy place called O'Malley's about three blocks over from the yard.

She'd never have gone into one of those places before she spotted—no, she didn't want to think about that right now.

Mary's laptop had died a few months back and, given her needs, she'd not bothered replacing it since her phone could pretty much do it all. Sliding back the screen protector on the obscene, military-grade case that kept her phone safe at work, Mary brought up an online dating site app, got annoyed, brought up an online animal adoption app, and then set to browsing a series of black Labradors while walking over to her bed.

"You guys are adorable but I don't want to fuck any of you." She sighed, crawling under the covers.

"Well, a few things, but mostly…" Arnold gave his lawyer the privilege of some direct attention, "I guess I'm wondering if the rumors I've heard are true about what happened at Byrne Investments over at Forty-Seventh Street?"

The sound of the lawyer sharply sucking air through his teeth was definitely something Arnold could have done without.

"Well Arnold, it's hard to say. I know something must have happened because I tried to get a hold of them yesterday by phone, only to hear a recorded message saying they're closed for renovations."

"Hmm, did you get a forwarding number? Or, like, did you just call someone's cell?" Arnold started thinking about how he loved the smoked meat sandwich at that deli. What was its name?

The lawyer busied himself filing the newly signed paperwork in one of his large desk's many drawers, staring silently for a moment at his hands as he did so. "Well, that's where it gets weird. I got an 'I'm away on vacation, please leave a message' message."

"So?"

"So I got that on every phone of every employee at the office and each time it was a computer voice— kind of like that old film critic who lost his jaw—that didn't actually say where they'd gone, when the person was expected to be back, or who to contact instead."

"Ha!" Arnold stopped trying to remember the name of the deli and slapped the desk. "You don't suppose they finally got caught laundering all that Guinea-Bissau drug money and the police actually did something, do you? They'd want to keep that under wraps for sure."

"Well, those guys over at Byrne aren't fond of being in the public eye. I know Gerald himself always says that's what sunk Fannie and Freddie. 'If the public knows your name, they can howl for your blood,' is how he put it to me once."

"Well, there you go…I guess. But—" Arnold's interest started to drift again. Shit, what was the name of that deli?

"No no no, there's more though." Arnold's lawyer may have been

3. SCHWEITZER'S

"Alright Arnold, just sign right there and I should be able to wrap this thing up pretty quickly, provided those greedy sons of bitches play ball."

Signing the paperwork his lawyer slid before him, Arnold sighed and leaned back in his chair, not really in the moment.

"Hey, I know it's stressful but don't worry. I expect us to be able to get a settlement of between twenty and forty million, which isn't bad on top of the bailout we already squeezed from those empty-headed shitstains."

Arnold let his eyes wander around the office, admiring the assortment of golf photos and paraphernalia decorating the walls. He eventually settled on a point directly above and to the left of the lawyer's face, so he could admire the view. Fifty floors up and it was easy to look across the city at the glittering peak of the Dunning-Kruger building. God, what Arnold wouldn't do to have an office there.

"Hello, Arnold? I'm talking about earning you an ungodly amount of money for very little effort. Usually that holds your attention."

"Oh, sorry. I'm...very pleased about this. I think it's really great you and the guys at the firm found a way for us to sue the government for additional funds because they didn't bail us out enough." Arnold kept his eyes where they were. "I am. I am."

"Okay, so what are you daydreaming about?"

comfortable cursing like a lazy standup comedian in front of his top client, but interrupting him was a whole 'nother ballpark. Snagging Arnold's full attention back with this unusual move, the lawyer continued.

"See, I actually had the home number of one of Gerald's little dickheads, Trevor, who likes to have a landline so he can give that to people he wants to make feel close but not actually bring them any closer. Like, 'Oh, hey, here's my home number. I don't give this out much, but you put your tongue in the right passage so here you go.' Then whenever the client tries to reach him he just says he was out of the house."

"Nice." Arnold grinned.

"Yeah, he pulled it on me once. Luckily, I still had the number in my phone so I gave it a try after getting no response from anybody at the office. Amazingly, his fucking wife picked up."

"Uh huh." The yo-yo of Arnold's attention started to pull away again. Something about breasts.

"I barely got my name out before she told me she didn't have anything to say to anyone about anything. I told her I wasn't a journalist, just a friend of Trevor's wondering if, you know, he wanted to go for drinks at Hamilton's later?"

"Uh huh." Back to that damn deli. That deli was tits.

"And she just makes this kind of horrible choking sound with her throat, mumbles something I can't hear, and then hangs up! What the fuck?"

KNOCK KNOCK

Without even looking at the hardwood office door, Arnold's lawyer raised his voice slightly, "Amanda, unless that's Gerald Byrne or his father or a Steiger sister, take a message. Okay?"

KNOCK KNOCK

"Man," Arnold half-whispered. "What is up with your secretary's knock? She pounding on the door with her dick?"

KNOCK KNOCK

"Seriously, no way is her hand making that kind of a sound."

Arnold opined.

"Jesus fuck," the lawyer muttered. "You ask for at least eight years' experience on their CV and this is what you get?"

KNOCK KN-

"Alright, come in!"

All thoughts of tits, deli sandwiches, and the Dunning-Kruger building vanished from Arnold's mind and were replaced by what he saw come through the doorway at top speed: a figure whose entire head and body was covered in leopard-print Lycra. Worn over this were a short, shaggy fur coat, left open, and a belt made out of differing sized, white leather squares.

Under normal circumstances Arnold might have tried to read what the letters on the belt spelled out but this unexpected figure was quickly crossing the short distance from the door to his swivel chair. Right now he was more concerned with the twenty ounces of steel swinging toward his skull.

Three fingers were able to get between the head of the claw hammer and Arnold's forehead, only to be broken and pressed backwards along a new indentation. Before blood could even begin to flow from the wound, the hammer returned to push a mangled index finger's tip directly into the part of Arnold's brain that had been holding out on him with the name of that deli.

Leaving the hammer to keep the index finger company in its new home, the intruder grabbed a long, dark-blue crowbar from her belt and leapt toward Arnold's lawyer. Starting by shattering the wrist of the hand sent scrambling for a desk drawer snub-nosed pistol, one curved end of the tool quickly made its way into the lawyer's mouth to press against the soft palette. Carbon steel clicked against bleached teeth, silencing the sea of questions swimming in his head. A spotted leg swung over each of the seated, terrified man's shoulders as The Figure sat on his chest—pushing the lawyer back in his chair to lean against the window with that great view of the Dunning-Kruger building. Both hands gripped the crowbar and, muscles writhing beneath Lycra and fur, she put all of her strength into one full-body *heave.*

4. Junkyard

Not owning a car of her own, Mary had to get up early to arrive on time for her shift at the junkyard. Her packed lunch consisted of two Shen-Yung ramens, a banana, and some crackers. As usual, she didn't have any cheese to go with that last item. This was all assembled carefully inside an antique lunchbox she'd found in the trunk of an old Toyota Camry some kitsch collector had to junk. Mary was happy to be using it for its intended purpose, sincerely and without any desire for audience.

It's not like she could really feel the coffee-house loyalty card sitting in the back left pocket of her denim overalls as she crossed the river to work, but she wished she could. She wished it was warm like a friendly tongue or maybe a little cold like the nose on a dog that's just come inside. Maybe it could make her less afraid of going back to where it came from.

Pausing as a bus passed uncomfortably close to the sidewalk, Mary cleared her head and finished the last ten minutes of her hour-long walk to the front gate of the junkyard. It was a bit chilly, so she was glad that the thick denim covered her body and the work gloves insulated her fingers from the cold handle on the gate, as she pulled it open barely enough to slip through.

Having dodged any street harassment on the walk over, Mary didn't find herself needing a quiet moment in the small, heated shack they used as a break room during the late fall and winter. She popped inside, plunked her lunchbox on the windowsill, and looked across the yard to see Vance see her. She acknowledged him with a quick nod and he waved.

Hard dirt caught in the grips on Mary's work boots as she half-jogged over to where her employer stood beside a row of cars that looked fresh to the yard if not to the world. Waiting for her to get closer, Vance took off a glove and ran his fingers through a hairline that wasn't too thin for a man his age.

"Alright Mary, we brought these in on the late shift last night." Vance gestured toward vehicles the latest round of police impounds couldn't sell, or couldn't be bothered to sell. "I want you on trunk-clearing duty to start, okay?" Even though the police had gone through for anything they'd consider evidence, it didn't mean there couldn't still be the odd small animal seeking shelter or loose objects that might damage their crusher.

This had been a common chore of Mary's since she started at the junkyard and, even when she was going through cars like these ones, she almost always found something interesting that could then be either recycled, thrown out or kept—like her lunchbox. Vance called it *trunk*-clearing duty but, of course, this included a thorough checking underneath seats and even rolling beneath the vehicle to see if some nut had hidden a gun or something else by taping it inside a wheel well or behind the bumper.

"You oughta be done with these by lunch, so in the afternoon I'm going to show you again how to safely drain battery acid and all the other fun things we have to dispose of before these cars can be turned into cubes. That'll be with some of those cars we got last Thursday, since I just finished inventory on all their parts."

Mary nodded enthusiastically at this, anxious for more useful skills she could employ to justify her being kept on at the junkyard.

"Hey, Vance!" a nasal voice that could only be her senior co-worker, Carmine, called out from the shack. "You want me to get on those—"

"Come over here! I don't feel like yellin' this morning."

Mary watched him drift over. As Vance once joked to her, Carmine might have been handsome if he had someone else's looks. A couple of years older than her, Carmine was decent enough company even if he couldn't stop talking about the news some days. She had plenty of time to look him over, since his pace in crossing over to where they stood wasn't in danger of being described as speedy by anyone other than narcoleptic snails. However, Mary preferred to look a little bit past him, toward the shack. Was it bigger than her apartment? Carmine arrived and began to open his mouth, but Vance cut him off.

"First things first, you go get us all some coffee. Good stuff, from that new place."

Carmine put one hand on his boss' sloped shoulders.

"Vance, send fuckin' Mary— no offense, Mary—send fuckin' Mary to get the coffee, would you?"

"It's your turn, Carmine, don't be cheap."

"I think you're forgetting, if I don't finish repairing the crusher today, then we're gonna get backed up like all the fuck out."

"Like 'all the fuck out,'" Vance repeated slowly, feigning trouble with the words. It was his way of getting under Carmine's skin as retaliation for being forced to hear such borderline incoherent crudeness.

"Yes." Carmine over enunciated. "That is what it will be like"

"Well, Mary, what do you think?" Vance turned to her.

Mary could feel her guts twisting a bit inside. She wanted to be the helpful new hire but she also, well, um.

"I think it's Carmine's turn," she replied, scratching behind one ear.

"And I know it's Carmine's turn. Come on boychik, if you hurry it up there'll be plenty of time to fix the crusher."

Carmine's sigh of resignation masked Mary's breathing out the air she hadn't realized she'd been holding in for the past minute.

5. KO-WEL-YU

"Listen, Mr. Coalyou—"

"It's pronounced ko-wel-yu, spelled Coelhu but pronounced like I just said it twice now as well as three times earlier."

Rebecca looked across her desk at the thirty-something Mr. Coelhu in slight disbelief. Did Mr. ko-wel-uh go to Arthur Stevenson finishing school? Did his gold watch cost six figures, something that could easily be afforded even before taking into account this year's bonus? Was there a framed picture of him shaking hands with Karl Dunning at a humanitarian charity event? It certainly didn't say so anywhere in the paperwork.

"Yes, well, I've looked over your case three times and I'm afraid your mortgage is currently owned by four parties, none of whom are AFPB."

"I'm aware, but what I want to know is, how can that even be? I purchased my home through your bank and your bank alone." Mr. Coelhu smoothed out his pants legs with shaking hands, taking pains to stay polite. "I didn't have any say in you selling my mortgage on to other parties and I especially don't see how on Earth it can be legal for you to sell the same product four times to as many parties."

Rebecca could tell him but her boss might get mad. Maybe.

Then again it would run along the lines of some great advice Mr. Dunning gave her at the charity event, right before going on stage to let everyone know what he supposedly thought should be done to help all those poor people in Greece trying to recover from the psychological effects of having had to resort to mass cannibalism. Rebecca would have given her left breast—the smaller one—to know what Mr. Dunning actually thought should be done to help those people.

"I tried to address this at my local branch and after a lot of time was wasted—time that cost me money, since you are only open during my own working hours—I was told that the answers to my questions could be provided in person if I drove downtown to come to this very office."

"Yes, that was…" Rebecca paused. "…considerate of the teller and his manager to redirect your line of inquiry to my office."

"I drove downtown, once again having to take a half day off from my job, after waiting seven weeks for an appointment and all you're doing is giving me a more complicated version of the same runaround I got at my local branch. Now what do you have to say to that? What do you have to say to that?"

"To be honest with you, Mr. Coelhu, I'd say the following two things." Rebecca leaned forward and gave him her most authoritarian face, knowing the lighting in the office would cast foreboding shadows across her features. "First of all, I'd say your primary concern should be the fact that your mortgage is underwater. Do you know what that means? It means—"

"Yes." Mr. Coelhu glanced at the art on the wall to his left; he couldn't stand to look at her anymore. "Yes, I know it means I owe more on my damn mortgage than the actual value of the house."

"Hmm." Rebecca continued. "Yes, exactly. That's a very dire situation that needs to be resolved before anything else, wouldn't you agree? The other thing, if I may add…" Rebecca gathered up a little bit of courage she'd been saving for a moment like this, a bit of courage she'd been saving ever since that transformative moment with Karl Dunning. "I'd like you to consider the fact that, of course, if what we've done with your mortgage was illegal then certainly the appropriate government regulatory bodies would have, by now, done their job and sorted out the situation with a suitably large fine, amongst other legal penalties."

Mr. Coelhu let out an anguished cry of frustration, high pitched and long. Tears began to fall from his face. His hands scrunched up the pants legs they'd been smoothing out only a minute or two before. Rebecca kept her eyes on this show while turning her head slightly toward what might have been a second cry, somewhere beyond her office walls.

"Mr. Coelhu, did you…Did you just now—"

"I'm sorry, listen, I'm sorry but you have to understand this is my life and you are…you are not respecting that fact." Mr. Coelhu stood up, doing his best to keep his whole body from trembling. "You have to understand you are ruining me and I am running out of options and…and…and hope…and—"

Jesus, did she hear something again? Couldn't this miserable man hear it over the sound of his big, cathartic moment here? Rebecca could no longer be bothered to even keep her eyes on him, letting them shift toward the same direction her entire body now faced.

"And…and…" Noticing her distraction, Mr. Coelhu gave up all pretence of controlling himself. "I'm not even going to be able to eat meat for the rest of the month." He slammed his hands on the desk, causing stationary to jump. "Because of the time I had to take off from work to see you!"

"Mr. Coelhu, can you not hear that?"

Confused, Mr. Coelhu sniffed back some errant nasal fluids and stopped to listen. The northernmost wall of Rebecca's office vibrated heavily as something thudded against it, causing the distraught homeowner to recoil in the opposite direction. Exasperated, Rebecca stood up and gestured at the wall.

"Oh, I don't know. That?"

Striding around first her desk and then Mr. Coelhu, Rebecca opened her office door and stepped out into the hall, pivoting on her right heel. Her vision was suddenly filled by an uncomfortably close faceless head covered in a style of leopard print she hadn't seen since her mother had last shown up at the office insisting they go cruising for men together.

Leopard Print raised a thick plastic Nalgene bottle with a forward-facing nozzle on the end, her thumb firmly planted over the rubber button on top. The woman's other hand held one of the many AFPB water glasses scattered around the office. With a quick flick of the wrist, she splashed Rebecca's face.

Instinctively, Rebecca brought both hands up and pawed away what she could of the water. She opened her mouth to protest this but as her hands came down, another liquid squirted directly into her eyes and the world vanished to dark gray as abruptly as if someone had flicked the off switch on a computer monitor.

Mr. Coelhu covered his ears at the sound of Rebecca's screams and looked out through the glass frame of her office door to see her fall back onto the ground, clawing at sockets venting acidic smoke toward the ceiling. The leopard-print woman with the thick gloves stood at arm's length from the toxic vapors and emptied the last of a glass of water over Rebecca's stomach, then unscrewed the Nalgene bottle and emptied the rest of its contents in the same place.

Even covering his ears and screaming, Mr. Coelhu couldn't block out the inhuman noises coming from Rebecca. Despite his earlier outburst, and the feelings that inspired it, he would never have wished this upon her.

The banker's body writhed as she lost mass by the second, turning black and dehydrated, producing a wall of toxic gray smoke containing corrosive elements along with several molecules of a stylish men's dress shirt by Hugo Boss. Hearing Mr. Coelhu, the leopard-print figure stepped through the cloud to enter the office the young homeowner wished he'd never entered.

Trying to make himself small, to make himself unnoticeable...oh God to make himself not there...oh Jesus to make himself nonthreatening...oh Lord to make himself young and free and anything else but here, Mr. Coelhu crouched down behind Rebecca's desk, where The Figure quickly found him. She raised one neoprene-clad index finger over an unseen mouth.

Removing her right glove, The Figure then put a hand still covered by Lycra into a pocket which Mr. Coelhu did nothing to defend. She quickly removed and pocketed the battery in a small pouch attached to a belt whose letters might have spelled something out to Coelhu, if he hadn't been too scared to open his eyes.

When Mr. Coelhu finally did open his eyes, The Figure was gone. Openly trembling, almost reveling in the freedom to display his fear, he stood up and collected his battery-less phone. Unsure if he was truly alone now, he still covered his mouth to stifle the high-pitched sound forced out of him by the sight of Rebecca's remains.

Only her gold watch was unscathed, ticking away just as the manufacturer guaranteed it would.

6. Mary's Turn

Mary took small steps crossing the bridge on the way to work that morning. Her muscles were sore but that wasn't it. Some horrible old homeless guy laying on a bench had flashed his crotch at her out from under a moldy, puffy winter coat that hid his aggressively flaccid penis and several competing rashes covering everything from knees to belly button. This hadn't helped, but that wasn't it either.

She even had a decent lunch to look forward to, a low-sodium beef and potato soup she'd actually found time to make a batch of on the weekend. The slight burn on her right index finger was sore, though not anything worth staying home for. Hell, it's not like Vance hadn't shown her how to be careful around all of the different poisonous or flammable crap they had to drain out of a car before it could be recycled.

Crouching down in the shack, Mary leaned against the metal sheet wall and couldn't help remembering how much time she spent hiding in bathroom stalls while feeling this way. Usually it was to get a tiny extra break while interning at McDonalds, where she was before the junkyard, but sometimes in high school it was to—

"Hey, Mary."

"Oh, hey, Carmine."

Carmine placed an immaculately assembled sandwich in the fridge.

It was one in a long series Mary was surprised to learn were actually made by Carmine and not his girlfriend or a sandwich artist. This left Mary wondering about Carmine's priorities since his fancy deli-style sandwiches were such a constant, while brushing his teeth was more of a "sometimes" thing. In the tight confines of the shack, she could smell the results of both routines as he literally spoke down to her.

"I'm not sure how you're going to take the lights off those three old buses while sitting down there."

Mary looked to her left at a calendar Vance had custom printed with different nephews and nieces for each month.

"Well," she focused on a toddler in red overalls as she replied. "You know, just trying not to think about some gross homeless guy that flashed his shit at me this morning."

"Let me guess." Carmine chuckled. "You told him you'd seen better?"

Mary looked back at Carmine, standing up with habitual self-consciousness even though she didn't have any cleavage on display for him to look down.

"You *have* seen better, right? For your sake, I hope you didn't just see the most beautiful dick of your entire life."

Mary chuckled uncomfortably, paused, then turned to leave the shack.

"I better get started on those buses."

"Not just yet. It's your turn today."

The little loyalty card in her back pocket seemed to heat up as something like an unwelcome sugar rush shot through her veins.

"I'll have a large Americano in my thermos, if you please," Carmine said as he fished for change in his right pants pocket. "And get me one of those blueberry muffins—but not the low-fat kind. I gotta make sure I keep all this great junk in my trunk, you know, for my girl."

It was hard to say which dragged more as Mary found her way to the coffee shop, time or her feet. Fall leaves glided down. Mary's hopes rose alongside her anxiety, intertwining to form the DNA helix of a new feeling that had been born inside her only a few days ago during the last trip to the coffee shop.

Her destination sat right at the intersection of fashionable Bohemia, low-income housing and a light industrial estate holding, amongst other things, the junkyard. O'Malley's location had been carefully chosen by its owner. He was a big fan of old Will Eisner comics that would turn a single location into the head of a needle through which the surrounding neighborhood characters' stories would be threaded. Yes, money. Yes, being surrounded by the artifice of his favorite beverage. But mostly he hoped, as a frustrated writer, to create a nexus of nonfiction to soak in like a hot bath.

Mary stepped through heavily stained wooden doors that had been salvaged from a two hundred year old brewery, right before its recent demolition. Immediately, the young junkyard employee found herself in the line-up, over a dozen people between her and what she'd begun to think of as "ground zero".

There were two cashiers; one put nothing more inspiring in her mind than a blank, beige void, the other was himself a light brown but the colors he put into Mary's head were varied, rich and textured. Here he was again, on the morning shift. Here she was again with Carmine's order, Vance's order, and a five-car pile-up of thoughts, emotions, and imagery all sharing space between her ears, behind her eyes. Other than her co-worker and boss' orders, she wouldn't be sharing any of this with anyone.

Jesus, if that short piece of shit keeps taking so long with his busted-ass debit card that's going to fuck up the rhythm of the line, Mary thought, staring holes in the side of the short man's head from her place ten people back. *I don't want to get the other guy. Come on, I can see from here your shit's only $1.50.*

Five people from the cashiers, Mary's hopes swung the other way when it occurred to her she had no idea how to perform the right conversational alchemy to transform a routine exchange of currency for coffee into a non-threatening, inspiring, romantic time with....*Ahmed*, his name tag read. Why hadn't she read it last time? Maybe if this girl with the terrible weave just took a little more time fishing cash out of...nope, it looked like her pink, plastic purse was too well organized for that to happen.

She was only two people from the cashiers when self-loathing joined the pile-up in Mary's head, somehow spurred on by a renewed appreciation of Ahmed's haircut. She'd done nothing special. She wasn't ready. She wasn't the one who got to make that connection with someone. She wouldn't be the person they were singing about in the song coming over the coffee shop speakers. She'd never be one of the happy people in the street, in the photos, in the movies, in the lives of those around her. She wouldn't get this. It wasn't for her.

With the one person in front of her finishing their transaction, it became apparent only an act of God would keep Mary from being served by Ahmed. Mary closed her eyes for a moment and tried to find strength by imagining scenes of the two of them together as a couple. Sex on the regular. Splitting bills at dinner and at home. No more sitting alone in movie theatres. The last image that popped into her head was of the index card sitting in her lunchbox. She hadn't even looked at it, but she remembered writing *DO IT* on the card in thick black marker.

The line moved and so did she.

"Hello, I haven't seen you in a few days," he said.

"Well," Mary told him. "It's my turn."

7. JESUS, TONY

Tony was careful to hold the smoke in his lungs correctly. He'd thought himself immune to its effects for years but Janet had just informed him it was his flawed technique creating an illusion of invulnerability. The two of them were nestled into the cozy, heated seating of his deep maroon, Ferrari 458 Italia. Underlit by faint red LED lights and displays, the two colleagues grinned at each other as Janet took the joint back between her fingers with practiced ease.

This pleasantly smoky cocoon sat on the sidewalk just far enough away from the Dunning-Kruger building for them to feel comfortable doing what they were doing without being spotted by their employer. Not that Mr. Kruger was one to wander the financial district, looking into the tinted windows of classic sports cars. But his paternal approval was so valued by Janet and Tony, they didn't dare take even the slightest risk of losing it.

The cold wind was stronger here; a perfect ten block long tunnel of tall buildings turned the street into an amplifier of aggressive weather patterns. Even beneath the music coming out of the speakers and sub-woofers encircling them in the car's body, the two executives could hear the wind whistling and buffeting their shelter.

"Jesus, Tony." Janet half-coughed, despite herself. "Why do we want to go to this thing? Why do we even want to leave this beautiful friggin' car?"

"Well..." Tony closed his eyes, enjoying the excuse to repeat the following. "Having recently been profiled in that *Top 40 Financial Execs Under 40* article as well as having my beautiful friggin' car featured on—"

"A print magazine. Jesus, Tony."

"Uh, this magazine has over four-hundred thousand subscribers." Tony pointed with a rolled-up copy he'd pulled from under his seat to show her. "And I'm pretty sure Mr. Kruger reads it."

"I'm pretty sure that's a fantasy." Janet carefully put out the remains of the joint, stashing it in a breath-mint tin she'd picked up from some luxury scale approximation of second hand knick-knack stores you'd see in areas she'd never go to without a key-ring Taser.

"So, yes, I know you think you've got some kind of image to maintain but that's not enough to make me want to get out and walk two blocks to some art installation hoo-ha."

"Well." Tony opened his eyes, turning to look at Janet. "I heard Gerald Byrne might show up. I mean, he only sponsored the whole event. He's only the artist's, uh...patron?"

In an alley some three blocks away, a young woman carefully adjusted her tear-away track pants and grimy Notre Dame hoodie. The strap on a found gym bag was shouldered and, with a quiet, involuntary "Wuf." The Figure began to scrape sneakers on sidewalk again.

"Gerald Byrne? Didn't his assistant cancel a meeting with Mr. Kruger just this afternoon?" Janet asked as she blew smoke up against the ceiling of the car, watching it hit and then spread outward. "I mean, you kind of have me here, but I don't see how the guy could have balls enough to cancel a meeting with The Nightmare on Wall Street, yet still come to some art show, even one he sponsored, that's happening so close to the Dunning-Kruger building. It seems disrespectful. Byrne's got more sense, I thought."

"Uh, well, yeah I guess. But shit, he sponsored the damn show." Tony shrugged.

"Hmm, good point." Hearing a beat come through that spoke to her in ways she'd not known since her MBA grad party, Janet took a break from giving Tony some good-natured shit and turned up the stereo a little. An empty Pepsi can blew into the rear windshield and bounced off; neither she nor Tony heard it.

The Figure turned a corner and saw the parked Ferrari 458. Pausing, tilting her head, she stood for a long moment.

"Christ, Janet, come on." A little hurt and frustrated, the weed taking him somewhere else than he'd hoped, Tony's voice cracked slightly. "I feel like I'm pulling teeth here." Turning away from her, he glanced across the street at someone whose face was covered by the down-turned brim of a baseball cap and a phone. Track pants and a hoodie. Tony guessed it wasn't that weird to see a homeless person with a phone but who the hell was paying for his plan? Had America really become such a welfare state?

Seeing Tony cling to the magazine like a security blanket, Janet took advantage of his distraction and snatched it from his hands. Opening her door a crack, she flung it up high above the car. Spreading its papery wings wide, the magazine caught a powerful gust that sent it on a spiraling path over the roof of the car and across the street. After swooping down to skim across the middle of the road like a bird checking for tasty insects on the surface of a pond, the magazine finally arced back up to flatten against The Figure's midsection.

"Why'd you—oh great, now that hobo has it."

"Lighten up, guy." Janet laughed. "Maybe she'll take it for a ride on the rails, spreading your legend across the land." She gestured with her hands to illustrate this grand journey, weaving loose lines of smoke. Tony kept his arms crossed, staring hard at the steering wheel.

The Figure pulled the magazine from her torso and found the coincidence of seeing the exact same car in the magazine as she saw across the street too much to ignore. Even with the tinting on his windows, it was easy to recognize the grinning car owner from the article. Using her phone, The Figure did a quick search for his name and found some other articles, the first being about how Tony and executives like him had been taking people's mortgage payments, setting them aside in a separate trust, then letting the mortgage itself grow ever more bloated while ruining the individual's credit rating.

Several people, with mountains of evidence on their side, had attempted to take Dunning-Kruger to court. All of them had lost. The case. Their homes. Their businesses.

"Oh Jesus, Tony," Janet muttered, reaching out to insincerely stroke his shoulder. "Don't get upset, I'll go to the art thing with you. Let's just enjoy our little artificial environment here a few minutes longer, okay?"

The Figure crossed the street in an arc, like an ellipsis closing off a horrible, private thought. Both thought and path took The Figure around and behind the car.

"Tony, come on," Janet pleaded, some genuine concern starting to creep in. "What is this? Are we on a date? Is that what we're on?" The muscles in his shoulder stiffened under her touch.

Tony kept his eyes closed, not wanting to be in the car, feeling anything he might say or do could only make this worse. It was his personal policy not to get too attached to women, to work out his needs with paid professionals. But there had been something irresistible about the way Janet had crushed those assholes trying to put together a lawsuit on behalf of the unpaid interns that kept so much of the paperwork moving through the D-K ether.

Part of what had let her do that was footage she'd recorded with her glasses. Was she recording now? He would have turned on the car's jamming device if he'd bothered to have one installed, but Tony had been too focused on form over function to get something so useful. Plus, there were etiquette issues which still hadn't been resolved. Are you suggesting the person in your company would be so rude as to record without asking first? Are you suggesting they might do anything untoward with what they recorded if they did so? It might be easier if there was only the one brand with its bulky recording unit, like in the good old days. Now there were so many more brands, more stylish and with much better concealed cameras.

Having found her way into an alley on the same side of the street as the car, opening not three feet behind, The Figure stood still for a moment as a chill wind whipped around her legs and pushed in through the gaps of the tear-away pants. The sensation blended with something else, something both integral and internal, causing The Figure to stop moving for a moment and focus on feeling a powerful shiver. Even the singular, driving imperative was temporarily wiped away.

Janet had a goal of her own, one Tony would have mixed feelings about, to say the least. Taking advantage of his closed eyes, she deftly pressed an embedded button set along the right temple of her frames.

Seeing nothing useful in the alleyway, The Figure glanced around and—failing to find any cameras—pulled the gym bag's zipper open. She had to give a second, harder pull when the teeth caught about halfway. Luckily, the weight of the bag's contents kept it steady against her hip. Looking inside, her fingers traced along a crowbar, then a length of chain, followed by wrench and then back to the crowbar again. Each item could only be used the one time and identical replacement items were not acceptable. Not often, anyways.

Tony opened his eyes as Janet began to massage his shoulder with the one hand, letting the other rest in her lap for now. He only stared ahead at a cream leather section of the dash.

"Listen, uh, Janet. I…I was very impressed by how you handled that little intern revolt and, well…"

Shit, Janet thought. *A crush. He's got a little crush on me. That's no good, that's not a recipe for keeping tonight within the boundaries of tonight.* As Tony prattled on with his mixture of sideways lust, affection, vanity, and clumsy misdirection, a choice was made only a few feet away. It was a choice Tony would have a different cocktail of conflicting reactions to, were he aware of what Janet had been hoping to do with him instead of going to the art show.

Lycra-coated fingers nimbly pulled at the rim of a rolled up leopard-print, skin-tight hood with its edges barely poking out from beneath the bottom of The Figure's baseball cap. In a few seconds, the hood was fully drawn down and fastened to the matching bodysuit just above the collarbone. Some quick rips, zips, and the flip of the cap left a small pile of well-worn clothes at the foot of a fully revealed Figure who wasted no time in removing her choice from the gym bag.

Tony was beginning to babble and Janet was becoming bored. It was tempting to turn off her glasses recording function but Tony was alternating between looking at the dash in embarrassment and sneaking little glances at her, hoping for approval that was less and less likely to be forthcoming. Not that it was so much work, she supposed, to delete the file later, except the user interface for that was such a pain in the ass. Plus, there was the live streaming to consider.

Janet turned to look out the passenger side window, thinking she could get away with a quick button press. Tony was staring at the dash when he heard her say, one more time, "Jesus, Tony!" before tiny pebbles of shattered safety glass shot around the edges of Janet's silhouette to pelt his face and shoulders. The financial executive had barely closed his eyes when he felt something angular and heavy tumble sharply into his shin.

His head a mess of screaming reflexes, Tony opened his eyes to see a bloody cinder block resting against his leg. Small, broken bits of what looked like white enamel mixed in with the safety glass pebbles strewn around his car's beautifully crafted interior. Janet was making a low, gurgling sound that discouraged him from looking off to her side of the vehicle. Instead, he looked to his left as the colorful contour of a woman pulled open his car door.

She was wearing a short, white fur coat and a belt with type on it he had only begun to read when the butt of a power drill drove into his forehead, the bit already spinning.

This was not the end of Tony's discomfort.

8. Meatstream.gov

Downstairs with dirty glasses, dishes, and empty bottles. Upstairs with whatever the bar needs. Over and over, this was James' life for three hours extending into the past and about six hours extending into the future. Sandwiched between monotony, James felt a bit better when he realized he could sneak about three minutes of private time in the space between bar and downstairs kitchen.

It was tough being a temp barback, sent to pop-up galleries and other events held all over the six boroughs. The pay was barely enough to cover expenses, but it was the only work James could get. With two-hundred grand of student loans for an unfinished business degree and the last of the international debt refuges purged by German flamethrower drones over a year ago, James didn't see any avenues out of this life.

Tonight could have been a bit more chill, in his opinion. Normally by ten pm, the evening had started properly. People would be dancing, talking, drinking, and relaxing. The DJ would have found the rhythm of the room. The staff would be in their respective grooves. But not tonight.

First, the artist had been a tremendous dick to Sarah, the nicer of the two bartenders. James had run into Sarah at a few events and he knew that while she could handle all kinds of abuse from customers, she was sensitive about her intelligence and a guy like the artist could tear down her self-esteem with his accent alone. Rattled, she wasn't offering any of the gentle banter and kind looks that could help him get through the last few hours of a rough night.

Several of the guests seemed distracted or even on edge. Chatting with the other bartender, James had managed to suss out that, though this evening was about celebrating the artists' new work, it had been hijacked by the rumor of how some big financial whiz, who had sponsored the whole thing, might actually show up in person. Thus the usual crowd became diffused with uptight bankers and their ilk, all hoping for a few moments to make their faces known to him. This created an odd crowd that wasn't mingling all that much, almost half of which were getting little enjoyment from the music or the art itself.

Hence the artist's foul mood and his being such a shit to Sarah when she'd asked an innocent question about a painting with a dog in the bottom left corner. A large, husky-type thing, the dog had a speech bubble coming up from its head that contained a picture of a hot dog. Sarah had thought this was cute and asked the artist if he'd drawn any other animals "speaking" about food. This was a crime worth five minutes of his venting stress all over her face, apparently.

"I bet the hot dog was supposed to symbolize his father's dick," James said to Sarah as he crouched down beside her to switch out some spent vodka bottles. Not really hearing what he said, only seeing her looking up at him, Sarah gave James a blank expression before someone rudely waving a hundred dollar bill drew her attention away again. Unsatisfied by the immediate world around him, James decided to check his phone on the way back to the kitchen.

His tray of bottles balanced atop an old wooden crate that had been re-finished and used as a coffee table by whatever this place had been before the art gallery pop-up, James quickly thumbed in the first few letters of the URL for his favorite live porn site. Meatstream.gov first got his attention by the cheekiness of its domain; what kept him coming back was this one amateur performer that went by the username of Belle Buster.

A woman herself, some banker type like the ones who'd invaded upstairs, she had a taste for being kind to soft types and then surprising them with a strange mix of encouragement and emotional abuse that generally led to some S&M activity well out of her target's usual comfort zone. As the username suggested, her partners were pretty much all lesbians. A little red-light-bulb icon let James know she was currently broadcasting live.

He was only able to see she was putting the remains of a joint away in some tin before he knew he'd have to get down to the kitchen right away or be yelled at for tardiness. The tallest bottle threatened to tip its way over the side of his tray as the young barback took the first white-tiled step around the corner and into the steamy, ad-hoc mess of a room where tired men only a little older than him prepared dishes their mothers had taught them. Comfort food was bar food this season.

Back up the stairs with gin, whiskey, and a dozen bottles of beer. James was extra careful going up the stairs, thanks to those beers, seeing as how they were from the last batch done by a brewery demolished a little over a year ago. It was a winter ale, punching hard at 18%, and had been the pride of the brewery's seasonal beers.

James knew all this and more as he'd once boned up on the local beer scene in hopes his knowledge might help him upgrade to bartending. It hadn't. Putting the bottles, numbered #27-33, on the counter beside Sarah, James thought bitterly upon how the only paid bartending work available demanded you have at least three years' experience and the rare entry level positions were all unpaid internships he didn't have the financial fat to hibernate through.

Back at the old wooden crate in the crook of the stairwell, there was just enough time to see that Belle Buster was working her thing on a man tonight. He was already looking pretty upset.

Wait until she gets out that key-ring Taser she likes to use, James thought. *Then things'll heat up.* James wasn't even into the key-ring Taser stuff, but he felt like he should be.

He crouched by Sarah again, this time laying down a dozen bottles of red wine the artist had asked for. The sound of Sarah laughing at a joke, using her genuine laugh, caught James' ear and made him smile as he turned to go grab another few minutes by the old crate.

Squinting over the glow of his phone's screen, James grew confused as Belle was staring out her passenger side window—looking in the exact opposite direction of the guy when she'd usually be doing things by now. He realized his default settings had been to download the stream as it happened and the sheer dullness of what he was seeing from Belle's point of view caused his thumb to slowly migrate toward the icon for ending it.

His thumb froze in place as his phone's tinny, tiny little speakers spat out, "Jesus, Tony!" followed by the sound of shattering glass, a sick thud, and the beginning of a low, agonized groan that left James grateful Belle's glasses fell to the ground and got crushed by the same large brick that had knocked them off her face.

James, ignoring calls from the downstairs kitchen to hurry up, quickly opened the recording and thumbed ahead to what he'd seen through Belle Buster's glasses right before the brick came flying toward them. Even though the contrast, resolution, and lighting were awful, it was plain the person that had been holding the brick didn't have a face. It was just a figure.

Then James experienced an impact of his own. Unwelcome self-awareness crashed through his consciousness, bringing about what he referred to as "Gary and The Existentials". Their familiar song played, the lyrics adjusted to his situation. The darkness of what had played across his phone wasn't edgy, it wasn't some secret world only he and a few others were privy to, it was just horrible. He was wasting his life, going nowhere with no great plan or purpose, just an ever-more desperate and depraved quest for distraction.

Blanking the irritated staff in the kitchen, he finally brought down the latest empties and collected some more gin. Each step back up the stairs came slowly, James' mind a tangle of self-loathing, fear for the future and creeping fascination laid across a leopard print canvas with white fur fringe. He had to do something. This had to stop, whatever "this" was exactly.

Standing up from the usual spot down by Sarah's shins, James glanced outside, hearing the powerful engine of a deep maroon sports car tearing past the front of the gallery at what had to be at least twenty over the speed limit.

The front passenger door window was missing.

Cold streetlight streamed across the smooth featurelessness of the driver's head. Safety glass pebbles nestled in her fur coat, glittering.

Two inanimate bodies sat in the back, propped against each other. Shadow spared James the grislier details of a sight he'd carry with him for the rest of his life.

"I quit," James said aloud.

"What?" Sarah answered.

"I said…" James began, already thinking of making rent this month. "I said 'Shit'. Just swearing."

Downstairs.

Bottles.

Upstairs.

Empty bottles.

Thinking.

9. Surfacing

Sweat pants. Sports bra. Hoodie.
Jogging. Street Lights. Three am, Friday.

Turning a corner, Mary took note of an abandoned hat and begging sign as she leaped over both.

She'd just read a short article about the recent Olympics in Baghdad, a profile of a runner she'd found both cute and inspiring. In it, the young man had talked about many things, epic and mundane. What he'd mentioned that was currently sitting between her ears was a simple fact about exercise and training, something he'd had to discover through the Internet instead of teachers as so little of Iraq's educational infrastructure had recovered from war by the time he was in his early teens. After serious physical exertion, the best thing you can do is not to just flop on the couch. Instead, do a few minutes of light stretches and jogging to gradually come down. This removes toxins building in your system during exercise that can leave you feeling worse for wear.

So here was Mary, trying to keep her system clean as can be. She knew she'd be tired walking to work tomorrow, she didn't need to be sore as well.

It was hard not to chuckle, coming across the bodega where she picked up her Shen-Yung ramens. With no real route in mind, she'd instinctively gone for some noodles. Jogging on the spot by the storefront, Mary peered through a window half papered over with various deals written on the kind of construction paper she'd used in grade school projects. One of the owner's sons was behind the counter, the one who never said anything when he served her. Fuck him.

Still, she remembered coming up with little excuses for dropping by the store even when he was working. The early days of living in the city had been so lonely that store clerks became her social life and the hairdresser's fingertips pushing her earlobes out of the way had become the sum total of regular human contact. Man or woman, it had just been nice to feel their touch. Mary remembered this as she softly ran a few of her own fingers along her right ear, unimpeded by any of the shoulder-length hair she'd long ago chopped off by inches over several carefully spaced visits.

Mary's phone, currently nested in her bra with earphones trailing up to her ears, sensed her slowing heartbeat and did what it had been told to do. It switched to one of the more kinetic playlists she'd made, goading its tired young owner into picking up the pace. Crossing the street it occurred to her she hadn't checked the lights, even though it had only been a few weeks since someone was last hit at this intersection.

Coming down the hill to her building, Mary felt exactly the right breeze against her cheek. In an instant she was standing by that tree…she was standing by that tree…she was standing by that—

HONK

"The fuck, bitch?" an ageing Puerto Rican man with tired eyes half-heartedly yelled at her, having swerved his rusty pick-up truck to avoid running her down where she stood perfectly still. Staying in the dead center of a T-junction wasn't what Mary called fun, so she took a few more paces and slid around the corner of her building to the side entrance.

Stepping into her studio apartment, Mary shucked off two fat white sneakers before taking a step forward and peeling off her sweaty clothes to toss them directly into the hamper by the end of the bed. It's not like anybody would be walking down the alley by her window at this hour. Screw them anyways, if they were so desperate to see a body.

But then Mary thought of something else that was exposed.

Reaching down, Mary brushed aside the pile of deeply creased denim work clothes and quickly scooped up the pile of leopard-print Lycra along with a ribcage-length, white fur coat and custom belt. Keeping an eye on the window, Mary almost stubbed her toe while walking over to the bathroom. When the hell was she going to get some blinds?

Once there, she bent down to spin the digits of a cheap combination padlock she'd installed on the cupboard doors underneath the sink. 12-24-15, pushing some cleaning products aside and then she felt safe again. In an instant, the costume, combination, and action were forgotten.

If only it had been so straightforward to feel confident enough to ask Ahmed out. Her failure this morning to turn a purchase into the promise of a first date had haunted her all day. Anxiety had made her too tense and virtually turned off her ability to use words. After giving the order there had only been a slight quiver in her jaw, and his friendly looks, which Mary had hoped meant the barista was trying to think of something interesting to say as well.

Rolling over onto one side, Mary's fingertips brushed along her exposed ear as she blew softly against the inside of the same forearm, experimenting by mouthing different shapes while pushing out less or more air each time.

10. ₀.*: • $'° :₀ '(((+_+)))₀.*:ⁿ •'$ⁿ ⁿ :₀ ' • °

Gerald Byrne woke up and for the first time in two weeks, it didn't make him feel strange to see nothing at all when he opened his eyes. His other senses hadn't yet become sharper, to compensate for being whittled down to just the four, but Gerald didn't need a sharper nose to recognize that particular hand sanitizer.

"Hello, Mr. Kruger, it's nice of you to take time out of your busy schedule to visit me."

"Gerry, it's only the two of us right now. You can call me Dad."

A third generation financial man, Gerald believed in his own version of The American Dream and felt that making it through life on your family name was too akin to European aristocracy. In his eighteenth year, he changed his last name to Byrne, right before heading off to Harvard. Search engines and word of mouth rendered this change all but meaningless in short order. Still, Gerald insisted on maintaining the illusion that nobody knew where he came from.

"Dad," Gerald began again. "You know I haven't had it explained to me how it is I'm alive, which is a rather large oversight, I think."

"I told them not to get into that with you yet. It's bad enough you're…" Kruger paused. "You're blinded for life."

"For life? Really? We can't even look into—"

"No, the optic nerves were too thoroughly damaged. That…that person really worked their…implement around inside the sockets."

Kruger expected his son to tense up at such a carefully worded reminder of the person who attacked him. Gerald just got annoyed.

"*My* sockets, Dad. She really worked her…shiv, I think it was? *She* really worked it around in *my* sockets."

The weight of his father made itself known to Gerald as the bed sagged a little on his left side, right by the waist. Surprisingly craggy hands for a fifty-eight year old financial mogul took Gerald's own, smooth palm. The Nightmare on Wall Street had always been a tender, caring father.

"I already have people installing the necessary electronics in your main residence so you'll be able to use this sort of GPS thing to help you navigate your way around. I'm also looking into having the system installed in the upper floors of my building."

"I appreciate the thought, but I'm not moving Byrne Investments into the Dunning-Kruger building. You don't rent office space to other companies, I don't see why I should be any different. As soon as possible I'll be—"

"Yes, but things are different now and—"

"Dad, I'm not moving into the building."

"Alright son, but I insist you upgrade security on wherever your new office will be."

"Why do I need a new office?"

Kruger stopped stroking his son's hand and held it firmly. Gerald, figuring he was in a private room, still found it remarkable he couldn't hear one single hospital sound from the hallway. There was only his father's carefully measured breathing and the pulse he felt quicken through those hands wrapped around his own.

"Because this human meat grinder managed to murder every single one of your employees on that floor. You're the only survivor."

Gerald thought for a moment about how his personal office had been soundproofed, both so he could have total silence for thinking and so he wouldn't disturb people when he blasted music to stimulate the same activity. Gerald had no clue anything was wrong until he tried to buzz his secretary. It was only seconds later that a figure had burst through the door and into his eyes.

Instinctively, Gerald looked away from his father. *What am I "looking" at now? Maybe a plant, maybe a Rothko print.*

"Are you sure?"

"The police said you're lucky to be alive. Each killing was very effective, brutal, and quick. I'd say something about having to admire the efficiency of her work, but I don't. I damn well don't."

Gerald paused to think, using his free hand to feel two weeks of beard on his chin.

"I'm guessing she didn't use guns? I would have heard guns."

"No. She started by using a goddamn sledgehammer on the young man at the front desk, then took his stun gun and used that along with a tire iron, a hammer, and a wrench to kill all except Diane and Jamie. We don't know why, but she would discard a weapon after using it once or twice. By those last two she was improvising with objects found on the premises."

"Found on the premises?"

"I'm paraphrasing the man from Avalanche we had go over the office before alerting the police," Kruger replied. "By the time she got to you, she only had the remains of a steak knife that'd been partially snapped off between Jamie's ribs."

"It was my idea to have that kind of stuff in the kitchen, proper cutlery." Gerald frowned. "I figured people deserved it for those late nights we'd have to order in."

"Yes, well, it was the reduced length of the knife that kept it from penetrating all the way to your brain. Judging from the security video, the pain made you pass out and unintentionally play possum."

"So why didn't I bleed out?"

"Your health insurance bracelet did its job, that's why. Now you know why I insisted you accept the damn gift."

"The medics really homed in on me first, huh? I still don't think men should wear bracelets but I guess I'm glad I gave in on that argument."

"It's like I've always said," Kruger lectured. "The money will protect you."

Gerald's chest began to heave.

"Oh come now, Gerry, it's nothing I haven't said to you a thousand times before."

"I know, I just, I was thinking about how often you've said that to me…" Gerald swallowed. "…my whole life, and I just…" He pressed his chin to his chest. "I just tried to roll my eyes."

Father and son uncomfortably choked down a mixture of sadness and bitter laughter. Neither man even considered how Gerald's career might not continue, that he may cease to be the wunderkind of their lofty world. After a full minute of this, Kruger opened his mouth again.

"Fuck." He gently breathed out. "I guess this horrible creature must be the last thing you saw. Of all the—"

"Hell of a sense of style she's got there." Gerald's shoulders still shook as he spoke. "That belt was something."

"You were able to read it? It might be helpful if you could remember what it said. The cameras never got a good enough angle."

"I think it said, in all caps…" Gerald paused, working to keep his tone even. "'SLOW DOWN & SHUT UP'."

"Do you have any idea what it means?"

The two men sat quietly as Gerald thought. After a long moment, he shook his head side to side in a small arc. Kruger wished his son would swear, yell, maybe even slam a fist down on the mattress. He did none of those things.

"You know, I don't want this to change my life any more than it has to," Gerald said. "But do I, like, was this thing targeted at me? Is whoever hired her going to come after me again, once they learn I'm alive?"

"We can get into the details of all that later. For now, keep one thing in mind." Kruger gripped his son's hand tighter, for emphasis. "The money will protect you."

11. التَّـــــاريخ أولا

Ahmed had turned his phone off for the evening and he didn't want to break that little unspoken promise he'd made to the awkward girl who'd come by the shop yesterday even though it wasn't, apparently, "her turn". He read the wrinkled, laminated menu once more. The minutes passed and Mary continued to be…well, so far she'd be early if she showed up, just not as much as Ahmed. Not wanting to be late, he'd left early and taken extra care to get on the right bus in case rush hour slowed him down by the usual margin.

Today, however, people got their asses home from work in a calm, orderly fashion for a change. So here he was, ten minutes into being twenty-five minutes early. He wasn't sure why, but he'd kept the full loyalty card she'd passed him yesterday morning. It had her phone number on the back, written under "Mary"—a name she'd never given him in all their past little interactions. Well, transactions more like. This was not a girl who got into small talk at the counter.

Letting his imagination wander, Ahmed traced with his eyes the rows of little blue Christmas lights strung about the pub. He wondered how she'd look in the mix of pale light from their cool blue bulbs and the warm under-glow of the hundreds of tea lights scattered across every counter, table, and windowsill. Surely she'd have something on that would be a bit more interesting, a bit more feminine than all that filthy denim he always saw her wearing in the lineup.

He'd chosen this bar because its familiarity helped him feel at ease. It hadn't been that long since his last first date, but it had been far too long since a first date had gone well. Ahmed had a completely unfounded belief that this one would.

Oh oh, shit, yes, yes that was her that just stepped in under the beam the bar owner swore was taken from an old whaling ship. Nothing like some reminder of the wanton slaughter of innocent giants to give a place some charm. The moment where Mary stood still, slowly turning her head to scan for Ahmed, gave him a chance to look her over.

Her short hair must have been recently combed and was maybe even still a little wet from the shower, framing features he imagined himself admiring from the other side of a queen-sized bed. The long-sleeved, tight white sweater appeared almost luminescent in the bar's low, mixed lighting. And while denim made its return in a pair of jeans, they looked like what must be The Nice Pair in her wardrobe. Ahmed couldn't quite see her shoes, though they were carrying her toward him at this point, so it was probably a good idea to look up and meet her gaze.

Silently, Mary took a seat opposite him and was clearly a little embarrassed at how the chair caught a bit on the floorboards when she pulled it out.

"Hey," Ahmed started. "Early, but not quite as early as me. How'd you get here?"

"Oh, sorry, am I late?"

"No no, I was just sort of making fun of myself. I tried to compensate for traffic but rush hour was pretty civilized, so I ended up waiting for a little while before you got here."

The waiters there were all paid under the table in cash, which often had the effect of making them feel pretty laissez-faire about their work. Ahmed was almost startled when a young woman sporting a long ponytail and a full sleeve of tattoos on her right arm, actually showed up before Mary even had a chance to look at the menu.

"Are you ready?" she asked the two of them.

"I am, but I think—"

"Uh, no, I got it." Mary interrupted, quickly scanning the menu. "I'll have the home-style chicken noodle soup with grilled cheese sandwich on the side."

"Crusts cut off or no?"

"Oh, um, crusts cut off please, and a half pint of something dark." Mary tapped one index finger on the menu. "Do you have that Eat My Schwartz thing the North brewery puts out?"

Ahmed quickly ordered himself some Mujudara with a side order of Kraft dinner and a pint of something blonde he'd feel guilty for later, maybe. As soon as the waitress left, he felt compelled to ask, "Are you into micro-brews and all that stuff, then?"

"A little while ago, I started at the junkyard and my coworkers are these two guys I have nothing in common with, so I had to find something to talk about with them." Mary shrugged. "I'm no beer snob, but it's nice to know a little about what I'm drinking and where the good stuff is from."

"Still, that's cool." Ahmed leaned back in his chair. "I don't really know much about beer at all."

"Are you allowed to, I mean, you ordered a pint I guess, but…" Letting the sentence trail off, Mary wasn't sure about the current, exact relationship between her foot and her mouth.

"I'm more ethnically than religiously Muslim. It's been a few generations since my family lived anywhere but America and, honestly, I'm not even sure if there's a Qur'an in my apartment."

"That's okay, I wouldn't know what to do if I had a Bible in mine," Mary replied, relieved that she hadn't offended him. "Religion's…" Mary waved one hand around, hoping it'd catch the right word for her. "…tricky."

"Yes, yes, I suppose that's a fair assessment!" Ahmed laughed, putting a slight smile on her face.

Their drinks arrived. As Mary reached for her beer, Ahmed

noticed a curious ring on her finger. Its band was made from over a dozen inter-woven copper wires and the "stone" looked like a little button with a light bulb drawn on it.

"This is neat," he said, pointing at the ring. "Where'd you get that?"

"Oh, this?" Surprised, Mary looked at the ring as if seeing it for the first time. "I uh, I sometimes make things out of what I find at the junkyard. The 'stone' is an old Check Engine light I pulled out of a dash."

"Huh, I didn't think anybody was into steampunk anymore."

"What? I don't know about that, but I've also made a pretty good coffee table from these crank-shafts and shit. Not much fun when I stub my toe on it, but still."

"I'd love to see that some time." Ahmed looked Mary in the eyes, calmly, steadily. He wasn't sure where the confidence had come from, but he was grateful for it.

Mary blushed slightly, glad for the distraction of their meals arriving. For a moment, she wished she'd had them leave the crusts on her grilled cheese. They would have helped give the sandwich more structural integrity for what she was about to do next. Oh well, there was no going back now.

Dipping a smidgen of her sandwich into the chicken noodle soup, Mary took advantage of Ahmed's looking down at his food to admire his features more directly than she'd ever felt comfortable doing from the line-up of the coffee shop. Soft lips nestled above a strong chin, the border between smooth skin and stubble. Long, almost feminine eyelashes made movements Mary couldn't help paying attention to. Hands rested on the table with a gentle strength she wanted to become familiar with.

This feeling of focus looking at him brought was something Mary had lusted after more than any physical contact. His features pushed away the world, temporarily simplifying her existence so that Mary might as well have been sitting by a still, blue lake with nobody else around for miles.

If we become a couple, Mary thought, *he'll definitely be the better looking one.*

Ahmed looked up, chewing. Mary spoke, compelled to fill the momentary silence.

"So what do you do when you're not at the coffee shop? Are you in school?" Mary asked around half a mouthful of soggy sandwich.

"I was. But, about six months ago, I left," he replied. Mary swallowed, then gave an inquisitive look that made Ahmed put his cutlery down and do a little eye roll.

"Well, I was studying to work in international law, but the more I learned the less I wanted to interact with that world. The final straw that broke my academic back was learning how a professor of psychiatry at the school was running this really unethical program in partnership with the DOD."

"Oh." This wasn't where Mary had hoped her question would lead. She'd wanted to learn more about him, which she was, but more hopes and dreams than along the lines of fear and hate.

"Basically, they were using university facilities to experiment with new interrogation techniques." Ahmed's voice rose slightly. "Specifically using immigrants so that the interrogators could practice their techniques on 'someone they wouldn't necessarily identify with'. So, you know, non-whites. Because we lie differently, apparently."

Mary stopped interacting with her meal as Ahmed stopped interacting with her, speaking more to a rhetorical crowd in his head than anybody actually present.

"And none of this was run by the student body. We only found out about it by accident when a busload of suspiciously non-student looking Haitians were brought in." Ahmed took a large swig of his drink, noticing a small drop falling on his shirt. "That was it. I know I sound like so many angry young men before me, but the whole thing really is just so damn ugly and designed to hold you down. It's like a plague of short-term thinking and willful ignorance has become the only real connectivity between education, the military, and the government. And, oh man, the financial sector? They're like kings who don't realize they're—"

Lowering his gaze from the hypothetical audience in the rafters, Ahmed came out of his self-induced trance long enough to notice Mary's body language, which seemed to have been opening up since she slipped in under that beam, was closing down rapidly. Shoulders folding in, slightly watery eyes casting brief, furtive glances at him before retreating to the safety of her lap.

He couldn't help but be reminded of a brief stint spent working inventory in a large shoe retailer. Stuck somewhere between barcoded crates of consumer goods, holding his little scanner like the ray gun in an old science fiction show, Ahmed had been so quiet that the manager hadn't realized he was still in the building when it was time to close. Ahmed saw in Mary the same mixture of panic and loneliness he'd felt as rows of hanging lights had begun turning off one by one.

"I'm sorry, I'm just angrily rambling off in all directions here. Never mind me, never mind me."

"It's okay. I just, I try not to think about all that stuff. It's overwhelming." Mary spoke without looking up at him. "I got anxious enough over spending money on eating out tonight."

"The prices are pretty cheap. To be honest, it's part of why I suggested we meet here. That and it's the first bar I really got to know when I was old enough to go to one."

Mary's limp hand moved toward a soupspoon with no great enthusiasm.

"So, working at a junkyard must be interesting, fixing up and messing around with all those vehicles." Ahmed shot this sentence across like a safety flare, hoping to guide Mary out of whatever dark pit it was he'd accidentally pushed her into. It took a moment, but she eventually looked up from her lap.

"Oh, I don't really fix things. I just tear them down."

12. infohose.com

A long, thin metal wire slipped under the throat of the security guard and the increasingly familiar figure quickly threw herself over a cubicle partition, still holding onto both ends. Protected by the partition, her body's full weight yanked the struggling guard a short distance off the ground. An expanding necklace of blood seeped from underneath his hands while he tried to free himself. As he finally stopped moving, two fingertips that had gotten under the wire gently slid off like melting ice cream from on top of the cone.

Unaware of any of this, a young woman in a ruffled blouse came back to her cubicle to be greeted by The Figure. Not seeing the gory spectacle on the other side of her partition, the woman was only confused at first. This soon changed as The Figure released the metal wire and swung a claw hammer so fast that both the young woman and the dead security guard hit the ground at the same time.

A long, thin metal wire slipped under the throat of the security guard and—

James sat on his old futon, hunched over a tablet that framed this looping video clip with heavily scratched, gunmetal gray plastic. Shrinking the video, he went back to the forum where he'd downloaded it. It was one of those sites which was occasionally mentioned in the news yet still retained an underground feeling due to its niche user base and almost bottomless reserves of unregulated content. Intense, adult discussions of the latest cartoons rested side by side with pornography of all stripes and leaked security camera footage of vicious murders.

James swiped past claims made by the thread's original poster, saying how his cousin worked for Avalanche security and not only gave him these clips but also supplied the latest in self-defense techniques. Some member of the company had to have leaked the footage, but this turd probably just found it in some other corner of the Internet. For as long as James could remember, finding information hadn't ever been a problem. It was knowing what to look for and what to do with it that was tricky.

Obviously, most people weren't looking for this woman, or surely there'd be greater public interest as well as coverage in more mainstream venues. Four weeks on from the oldest post about her, there was only a modest club of people collecting images, video, and artifacts to go with the inevitable theories. James tapped on another video, one with a thumbnail that gave away the ending a bit by showing her cramming the tip of a crowbar into some guy's mouth.

James' features creased slightly when he got to the payoff.

This wasn't the movies. The camera didn't cut away right before the horrible act, and nothing about what she did to these people was implied. The void lay in what movies usually did give you, motivation and personal details. Who was she and why was she doing this? Was it even always the same person in the suit?

More than a few felt the answer lay in radical left-wing groups, since her targets were all involved with the upper echelons of the financial sector. Perhaps some old Occupy, Black Bloc, or Debt Head had finally decided a more focused, individual action was necessary—that violence was more difficult to argue with than rhetoric. To some people this meant terrorism, which brought up a multitude of conversational cul-de-sacs trying to rationalize how a Middle Eastern group could use a woman as anything other than a suicide bomber or what African culture might spawn such a costume.

A few wags likened her to a superhero, albeit more in the vein of a violent anti-hero than your square-jawed Superman types. These people made some interesting points regarding how the only survivor of her attacks was someone who was in no way a part of the organization she chose to visit. However, the slaying of three delegates from a financial think tank visiting AFPB had made it clear she was open to targets of opportunity.

The survivor of that attack was, strangely, not being interviewed by any major news networks nor was he writing about his experiences online. Private security hadn't processed him, which was a shame since they were so much more prone to leaks than the police. There was already an informal petition by the thread's participants trying to get the fraction of a percentage point of the site's users who actually had any real hacking ability to seek out the survivor's statement to the police.

So far, no results.

Conspiracy theories about her being a paid assassin in the employ of virtually every organization on Earth swirled around half-serious tangents about zentai costume sex fetishism. However, James reasoned that if she was getting off on the violence, she'd surely linger more over each kill. If she was highly paid or supported by a large organization, then why were her tools crude, irregular, and so often improvised?

James found himself drawn to theories where she was a lone individual who had decided something. Money, sex, politics, these weren't her motivations. It was revenge against those who had traumatized the society she lived in, had made it almost unbearable to try to succeed, had done so much to make her feel pushed out and so very trapped within. But wait, weren't the security guards and secretaries she killed as much a victim of this as her?

James just wasn't quite getting everything he needed from any one theory. He had to figure out exactly what it was she was doing and her reasons for doing it. Looking up from the tablet to gaze out his one window—a mediocre view filtered through gauzy brown curtain—James also needed to know more about why he was so fascinated because he could feel this fascination taking him somewhere. Even James knew if someone was leading you by the hand, they shouldn't be a stranger.

13. (-_-)$$$$$$

Gerald focused his mind's eye upon every inch of an inner gallery filled with murals painted by a brush dipped in memory. Rowing at Harvard. Ballooning over the Bay Area. Fingers sinking into Martha's fleshy hips.

Feeling a slight breeze come through an open window on the forty-second floor, at the corner of forty-seventh and fourth, Gerald sat there wondering why he hadn't done more of this before. He couldn't help but wonder what other gifts his new state might give him. Since his injury, he'd yet to sit down and do any of the kind of meditative planning that had helped him make his fortune thus far. Would the benefit of added focus from losing visual stimuli compensate for reduced ability to take in information?

"Hello, Gerry."

"Mr. Kruger, don't you have business today regarding the destabilization of Nigeria?"

"Oh, don't worry about Nigeria." Kruger replied. "I've got people for that."

Chemically approximated eucalyptus found its way up Gerald's nose moments before Kruger's hands perched on his shoulders. He assumed his father was admiring a view of the city the young financial maverick would never see again. Incorrect. Kruger was gazing down upon Gerald's head, partly out of love and partly with hopes that he might be able to steal a glimpse at his child's inner workings.

"So," he began. "You'll be pleased to know the media blackout has been successful and is holding."

Gerald didn't have any strong feelings about this one way or the other, not having asked for or even been aware of it before now. He nodded all the same.

"You were too young when that Occupy crap happened and I had you safely ensconced at Harvard when the Debt Heads did their thing. Trust me, we can't have what this woman does catching on."

Gerald clued in from the mention of Harvard that they must be alone.

"Alright, Dad, so what comes next?"

Kruger's grip tightened.

"Well, Gerry, that's a good question." Kruger's idea of a good question was one he didn't immediately have a definitive answer for; to be fair, these were few in number. "I know it's important to you that you be your own man, out from under my shadow, and it's your company that this woman hit."

"Didn't she kill Janet and some chump from D-K acquisitions?"

"Possibly. Someone certainly did. But she wiped out your staff and took your eyes, so I feel it's only right you decide what's next."

Gerald sat quietly, turning things over in his mind.

"I think I'm in the business of business, not doing the police department's work for them."

"Well, Gerald, that's true." Kruger's hands left Gerald's shoulders and, from the sound of his voice, it seemed Gerald's father had begun pacing around the room. "However, you might want to keep in mind that you're the only survivor of what my people at Avalanche have confirmed as at least six similar incidents, all perpetrated by the same woman."

"Six?" Gerald raised an eyebrow, even though his father was pacing behind him.

"Yes, all financial institutions. All of her victims were employees of the companies or visiting employees from other financial companies. The only other survivor is some idiot who'd come into AFPB to complain about his mortgage, but he called the police—who actually showed up before Avalanche, so."

"That is distressing." Gerald leaned closer to his open window, enjoying the breeze. "But I've still got a few higher priority, actionable items on my agenda. On top of learning Braille et cetera, I need to make sure the immediate family of all my dead employees are attended to, as well as find suitable replacements."

"You're welcome to rifle through my HR database."

"Thanks, Dad, I wouldn't normally take you up on that but there's one other urgent matter where I'll just have to have a couple of people with me. A few gentlemen from Guinea-Bissau are supposed to be coming by in a week to discuss something they say is very important."

The sound of Kruger's pacing stopped.

"I'm sorry, what? I thought you kept those maniacs at arm's length."

"Normally they stay on their side of the Atlantic, it's true. They emailed me just before my special visitor came by, letting me know they were coming to the city and that a meeting to discuss expanding our business relationship was, apparently, in order."

"Yes, well." Gerald could tell Kruger was close again, hands kept to himself if not their smell. "I can see that's not the kind of meeting you'd want to have on your own, especially in your new condition. Still, you really don't want to be more proactive with this horrible woman? Maybe get some bodyguards, at least?"

Gerald stood up and turned to face his father, Oliver People's sunglasses covering his wounds.

"I used to be fascinated by her kind. Now?" Gerald put a hand to his chin. "Now I find my opinions are evolving. I look at it this way. She tried to take my life, right? The more time and energy I devote to her, the more I change my life because of what she did, the more she prevents me from achieving my goals, the more she wins."

"She'll really prevent you from achieving your goals if she returns to finish what she started." Kruger put his hands back on Gerald's shoulders for emphasis. "Far as I know it wasn't anything specifically targeting you, but you should really consider slowing down and—"

"I'm not going to sit around waiting for the change I want in the world to just happen." Gerald added, tossing off Kruger's hands. "She certainly isn't!"

14. Ladylike

A thin line of trees wearing fall colors sat right outside the length of fence visible in a side mirror Mary was carefully prying off the body of an old Datsun sedan. Her mind churned over the night before as her hands moved with swift and sure motions, not requiring much input from the higher functions to do their work.

Like a car tire trying to get a grip on an icy surface, their conversation had struggled to find traction for a while after Ahmed's diatribe about why he left university. Noticing someone being served fish at another table, Mary had mumbled something about rotten potatoes and then gone bright red when Ahmed asked her to repeat it so he could hear. After much playful squirming in her seat, she'd finally told him how she'd never understood the idea of a vagina smelling like fish, especially since she felt that rotten potatoes smelled more like unwashed vaginas than anything. Ahmed asked how she knew this and Mary then got to relate the story of how her high school gym teacher's car trunk had quite mysteriously been full of the things. You never knew what would finally get you both laughing.

Old metal slowly began to give as Mary brought her shoulders' full strength to bear. She wasn't burly by any stretch, but the young woman had learned early on what could be accomplished when she didn't rely on just one part of her body at a time. As her full form focused, her mind became more and more lost in pleasant memories of the night before, as well as fantasies she wanted to turn into pleasant memories. It was like being buried beneath a pile of warm, freshly laundered blankets you'd never want to crawl out from.

"Hey! Mary!"

"Wha—?"

SNERRRR-AP

Mary lost her balance and fell back hard. A dust angel was violently birthed on the ground behind where she had been standing. The driver's side mirror flew and skipped along the ground like a small animal startled from its hiding place. Vance's washed-out features and clothing almost blended with the pale, overcast sky Mary saw behind him as she looked up from the earth.

"Jesus, Mary, open up your ears would you? You know I don't like to yell."

Lying down was so seductive, it took an effort of will for Mary to scrabble upright and dust herself off. Vance waited for the heavy slap of work gloves on denim to stop before he continued.

"As its Friday, I thought I'd bring a little treat we could all enjoy over lunch."

"Oh, uh, you mean you went out and got some of those, uh—"

Vance made a little twirling gesture with his right index finger, teasingly telling Mary to get on and spit it out.

"The, um, North brewery stuff? From their last batch of winter ale?"

"Yup." Vance grinned. "Bottles number fifty-six, seventy-two, and one eleven…I think. It cost a little bit, but I figure we've earned a treat this month."

Vance squinted at Mary, studying her features, then took a deep, theatrical sniff. Appalled, Mary looked up at her employer with wide, nervous eyes.

"What?"

"Just checking to see if the brewery didn't set up a new location somewhere in your guts. Were you drinking this morning? I can smell something on your breath."

"Oh." Mary blushed. "Sorry, I got in late last night and forgot to brush my teeth. Not very ladylike, I guess." Vance laughed and clapped Mary on the shoulder.

"It's nice to have a woman around but I'm hardly worried about you being ladylike. Listen, spend another fifteen minutes on this car, then join Carmine and me over at the shack."

Mary nodded enthusiastically, then watched Vance walk away. What would it have been like if he was her father? Tough love, the healthy kind, mixed with gentle understanding and perhaps a crude but intimidating vocabulary. Having come from a sperm bank, Mary liked to imagine different men as her father. It also made it tricky for her, though, to know whether certain parts of who she was were inherited or resulted from how life had shaped her.

Turning to something more tangible, Mary grabbed a crowbar and began prying open the trunk of the car. The stupid thing had sat for months in a pond on some idiot's farm and thoroughly rusted shut, rendering the keys they'd been given useless.

But yeah, Mary thought, mouth moving slightly while producing no sound, *For a first date, that went pretty well. Hopefully, I didn't email him too quickly. It'd be nice if he wants to get together again soon.*

Not wanting to fall on her ass once more, Mary leaned down and forward on the crowbar instead of down and back. It was a shame he was so ready to talk about big problems in the world. When she could steer him away from that, his charm had such a warming effect. It made her feel something like that morphine drip, in a good way, that morphine drip from when she—

CRRRRRRRRRRRRRRRRRRRRRRANK

The trunk popped open, scattering red flecks along Mary's lower torso and thighs.

"Nice," she muttered to herself before focusing on the contents of the trunk, her mind already wandering back to Ahmed.

Yeah.

She'd definitely found something special here.

15. SMILE

The old bus stopped to expel. Exhaust fumes. Sounds. Light. People. And then it sealed up again, right before carrying off into the distance. Those who'd just exited all hurried off to their destinations. One individual paused after a few steps, standing upon the crest of a rolling hilltop coated in pavement bearing numerous cracks from last year's frost heaves, the stretch marks of the city.

From under the worn peak of a found baseball cap, The Figure stared across several blocks of urban decay at its finest. On the near horizon stood the glassy peaks where she would fully become, for a while. For now, The Figure's hands were hanging on the steering wheel, like those of a trucker trying to keep his eyes open during the final hour of an overnight run.

With each step toward the financial district, The Figure gradually became more alert. Each breeze played across her exposed skin like fingers along a piano, summoning precise, intense sensations. These quickly became fuel for a machine that'd been slowly assembled over a lifetime, but had only recently been activated.

It would take about an hour to get there. Luckily, her load was not a heavy one tonight.

Forty-five minutes to go. Thirty minutes to go. Security bars still on some corner store windows but—

"Hey, lady, smile why don't ya."

With her focus on the foreground, the words of a parking lot playboy barely registered as sounds, let alone language. Anything peripheral was just that.

"What? Lady, you look at me when I talk to you. Come on, didn't your mama teach you how to have a conversation? Hey now, why don't you smile?"

The Figure started taking faster steps. There was some serious equipment in the faded, neon pink backpack she carried, though nothing for this situation. CCTV coverage in this neighborhood was poor, but still, but still.

"Why you got a little kids backpack, anyhow? All little animal stickers n' shit. You just got outta school?" Getting off his throne—an overturned milk crate—he wasn't that large. He didn't have to be.

Inside the backpack was an experiment, a blending of two recent finds. The backpack itself probably was once a little girl's. It had been found in the drainage ditch near a large grade school. Its former owner's age wouldn't have kept this man from saying similar things to her. It might have made things worse.

The Figure kept moving forward, cool breezes forgotten, momentum shifting. She had tools, but not the right tools. This was a problem, but it wasn't *the* problem. She wasn't at the rich, glass heart and The Figure was not made for this. The situation had to change and change soon.

"Goddammit!" His voice raised an octave, then came back down. "You don't smile, you don't look at a person, you even walk away when someone's TALKing to you!" The Figure put one foot in front of the other and so did he.

All alone for now, The Figure would have to improvise with what she had at hand. Seeing an alleyway with light at the end, she took a hard left turn. Away from the meager protection of streetlights and visibility, The Figure quickly scanned for opportunity.

"Oh, now, is that how it is?" he muttered to himself, seeing where the woman had slipped off. One hand crawled into a jacket pocket with a zipper that had broken long ago, and closed around a familiar handle. The other scratched at a constellation of eczema along the back of his neck.

Turning down the alley, he stood still after only a few paces. Waiting for his eyes to adjust, he listened carefully. There was light at the end of the alley but, being a local, he knew it was only a security light hanging above the dead end of a heavily secured back entrance for the short-term loan office that wouldn't speak to him anymore.

Scratching the back of his neck again, he looked up to see a bulky silhouette perched two stories high on a fire escape he wouldn't trust with anybody's life, certainly not his own. The ladder had been pulled up so he couldn't follow her and the light pollution in the alley only allowed him to make out her eyes.

They stared at him intently and he returned the favor, tilting his head side-to-side every few seconds, trying to figure something out. In one moment, it was as if an angry cat was staring him down but then he'd adjust, squint, tilt, and feel like there was nothing at all behind the eyes of this woman who was sitting up there, tightly holding white knuckles on black railing.

"Ah, you're not that pretty. Bet you have a big fat ass under those track pants, too. Fuckin' dyke, fuckin' waste my dick on your fuckin'..." Hand still in his pocket, he swayed back a few steps, turned and left. The Figure's eyes followed him until he was gone.

She carefully allocated and waited twelve more minutes before men's work boots hit the ground and began walking toward the workplaces of people The Figure knew how to deal with.

16. Aftercare

Jogging through her neighborhood, Mary's mouth was a straight line. When she passed the corner store and saw one of the owner's sons accidentally tip a tall display of potato chips all over himself, she refused to show her amusement. Hopping over the same hat some homeless person had forgotten about, she landed hard on an abandoned French fry. Examining the results on the bottom of her shoe, it was hard not to think about the potato story she'd told Ahmed the other night.

Still, her lips were sealed and stationary. Mary didn't want to risk giving that out to someone she didn't realize was watching, someone who didn't deserve it.

Back home, shedding her jogging gear into a pile on the floor beside denim and Lycra, Mary could still feel it: toxins gathering in her system.

Stretches. Over and over she performed a half dozen stretches she'd seen in a series of online videos. Combining too much urgency with too little experience, Mary succeeded in hurting herself, forming a small tear in her muscle. A small tear formed in her eye. Muscle tore from right beside his eye.

The Figure wrenched hard on the handle of her custom implement, a razor sharp grappling hook secured on the other end of a long-handled claw hammer. One of the blades pulled a length of muscle through the opening it had made in the man's temple—one jagged edge having caught on a particularly sticky stretch of sinew. Eyes open in shock, the man was forced to look along its length as this piece of him was pulled away in a fashion far from surgical.

Mary put a hand to her temple. Right calf stinging, she staggered toward her bed and flopped down so hard her phone bounced straight up off the mattress. It landed beside her outstretched hand, a small blessing. Thumbing through her contacts in less than five seconds, it occurred to Mary there were less than a handful of people she could call.

There were even fewer who could possibly help her feel better, and nobody she felt she could call at this hour.

And…

She should have tried harder to talk to strangers. With each passing moment, she felt stranger. A sound barely escaped her throat, strangled. The banker's vision, mangled.

A one-way road wasn't being respected. Something was forcing itself down the wrong direction.

And…

An out-of-focus picture of Ahmed she'd taken without his being aware, Mary pretending to be checking the online bus schedules at the time, appeared on her phone's screen. She should hang up, but he'd see that it was her dialing at three a.m. Well, he'd only see that someone with her phone number had called unless he'd put her name to the number like she had with his. Either way he could call back and then what? And then what?

"Hello?"

A low growling, gurgling noise escaped Mary's mouth but she covered the receiver in time.

"Mary?"

He'd saved her number in his phone!

"H—hey Ahmed, uhm." Mary bit her lip, failed to think of

anything rational to justify calling this late. "Are you…okay?"

"Yeah!" Ahmed laughed. "Yeah, I'm fine. A little tired, I guess. They had me working from open until close today."

"Were people not too bad today?"

"That pot-bellied guy you work with could brush his teeth more often but yeah, no, it was…" He yawned. "It was pretty decent. I didn't even have to stay after to close the till et cetera."

"Still, that's a long day." Mary rolled onto her back, eyes closed. "Hey, do they pay you when you close? Like, for the time after the store closes?"

"Nope." Ahmed replied. "To be honest, whenever I'm closing with someone I know has a car, I just leave right after locking the doors and let them sort it out."

"Isn't that kind of, well, uh…"

"Jerky? Maybe a bit, but fuck, they'll get home a lot faster than I will at that hour. Just because they're willing to go into debt for a hunk of metal that sucks all the money out your ass doesn't mean I have to feel bad for them."

"Sucks the money out your ass, huh? Quite the image."

"Ha! Well, sorry, I mean, I know cars are a part of your job. I just don't want to ever own one, you know?"

It was Mary's turn to laugh, a low chuckle that made a muscle in her chest twinge. Apparently, she'd hurt herself more than she realized.

"Don't worry, I don't own a car and my job is to tear them to pieces before crushing what's left into a cube. Still, it…it'd be nice to have one, but God only knows when I could afford anything."

"Mary?"

"Yes?"

"Are you okay?"

Mary scrunched her eyelids together and exhaled slowly. Half a minute passed before Ahmed spoke again.

"You don't have to tell me what's up if you don't want to."

"Thanks."

"Do you feel any better than before you called?"

Mary held still for a moment, eyelids smoothing out with calm. She smiled.

17. ARTiculate.com

James slammed the door to his apartment so hard it bounced back out of the frame. This might have made him feel stronger if the doorframe wasn't so weak, if he hadn't been trying to slip in quietly to avoid small talk with the other tenants. After a few minutes of cursing and struggling, the flimsy barrier between James and whoever might wander the hallways of the tenement building was back in place.

James had to carefully undress because he couldn't afford to replace any of his job interview clothes. A gift from his parents when he'd turned nineteen, they were starting to look a bit worn. Still, no tearing them off and tossing them across the room. Further denied satisfying release for his frustrations, he spat out, "Why don't they give all the details up front? There should be a law!"

His mood was all the lower for the heights to which his hopes had been raised. Sarah the bartender had called him and first he thought maybe she'd seen something in him she liked. No, but then wait! It turned out the artist had mistaken James' barbacking on total auto-pilot for hard work and focus.

In need of an assistant, the artist had bullied Sarah into contacting James directly—even though he could have contacted the same temp agency that sent him over for the barback position. Sarah casually informed James of an address and a time he could show up at if he wanted to be interviewed. James often thought about what it might be like to be an artist and anything had to pay better than temp work, so he agreed right away.

Unfortunately, Sarah didn't care much and wasn't receptive to his suggestion that they meet up some time outside of work. She pointed out that, while they sometimes worked at the same gigs, they were sent by different agencies and, as such, didn't really "work together". James tried to get across that that wasn't the main point of what he was saying, but this initiated a short bout of unsatisfying cross-talk, with her mostly saying, "Yeah, yeah, yeah, uh huh, yeah," before wishing him luck and saying how she really had to go.

James wished she'd hung up without saying anything, like people on television.

About ten hours ago, there he'd been standing outside the tall double doors to a large, old loft space. It had once stored manufactured goods people not only needed, but cared for and passed down to their children. Now the artist, and the few other occupants in this collection of lofts, fed off of an aura of authenticity this produced in their minds. James felt it, too, unsure if it was on his side.

Index finger on the bright red button. *Buzz. Clank.*

After pushing open the doors, James was greeted by a sight that rarely failed to get his attention: space. Whether in his half-bachelor, the cramped subway, the noodle shop with the saggy ceiling, or just about anywhere else he interacted with on a regular basis, James didn't have much space to move. Despite the forest of mannequins and other large-scale clutter, he felt like he could spin in a circle with his arms outstretched and not worry about hitting anything. This would never occur to him in a park or other public space.

Appearing from amongst a cluster of mannequins in Day-Glo Armani, the artist greeted James with a smile he recognized. He'd seen the artist wearing it whenever he spoke to someone important, who seemed like they could do something for him. Still, it was hard not to be interested as the artist led him around the loft while discussing various types of emerging art of which James was only tangentially aware. The names of people, places, and movements were little more than syllables to the young man. They held significance because of his ignorance, not in spite of it.

The two men settled down in a pair of slightly worn plastic chairs which had been drawn up by some European industrial designer who was unknown by most, yet royalty within her own little world. The artist continued to be friendly and open, asking James about himself and what he was working toward. Not being sure about either, James cobbled together a story from fragments of what he'd told other potential employers. It seemed to go over well.

Although mundane duties would be the mainstay of the assistant role, they were mentioned only in passing and the focus of the artists' pitch had been on ethereal opportunities to learn, network, and maybe even graduate to paying work.

"I'm sorry, this is unpaid?" James had asked, feeling a moment of familiar, unwelcome clarity.

"Well yes, that's just how these things go. But after the first six months…"

In bed, squinting hard at his tablet, James didn't care to replay the rest of what the artist had said in the short period of time between answering James' rhetorical question and their parting ways. Instinctively, James had been polite and nodded when the artist said he had a good feeling about James, that he'd normally sleep on the decision but it was obvious James was right for the position—if he wanted it.

"Can I sleep on it? I'm not comfortable making big decisions on the spot."

Flipping between several open sites, James passed his eyes over each. The taps and swipes of his finger grew quicker and sharper. He opened a word processor and began thumbing out his answer to all the other theories about this costumed killer preying on the financial sector, only getting three hundred words in before realizing he was largely cribbing from something he'd read online not too long ago.

He felt like a rocket with not enough fuel to escape the atmosphere, fast going through what little remained in the tanks. His aging parents would help him if he asked, but James couldn't bear to take any more food from their mouths. Besides, they couldn't possibly pay off the debts his incomplete education had incurred. He couldn't afford to go on a second date, never mind raise a family and—

"Stop it," James muttered.

Leaping back to the forum thread about the financial sector killer, James tried to distract himself from these horrible, familiar feelings by staring at pictures and video of this person who stirred in him something new and, if not totally unfamiliar, at least an unfamiliar mixture of the familiar. Something more intense. Something—

What kind of future could he plan for? What had he done with the time he'd had so far?

"Stop it!" James repeated. He pressed play.

A clip began, embedded underneath one of the theories about The Figure having some kind of Special Forces training. A private security guard came around a corner, interrupting The Figure as she finished off a guy in a charcoal gray suit who looked like he had a long strip of shredded bacon hanging from beside his temple.

Several theories about The Figure cited some kind of martial arts training, often the types that incorporated weaponry, like Pencack Silat. James didn't see it, even in this clip where The Figure managed to cross four feet of gray carpet and hook the guard's pistol out of his hand before he could fire.

Her movements were all about taking the straightest line toward whatever she was focused on. The swing of the strange grappling-hook-head and hammer implement she carried in this clip betrayed no graceful art, no ten-thousand hours of practice, no hesitation. This in stark contrast to the guard who, being startled, gave precious seconds The Figure spent on disarming him. James paused the video as The Figure brought her implement up high, the intended path between hammer head and guard's brow so clear it may as well have been drawn in with a dotted line.

She makes decision after decision, following through instantly, James thought admiringly, trying not to let the way the tights clung to The Figure's behind distract him. "I want that," he said aloud.

He closed his eyes, looking to the life ahead of him as he understood it now, and saw a thin gray line tapering off into an inky black void. Looking at his present, James could only see the next step along the gray line. A moment passed and it was as if a neon orange beam began to extend from beneath his feet, heading off in a different direction. James opened his eyes and knew what came next. Quickly, he went back and pared his three-hundred-word forum post down to a single sentence.

BECOME THE MEANS AND LET OTHERS WORRY ABOUT THE END.

18. التسجيل الثاني

There was a waist-high gate at this subway station, sitting with three turnstiles on each side and the mouth of a wide stairwell directly ahead. It was only supposed to be opened by maintenance workers when they needed to get larger tools or machinery through, and it was, except those workers had a regular habit of failing to secure the gate properly after they were done. Mary rarely took the subway but when she did, she considered it a good omen when that gate was unlocked, allowing her to slip through for a free ride.

That it should be this way when heading out to meet Ahmed for their second date felt so special. A warm sensation raced along her forearms as she passed through and went down the stairs to the platform. The tips of Mary's fingers tapped out a message along the wall tiles in their own personal Morse code, over and over.

"Hello, I'm excited!" they said. "Hello! I'm excited!"

Instinctively, Mary huddled in the back of the car in a lone single seat that had probably been crammed in after the train's original manufacture. On another day, it would have been claustrophobic. In this moment, it just added to the warmth and security Mary took in hugging herself while thinking of him. Mary, usually untrusting and anxious of where it might lead her, let her imagination off the leash this evening. It took long, loping steps and so did she, on her way out of the station, a few blocks down from where they were meeting. She imagined running her hands through his hair, tufts poking between fingers like grass between her toes. Not knowing how his eyes might wander over her. All the pleasant things she still might learn about him. His apartment! So many ways his bedroom could be…

Her right calf began to sting again. She didn't care. Blood pumping, temperature rising, Mary shed her thin coat and let the warm night air caress her bare arms. A sleeveless black vest had felt like a strange choice. Mary figured it was hardly her first.

The vest actually went nicely with her white jeans, its buttons matching the color of their brass studs. She bought secondhand clothes from thrift stores by necessity, but tonight Mary appreciated the stylishness of the practice, and hoped it impressed him. Lightly creased flats carried her across deeply cracked pavement. Mary wished jokes were more her thing, that she had the skill to practice some clever opening line while finding her way along the maze of stocky, red-brick storefronts and townhouses.

"This is alright, isn't it?"

Ahmed greeted her at the hilltop of one of the larger parks this lesser part of the city had to offer. Light pollution produced an even, gray ceiling that comforted them as they stood at the edge of a wide, deep depression where dogs played as their owners watched.

"Yeah, it is."

Mary stared into Ahmed's eyes and he stared back, playing chicken to see who'd swerve away into safer territory first. After a long, soft-focus moment it was Ahmed who looked down.

"That's not fair," he said, quickly snapping his gaze up toward a fir tree's peak. "The makeup around your eyes—it really has an effect."

Mary's eyes looked larger still as she took this in. Not only was she flattered, she was relieved. It had taken some courage for her to decorate herself to seek attention, even passively.

"Hey, what's that?" she asked.

Ahmed had a brown paper bag in one hand that she knew would have a few tall boys in it. They'd talked about this over texts while she was at the junkyard today, but it was fun to feign ignorance.

"Something we'll want to drink further from the edge of the park," he replied, checking the time on his phone. "Better hurry, the surprise starts in an hour and it'll take us fifteen minutes to walk there."

Ahmed walked ahead a few paces, wishing he felt confident enough to lead her by the hand, then turned to look at Mary expectantly. She smiled with her eyes and bobbed slightly as she took her first step along the grass. So...this was something.

Fiddling with his fingertips, Ahmed told Mary a story about one of his coworkers trying to get through a shift while high on mushrooms. She listened, giving most of her attention to the way his face and hands animated in the telling, soaking it all in. Eventually they found their way to a pair of blue plastic whales on springs and each took a seat. Ahmed pulled out two dark blue cans with intricate, orange illustrations of nineteenth century ships on them. Passing one to Mary, he took the chance to let his index finger rub against her hand. They silently opened their cans and each took a sip, grateful for something to focus on besides trying to impress each other.

"So what have you been up to since we had dinner?" he asked her.

"Oh, not much. Work. Jogging. You?"

"Obviously you'd ask me that." Ahmed laughed, took a sip from his beer. "But here I am, a little unprepared."

Mary allowed her whale to bend back slightly as she drank, using the moment to think about what he'd just said.

"Well, um, you can take a minute to get your shit together. I don't mind."

Ahmed did just that.

"I've been working, thinking about what comes next and other fun things like that. Mostly, I've been thinking about my uncle."

"Oh? Is he your favorite uncle?"

"For sure, which is why I was asked to say a few words about him at his funeral yesterday."

Mary let her whale settle back into its regular position and took another sip. Ahmed looked at her looking at him, then started to turn away. He caught himself and held his gaze.

"Sorry, Mary, I didn't mean to bring it up. A bit too heavy for a second date, right?"

"Very direct. Very honest." Mary paused. "Tell me about it."

So he did. Details about his family and the service, short anecdotes about spending time with his uncle while growing up, the works. Eventually, he got to the actual experience of saying a few words while standing in front of his uncle's collage of friends and family. It was only then that Ahmed needed to look away from Mary, to some point over the horizon.

"I couldn't recite for you what I said, I'd get too upset. I can tell you there was a feeling I was actually grateful for: clarity."

"You, um, could really see your uncle clearly, now that he's gone?" Mary asked. Ahmed looked at her again, an intensity in his eyes.

"Yes, but more than that. I had this incredible objectivity about…everything! All sorts of bullshit became so inconsequential. All the family squabbles, insecurities about public speaking, financial concerns—"

He paused to compose his next sentence. She ran her hand along the scratched plastic surface of her whale's forehead, then spoke. "I, um, I guess I can see how that feeling could be seductive. Personally, I—"

"Even the never ending stream of terrifying, depressing shit you see pour down on social media was blessedly pushed outside my peripheral vision." He interrupted. "That really blew me away." Ahmed finished his beer.

"Well, you could, you know, just not look at that shit?" Mary cautiously suggested. "I don't."

"True, I could." Ahmed swung one leg over to sit facing Mary. "But if you don't keep up with what's going on then how can you prepare for anything? How can you really be a member of society?"

"That's important to you, then? Being a member of society?"

Ahmed laughed, grinned, then spoke. "Yes, yes it is. I've got some opinions about that I'd like to share with you but…" He checked the time on his phone. "If we don't leave now we're going to be late for the show." Realization shot across his features. "Crap!"

"Don't worry." It was Mary's turn to laugh. "I'm not big on surprises anyway."

Ahmed carefully dismounted his wobbly whale. Perfectly capable of the same, Mary chose to extend her hand the way she'd seen Jane Austen characters do in movies. Ahmed knew what to do and they enjoyed each other's touch as he helped her off her springy steed. Once she was standing, Mary gently wrapped her fingers around Ahmed's hand and again, he knew what to do. Their bare forearms sparked off each other as they left.

"Right then, a friend of mine performs in this really creative, multi-faceted band and he said he'd get us into his show for free tonight." Ahmed chuckled. "And I'm a nice boy who works at a coffee shop taking you to see his buddy's band play. Jesus. I promise the music will be more original than I am."

"Oh, well, I'm sure it'll be wonderful."

A couple of hours later, a gentle fuzziness around her temples joined hands with lush, dark brown seats at the bar to hold Mary in a cozy embrace. Ahmed's friend had come through and then some, helping them in through a side entrance to claim one of the coveted balcony seats in the converted theater. Soon after, tall red curtains had parted to reveal a half dozen people with twice as many instruments at their command. Neither Mary nor Ahmed were sure exactly what genre fit the music they played, but both agreed it was more than worth their jog from the park. Skin tingling pleasantly across her cheeks, she stole a sideways glance at him as he took a sip from his drink.

"The music is a bit loud and I want to be able to hear you," he'd said, an excuse to slide right up beside her, an excuse she happily swallowed. Now his free hand was stapled to his thigh; it hadn't moved for over an hour. A window opened in Mary's mind as she realized something truly rare and glorious was occurring; someone was more nervous than she was, and this flooded her with confidence. Unaccustomed to it, she became drunk on the sensation.

Indifferent to all the other people sitting around them, Mary took his hands and guided them precisely where she wanted.

19. www.backyardmotherfucker.com/toughenupson

James dragged the oldest, most worn mannequin to the center of the room. The artist had told him to toss it out and he was going to do that, afterward. Music came out of wall speakers carefully positioned to provide top-quality surround sound, mostly drum machines spoken over by a breathy, Germanic woman speak-singing as if in a trance.

The other mannequins were arranged like a studio audience for what was about to occur while the artist was out of town for another gallery showing. James had been given a key so he could make the place appear lived-in. He had his shirt off and a streak of silver face paint stretched from one temple, across his eyelids, and to the other temple. Hands wrapped in strips of cloth, tonight James was going to do more than leave some lights on and play music while reading a book.

Glancing at the workspace where he'd propped his tablet up against several canvasses, James cursed under his breath. He'd already watched the video dozens of times in his apartment but stage fright had momentarily robbed him of what he'd tried to memorize. Looking back at the smooth faces of his audience, he mentally laid a leopard print pattern over their whiteness.

When his fist struck the old mannequin in the gut, it fell over instantly. So did James. Despite the wrappings, despite studying backyard fight videos, several fingers bruised. Pain shocked the young man. Aside from a few grade school scraps with bullies, James had next to no personal knowledge of violence and what it entailed. Thinking carefully, he stayed on the ground and enjoyed the soothing sensation of the cold, polished concrete on his bare arms and torso.

"Oh, you idiot," he said aloud. "She doesn't use her fists, so why should you?"

Because she's a woman compensating for lack of upper-body strength, while you're a full grown man? an unwelcome part of his mind answered. Returning to a standing position by pushing himself up on his sore hand, James chose to leave that thought on the floor. As he set the mannequin back up, his hands on its womanly hips, he couldn't help but mutter, "Christ, I'm lonely."

After looking around for fifteen minutes, sizing up various implements, James was delighted to find a short, metal baseball bat that had been a prop in a photo-shoot. Twirling it up into the air, he couldn't help flinching as the bat windmilled back down. Even though he was technically supposed to be in the studio, James felt an acid bath of anxiety when the bat clattered on the floor beside him.

Picking it back up, James took a few practice swings at thin air. After the fifth swing he began to worry about knocking the mannequin's head off, sending it to collide with any number of precious objects the artist would definitely notice had been damaged. This set off a montage playing behind his eyes, clip after clip showing The Figure rapidly dashing from victim to victim. The implements she bashed their skulls in with changed while the smooth action with which she did so was always the same, and always seemed to come from a place without hesitation.

"She just decides," James uttered like a brand new mantra. "And she does it!"

A spider web of cracks popped across the old mannequin's left cheekbone. James, overjoyed at the result, spun around and gave its right knee a grand slam. The joint blew out sideways, showering small plastic chips along the floor. The mannequin tumbled to the floor and James finished it off with three more blows to the head. He wanted it to shatter like something he'd seen in one of the old protests that used to happen. He ran out of steam before getting the result he sought.

"Yeah, there we go. That's some right vile action there, rude boy." A phrase he'd heard in a song he'd found intimidating for the first few listens. Checking his phone, James saw that he'd only been training for about twenty minutes and some of that time had been spent laying on the ground. Ah well, maybe it was time to take a break. Besides, there was more to what he wanted to do than being able to inflict damage.

Still huffing, James picked up some luxuriously printed art and costume supply catalogs from a stack on the floor. The stacks looked messy, one of his first tasks having been to arrange them that way on purpose. Given that the artist often brought clients or women back to the studio, there was as much art direction in the room as there was art itself.

For a moment, he focused on enjoying the smooth texture of the paper, the smell of the glue in the binding. Both were more pleasant than any free rag James found while using public transit. Rich, vivid colors and shapes drew his eyes along paths that felt spontaneous but were the result of precision planning by graphic designers building on decades of progress in their field. This was nice, holding beautiful objects displaying tools for making more beautiful objects while standing in a spacious room dedicated to doing just that.

Maybe there was a way he could use this to make money? Maybe take a Robin Hood angle that this woman didn't seem to be exploring? Not that there were many sacks of gold to be found in the upper stories of the financial district.

When the near impossibility of taking this or any other path to a place of material comfort became apparent to James, it brought back the strength of focus that had taken him here in the first place. He turned page after page, seeking the look that would confuse and frighten those who saw him.

I can at least hurt them, James thought. *I can do that for damn sure.*

A shift in light pollution caused the moonbeam shining down through the high windows to waver. The beam steadied again, needing only the movement of a cloud for it to vanish entirely.

20. $$$$$$(*-*) %

"Oh!" Gerald exclaimed to himself. "Christ on a crutch, there we go, there we go."

For the first time since The Escapade, as Gerald insisted on calling it, he felt in control. The lines of his body were running in the right direction. Problems needed solving and his was the mind to solve them. Ann handed him another mint, which he popped into his mouth.

Ann was Gerald's new assistant, the only new Byrne Investments employee carefully screened not to have any connection to Dunning-Kruger or his father in general. Her full name was Ann Veronica Marple, something she'd stitched together from fiction to replace the name her parents had given her. Gerald had dug up her birth name, something she'd referred to as "very Burning Man," which amused him.

It was this similarity to himself that had encouraged Gerald to bring her in for an interview, any additional similarities he discovered only pleasing him further. Like him, Ann was an enthusiastic problem-solver who loved flexing the financial muscles beneath the skin of their world. Talk of finance and competitive power relations brought from her tones of voice most people reserved for a favorite hobby they rarely found anyone to enjoy with.

Gerald had almost no idea what she looked like and refused to be told. It was more interesting that way. The one time Ann annoyed him in the two weeks since her hiring was when she made a bad joke about being a natural blonde. Given this information, Gerald felt the silver lining of his blindness chip away.

Imagining different appearances for Ann Veronica Marple was not what currently engaged his mind. What had Gerald excited was the prospect of meeting with the small group of envoys sent across the sea by the narco-lords of Guinea-Bissau whose money he had been laundering for the past year.

Learning how to navigate his new disability was boring. Choosing new personnel was satisfying, but only as much as picking out the day's clothes. Deciding upon how to spruce up the office had been almost literally paint-by-numbers.

"Clean up the blood, patch over the holes in the walls, and otherwise make it exactly the same as before," he'd told them. "That way I'll actually know how it looks."

But this? This was something that engaged Gerald, even as it made Ann Veronica just a bit nervous. Well, Gerald thought she was nervous, as this was the first time he'd heard her clicking her pen over and over. What he did know was that he had the skyline at his back, his new assistant was to his left, and any minute now, the new front desk person would buzz in some men. They'd provide Ann's first experience dealing with a side of business that wasn't covered in her classes at school.

"Ann, have you finished attending to the families of my employees who died in that bizarre attack?"

"Yes, Mr. Byrne, their life insurance claims have all been reduced to the absolute minimum and we even managed to evade any culpability for the front desk man as he was not technically employed by the firm."

"Excellent. Tell me, how are you feeling about the meeting we're about to have?"

"Prepared, Mr. Byrne. I feel prepared."

"Why's that, then?"

Click-click.

"I've read through the available files and even did some general research during my personal time."

"Can you say anything in Portuguese, Ann?"

"Um…Retorno sobre o investimento."

"Not bad. Any Creole?"

"No sir."

Click-click.

Gerald heard footsteps approaching his door. One small change had been the removal of all soundproofing in his office. Quiet used to be conducive to his planning, now it caused anxiety.

"That's okay, I don't speak any either. Might be worth brushing up, though, if we end up seeing more of these guys."

The door opened and Gerald was greeted by a sound his father had made familiar to him as he grew up—an employee being chastised. Even with a Latin American accent speaking Creole, there were familiar rhythms and cadences to be picked out of what was otherwise incomprehensible to Gerald's ears.

The floor's vibrations, caused by the approach of the visitors from Guinea-Bissau, suggested either several large men or an abundance of average-sized men. Gerald paused, then listened to how long it took them to be seated. That measurement, combined with how Ann didn't leave for more chairs, meant he couldn't possibly be sitting across from more than six individuals.

Unless some were standing, of course.

God, this is annoying, Gerald thought, then greeted them. "Bonjou zanmi."

"Not bad!" exclaimed the chastiser. "But I should warn you that Guinea-Bissau Creole is not the same as Haitian Creole, which you have just spoken. Though we do appreciate the effort."

"I try," Gerald replied, then tapped on his sunglasses. "I've recently been given a handicap when it comes to learning new languages."

"Oh, I'm sorry, sir," Ann blurted out. "You told me you didn't want to advertise your new condition so it didn't occur to me that I should inform these gentlemen."

Click-click.

"That's okay, Ann. Besides, these men have all seen some things in their time."

A few noises of agreement were made.

"So, yes, I suppose I should identify myself," the chastiser spoke. "I am Juan Pablo and with me are five of my best and brightest men."

"I listened to your latest email this morning and I must admit it was frustratingly vague. I gather you've come here on a longer-term visit?"

"Well, I'm sorry to cause you frustration." As Juan spoke, Gerald imagined the hand gestures he was sure came with such a forcibly relaxed manner of speaking. "But I am wary of being monitored, given what I hope to achieve."

Gerald knew he was supposed to say: *Which is?* but didn't like taking conversational prompts from others. After a moment of near silence, a mild office hum in the background, Juan Pablo continued.

"I only wish to discuss the overall concept today. We can get into the details if you find the idea agreeable. I am looking to set up shop here in America, in this very city."

Click-click.

"I think it's time for my organization to begin to do its own laundry. We'd like to pay you to help us set up white collar operations in the city for this purpose."

Juan paused, wanting Gerald to set up the next part of his pitch by asking why he would put a stop to the regular income of their current arrangement in exchange for just a onetime sum. Gerald tilted his head slightly, saying nothing. Juan cleared his throat and continued.

"The long-term benefits, replacing the regular fees you currently charge us for laundering, would be many. My people, for example, would put their unique skill sets and experience at your disposal."

"I don't have much need for smugglers and killers," Gerald said.

"You'll have to offer more than that for me to cut off one of my more lucrative revenue streams."

"You might be surprised what you end up needing on any given day. However, you are correct. That alone is not enough," Juan Pablo replied. "I am a proud man, so this isn't easy for me to say. Your most significant gain would be to eventually consider our North American operations a joint-owned subsidiary of Byrne Investments.

"This partial merger would benefit me by providing access to your financial experts and lawyers to help my operation grow more legitimate. You would receive steady dividends from every ounce of cocaine I sell in the northwest hemisphere—an amount that would grow rapidly I assure you."

Gerald tossed a "Hmm" to Juan Pablo so he'd know he was thinking, not patiently waiting for more pitch. He'd heard enough, really, and was already formulating ways to distance himself from these men.

"I'm sorry, Juan Pablo. I have a hard time seeing how this benefits me sufficiently to justify my becoming entangled with organized crime on a local level."

Click-click.

"Mr. Byrne, I mean no disrespect but I feel I must respond to that." Juan took an even, steady breath and continued. "I've done some research and I was not surprised to see that your father owns a controlling stake in Avalanche Security. He is forever funneling money to lobbyists fighting to gain increased autonomy for private security companies on American soil."

This was news to Gerald. He had to give his father some respect for managing to keep that from him.

"He even appears to be directly responsible for a bill—currently being debated in the Senate—to allow private security companies jurisdictional superiority over police on corporate property. Is this really so different from my personal army back in Guinea-Bissau?"

Gerald adjusted himself, sitting upright.

"Even if I agree that I play the same game as you, which I don't, but if I did, then I would have to say that I am playing it at a much larger and safer level from which I have no motivation to stoop."

"Money and power would be the motivation, Mr. Byrne." Juan Pablo might have been saying this through tightened lips. Gerald wasn't sure.

"Juan Pablo, I appreciate your travelling all this way to talk with me in person but an undergraduate's notion of how organized crime and big business are basically the same thing isn't going to sway me in the least." Gerald knit his fingers together. "I assure you, we are very different members of very different communities."

Click-click.

"If I may, how did you lose your eyes? I can see the edge of some scars that suggest this was no accident," Juan Pablo asked like he was curious what cell phone provider Gerald went with.

Click-click.

"I was attacked, that's all there is to it." Gerald drummed a few fingers on his desk. He'd guessed that people who carry AK-47s around like car keys wouldn't feel shy asking about his wounds, but he didn't want to get into the details in front of Ann and unnerve her.

"May I see you without the sunglasses?" Juan Pablo asked.

"Sure." Gerald turned in Ann's direction. "Ann, I'd like you to look away. Please do as I say, even though I no longer have peripheral vision to confirm you've done as you've been told."

Click-click.

"Yes sir."

Click-click.

"Alright, gentlemen." Gerald turned back to face them. "Do you think Forbes will still describe me as a visionary?"

Taking off the glasses, he imagined his darkened sockets set beneath expertly styled hair framed by skyscrapers and baby blue sky. Backlit—he'd be backlit by the sun at this hour.

Gerald's inner twelve-year old hoped for some kind of audible reaction from Juan and his men. There was deep satisfaction to be had in disturbing those who'd seen all kinds of horrors on the battlefields of the West African blood diamond belt. Gerald's inner child didn't get what he'd hoped for.

After a few seconds, Juan Pablo let out a "Huh" that reminded Gerald of a jeweller he'd watched appraising a gemstone.

"That's your professional assessment? Fair enough." Gerald put his sunglasses back on. "Well, I think this meeting has reached its conclusion. Ann, would you please escort these gentlemen out of my office?"

Click-click. Click-click. Click-click.

"Don't worry, Ms. Ann, we will find our own way out." The point of origin for Juan's voice was moving in the right direction. Chairs shifted. The floor vibrated slightly with the men's movements. Then Gerald heard Juan's voice come from what he identified as his office's doorframe.

"I'll leave you with two things to think about. One, we will be in town for a good while longer as we explore alternatives. Two, if you reconsider, I will happily provide you with an excellent bodyguard. Those wounds tell me you'll need someone who has done more than put in a few hours at a firing range and brutalized some protestors."

The door closed.

"In case you were wondering, sir, Juan Pablo was sort of a Latin American coloring while the others were all quite black. One of the black men had a rather distinctive suit and carried a union jack umbrella. I'm not sure if that plays into the hierarchy or not but—"

"Now, Ann, why did you feel I needed to know that?" Gerald asked. "Race doesn't matter to me anymore. Isn't it obvious I'm colorblind these days?"

Ann wasn't sure how to react.

"Sorry," Gerald said softly. "Too soon?"

Click-click.

"Anyway, try not to show your waspishness so damn much." Gerald clapped his hands together. "Now. What's up next?"

"Well, sir." The sound of a delicate thumb tapped and slid along the surface of a phone. "You don't have anything on your schedule for the next hour."

"I have a few calls I'd like to make." Gerald leaned back in his chair, enjoying the feeling in his arms as he stretched. "Would you mind giving me some privacy?"

"Certainly, sir." The springs in her chair creaked as she got out of it. Heels on hard floor stopped before they could have possibly reached the door.

"Ann?" Gerald inquired, feeling like a bat sending out a wave of sonar.

"Well, Mr. Byrne, it just occurred to me we haven't discussed how you'd prefer I address you. Those I've worked under in the past have all insisted I call them by their first name and I wondered if maybe you felt the same way."

"No." Gerald made a sweeping motion with his hand in what he hoped was the right direction. "I don't believe in false intimacy. 'Sir' will be fine."

Ann must have nodded in reply because all Gerald heard after he spoke was a moment of silence, then a few more footsteps and the door gently closing. Pulling out his phone, Gerald woke it up with his thumb.

"Mr. Dunning, business line," he carefully enunciated.

All the post-injury care and consolation had used up Gerald's tolerance for fatherly advice so thoroughly it would probably be months before he could stand to ask Kruger for anything more substantial than a holiday destination recommendation. Luckily, the other half of Dunning-Kruger had provided impeccable advice to Gerald ever since his Harvard years.

Dunning provided excellent advice to a lot of people. Hardcopies of his books, some on business and some autobiographical, could be found in desk drawers of businesspeople from all sectors and strata. On the rare occasions when he accepted speaking engagements, it was common for those attending—once he came down from the podium—to gather around him like a grateful congregation. There were many stories, some true and some more apocryphal, about people finding success after having even one calmly spoken sentence put in their ears by Dunning.

Gerald valued his close connection to the man yet did his best to keep it secret. After the tenth ring, nine and a half more than it would normally take to get a hold of his father, Dunning picked up.

"Hello, Gerald. You don't mind if we talk while I get a massage, do you? Biyu here can't understand English, anyway."

"Certainly, Mr. Dunning, that's fine by me."

"I love it that you still call me 'Mr. Dunning', like you're the paperboy and I'm your next door neighbor in some *Leave It To Beaver* type thing." Dunning laughed. "God, this spa is great. I'll have to get them to send you an invite for membership."

"That'd be wonderful."

"So, okay. What's up, Gerry?"

"My black collar Guinea-Bissau revenue stream looks to be drying up. They wanted to upgrade our relationship by having me help set them up here, bleach those collars white, and eventually perform a partial merger through a mutually owned subsidiary."

"Jesus, it's not like those types to be willing to give up any autonomy."

"Yeah. He said he's 'a proud man', so you know he isn't."

"Of course not. Proud men don't have to advertise the fact and proud men certainly won't commit the kinds of deeds he has in order to make a dollar." Dunning grunted as a troublesome muscle group was kneaded. "Oh, that's such bullshit. I hate it when guys say that in a proposal. Did they offer you a cut of the coke money?"

"They did. We didn't discuss specific numbers, but even a small cut at the kind of volume they'd be moving would provide me with a very significant return on my investment. However, I have to be honest, Mr. Dunning. I turned them down."

"Was it a hard refusal or soft?"

"Soft, though I don't know if they realize it. I need more time to think about this. It would mean entangling myself with a certain class of people in a way that would be very difficult to deny if anything came to light."

"If anything came to light?" Dunning snorted. "Listen, I could drown you in specifics but here's my feeling about the issue. If you crunch the numbers and they're seductive enough, go for it."

"Really?"

"Yes, then you have to go for something else daring. Maybe get more directly invested in Washington. Maybe take on some more black collar laundry jobs. Try to copyright a food group. Go hog wild."

"What? Why?"

"Jesus, Gerry, come on now. Haven't you listened to what I've been telling you all these years?"

Gerry had, yet Mr. Dunning had the uncompromising habit of expecting people to not only benefit from the direct meaning of his advice but also to weave a greater meaning out of the collective pattern. Gerald had first impressed Mr. Dunning back in university by deducing one of these patterns. Right now, he was stumped.

Having just heard some breathing noises and slaps of flesh on tiling, Gerald was at least able to deduce that Mr. Dunning felt the need to stand and pace while saying whatever came next. Swiveling in his chair, the blind businessman put both feet against the floor-to-ceiling window he could no longer look through and pushed his back against his desk.

"When you played rugby in school, did you send out one player at a time?" Mr. Dunning asked. "No, you utilized the entire team in an attempt to completely overrun and overwhelm your opponents. Can you tell me what the key word was there?"

"Overwhelm?"

"Yes!" Mr. Dunning's free hand must have slapped his thigh. "You overwhelm them. You fatigue them, which makes it easier to overwhelm them, which wears them out and so on. Make them underestimate you so that if they ever even begin to grasp the full scale of your accomplishments—and believe me, they are accomplishments—they'll reel as their senses are overloaded by what they could never have prepared themselves for."

Dunning paused to catch his breath. Gerald listened closely even to this, feeling like he had his ear held to the chest of a champion boxer filling his lungs right before lunging in for the final uppercut.

"Flood them with information. Flood them with actions both public and secret. Flood them with reasons to pay attention and flood them with reasons to look away. Don't spend forever staring at perceived percentile chances. Act!" Dunning's voice continued to rise as he spoke. "It's this capacity for great action from a great many angles that allows us to overwhelm them, that separates us from the animals!"

Gerald felt, as much as knew, Mr. Dunning didn't mean creatures of the wild.

21. DEEP CUTS

The air in the deep, glass valleys of the financial district was still and warm. Grids checkered with shimmering black and gold stretched up to the sky. The Figure walked down the middle of a wide road with purpose in her step and tools tucked into a piece of well-worn, rolling luggage. Carefully manicured trees and streetlights in the modern style stood evenly spaced along the sidewalks. In the hour-long walk there, The Figure had been slowly but surely coming online and it was at this point a last little kick was needed to become fully operational.

She wanted to run forward. Too soon. She wanted to simplify. Too soon. She wanted to feel impact shoot up along one arm, then the other. Too soon. From behind thin Lycra, dilating eyes scanned dozens of windows, settling on a corner office where a woman in a sharp suit paced while chewing someone out over the phone. All the other windows on her floor were dark.

Okay.

There was a pattern to how The Figure was drawn to this part of town, always with a general idea of what was to be done. But something more specific, more singular needed to be found to focus on. Without this focus, it was difficult for her to fully engage with the world, to fully take the reins from the anxious young woman she shared space with. Sometimes this meant a needed piece wouldn't fall into place and she'd have to turn back. Better that than finding oneself in the heat of the moment with no heat.

The building had an underground parking garage that The Figure knew would be easier to pass through than the large, open lobby. Two guards behind a front desk would demand unknown visitors sign in at this hour. The garage's sliding door required an ID card to open. The Figure stood a short distance down and across the street pondering this when it began to slide up, revealing the kind of car you might see in a European perfume commercial.

Moving quickly, The Figure opened the rear door behind the driver's seat and slid in with one smooth motion, pulling the luggage inside with her. The steel-gray haired man behind the wheel opened his mouth to protest, changing his mind when a vicious replica trench knife flashed directly before his eyes and came down to rest against his throat. Looking at the rearview mirror, he saw The Figure use her free hand to signal him to turn right.

Skin cold and dry, he watched The Figure make this gesture four more times to bring them around the block and back to the entrance of the underground parking garage. He thought this was the prelude to his family having to provide ransom in exchange for his safety. As The Figure gestured for him to use his ID to open the sliding door, he became unsure. The nose of the car dipped down, and in they went.

Too scared to speak until now, the words battered their way up his throat and out his mouth like passengers crawling over each other to escape a burning train car. "Listen, I did some time in our Brazilian office. I understand what you kidnappers are up to and I know from experience it is always best to cooperate. I assure you that I will, that I will—"

Confusion momentarily pushed fear aside. The Figure's free hand fondled the collar of his raincoat. Distracted by this, he didn't pay the heed he should have to the tip of her knife taking over the role of directing him. He followed its instructions, bringing the car into a corner of the lot where concrete pillars largely obscured them from security cameras.

Wordlessly directed to remove his seat belt and pass his coat into the backseat, the man did in fact cooperate. Her free hand fished his security pass out of the coat. The Figure was satisfied to see the man worked for Norquest LLC. They'd most recently made the news by fleecing thousands of the elderly out of their retirement funds in a manner much more grand and insidious than anything ever achieved by common identity thieves.

The Figure finally came fully online as the last spark of life left the man, along with several pints of blood seeping from the wound in his neck to pool in his lap and outstretched palms. Wearing the coat he'd handed her and a hat found on the passenger seat, she headed for the elevators with both the pass and luggage in hand.

The Figure's target was on the seventh floor, but she visited the top floor first. Just above the finest offices in the building would generally be a dingy area populated by the odd maintenance worker, possibly a security guard, and definitely plenty of large boxes and machinery related to heating and air. This building was no exception and The Figure quickly ducked behind a tall mass of cardboard boxes with the Norquest logo on their sides, a sterile sans-serif font chosen by some middle manager several decades ago to symbolize both reliability and futurity.

The Figure double-checked for a small item in her left glove, worn over the leopard print covering which kept her fingerprints to herself. Paper crinkled between Lycra bodysuit and thin, black leather. A security guard exited the same elevator and spoke into an earpiece.

"Hey, Graham, it's Eddie, just checking in. I'm looking at the maintenance floor right now. It's dusty as ever. What? No, I'm good, thanks. Maybe when I check in again."

A long moment of silence passed as the guard walked over to make sure an electrical panel was still properly secured. Focused on the task at hand, he was unaware of The Figure padding up behind him until a tire iron crashed into his right ear. Falling to his knees in pain, his right hand instinctively reached for his earpiece and, after the briefest of contact, pulled away.

Small pieces of crushed plastic and bent wire had been driven into his flesh by the impact. One thin strip of copper was dangerously close to rupturing his eardrum. Feeling as if he were underwater, Eddie didn't know what to think when he was rolled on his back to look up at a faceless woman straight out of a pop art painting. The Figure held the tire iron high with one hand, making it clear what misbehavior would bring, while her other hand held a small, typed index card.

CAMERA ROOM?

The guard squinted, grimacing from pain, his right hand still hovering near the impact site like an attentive parent struggling with a doctor's orders not to touch their child lest they make things worse. The pain stripped him down, immolating all the bravado he'd expressed in past discussions of what he'd do in the face of a violent intruder. He didn't want confrontation. He only wanted to be comfortable, to be okay, to be able to hear in both ears—

A sharp tap of the tire iron on the electrical panel brought the guard's mind back into focus for a moment. At first, he resisted saying anything, then an unsatisfactory hourly wage floated across his thoughts and the rest came easily.

"Tenth…tenth…tenth floor, right after the men's washroom. Unmarked…oh God, my ear, my ear. You fucker, my ear—" The Figure punctuated this sentence with three more quick blows to the same place.

After dragging it across the room, she left the body and the tire iron where she'd been hiding when the guard first entered. After grabbing his extendable baton and security card, she headed down to the tenth floor.

The room was right where it was supposed to be and the card granted her access. Two minutes later, The Figure came back out again. The replica trench knife was abandoned, along with the long coat and hat, like gum with no more flavor. Fully revealed to the world, mind clear as cut glass, The Figure found her way down the stairs.

By the time The Figure began navigating between cubicles on the seventh floor, she estimated another five minutes before the next security guard check-in. Soon after that, the nervous system of the building would know something was wrong and from there it wouldn't be long before the situation would escalate. The Figure was unsure if the private security company taking care of this building was arrogant enough to try to take care of her themselves rather than call the police. Feeling the satisfying heft of the extendable baton in her hand, she gritted her teeth and hoped they were.

It was simple enough to follow the muffled sound of the woman's phone call. Judging from her tone, it was either the same conversation spotted earlier through the window or she had to chew out more than one person this evening. Carefully avoiding the little whirring Roomba vacuums diligently eating up dirt from the carpeted corridors between workspaces, The Figure—carrying her luggage just above the floor—took a position immediately beside the glass door to the woman's office.

She listened.

"No, no that won't do. It won't…it won't. It—stop, it won't," the woman said in a British accent. "You'll just have to make it…no, there's no getting around it. We have to make some very deep cuts."

The woman kept speaking. The Figure didn't hear her. She was scraping clear any last thoughts not connected to her muscles, her bones, her blood, and the glossy, fully extended baton sitting in her right hand like the tail of a scorpion resting under a hot sun. Starbursts of relief pulsed out from the base of her skull as The Figure achieved a degree of focus others could seek for decades in monasteries and on mountaintops. For a moment, there was pleasure. Then, better still, there was nothing.

It was too brief. It always was.

Information began to flow into The Figure's mind once more as she soundlessly pushed the office door open and slipped in. The businesswoman faced away from her, free hand wedged between her right side and the elbow of the arm keeping a phone pressed to her ear. Seen closer still, it was now possible to tell The Figure's prey was about half a foot taller than her—almost six foot four. They weren't broad, yet there was a strength and confidence in the way her shoulders sat underneath a coppery orange blazer. Straight, shiny black hair arced down between those shoulders like the stroke of a master's paintbrush.

It was easy to imagine how she held her own in a boardroom, but imagination wasn't The Figure's game.

Springing forward, baton raised, The Figure didn't know the businesswoman was able to see her in the reflection from a picture frame until it was too late to change course. The businesswoman's free hand wasn't so free, it turned out. A sharp letter opener with an unusually long blade swung around at The Figure's face. Both women twisted to avoid the other's weapon, resulting in the baton weakly knocking the phone away while the monogrammed blade of the letter opener flew by less than an inch from eyes that had zeroed in on this office just fifteen minutes ago.

"Cunt!" the woman barked, taking on her best approximation of a fighter's posture. "I've heard about you!"

Tactical thinking, not fear, moved the woman behind her desk—all the while facing down The Figure, who had taken on her own stance and was trying to work out the best angle of attack. The nameplate on the desk read *Sharon Carter, CFO*. Well above the nameplate, a pair of green eyes looked at The Figure like a lioness staring down a hyena. The faint sound of the phone, still dialing, trying to get through to another line, was the only sound. The Figure paid it no heed, even after Sharon nodded in its direction.

"Hear that?" she asked. "I dialed security. Whenever that miserable streak of piss feels like picking up, he'll hear what's happening and send ten men down to throw themselves upon you." She glanced at the phone. "Anytime now, Harold!"

Harry sat in his chair up on the tenth floor, blank eyes still pointed at screens. On one display, he would have seen Sharon hastily shouldering off her blazer and kicking away a pair of heels, had he not been given an extra mouth three minutes prior.

"I fenced at Cambridge," she announced." I feel it's only fair to let you know that." Lean, firm arms moved beneath cream-colored silk as Sharon limbered up. The Figure took no notice of this, could only think of how the businesswoman would look flying through the window at her back. The desk was in the way, though, and the kind of attention that'd bring was more than could be easily escaped. This was frustrating, and her target—an expert at reading body language from years of jostling for power—could tell.

"Infuriating, isn't it? You mustn't like it much when one of the sheep turns out to be a wolf." Sharon continued from her place of relative safety. "Is that how you see us? As sheep? Little corporate drones or whatever your college boyfriend calls us while clumsily fingering you?"

The Figure paced to the left, Sharon stepped to the right. The Figure paced to the right, Sharon stepped to the left. Always the maximum amount of desk remained between them and, even if Harold wasn't ever going to pick up that call, it wouldn't be much longer before a guard tried to check in and felt compelled to investigate when no answer came. Eventually they were back at the start, both standing on opposite sides of the broad desk's middle.

"Or are you really an assassin?" Sharon pondered aloud. "Have I actually become that much of an obstacle to my competitors?"

Even with sweat beading on her forehead, Ms. Carter allowed a grin to encroach upon her sneer. Hoping Sharon's musings distracted her, The Figure attempted to leap over the desk and strike her across the face—aiming for a cheekbone. Sharon raised her left arm, getting a broken wrist for the effort, while lunging forward with the letter opener. The Figure had to retreat, dripping several dark drops on the mahogany as she did so.

Crazed with pain, Sharon clutched her left wrist to her breast and stared at the wound she'd traded to her would-be killer. The Figure was more concerned with the opening in the bodysuit than the one in its flesh.

"So, you're Caucasian," Sharon struggled to get out. "That…that narrows it down a bit. The DNA you just left all over my desk should help even more."

Once more, The Figure rushed forward with the baton, failing again to connect with Sharon's skull. Fracturing the forearm Ms. Carter raised in her defense, The Figure avoided another wound on the left shoulder only to take a long cut along the collarbone. The Amazonian businesswoman let out a growl laced with frustration as well as pain.

"You cunt, you cunt, you cunt…"

The Figure took a step back, then another. Sharon's left arm hung limply now, though it seemed possible she might raise it to be battered over and over—if only out of spite.

"Even if you're not a terrorist, I'll make sure they classify you as one," she said, as if willing the scenario into existence. "Don't worry, though. Even when you've been deprived of daylight, sleep, food, and every other comfort, you'll still have more than any of the people you've killed—you'll be alive."

The Figure took two more steps back.

"That's it, get out of here. They'll be on you soon! Run!" Sharon screamed. "Do you hear me? You should run!"

Body shuddering with adrenaline, The Figure ran toward the desk. Sharon screamed again, half-battle cry, half pure rage. Throwing the baton at her open mouth, The Figure dived down to slide her hands underneath where the desk met the carpet. The baton bruised the businesswoman's jaw as it bounced off, reducing her to guttural cries as the desk swiftly tipped over to crush one foot and pin her against the windows of a corner office it had taken years to earn.

Her one free hand sitting on the end of a broken wrist, Sharon was unable to push back without having to drop the letter opener and she was too busy using it to slash at her attacker. By the time The Figure pulled back out of reach, she'd gained six more openings where leopard print gave way to bloody, ruined flesh. Behind her featureless face lay a glitching program, struggling to process the data at hand to best fulfill its function.

This was resolved by the remembrance of two emergency items kept in the luggage left just outside the office. Spittle and sounds hurled at her as she left, The Figure fetched these items and marched right back in. Had their places been switched, Sharon might have stood in front of The Figure trapped behind the desk and waited a moment for the horror of what was to come next to sink in. Then there likely would have been a short speech designed to further break down her opponent's morale.

But The Figure didn't waste a moment getting close enough to start tossing the gasoline she kept in a heavily scratched plastic thermos all over Sharon. Carefully staying out of reach, she easily dodged the letter opener when it was thrown. Even with only one hand, radiant with pain and pinned to the glass, Sharon began to push the desk back. The Figure tried for a moment to push in return, only to be taught how much stronger the businesswoman was.

The Figure quickly stepped aside, crouching to fetch the baton from where it had landed to the side of the desk. Like a teacher of decades past disciplining a schoolchild for bad handwriting, The Figure struck Sharon's good hand until it was good no more. The desk fell back into place, keeping the CFO of Norquest LLC where she stood.

Mindful of setting off fire alarms any sooner then she had to, a thin trail of gasoline was left running from the desk, out of the office, and all the way to the stairs. A Roomba dutifully, vainly sucked at darkened carpet as Sharon screamed. The Figure hastily sealed the wounds in her bodysuit with black electrical tape taken from the rolling luggage's front pocket. Satisfied, she traded the roll of tape for a cheap plastic lighter, bent down, and sent a bright, flickering visitor on its way to Sharon Carter's final meeting.

The Figure ran down as the building went up, soon driving away with a corpse in the passenger seat. Security would either have alerted the police, their head office, or both, but that wasn't why her foot pressed the accelerator flat to the floor. Blood continued to leak out from several wounds, but that wasn't it either. Far sooner than normal, The Figure herself was starting to fade and her counterpart was not equipped for the last leg of the evening.

Biting down on her tongue so hard it hurt, she drove onward, desperately trying to hold onto faint wisps of what she'd felt just before entering Sharon's office.

22. Chrysalis

Trying not to think of the impact on her food budget, Mary anxiously passed her debit card over the scanner. It felt like the bus driver was staring at her, even though his eyes were pointed at the road. The chip in the card was read and the scanner made a sound selected from a shortlist of over a hundred electronic tones that highly trained behavioral psychologists—just before breaking for lunch—had decided was reassuring.

Creakily, like someone fifty years her senior, Mary managed to grab a seat. Ignoring the glare of early morning sunlight through the windows, she tried not to think about the dull pain all over her upper body or the gauze she'd purchased from an all-night drug store at some ungodly hour the previous night. Mary wasn't wholly unaware of how her body had reached this condition, though she was trying to be.

Eyes closed. The Lilliputian percussion of someone's iPod turned up way too loud, escaping the personal bubble it was creating for its owner. Two very slow people speaking to each other very fast. A mother encouraging her daughter to sit beside a stranger while she stands. That reassuring sound from the scanner. Brakes expelling compressed air. The engine never managing to roar as loud as it wanted to.

Grateful for the long-sleeved black shirt under her usual denim uniform, Mary took her lunch box and stepped off the bus to see Vance fiddling with his keys by the gates to the junkyard. Silently walking up alongside, she startled him just as he finally found the right key. "Mary!" he exclaimed. "You're early today."

"Yeah, well, the bus schedule means I, oh man…" She yawned. " I can either be twenty minutes early or forty minutes late, so…" They walked in.

"You usually take the bus?" Vance asked. Mary shook her head and he let it go, as his other employee was also early this morning. Carmine sat on the steps of the shed, eating one of his sandwiches. He was unshaven, while both the ingredients and bread were fresh. Vance knew his presence signified a night of bad rest abandoned in frustration at the first sign of the sun.

"Your guts keep you up again?" Vance inquired. Carmine, mouth full of egg, bacon, parsley, and mushroom, nodded slowly.

"Geez…" Vance continued. "I've got a couple of really upbeat individuals to work with today."

Mary put her lunch in the fridge, grabbed a toolbox off the counter and the crowbar by its side. She paused, trying to think of something. Whatever it was got shot out of an airlock when Vance's hand landed painfully on her right shoulder.

"Alright, Chatty Cathy, we have ten new cars from the police impound lot that nobody felt like buying. They're down by those old buses we got on Wednesday. Can you start on those, please?" Mary nodded, then tried to be more upbeat.

"Sure thing, Vance!" Her reward was another painful pat on the shoulder.

"There we go! That's what I like to see at this hour." He grinned. Walking past Carmine, Mary couldn't help noticing a smell backing up Vance's assumption that his senior employee had gut problems. Carmine noticed her noticing, shrugged, and finished his sandwich.

"Nice," Mary said, turning her head as she walked toward the new batch of vehicles. Carmine squinted and gave her his best Cheshire cat grin.

The earth was getting colder and harder. Nothing broke off in the grips of her boots now. The light wind blowing against Mary's face wasn't unpleasant yet, but it soon would be. Trees just the other side of the junkyard's perimeter fence were a mix of bright color and dead patches, with more of the latter each passing day. She came to a heavily dented sedan with doors a different shade of red than the body. There were discolored spots all over—some were rust and some were smears of poorly painted Bondo. With her own bruises, cuts, and bandages it wasn't hard for Mary to feel sympathetic toward this vehicle she was about to break down.

She was about to break down.

No she wasn't.

Far from the shed, Vance, Carmine or anyone else, she was alone, and being alone made it easier to be brave because nobody could contradict her. Mary told herself the weather was lovely, her cuts would heal without scarring, and she'd figure out what would come next. She told herself to get to work.

The contents of the trunk were few and easily categorized. Side mirrors came off smoothly. The battery was heavy, but removing it wasn't so bad. There was virtually no gas or oil to drain. Underneath the car looked about right.

No it didn't.

The rear axle looked twice as thick as it should be. Fetching a small flashlight from her overalls, Mary carefully worked her upper body beneath the car and took a closer look. Duct tape, painted the same gray shade as the axle, secured and obscured something about two feet long. Pulling out a pocketknife with her other hand, Mary carefully worked the blade through at least three layers of tape as she carefully freed the object—all the while wondering if this was something a bomb squad should be dealing with.

Wiggling out from under the car, Mary got some karmic payback for startling Vance earlier. "Jesus Christ, Ahmed!" There he was, standing over her with a disposable coffee tray holding two drinks.

"Is that his full name? If so, I'm flattered!" Still holding the strange object, Mary stood up and looked at him quizzically. Ahmed was not of the junkyard, yet here he was. "Anyways, if I've been following correctly, then today would be your turn to get coffee. I don't start my shift for another hour, so I figured I'd surprise you with a delivery."

Mary stretched, then took the cup with her name on it. "Geez, uh, everybody's early today. I was early, Carmine's guts made him come in early—"

"His guts? You wouldn't guess it from the way he threw back his Americano."

Mary pushed some hair back. "It's weird seeing you here."

"It's weird being here. You've told me about this place a few times. I passed it once or twice when I tried to shake up my usual route to work. But yeah, all these decaying vehicles. Did you know you work in a metaphor for the decline of the American empire?"

Mary grinned, then had to catch the strange object as it nearly slipped out from under her arm. Placing her coffee on the roof of the car, Mary secured the thing with her other hand.

"What's that?" Ahmed asked.

"I don't know. I just found it against the rear axle. The previous owner really taped it on there like a motherfucker." Mary worried for a second about being crude. If Ahmed was put off, she couldn't tell for the curiosity on his face.

"So, you gonna open it?"

"Shouldn't you be getting to, uh, work?"

Ahmed checked his phone. "I've got time."

"Okay, but if it's a bomb, you have to protect me by heroically throwing yourself on it." Mary smiled mischievously. Having had a moment to think, she wasn't too concerned about it being anything so dangerous. It had been taped to a car axle, not left in a backpack on the sidewalk. Using a small ice scraper found in the car's trunk, Mary removed enough tape residue from one end of the tube to reveal the seam of a cap. Dropping the scraper, she put on work gloves for extra grip and began to twist the cap.

Six turns and it popped off, almost pushed out from within by something shiny and black that was struggling like an insect escaping from its chrysalis. Mary looked at Ahmed. He raised his eyebrows while his lower lip twisted down to the left. She slowly pulled the object from the tube. It appeared to have a flat head with several buttons along one side and a mounting plate right across the top. As it found its way out further, three extendable limbs struggled in their effort to expand outward. Mary yelped when, having pulled the object out a little over two-thirds of the way, it leaped out of the tube and one of its limbs swung out and knocked her in the forehead. A modest blow, it was more jarring than painful. When she opened her eyes, again the object had revealed itself. Even on its side, it was obviously a tripod of some kind.

"Filmmakers?" Mary put to Ahmed, who didn't look as confused as he had before. Bending down, he tipped the tripod so it stood upright and the device quickly adjusted its footing for the firmest purchase possible on the hard, uneven earth.

"Holy crap! I can't believe someone taped one of these under a car. Where'd this old junker come from?" he asked, still staring at the tripod.

"Police impound. When they can't sell the stuff they take from criminals they send it here to be broken down and we give them a few bucks for the scrap."

"Well you better give them a call, don't you think?"

"Why?"

Ahmed looked at Mary in genuine surprise. "Haven't you been paying attention to the news lately?"

Annoyed, she looked back down at the tripod. "No. Not really. There's a lot of news, Ahmed."

"I know but, man, this is kind of the big story right now. One of those Assange Acolyte assholes thought it was only right if the people of the world had free and easy access to printing files for this new toy. Some mercenary bastards—sorry, 'private contractors', like they fix your goddamn porch—anyway, these contractors had their

R&D arm develop it. There's been a clampdown but once a file is out there it's out there, you know?" Ahmed kept looking between Mary and the tripod, as if trying to draw a line of pure interest from the former to the latter.

"So what does it do that's so revolutionary?" Mary asked, still looking down. "What's the big deal about a tripod?"

"This is more of a semi-autonomous drone that happens to double as a tripod." Ahmed pointed at some of the buttons along the side. "I think I read something about these militia freaks developing an app so you can use your phone. You just rig a gun on this thing and either direct it at specific targets or…"

Ahmed paused as he reached for the tube and tipped it so a chunky, olive green case fell out. It looked like the sort of thing you'd use to display a rugged, outdoorsy watch for people who are more into the look of adventure than adventure itself. Inside was a pair of slim gold rectangles, like a pair of memory cards. "These must be the transponders."

"So, what?" Mary squinted. "Like, you wear one of these and it can't shoot you, I guess?"

"Yeah, it'll rotate 360 degrees and pull the trigger on almost anything you attach to it, unless it's pointed within a meter of a transponder. Stick a high capacity machine gun on the thing, drop it into an area filled with 'enemy combatants', no innocents of course, never any innocents, and just…" Ahmed looked away, across the junkyard. "This fucking thing is for murdering brown people by the dozen. Preferably poor, foreign ones."

"Listen it's, um, it's not the end of the world or anything." Mary came up behind him, started to give an inept yet well-meaning shoulder massage as much to calm herself as anybody. "I'll contact the police like I always do when I find something dangerous. They'll pick it up and destroy it or whatever."

He was so passionate and she understood why, but Mary still wished he could be passionate about almost anything else. Drawn and repelled at the same time, she froze. He turned to face her.

"Do you always find stuff this dangerous at work?" Ahmed asked, concern in his eyes. "What if a bomb or some chemicals spilled out or—"

Wary of her wounds, Mary pinned Ahmed's hands to his hips and slowly kissed him. The contrast between his warm lips and the cool wind was all she wanted from the day. Leaning on him slightly, she held them there for half a minute before pushing back to admire his face, still holding his hands. "You're…" She sighed, choosing not to finish the sentence. Judging from the look on Ahmed's face, she didn't need to.

"So," he eventually said. "You're not worried about your co workers hooting and hollering?"

"Uh, no."

"Not even the guy with the bad breath?" Ahmed stole a small kiss. "The least popular Mario brother?"

"I know from what I tell you that Carmine might come off like he's only a collection of stereotypes. He's more than that."

"Yeah." Ahmed nodded, feeling calmer. "Most people are."

"Listen, I don't like it either. Guns really aren't my thing. Don't worry. I'll handle it. You go to work, okay?"

"Sure. That reminds me, they switched a bunch of my shifts around so I can't do Thursday anymore. I'm on all evenings for the rest of the week, actually."

"Fuckers. Well, what about Monday?" Mary frowned. She'd just been worrying about being crude.

"I won't get my hours until Sunday afternoon. I'll let you know as soon as I know, okay?" Ahmed started walking away. Mary shrugged in acceptance and gave him a little wave before turning back to her find. She hadn't been worried about Carmine or Vance's reaction to her kiss with Ahmed because both of them were clear on the other side of the junkyard. With Ahmed gone, nobody could see her or the tripod anymore.

After a little experimentation, Mary figured out not only how to collapse the smart tripod but also how to lock it so the thing wouldn't try to expand back to its fully deployed position. Stuffing it back in the tube, Mary felt a renewed ache in a cut along her right shoulder blade, another part of her life outside the junkyard intruding on her workday. She hoped she could see him Monday. She hoped she could manage the world between now and then. She hoped she'd make the right choice with this bizarre find from underneath the car.

Mary closed her eyes, trying not to think.

23. olddognewaesthetic.net

Ignoring his unopened mail, knowing it had to be bad if they were sending him something physical, James put his tablet to sleep. There were a few more dead pixels on its screen than a week ago and no money to get a new one; something else he tried not to think about. It was starting to get cooler in his apartment but he didn't dare turn on the heat. The electronic discord of several loud sirens came through his small window and ricocheted off the walls, letting him know the nearby fire department was spilling its contents in response to some emergency somewhere. Now felt as good a time as ever to take the next step, or what he assumed was the next step.

Getting up from his bed and putting on some underwear without any holes in it, James thought about how he'd read that serial killers often worked their way up to people by murdering animals. He wasn't sure he fancied what The Figure did as serial killing, mostly because he didn't want to identify himself as a serial killer. He also wasn't sure he could just start off by walking into an office and doing what she had been doing for the past two months.

However, the idea of intentionally hurting a cat or a dog gave him the chills. Just imagining an animal's yelp of pain made him uncomfortable. Standing in front of his tiny bathroom mirror, James let out a brief snort of amusement as he wondered whether a fish would be any help. No, it had to be something more substantial than a fish, something less innocent than a four-legged mammal.

Pulling out his clipper, James buzzed all of the hair on his head right down to the stubble, hoping that would help. Seeing his hair fall to the ground reminded him of a documentary he'd seen about cults, about how extinguishing personal identity was such an important part of the process for new members. Special clothes, of course, were another part. Luckily, he'd prepared for that over the past little while, hiding extra purchases on the artist's credit card amongst the dozens of other orders for materials to be used in his employer's next installation.

Can you really call someone an employer when they don't pay you? James thought as he swept up loose hairs to deposit in the garbage under the sink. Maybe killing the artist could be his gateway drug. Except, of course, it'd take the police about five seconds to figure out who did it. He wasn't even sure he could push himself into the right headspace for the act itself. The artist was a dick and he was definitely taking advantage of James, but…

Having used his hands to collect the last of the hair, James stood up again to wash off the few strands that had stuck to him. The haircut helped, yet more was needed. Stepping back into the main area of the apartment, he woke his tablet up and plugged it into some cheap external speakers with tape holding one of the connecting wires in place. An appropriate song was chosen, something with flat, drum machine percussion rising and falling in waves, building, building, building.

Looking about the room, James thought about his parents for a moment. He'd intentionally avoided contacting them since he'd made up his mind about all this. He loved them. He couldn't do anything this terrible. He loved them. Maybe when they died of old age or whatever then he'd be free to…

That's horrible, shut up, James thought.

How did she reconcile murdering dozens upon dozens of people with whatever her mother and father had taught her, what they'd think if they knew, what their faces would look like the next time they set eyes on her? James didn't know, but he realized he'd have to work out his own way. For a moment, he found himself looking at the unopened mail again. It filled him with dread, a feeling whose power he could harness.

As the music hit a crescendo, James took a makeup kit filled with loud colors and returned to the bathroom. Neon and metallic tones were all there for the taking. He started with basic black and white. After five minutes of careful work there were two upside-down triangles with wide bases and rounded corners hanging down from his cheekbones. The left triangle had black along the lower two sides and the rest filled in with white, while the other was its exact opposite.

Like pagan charms to ward off demons, these patterns were intended to confuse facial recognition software used by security cameras. James had led a calm enough life that he wasn't registered in any databases as a criminal or other potential troublemaker. Still, they made him feel safer while further distancing him from the face he wore an hour ago. The online source where he'd learned about them was reliable enough for him to trust that there was something to the markings.

A band of silver came across from the left temple, covering both eyebrows as well as the upper half of his eyelids and over to the other side. Night blue followed, arcing back across from the right and over the lower half of his eyelids to stop just beneath where the silver started. A broad brush stabbed at the right corner of his jaw and worked back steadily, covering both lips and eventually coming to a rest on the left corner. None of this would have any effect on cameras. It made him feel braver all the same.

Looking in the mirror, James took it all in. A flash of memory, a Goth phase, a high school bully calling him a faggot. Anger flared behind the young man's brow and he wished he knew where that bully was now. Thoughts of driving a crowbar against his body came easily, provoking no squeamishness.

Back by his bed, James took a minute to stretch his limbs, to try to get out of his mind and into his body. Arms behind head. Fingers extended and bunched back up into fists. Lunges brought him down low to the carpet. A failed attempt to touch his toes coupled with rationalizations about relative limb length taking precedence over limberness. A stray thought about the owner of a Cash 4 Gold store whom he'd seen more than once while walking home late at night from a barbacking gig.

Leaning against the windowsill, staring out through the branches of a tree at the brick wall that made up most of his view, James dug deeper. He didn't know the man's name. That felt like a good thing. He wasn't exactly the kind of person she went after, but maybe he was in the same general category. A man who offered desperate people the chance to sell family heirlooms for rent money wasn't in the same league as an executive overseeing thousands of shady mortgages, yet James was, after all, trying to walk before he could run.

Okay, so what else did he know? Looking at the time on his tablet, James knew it was about thirty minutes before the man would be closing for the day. Tack on another thirty minutes to lock up and close the till and he had about an hour to figure out his exact plan and head over there. James turned to the white plastic shipping envelope with his employer's address on it, resting by the end of the bed.

He knew there was a camera watching both the front and back entrances to the place, both designed for intimidation, easily large enough for any would-be thief to spot. Thanks to clips he'd seen of The Figure, he also knew it didn't take much in the way of injury to kill a person; he wouldn't have to be on the scene for long. Thoughts about not shitting where you eat came to mind. They were pushed away by the dour remembrance that nobody in the neighborhood had ever had even the simplest, shortest conversation with him. Nobody other than his landlord knew his name or where he lived.

James shook his head, then tore open the shipping envelope like a bag of chips and spilled its contents onto the bed. Cut to resemble form fitting army fatigues, his custom-ordered uniform came with several creases he'd never take the time to iron out. If glanced at peripherally, one might mistake the uniform's pattern for urban camouflage.

Looked at directly, the patterns revealed themselves as a much sharper-edged and chaotic pattern created by randomly generated fractal shapes. Scattered amidst this mathematical riot of dark, medium, and light gray were thin, dotted lines of pale orange that never curved, only bent at forty-five degree angles. It was like looking at the inside-out hide of a computer-generated man from some early 1990s first person shooter, pixilated veins still attached.

James had designed the pattern during one late night on a powerful drawing tablet in the artist's studio, then sent it off to an automated merchandise manufacturing plant in China. The company's software had scanned James' design for anything containing hate speech or copyright infringement and, finding none, had instructed the correct machines to translate the digital into the physical.

Eventually, some poor bastard, who wouldn't blink if presented with the chance to take James' place, had carefully folded the garment and shipped it off to America. He or she would have entirely forgotten about it, understandably distracted by malnutrition or even suicidal thoughts, the latter of which the company had had to establish several countermeasures against.

Putting on the costume, James stretched and flexed so he could feel the material go taut across his body. Taking a deep breath, because it felt appropriately theatrical to do so, James stepped back into the bathroom and in front of the mirror.

This felt right. This felt correct.

In an attempt to push back against a recurring sensation of accelerating time, he'd recently begun taking as many different paths as possible during routine trips like his temporary barback commutes or picking up milk from the local supermarket. It helped that James had excellent spatial awareness and could remember any route he'd taken even once before. He wasn't sure if it did much to keep time from passing too quickly, to keep feelings of mortality at bay, but it did teach him his neighborhood's every nook and cranny. Twenty minutes later, James was wandering through back alleys, taking the least visible, most circuitous route to the Cash 4 Gold.

Narrowly squeaking through a gap between dumpsters, James wondered if it was time to put up the hood on his jacket. He'd correctly guessed there would barely be anyone out at this twilight hour between when most people have gone to bed and when the bars would close and spill their last customers out onto the sidewalk. Still, if spotted at a distance, would he look more or less noteworthy with his face covered? He wasn't able to tell and there wasn't exactly a wiki for this.

Close to the back entrance of his destination, it was as good a time as any for James to cover his head. The hood on the jacket came forward a whole two inches past his face, then tucked back in to form a mask that zipped directly up the middle. Two mirrored, flexible plastic lenses sat roughly over where his eyes looked out. These lenses were rounded triangles pointing downward, just as his anti-facial recognition makeup did, and were the only interruption in the outfit's pattern other than the zipper leading from crown to waistline. Crouching low around the corner just beyond the Cash 4 Gold rear security camera's reach, it occurred to James the hood made the face paint redundant. *Well, maybe my hood gets pulled off. I'd be harder to recognize on the street without any paint across my features.* he reasoned. *And it helped me get it together enough to even be here. Shut up, already.* James' mind turned to the matter of a weapon. Checking his phone, he saw that it would be about twenty minutes before the owner would likely leave. Maybe the shitty little man came out the back and was murdered, maybe not—that was the best James could do tonight.

Rummaging through garbage, wary of staining his sleeves, it occurred to him that people generally didn't toss hammers or butcher's knives in the garbage. Buying something from a store felt like leaving a trail of breadcrumbs for the police and shoplifting just risked getting them involved even quicker. Bringing something from home had occurred to James but he didn't have anything suitable to carry a weapon in. Besides, he didn't own any tools or blades larger than a steak knife that had never actually cut steak.

He didn't even find any plates or cutlery. Someone had thrown the mountain of dirty dishes in his floor's communal kitchen out a window earlier that day. Peering down from several floors up, James had been able to spot the pieces of his bright red plate amongst the mixed media, abstract mosaic formed along the sidewalk.

Thinking back to the infohose.com forum where theories about The Figure continued to grow and interbreed, there hadn't been much information on her tools other than the fact that they were only used sparingly before being abandoned in favor of something else. Appropriate kitchen cutlery. Fire extinguishers. Executive's golf clubs. Security guard's various "non-lethal" weapons. None of these would be found in a back-alley dumpster.

Checking the time, James saw he had only five minutes left, if his guess was correct.

Jesus, should he take some money? Mask the act somewhat by making it look like a robbery gone wrong? It's not like he couldn't use a few dollars. Wouldn't that muddy the meaning of what he was trying to say? What, indeed, was he trying to say? No, wait, BECOME THE MEANS AND LET OTHERS WORRY ABOUT THE END, right? That had felt so purposeful when James had first thought of it. However, upon closer inspection…

The back entrance swung open and a flood of imagery rushed into James' mind. Over a lifetime, his head had been filled with bizarre and distorted notions of violence—real, imagined, filmed, illustrated, photographed—none of which could be combined to form a perfect substitute for actual experience. These blended with deep-seated frustrations and fear, forming a frothing wave that washed him right up to the precipice of action only to stop right there, evaporating to leave James lonely and scared. The flesh was strong but the will was weak.

When it came to romance, something similar often occurred.

Terrified of being spotted, James scampered back between the dumpsters. The only thing threatened that night was the paint on his face, nearly streaked by tears that failed to find their way out. The only brutal beating was the one taken by his ego, though the pain was dulled by a thick scar tissue of familiarity.

Neatly folding his new clothes and putting them back in the envelope, James turned off the bathroom light before stepping in to wash off his face. He didn't want to see himself at the moment. Finding the hand towel by memory, he dried off and crawled into bed. Over and over, he fended off self-lacerating thoughts and concerns for the future by mentally repeating a freshly minted mantra.

THE OFFICE IS CLOSED.

Over on his tiny desk, a small pile of mail remained unopened.

24. التسجيل الثالث

When he finally got his schedule, Ahmed discovered he wasn't available in the evening until the following Tuesday. This worked out since Vance had reluctantly told Mary he'd have to reduce her hours to only the first and last two days of the work week. There just wasn't the same volume of vehicles coming in for them to process, and though Vance tried to assure her this would be temporary, he couldn't provide any evidence for why that might be the case. Fewer and fewer people had been buying cars long enough for the results to finally trickle down to the last stage of an automobile's life cycle.

Ahmed didn't have to work until late in the afternoon on the Wednesday, so between that and Mary's new schedule there was the potential for a truly wild night. Normally Mary didn't get too excited about *potential*, a word her mother had long ago taught her might as well be synonymous with *empty promise*. Right now though, she allowed herself to love the word and its original meaning—if only to smother any anxiety over her new financial circumstances.

Mary spent some of her time at work on Monday looking for something special among the cars she broke down. Not having gotten up to anything in the evenings since she last saw Ahmed, Mary had had plenty of time to debate giving him a small gift and finally decided that if Ahmed thought it was weird to be given something on a third date then he could kiss one hundred percent of her ass. She wouldn't normally be so assertive, but the same anxiety she was trying to smother left her less patient with any possible, additional negativity in her life.

Thirty minutes before quitting time on Monday, she found something suitable in the dashboard of a 1991 Ford Taurus station wagon and yanked it out with a set of needle-nose pliers. Mary had to stay up a little later than usual while working over her crankshaft coffee table; it was worth it to fall asleep thinking of all sorts of ways she could weave the gift into the following evening.

After a day at the junkyard where Mary's hands had taken care of everything, her head floating in the clouds, she defiantly spent a few dollars on a bus ride home to conserve precious energy so that she might be better able to smile, to laugh, to say the right things.

The usual pile of denim sat by her door as she stood in the kitchen area eating leftovers, wearing only sweaty underwear and a furrowed brow. The buttons on her overalls had settled to stare up at Mary like the eyes of a devoted pet. She didn't notice as her own eyes were focused on the closet on the other side of the apartment. Not having a lot of money, Mary only had two pairs of good jeans, and the white ones were out of the running for having been worn on their last date. Not being the type, there wasn't a single skirt in her wardrobe and the season for shorts was several weeks departed.

The irony of being too self-conscious to wear tights as pants was lost on her.

With Tupperware left in the sink along with a dirty fork, Mary sat on the end of her bed and carefully scrubbed small stains from below the knees of her good blue jeans. Lying on the floor in front of her were a few pairs of socks, underwear, bras, and tops to mix and match. Dutifully lying beside her right thigh, her phone displayed a website showing several color wheels for working out complimentary color combinations—a tool intended for artists and graphic designers.

Was the shirt shrunk enough to be tight in a sexy way or did it just bunch uncomfortably in the armpits? This was the thought floating behind Mary's eyes as she stepped out of a rooftop exit six stories above a neighborhood she'd often passed through on the way to work, but which she'd never properly explored. Not wanting to go to a park twice in a row, Ahmed had suggested they meet on the reasonably well maintained rooftop of the Emerson Mall.

Walking by rock gardens, trees, and teenagers sneaking drinks from paper bags, Mary furtively looked around for Ahmed and didn't find him. Carefully considering lines of sight from the two points where Ahmed might appear, she settled on a park bench and was left alone with her thoughts.

In her head sat a Roman senate of Marys and they immediately began to debate whether the gray hoodie was form-fitting enough. Was the pulled-down zipper combining with the red T-shirt to draw too much attention to her bust? The black, floral lace bra seemed a nice choice in case the evening went the way she wanted it to. Then again, why didn't she realize those same flowers were going to create a strange effect with the T-shirt stretched across them?

To Mary's relief, this didn't last long. When a hand rested upon the point where her neck met her shoulder, she didn't have to look to know who the owner was. A large, brown paper bag with the logo of O'Malley's Coffee landed to her left and, judging by the smells coming from it, the bag didn't actually hold food from Ahmed's work. Taking his hand, Mary led the person she was tentatively thinking of as "my fella" to sit on her right side so the bag wouldn't be between them.

"Hope you're ready for a little something different. I had to call my mom four times. Still, I think I managed to cook up some tasty stuff you've probably never tried." Ahmed smiled cheekily. "Unless you've been to a restaurant that serves Syrian food, in which case, fuuuuck me." Ahmed kept smiling as he leaned close, reaching across Mary to grab the bag, his warmth the payoff for her guiding him to her right.

Bringing the bag to his lap, Ahmed pulled out some paper plates and napkins with his work's logo on them. Plastic cutlery followed, along with reassuring smells Mary made a point of deeply inhaling.

"Okay, so..." he began. "I don't want to make you feel any pressure, but this is a fancy dinner. Never mind the paper bag, never mind the plastic cutlery."

Mary grinned, enjoying his playful tone and the energy that came with it. She looked at him with bright eyes as he continued, laying paper and plastic on their laps with the reverence you'd give ceramic and silver. Next came two long sticks of something wrapped tightly in aluminum foil, one on each plate. Then two cans of beer, the ships printed on their sides bringing back pleasant memories from the last time they were on a date.

"For the first course, we'll be having something I'm sure you've never seen before in all your years." He pulled open the foil on her plate. "Kebabs! That's some Kebab Siniyye right there and, yes, I did have to look up that name on Wikipedia. It's lamb with chili pepper, onion, and tomato."

Mary laughed. "I, uh, I've seen kebabs before. Geez, how white trash do you think I am?"

"I don't know. That depends on how much no-name Kraft Dinner you eat in a week." Ahmed teased. "Anyways, the next course is definitely something you haven't seen."

"What, a shawarma?" Mary teased back, chewing on her first bite of the kebab. "Shit, this is good."

Ahmed nodded in agreement as he tore into his own kebab. Both of them ended up sitting in the same position, hunched over with a wide stance, to avoid getting kebab drippings on their clothes, and set to eating in that self-conscious way you do when in the company of someone you want to impress.

Eventually, they moved on to the second course, which Ahmed correctly guessed Mary had never seen before; Mehshi. Mary looked at the pair of stuffed eggplants and felt a brief worry she'd have to do something she'd never been good at, eating food she couldn't stand in order to please another. Thus, it was with both pleasure and relief that Mary discovered the eggplant contained rice, ground beef, and some nuts she couldn't name but that tasted as agreeable as her company.

Eating this part of the meal, they sat upright and turned toward the middle of the bench, each filling their vision half with the other and half with the city vista. Aside from a sincere "Mmmmmm!" Mary used to let Ahmed know she was enjoying her Mehshi, the only sounds they made were those of eating. She felt something it usually took a long time to feel around someone, total comfort with not talking for a few minutes.

As the nearby teenagers wandered off and the city mercifully quieted down to a dull rumble of the softer traffic sounds, Mary felt her comfort begin to evolve. It was almost walking up onto land, the shadow beneath the water was becoming clearer, increasingly resembling a feeling she'd only found through altogether different means, through—

"Mary?"

She snapped out of her reverie. "Wha… uh, yes?"

"Well, here we were enjoying our meal and…" Ahmed paused to swallow. "Enjoying the view. Then I saw your eyes glaze over some, drifting down a bit, and it was obvious you were looking at something else, somewhere else."

"Oh, well, I'm enjoying myself, I really am!" Mary sputtered, "I wasn't—"

"It's okay, don't worry. I was just curious where you went there, you sort of sunk beneath the surface for a moment."

"Yeah, I do that on the regular." Mary finished the last bite of her meal and wiped off her hands with napkins from Ahmed's work. "What's for desert?"

"I was thinking we could get some ice cream?"

"S…Syrian ice cream?"

"Maybe the Baskin Robbins guys were from Syria?" Ahmed grinned. "Honestly, I could have brought some of these rolled pastries with cheese and syrup or maybe some Baklava. I don't really like that stuff."

"Ah ha!" Mary pointed at him. "We've, uh, corrupted you with our decadent Western ways!"

"You corrupted my dad. He's the one who always insisted on two scoops of Rocky Road after dinner." Ahmed chuckled. "He doesn't have a lot of pleasures in life but that's always been a constant."

They stood up and Ahmed started toward a nearby garbage can with the cast offs from their dinner.

"What does your dad do?" Mary asked, staying by the bench.

Right after Mary finished her sentence, Ahmed slammed the ball of garbage into the bin a good deal harder than necessary. "Dad SHOULD be working at…" He sighed. "He runs a corner store, like a good little brown person."

Even as the words came from his mouth, Ahmed knew this wasn't going to exactly lift the mood. He couldn't stop himself. Turning to Mary, her unsure expression made him feel even worse. He breathed in, setting his backside against the edge of the garbage can, and exhaled slowly.

"Sorry. You don't need to know all the details. Dad used to be doing something he should still be doing and now he's not and it makes me feel kind of…overwhelmed and awful and unable to cope and…"

Mary had never heard Ahmed sound so unsure, never heard him speak in such a tremulous voice. The slight quiver this put in her chest drew her toward him. She came over and stroked his hair, some small corner of her mind worrying her response was a bit melodramatic. He looked up and opened his mouth to speak. She cut him off.

"Hey, I totally understand feeling that way and, like, uh…" Mary carefully considered the next word to come, then leaped into it. "We don't have to tell each other every little detail about our lives, certainly not if it makes you or I uncomfortable."

Ahmed had smiled at her use of the word and she returned the smile when he used it, too, replying with, "We don't, do we?"

"We should get some ice cream." Mary suggested.

"We should," Ahmed replied, pushing away from the garbage can to steal a kiss on her cheek.

They were silent for almost the entire walk to the ice cream parlor. Quiet contentment tasted better than any ice cream she could have ordered and Mary savored it. They observed all the little details around them as one, both noticing things they would never have picked up on in a more solitary, lonelier state.

Lips pursed in a barely contained smile, Mary figured Ahmed must be feeling the same way and this fed further into her contentment. We. Us. These were words she looked forward to further shaking the dust off. There were others she dared to imagine using, but decided they should be left in storage for now. Still, just the possibility…

Ahmed chuckled. "Wow, you do like to drift off."

"What?"

Mary came out of herself and realized Ahmed had led her by the hand into the ice cream parlor. A tired looking older man behind the counter, wearing the same uniform as a teenager up at the till, held a scoop while looking at her expectantly.

"Uhm, uh…oh, er…" Mary scanned the flavors briefly before looking up to stare intently at prices on a blackboard high on the wall behind the older employee. Ahmed saw this and used one hand to draw her attention back to the ice cream.

"Don't worry about prices, get whatever you want."

"Are, are you sure?"

"Yeah, I got some good tips this past week, don't worry about it." Ahmed smirked. "Just don't get the lobster, caviar, and diamond flavored one."

Worries about not holding up her end of the date—whatever that meant exactly—were pushed down by the pleasure of letting go. Getting three different flavors stacked on a chocolate-coated waffle cone might not have been a thrill for a lot of people; for Mary it may as well have been riding a motorcycle over the gap between two raising ends of a bridge as it let a tall boat pass through. Taking pleasure in treating her, Ahmed paid the teenager while betraying no hint of the thought in his head, how next week's tips better be good as well.

A minute later, they were seated outside in white plastic furniture that had seen better days, part of a mock patio the ice cream parlor had created simply by placing them on the sidewalk. Even with the cooler weather, the two of them had to chase melting streaks running down their cones, pushing them back up to the scoops with their tongues.

Looking away from Ahmed for only a moment, Mary took some of their surroundings in.

It was all bars, restaurants, and shops on the ground floor of short buildings whose upper floors were storage or living space for whoever ran what was beneath them. Laurels of graffiti lay along the edges of their rooftops, loudly proclaiming the aliases of artists in barely legible letters. For a moment, Mary wondered about the weak legacy these provided, then she got back to admiring what Ahmed's dress shirt revealed with its three undone buttons at the top.

"Oh fuck," he muttered.

Mary looked at him. After a moment, he shrugged and quickly said, "I just noticed those guys sitting on the patio across the street from us are reading about that terrorist attack in Chicago, then taking little glances at me."

"I haven't really been reading about that."

"Seriously?" Ahmed replied, keeping his eyes on the men across the street. "I know the news isn't your thing, but that's been just dominating for the past week."

"Well, I know…I know it happened and the gist of it. It's just there's nothing I can do to change that shit."

"You know those assholes who took out the Sears Tower weren't even Muslim? And they were of Saudi, NOT Syrian heritage. But, brown, so…" Ahmed's expression soured further. "Look at them, they're obviously talking about me. Jesus, one of them just pointed, I swear he just pointed." Finishing the last bite of his cone, Ahmed stood up ramrod straight. Shoulders pushed back, feet firmly planted, his mind telling him something sensible and his body favoring something less so, albeit far more satisfying. She never had to deal with this kind of hassle, yet she knew what it was like to be made uncomfortable by unwelcome attention. Mary felt her temper rising in sync with his, a pleasure and a pain as anger blended with righteousness.

This gave Mary the confidence she needed to ask Ahmed something she'd rehearsed in her head over and over since they first spent time together. Maybe it wasn't the healthiest path, but where she was concerned it often took the spark of anger to light a way out from her shell. She ran the fingertips of her right hand across the distance from Ahmed's shoulder to where his shirt was open. He watched, rapt with attention, as she curled her thumb around and under the material, against his chest.

"Ahmed, I want to see your apartment. I know we had plans for after dinner...can we go there instead? Now?"

He replied with a long, slow kiss, as much for the men across the street as for her. Mary picked up on this, thriving on the act of spite. Eyes narrowing, the men held their free shitrag of a paper like a floating beam left from wreckage of the days when their views were mainstream. Ahmed didn't want to acknowledge the men any further and began to move toward his home. Mary stared them down while she let herself be led away, her request silently granted.

The walk to Ahmed's building was so short that Mary couldn't help but enjoy flattering herself with the idea of his setting their evening's plans so close by because he'd intended to invite her over at the end of the night. It was a shame about the unpleasant interruption to their date, though she was happy to fast-forward to this. Letting go of his hand, she skipped ahead to the front door and turned to face him with an expectant smile.

She got another, quicker kiss for this and was glad to have been able to get what she wanted with just a look. Theoretically, this was something in every woman's arsenal, yet Mary had rarely been able to find it among all the clutter of self-doubt in her emotional closet. Ahmed used the small blue fob on his key ring to let them into a tiny lobby containing furniture that suggested a much nicer building than they were in, part of the landlord's effort to impress prospective tenants. Soon enough they were heading up in one of the elevators, hearts beating a little quicker beneath each of their breasts.

"I wish I could tell you why it is almost every apartment building hallway uses lights that coat everything in dental plaque yellow," Ahmed lightly remarked as they stepped out onto his floor.

"I don't care," Mary replied.

Stepping into his apartment, Ahmed allowed himself an internal sigh of relief that none of his three roommates was in the common area. Mary became an information sponge, taking in everything she could not only because it was Ahmed's home but simply because it was someone else's home; she almost never saw anywhere other than her own. Details as small as the relative location of the kitchen sink to the fridge were all filed away with a note of genuine interest. Still, he could give her the five-cent tour later.

Mary turned to him and got as far as, "So, um, which room is…" before feeling the neon of her nerve begin to flicker. Comfortable in his own home, Ahmed's own confidence rose to compensate.

"Mine? Let me show you."

It was clean enough, while still smelling strongly of him; the best of both worlds. Posters in cheap frames gave her more of an idea of his tastes in film and music, but that wasn't the part of him she wanted to learn more about right now. She definitely was curious about the small collection of ceramic figures by the window and she'd have to check those out…later. She felt safe with him, with a man she barely knew in a place she'd only just come to for the first time. It was a thrill and a comfort, the two feelings mixing to paint a bold tint over everything Mary saw.

Ahmed carefully fell onto his double bed and pulled Mary with him, setting the two to a brief bout of smiles and giggling. In the minutes that followed, she felt all sorts of wonderful sensations, the brightest being one of absolute serenity. The men with their newspaper, gestures, and glances. Her reduced hours and constant concern about money. Her loneliness. Even fractured memories of what happened some nights in the financial district were pushed down, down, down into a soundless, colorless space within. At the same time, it felt as if she was being lifted, floating higher and further away from all sensation, toward some unknown nirvana where everything was beautiful and nothing hurt, where the walls weren't closing in.

If it could happen with this man, if it could keep happening, then maybe—

Mary snapped back to a more a visceral state of awareness as Ahmed pulled her T-shirt up over her head. She saw his welcome look of desire, then a field of red followed by Ahmed wearing a confused expression. Confusion was soon joined by concern as he moved a hand close to the still-healing wounds on her upper body. Irritated pink lines marked her lightly tanned flesh and two white plaster rectangles lay across each of her shoulder blades, covering the two deepest wounds.

Mary felt a small rush of fear as she inwardly cursed herself. She couldn't have come out tonight if she hadn't forced herself not to think about the cuts. She couldn't think of a good excuse for them. She couldn't think of a good excuse for why she shouldn't have what she wanted with Ahmed.

She couldn't think.

So she didn't.

Now here she was, so close and yet so far, tears threatening to erupt. Mary did something she was getting better at all the time, she fought back. She looked Ahmed right in his eyes. Words swirled and churned deep in the pit of her, but she couldn't manage to pull them out. She couldn't retreat, either, by looking away or letting those tears go free. Ahmed eventually broke the silence.

"When people have a conflict within themselves, they can think it's all internal but there's always external results that push through." His voice cracked, he pushed on. "Are these those? Do you cut yourself? Do you ever feel suicidal?"

Mary's laughter was long and deep. Pushing hair away from her eyes, hair that had been allowed to grow in the time since she first tried to ask out the man whose bed she was sharing. Mary paused to put together her reply.

"No...no, I've never really felt, um, suicidal. If I ever had, then we wouldn't be having this conversation, I'd be gone."

"Oh, oh, Mary. Please, don't say things like that. Besides, cutting isn't necessarily anything to do with suicidal—"

"Shh. Listen." Mary closed her eyes, opened them. "Remember what we agreed back on top of the mall? Well, the story of these are something I don't really want to share. Not now. Is that okay?"

Ahmed struggled within himself, unable to take his eyes off her, hoping she'd give away some clue with her body language, some hint that would let him unravel whatever mystery it was he'd stumbled upon. He realized he still had one hand resting on her hip, two fingers on denim, two and the thumb on flesh. He looked at this, drawing her vision to the same spot. Soft light from his bedside lamp cast streaks of shadow across her.

No longer staring her down, he was able to answer. "Well, this is kinda... but yeah, okay. Okay."

"You don't have to worry about me," she lied.

"I guess you'd like me to stop, huh?" he asked.

"No, no. We don't have to stop. Maybe we just don't go all the way tonight? Only tonight." Despite where she'd steered the evening, Mary didn't want Ahmed upset during their first time.

"Okay."

He felt her against him, wounds and all.

Blessedly, they slept without waking up in the middle of the night. Opening her eyes first, Mary blew softly on the back of his neck to wake him. Ahmed reached behind to pull her closer, holding her hand tightly as she continued. He could feel the red T-shirt had been put on before she'd woken him. By covering up the cause of their late night discussion, she only succeeded in pushing it to the forefront of his mind. He kept his thoughts to himself. After they'd stopped speaking, all Ahmed had wanted to do was make her feel good in any way he was able. Every caress, every kiss wasn't just affection, it was an attempt to soothe and to heal.

While he slept, he had a muddy, confusing dream from which he could only remember some terrible pressure building inside Mary. Eventually it pushed outward, bursting through her wounds. Staring in mute horror was his only recourse as tendrils of gore pushed out further and further and further.

After Mary left, Ahmed noticed one or more of her cuts had re-opened in the night, leaving blood on the side of the bed where he usually slept. Stuffing the sheets into an old gym bag he used for hauling laundry to a place two blocks south and around the corner, he couldn't help thinking about his dream and hoped his subconscious took him somewhere more pleasant when he next slept.

Emptying his hamper into the bag, figuring he might as well do the whole load before going to work later, Ahmed spotted a small ring box on the floor. After a second's thought, he realized Mary must have left it on the bed for him to find and he'd missed it, sending the dark brown cardboard flying when he pulled off the sheets. Crouching down, he opened the box to find a ring much like the one he'd spotted on her hand during their first date, bent and twisted wiring with a dashboard light for a gemstone. While Mary's ring had a "Check Engine" symbol, this image was both unfamiliar and instantly recognizable. He later had to look online to discover it was an "Attention Alert Indicator" symbol, the perfect outline of a steaming cup of coffee.

25. bark.com/bars/spokes

James looked down at the costume on his bed and felt worse than he'd ever felt at any of the Halloween parties where he'd failed to charm the costume off a Sexy Nurse, Sexy Batgirl, Sexy Cavegirl, et cetera. Twice again, he'd failed to consummate the path he'd chosen. Twice again, he'd waited near the rear entrance of the pawn shop and lost his nerve. Only one thing had changed; beside his costume there now lay a rusty, grimy lead pipe he'd found on the ground behind the truck of an absent-minded plumber.

That pipe had recently destroyed the artist's second oldest mannequin, whose absence had luckily gone unnoticed. Feeling its weight in his hand, and the way the heavier end of the pipe wanted to keep going when he swung it, James had the feeling of power swinging a big stick tended to give a young man. For that feeling, he kept the pipe instead of disposing of it as she might have done.

How did she keep up the intensity of feeling required to do what she did? James stared at his costume and his weapon, only able to feel a wisp of what had pushed him to try to walk her path, the mold. He knew he had been angry. He knew he could whip himself up to be angry again, with diminishing returns. He tried reading more news items about the kinds of people she killed committing the kinds of misdeeds he assumed she was punishing them for. This left him depressed and tired, not angry.

Neatly folding the costume to put it away, James tried to use his own situation as fuel for the fire. He didn't see any real future for himself, true, but he could always move back in with his parents. Unpaid as it was, he did in fact learn some interesting things and occasionally meet some interesting people while being the artist's assistant. Workfare, serfdom with a smile, hadn't caught up with him as it had so many of his peers. Reagan Debtor's Prison—

James sucked air through his teeth, jerking his head back in a way generally reserved for when thoughts of his own mortality cornered him at some terrible, sleepless hour in the night. He put the bag with the folded costume on top of the slightly larger pile of mail on his desk. Next, he put the bathroom door between him and the unwelcome paper he couldn't bring himself to kick out of his home.

Staring in the mirror, James tried to remember how he'd motivated himself to do other difficult things in his life. The few dates he'd ever been on, he'd gotten by forcing himself to send an online message or just say "Hello" before thinking about the next step—since that was what so often stopped him. It wasn't the worst trick, but the consequences of being ignored or having his feelings properly beat up were nowhere near as dire as the penalties for ending a life.

Going to school had been another example of what he privately called "The Raggedy James-y Technique", where he imagined simply opening a door and tossing a Raggedy Andy style doll of himself into a room, waiting a few minutes, then checking to see if the doll was better off than before or if it needed an arm sewn back on. He figured the pressure of all the debt he'd accrue by going to university for an MBA would force him to achieve, make it impossible for him to go in any direction but up, so he'd opened a door labeled "University" and tossed the doll in.

Three years and several minor panic attacks later, he discovered that that same pressure could force him down, could leave the doll a wet pile of stuffing and cloth strewn about the floor. Lurking deep within the same corridors as those three am mortality panic attacks, there roamed a knowledge that maybe under-thinking a choice could be just as damaging as over-thinking a choice could be paralyzing. Hell, at least someone who's paralyzed just lays there, not provoking anyone or anything into hurting him.

"Fuck. Off!" James told his reflection, putting down a freshly prepared toothbrush. Carefully balancing the brush so it would be ready for when he came home, not having much left in his heavily wrinkled toothpaste tube, James burst back into the other half of his apartment and began rifling through his clothes for something decent to wear. Eventually, he managed to find a T-shirt with a flattering cut, deep blue jeans he saved for special occasions, and a pair of nice black leather shoes he'd only worn for work. James' lips curled. Why should his nicest clothes be worn for the part of his life he cared about the least? The part that cared about him the least?

He gave the shoes a quick polish, the shirt a quick ironing, and the pants a quick spot check for any small food stains he might have missed the last time he took them off. Six quick phone calls later and it seemed anybody who might join James for a drink was either broke, tired, or both. Throwing his hands in the air, James decided to go out on his own.

Stepping onto the sidewalk, James was careful not to drag his feet as he usually did, mindful of wearing out the soles on shoes he couldn't afford to replace. Breathing in deeply, he headed off toward an intersection of town he'd loved during the relative freedom and financial laissez-faire of his student days. Being broke was romantic then, full of games like inventing meals out of whatever was on sale at the super market that week. But when broke started to look like a lifetime commitment, the romance dried up and the games stopped being fun.

Animated conversation wafted out the windows of bar after club after restaurant after coffee shop, tickling his senses with possibilities for the evening. This was always what got James out on the town when he was in his school days, the possibilities. A momentum began to seize him and he let it, enjoying the purpose with which his feet met the pavement. Then, a happy couple turned a corner and was going to pass him on the way to whatever they had planned.

James had a well-practiced move for checking out the female half of a couple. He'd flick his eyes over her and then back to some point on the horizon, a lamp post or maybe a parked car's license plate, chosen to simulate the eye line of someone lost in their own world. The goal was to hold his gaze on her long enough so it was actually satisfying, otherwise he risked being spotted for nothing. Staring too long turned a look into a leer and James wasn't ready to give up on himself that much, not until he was a great deal older at least.

He couldn't help noticing the held hands and the expression on her face as she listened intently to what he was saying. At the same instant, both he and the guy saw some leftover ice cream on her lower lip; only one of them got to kiss it off.

Brown bastard, James thought, immediately chastising himself for hatred that wasn't truly in his heart.

Quickening his pace, he walked past them as she chuckled at her man's ice cream removal method. Trying to atone for the terrible remark nobody heard but him, trying to lift his mood again, James decided he'd had enough with being frustrated and wanting to lash out.

Good luck to them, he thought, glancing back over his shoulder to see them moving on. *They should be happy. We should all be so happy.* A saccharine, tight-lipped smile spread across his face as he carried on his way.

Two more blocks and James arrived where his favorite bar from his university days should have been; it wasn't. A quick check on his phone revealed that the old place had phased out of existence in the way bars and restaurants do, only to be replaced with another. Looking up from his little glowing guide, James saw more than a few places around this intersection had changed. Like picking an item from a menu, he decided to take this as a positive sign. New places, new people, new direction. Glancing at his options, James chose a bar diagonally across from where his old hangout used to be.

The name, Spokes, arced across the tall window framing the bar's interior like a widescreen television. Beneath it sat a bicycle with glowing light bulbs where the ends of the handles would normally be. Bookending the bike were two tall ferns. Behind this display were a pair of seats bordering on small couches, placed opposite each other so one faced out toward the street and the other faced in toward the bar. Each seat had a little growth on one side that sprouted a large wooden surface clearly intended for you to put your drinks on. James could see himself sitting in the couch facing the window, looking to those who came in as if he were the star of the show.

Inside it became even more obvious how narrow and deep Spokes went. Maybe five people could stand abreast from one side to the other, while a line of more than ten times that could extend from the front entrance to the back. The bar itself ran for a good two thirds along the right side while small, two-person booths filled up the left. Those couches by the window were clearly the premium seating and worry over losing them to someone else made James a little anxious as he picked up his pint.

Not that he had much to worry about, given the hour. There were only a half dozen people present and none of them was looking at those couches. *Their loss*, James thought as he took the couch facing the window, making himself part of the display. While sitting at the bar or one of the small booths on his own made James imagine himself providing a pitiful sight, this did feel like he was just waiting for some friends or even a stylish woman to show up. He leaned back in his seat, stretched out his arms along its back, and waited.

For the next hour, James found himself performing a pantomime whenever someone came in the front door. First, he looked up to see if it was a woman he'd like to talk to. Whether it was what he was looking for or three guys in plaid shirts joking with each other, he put on a face he hoped conveyed "Woops, not you then." The next step was an exaggerated removal of phone from pocket, followed by pretending to check for texts from non-existent pals or ladies who were theoretically running late. When satisfied he was no longer under any scrutiny, the phone went back and the loop would close as he resumed his relaxed posture with a carefully constructed, casually curious expression.

Watching people pass by on their way to other evenings in other homes and venues, James wondered what he'd do if he actually got to meet The Figure. Maybe, instead of becoming her partner in whatever crazed crusade she was on, he'd be for her what he wanted someone to be for him tonight. Maybe she'd take off her mask like the studio-executive's-idea-of-a-nerd in a romantic comedy removing her glasses and letting her hair down, revealing the kind of beauty wars used to be fought over. Her arms around him, his arms around her, either would be fine so long as—

"Shit."

After checking that he'd muttered that to himself at a level others wouldn't hear, James turned to try and properly register the three women he'd missed entering. They were taking a place at the bar and one in particular caught his eyes, all curves, glasses, and confidence. Usually, he'd keep his eye line low in this situation, but James just had to see her face. An icy flower of panic quickly blossomed in his chest as she noticed him noticing her. Trying not to whip his head back around so fast that what he'd been doing would be obvious, never mind his already having been caught, James turned to face the window again.

Unbeknownst to him, the result of his conflicting panic and desire to appear cool resulted in looking almost like he was making a firm, nonverbal gesture that told Glasses to join him. As he sat there working overtime at nonchalantly looking out upon the street, she looked at him out of the corner of her eye. The fact that he made the gesture just the once and never checked back to see if she was coming made her curious. After asking her friends to keep an eye on things, she paid for her drink and headed over.

Glasses took the couch opposite to James, her curly, strawberry blonde hair adding to the diorama he looked through at the world outside. Ferns arced over her and one of the light bulbs positioned itself just right to suggest she had a big idea. James couldn't keep his eyebrows from briefly fluttering up a fraction of an inch. She noticed.

"Oh? You didn't think I'd come over here, huh?"

"No." Truth.

"But, you wanted me to, right?"

"Yes." Also truth.

"Well." She took a sip from her drink, something orange with a cherry doing leisurely laps around the glass. "I'm slumming for tonight. Usually, I'm somewhere downtown, somewhere with bottle service, you know? How about you?"

James had figured what made her clothes look so good on her was the way he was seeing her, through the lens of his loneliness. As with food, hunger was the greatest spice. But no, she must have spent some money on that dress, that coat, those shoes, even the chunky black frames of her glasses with a name along their sides he recognized from billboards displaying dispassionate Aryans in black and white.

"Oh, I live not too far from here." As with job interviews, James found it impossible to lie in these situations even though there was so much advice in the world telling him it was the clever thing to do. "I work for a successful artist, which can be fun, even if it doesn't pay that much."

He'd thought, *Doesn't pay much*, would make her interest crumple up like the face of someone who'd bitten into an old lemon, so it was to his surprise and delight that instead she came forward in her seat, eyes wider and mouth open in a smile.

"Oh?" she exclaimed. "Does he do a lot of gallery showings? I've always wished I was an artist myself. My talent has more to do with boring stuff like corporate oversight. I make myself feel better by trying to be a patron, you know?"

Not sure where to start with his reply, James bought himself a few moments by going with, "I'm James, by the way."

"Yeah, right, names, names." She grinned, reaching out to shake his hand. "I'm Anita."

James found the foothold he needed to begin discussing the artist and what he did for him, focusing on more interesting parts and leaving out his being unpaid. Lying was tricky for James, but he could omit with the best of them.

This delighted Anita, leading her to then decide it could be nice to sleep with this guy who spent his days adjacent to something she glorified all the more for how she felt she didn't understand it—as if all art were a puzzle she was too intimidated to try and solve. James, unaware of her decision, continued to do his best to impress her with specifics about himself, his general nature having already gotten him to his desired destination.

Eventually, Anita excused herself to go to the washroom, saying she'd bring them each a fresh drink upon her return. James pushed down the nervousness this brought up in him when he remembered he only had enough cash for two drinks, that returning the favor would mean having enough for three when you included the one he'd been nursing for the hour before she'd arrived.

As the two of them were talking, James had assigned a few brain cells to solving the mystery of how he'd drawn her over and they'd successfully deduced the way his head movement had been interpreted. Should he be more firm with her, maybe even a bit of a jerk? He didn't think that was how you were supposed to act with women. Then again, James had read here and there some women liked to be submissive to a man. Some didn't, of course. It was like they were people, each with their own personality, or something.

If she'd just kiss him, if she'd just save him, if she could just do that. Could she just do that for him? There was that anger again. Oh, God no, he'd never hurt her, he'd never even say anything, but the hell with her, the hell with her, unless she'd touch him. Then? Anything for her.

Anything he could do, which didn't feel like much.

"Miss me?" Her dress rode up a little bit as she sat down. That was all right.

James took a pint of something he guessed was Belgian, unfamiliar and a few bucks more than he usually spent. It was nice, so was she. His glass clinked against hers and they each took a sip; James rushing his as even these few moments of silence were making him feel anxious, like each second he wasn't actively keeping the conversation afloat meant it was drifting downward toward a puddle of disappointment.

"So what do you do?" he asked, refusing to be annoyed by the unoriginality of the question.

Anita's dress drew tightly across her chest when she took in breath for a slightly exaggerated sigh. That was all right.

"Well..." She sighed. "I don't really like to talk about work, to be honest. There's a lot of specialized vocabulary even I can barely care about. Basically, I work for a successful hedge fund and I directly oversee one of their larger investments to make sure they stay on message."

"On message?" James couldn't help himself, even though he knew he should change the subject. "Who's that, then?" Yup, he could see in the way her body language changed, he shouldn't have asked.

"So, okay, the fund is run by the Steiger sisters, who own about thirty-five companies in ten different fields." She sipped her drink, reappraising him across the glass. "One company is called Trinity Media and they in turn run three dozen newspapers, a few television networks and four of the more popular online aggregators. I spend a lot of time at the Trinity Media office near forty-seventh and ninth street, making sure none of those media sources say anything against anything the Steigers support. I'd kind of like to oversee another property, though. Maybe Kensington Odyssey, they do luxury travel arrangements!"

"There must be something you like about Trinity Media," James said, not sure if she wanted reassuring about her current position.

"I guess I enjoy how much I fit in with the people there, even though I'm not a journalist," Anita replied. "You have to do so much unpaid or low-paid work to get a career going in news these days that you can count on anybody you meet being from the right kind of families, you know? They're the people who don't have to do it for the paycheck, which I think results in a more pure kind of journalism."

At this point, it would have been more appropriate for one of the bicycle's light bulbs to be floating above James' head.

"Wait a minute, you must have to check over a lot of news stories before they're even reported, right?" he asked, she nodded, he continued. "I'm curious, have you heard anything about this costumed killer who's been tearing through dozens of victims in the financial district?"

Anita frowned, then took her drink and came over to sit beside him. James didn't know what to make of this.

"My official position is 'no'." she half-whispered into his ear. "How is it you've heard anything?"

"Um, the Internet?"

"Yes, but which sites? And on which one?"

"On which—which Internet?" James replied, incredulously.

"Yes, which Internet? You seriously don't think there's just—" Anita caught herself, leaned back from him a bit. This caused her dress to fold and show off more cleavage. That was all right.

"Listen, I have to go to the bathroom again. Why don't you grab us some fresh drinks and when I get back we can talk about something else, something more 'Friday night', you know?" And up she went. James still had half a pint, which he silently supped back at some speed.

He could maybe press later to try to find out more about The Figure. He could maybe find out more about Anita. He could maybe not feel so solitary, at least for a few hours. But to do all that, James reckoned, he had to be able to afford two more drinks when he could only manage one. There wasn't anything left on his credit card, nor was there any more overdraft on his checking account to dredge up. The words *Savings Account* didn't occur to him at all.

His frustration redirected inward, James was flogging the flesh off his self-esteem's back. By this point, were this part of his psyche a person, pink-tinged bones would have started to become visible. Some other Spokes patrons wondered why the guy sitting by the front looked so anguished, almost ready to cry. James planned how he'd have to weave his way through the neighborhood before Anita would be unable to step outside the bar and deduce which way he'd left.

Unaware he was being monitored by two of her friends, both confused by his pained expression, James put his glass down and felt tension turn his shoulders into birch wood as he stepped out the bar and took a perfect, ninety degree, hard right. He didn't run, but he was almost power walking as he worked his way back home. It was only after James was certain he was further away than any sane woman would follow him that he slowed down.

James' hands trembled slightly with low blood sugar, despite the two beers. He felt run to the ground, a fox with no more energy to escape the hounds. He idly considered taking his pipe and just murdering someone, anyone, never mind the costume. He dismissed the thought as quickly as it came, each and every time it came, as his tenement building grew nearer.

Approaching the front entrance, James couldn't help remembering something that had happened at a New Year's party once. He'd been making out on a couch with a girl who had been so obviously into him even he had noticed. Then, for some godforsaken reason, he'd pulled back and started quizzing her about her future. The phrase "five year plan" had been deployed and what came next wasn't pretty. She'd replied with some quip about how while she did trim down there, this didn't mean her vagina had a moustache like Joseph Stalin, not that he was going to be able to find out now anyway.

Over thinking. Under thinking. Where was the middle? That focus? Where was a lasting drive?

James felt he knew the answer, that he'd known the answer for a while; he'd just been blanking it as hard as that girl had done to him after making her Joseph Stalin jab.

Coming into his apartment, he shut the door with theatrical

carefulness before swiveling left and punching down into his desk as hard as he could. It had felt James' frustration a few times before and the crack along its midsection finally gave way. Laminated, compressed wood foam awkwardly collapsed to the floor, spilling the costume and the small pile of unopened envelopes.

He reached down for the mail, throwing the Raggedy James-y doll into a dark room one more time.

26. Sunflowers

Closing the door to Ahmed's apartment behind her, Mary knew some decisions had to be made. Leaving the lobby, she felt he would respect her request to not ask about the healing cuts on her upper body, but plainly, any further injury would make it impossible for him to keep that promise forever. Saving money with a sizable walk home, almost two hours long, Mary alternated between treating what she now felt comfortable calling "my new relationship" as a puzzle in need of solving and seeing it as a perfect tool for pulling up some of the finest sensations the chemicals in her body had to offer.

Sunlight beamed through the gaps between falling leaves. Colors were sharper. The air had a cool, palatable taste to it. She felt each breath from start to finish, a pleasure. Even the concrete brought back snapshots of blissful imagery from her earliest memories of Ahmed's face framed by the sunflower-patterned pillowcase he said his aunt had bought him. What a sign that case had been; it almost made Mary let herself believe in fate.

Walking past a men's clothing store, she saw one mannequin wearing an outfit she rather liked and fantasized about being able to buy it for Ahmed. Mary enjoyed the idea of making him look nice not only for herself, but for the world at large. Maybe she'd give him more than the clothes: the confidence to find something better than slinging coffee. There was certainly some appeal to helping him, giving him strength and other things as "the woman behind the man". That being said, she certainly enjoyed imagining what he could give her as "the man behind the woman".

Mary went a little red for a moment.

Correcting the course of her thinking, silently mouthing, "Okay, but seriously?" while taking a left turn by an empty skate park, Mary drew strength from the idea of Ahmed's continued presence in her life. Would he watch the cartoons of her childhood with her? Maybe on a Sunday morning after a Saturday night first spent exploring the city, then each other?

Surely he would. Surely his hair would be just right as he did so, his fingers intertwined with hers from start to finish. Maybe they could eventually live together, moving into a new place nicer than anything they could ever afford individually, making their new home into a perfect expression of who they were.

As she slid more and more artistic creations into the carousel of her mental slide show, the fantasies of the relationship quickly outnumbered the memories. Mary paused, not far from the convenience store where she got her Shen-Yung ramens, hoping that stopping her body might help slow down her imagination. This was starting to feel dangerous, in an exciting way. Staring directly down at the sidewalk, Mary gathered her faculties.

If she wanted what Ahmed's presence in her life provided, she'd have to bridge the gap between now and whenever he might become a real partner in her life. Right now, he was barely a boyfriend and that helped, but didn't eliminate the need for what she kept locked beneath the bathroom sink. What she kept there threatened the relationship. Could she cope without it? Was being with Ahmed actually something she should pin her hopes to?

She had to talk to someone about this, about what came next. Lacking siblings or close friends, Mary knew this left her only one option.

Kicking worn shoes from sore feet, she flopped onto her bed facedown into the pillows. This was too much. She just wanted to sleep, even knowing it would all be waiting for her when she awoke. Eventually Mary rolled flat on her back, pulled out her phone, and selected one from the handful of names in her contact list. A familiar gray-faced, default avatar came up on the screen with the word "Mom" underneath it.

Six hours drive away, a tired woman working in a small garden felt the back pocket of her overalls vibrate. Walking to the end of a row of carrots, she removed yellow work gloves. Pulling out her phone with one hand, she used the other to touch the screen of an old tablet attached to some portable speakers that had been radiating BBC News through the air while she worked.

"Mary?"

"Who else would it be?"

"Someone else using your phone? Maybe it got hacked."

"Who would want to hack my phone?"

"You'd be surprised. I was just listening to a report about how…"

Mary wanted to interrupt her with the news that she'd found someone, but lost her nerve for a moment. Even though her mother was only doing her best recital of some news story designed to whip up fear in people over a certain age or under a certain level of technological literacy, it was nice just to listen to her voice for a little bit.

"Mom, Mom, I'll keep all that in mind, okay?"

"Good, good. You know Mrs. Cooke was asking about you the other day? Wondering about your adventures in the big city. You remember Mrs. Cooke, right?"

"Ssssort of?"

"Well I told her about your job at the junkyard and she asked if you had full time with benefits and I wasn't sure about the benefits but I told her you had full time and we both agreed you're very lucky and—"

"Mom! Don't you want to know why I called?"

Mary's mother sat down, bum on the grass and feet in the deep trench between carrots and potatoes. "Of course, it's just you barely call and I have all this news I want to tell you before I forget it."

"Well, I don't work full time anymore. They've cut me down to four days a week." Not ready for The Problem, Mary decided to relate A Problem, "I'll still be able to cover my expenses, but I was actually managing to save a little money. Not enough for retirement but maybe I'd have a tiny cushion if I ever got hurt badly or—"

"Do you need help?"

Mary knew her mother couldn't give her any meaningful financial aid. Mary grimaced as she was reminded of how the woman who birthed her had to work six days a week at a supermarket as well as try to maintain a small home garden, the only way to be able to afford any healthy vegetables in her diet.

"Mary? Mary, don't go quiet and disappear down a dark hole. You know that's not good for anyone. Do you need money?"

"No, Mom, I don't need any money." A half-truth. "I kind of have a problem I could use your help with though."

Several moments of silence. "Mary? Are you still there?"

"Yes, Mom."

"Well, what is it?"

"I met a boy and he makes me really happy."

Mary's mother laughed so hard her face ached from smiling.

"There are worse things," she eventually got out. "There really are. Did you hear about those poor souls in Chicago? You'd think all the rights they've taken away and the militarization of the police would actually help prevent crap like those nuts at the Sears Tower. But then we all know what it's really about, don't we? It's so galling how they don't even seem to want to hide their moves behind a conspiracy; it's all out there in the open!"

"Mom, stop, okay?" Mary's brow tensed. "I don't want to hear that stuff."

"Head in the sand as always. I can't believe someone your age pays so little attention to the news. Don't you use the Internet?"

"Yeah, I, uh, do in fact use that there Internet."

"Not looking at the world doesn't keep it from happening. Just like moving out didn't magically make the dog come back to life."

"Mom! Heisenbark wasn't just 'the dog'. We had him for eighteen years!" Mary turned on her side, staring daggers at the short dividing wall between the main area of her apartment and her tiny kitchen. "And I wish you'd stop being mad about my leaving home. I couldn't stay there forever."

"I wish I'd stop being mad, too. I really do, my darling. It's just hard here all on my own."

"Nobody forced you to have a test-tube baby. You could have made one the old fashioned way."

"Not with any of the men I ever met. God, the awkward ones always complained about how easy it is for a woman to get laid when sex isn't even the issue, is it?" A pause as she struggled to remember the point of the call. "What's this boy's name?"

"His name is Ahmed," Mary answered. "He works at the nice coffee shop the guys and I get our morning fix from."

"The coffee shop you—okay, I was wondering how you might meet someone. Has he introduced you to his friends? Maybe you could make some friends, too. You've been so lonely."

"Mom!" Mary caught herself. "Not really. Only this one guy that got us into a show. It's okay. I like it this way, while we're still getting to know each other."

"Keeping your world small and manageable, then." Her mother sighed. "Have you at least considered my suggestion? Volunteering somewhere, maybe the library?"

"I haven't got time to work for free!"

"Well, you have two extra days off now, don't you?"

"That's not the problem I want to talk about."

"So okay, my love, tell me what it is why don't you?"

The Figure might have been able to throw herself into situations with only the lightest outline of a plan, but Mary just couldn't. She thought she'd think of some way to talk about the conflict between her needs, her wants, and her situation without giving away the delicate parts of all three. She didn't.

"I don't know." A lie. "I don't know, I don't know, I don't know."

"Mary—"

"Mom, never mind. I shouldn't have called. I'm just a fuck up, I'm just doomed, okay? It doesn't matter that some guy has finally taken an interest in me."

"Mary, lots of boys notice you. You're so nice and tall."

"With dry skin and beady eyes and and and besides, most guys don't like tall girls and what does it matter anyways when I'll never be able to retire or have a kid or a house or or or—"

Mary sat in silence with her eyes scrunched closed, breath shallow, hand holding her phone so tight the case separated slightly and made a small plastic-on-plastic sound in her ear. She wasn't the crying type. Mary wished she was, if only for some catharsis from a vice of frustration which had begun squeezing the day's good mood into a pulp.

Desperate to end the call on a positive note, her mother wrenched the steering wheel on the conversation. "Mary, did you know this year's sunflowers are still standing tall and proud? You've always liked sunflowers."

"I love them." Mary swallowed.

"I'll never forget that time you were six and we got the first real snowstorm of the season. We had over a dozen sunflowers all standing at the end of the yard and you saw one fall over. So I had to dress you in your little snowsuit and watch through the kitchen window as you ran out to them."

Mary remembered; her face relaxed a little bit.

"You were so sad they were dying, you actually ran up and hugged one."

Mary felt a soft laughter brewing inside, knowing what came next.

"You hugged one so hard, and its stem had grown so brittle in the cold, the top half broke off and fell on your head. You cried and cried and cried, you poor little thing." Mary's mother sighed fondly.

"No matter how much I explained to you just because one good time was coming to an end, it didn't mean there'd never be any more, it didn't mean there wouldn't be more sunflowers. You just kept crying until you tired yourself out."

"I really loved them." Mary smiled, laughter never finding its way out yet warming her all the same.

27. (⁻ - ⁻ >)>

Gerald knew he was asleep almost immediately. Even if not for years of practicing lucid dreaming, his being able to see was a pretty big tip-off. As tended to be the case, he was walking through a Frankenstein's monster of various offices he'd been to or owned at one point. Sometimes a hallway from Harvard or a room from his parent's primary residence during his childhood would pop up, but not tonight; tonight was office after office after office.

Being aware of dreaming, he had at least a little control over which direction he took; not so much where his vision was pointed. Gerald liked the idea of more control and, essentially, life—because even though the results dried up upon awakening, surely several hours spent in control of your actions counted as something approximating more life? As a result of this, late in his last year of prep school, Gerald had begun studying the discipline of achieving conscious awareness during a dream state.

He'd sniffed at the promotional copy on the back of a guidebook he'd picked up, yet lucid dreaming had in fact left him more rested while helping him gain greater confidence, overcome fears, and even improve his creativity. It was that last one which had given him an edge in the boardroom as creativity was in pretty short supply amongst a pack of MBAs.

Since he'd lost his eyes, Gerald hadn't been able to keep up the mental exercises required to maintain regular, fully empowered dreaming. At first, he'd found it difficult to focus on a white dot in his mind or perform specific breathing exercises because of the painkillers. Even after getting off the morphine pills, there was still a major obstacle in his way. Almost every technique that would set up his mind for lucid dreaming required being highly aware of his body, shifting focus from one part to another as he built a copy of it in his mind for him to pilot around the dreamscape.

Invariably, this meant being highly aware of his empty eye sockets, and not only was this unpleasant to dwell upon, but Gerald worried it could lead to being blind in his dreams as well. For this, he paid a price that truly galled him. He'd surrendered total control.

Well, Gerald thought. *Let's go to the office.* Gerald may have found greater creativity through lucid dreaming, but he hadn't exactly turned into Salvador Dali. He was pleased to find his office fairly quickly and on some level he understood that keeping everything in his real-life office the same helped him find it in his dreams. While he couldn't see the real office anymore, he still felt the same chair beneath him and walked the same amount of steps to reach it.

In the dream, he did just that, turning his seat to admire the view. The shimmering outline of the Dunning-Kruger building was the right coppery-gold tint. The four black glass towers of Norquest, LLC were arranged to the far right. And between them, he could see some ocean along the skyline. Next, he saw the Millennium Falcon swoop down from the clouds, pointing directly at him for a few moments before pulling up to fly over his building. Still, not bad.

The upsetting thing came soon after, when the dimensions of the room as he established them in his mind were not respected. He knew the strange figure who had taken his eyes had come in through his office door, which currently sat several feet directly behind him. Regardless, she burst in through the window in front of him, pushing a section of it open as if shouldering through a door—because that's what she'd done that day in the real office, shouldered his door open.

It didn't make complete sense, it didn't have to. A psychiatrist at the hospital had warned him he might suffer nightmares and other symptoms of a variety of post-traumatic stress disorder. Gerald had certainly seen enough of this in stories that he expected the sheer predictability, the cliché of the whole thing, would render it powerless.

He was wrong.

Oh, the first few times he'd been able to simply will her away, as if waving a hand to dismiss an over-attentive waiter. After a while, he found he had to imagine actually grappling with her in hand-to-hand combat, always winning because he decided he was strong enough to break her neck with ease. When the neck wouldn't stay broken he had to escalate to placing guns in his hands, and the last time she stalked him through the hallways of Byrne Investments the guns were frustratingly ineffective, bullets simply passing through her until she was unbearably close.

Not having had the time to study her closely, her proportions always shifted from dream to dream and even from moment to moment. Tonight she was much, much taller than she had been in real life and her right hand was nothing but shining, blood-streaked blades. Looking to his own hands, nothing would appear no matter how much he willed it. As she leaped up to sit on his chest, jagged knives raised high to strike, Gerald couldn't even make his hands move.

This was it, she was about to take the final inch. Furious with the situation as well as the voice inside him that had started to wonder aloud, "What else will she take?" he tried to end the dream. Gerald watched his left eye pulled back away from his face, split in the middle like a grape, while he shouted in hoarse tones, "Wake up! Wake up! Wake up!"

And he did, right as she began to take the other eye.

Throat dry from mouth breathing in his sleep—something he'd inherited from his mother—Gerald reached for a glass of water and pushed it over onto the carpet. A knock at his bedroom door.

"Mr. Byrne, are you alright sir?" It was Ann. Lacking any long-term partner to help him with all the little things that were so much more difficult now, it had been necessary to make her his caretaker as well as his assistant. This was the kind of liberty you could get away with when you had enough prestige and a new hire.

Getting two jobs out of Ann for one paycheck helped Gerald feel a little bit better about having to rely so heavily on another human being. Having internalized the promise of what a stepping-stone this could be, Ann felt a little better about being so heavily taken advantage of by an employer.

"What time is it?"

"It's six twenty, Mr. Byrne."

"May as well get up then. I'm going to shower first. Please have my breakfast ready in fifteen minutes. Oh, and what's the first item on today's agenda?" He knew the answer, but wanted to know if she did, too.

A pause while she checked her phone. As Gerald was about to chastise her for not knowing off the top of her head, she answered. "All I have is 'D-K building, special meeting' for nine on the dot."

Getting out of bed, Gerald remembered how his father had made a point of verbally extending the invitation over the phone—as if that was any safer than sending an email. This was a meeting that had been canceled twice before, something big his father and Mr. Dunning had been trying to organize with several other CEOs of large banks, investment firms, and the like.

He wouldn't have quite rated an invitation if not for his father; and, as it was, he'd be expected to sit quietly on the sidelines. Dunning hadn't been willing to spill the beans on the actual subject of the meeting, even though he was usually happy to tell Gerald anything Kruger wouldn't. While the concentration of powerful individuals in one room was a strong pull, Dunning's silence was what had really seized Gerald's interest.

"Fffffuck!" Mulling this over, he didn't pay enough attention to his surroundings and stubbed a toe on the dresser so hard he could almost hear the nail go black. Ann's heels on the hardwood of the hallway. The latch turning. "Mr. Byrne, I heard a noise. Are you okay?"

Gerald had quickly established he didn't have one ounce of self-consciousness about being seen in a state of undress by Ann. She'd sounded sure enough when she told him she was a professional and all that; still, Gerald had to wonder. Did she look at him like a dispassionate nurse or did he intimidate her? Arouse her? Both? Sitting back on the edge of his bed, the hurt toe palmed in one hand, Gerald put on an act of grimacing in pain. It felt appropriate.

"Just stubbed my toe. I guess I was still disoriented from sleep and forgot how many paces to take before turning left into the en-suite."

Her weight on the bed, sitting beside him. This casualness was to be expected, given the kind of access to his life Gerald had allowed Ann. He almost wanted her to stroke his hair; it had been some time since a woman had done that for him. Instead, she took his chin and turned his face to her with all the intimacy of swiveling a faucet head.

If his eye sockets disturbed her, she didn't show it in any way he could notice.

"Sir, I hope you don't mind my saying but you look like you didn't get a lot of rest."

Gerald barked a short laugh. "Bags under my eyes?"

"Just in general, you don't look like someone getting much rest. Did you have trouble sleeping?"

"Nightmares, totally boring nightmares. Don't worry about it."

"About—"

"Yes, the horrible bitch who took my eyes. La dee da. What else is new? Can you help me to the bathroom, please?"

She took his hand, leading him along a path that confirmed he had forgotten the two extra paces needed before turning left to go around the dresser. Ann held his hand like you might hold a little boy's as you led him to the washroom and this annoyed Gerald. However, he knew he'd only sound as small as he currently was being made to feel if he gave her grief over this. When she spoke again, her tone was perfectly even, yet came off faintly patronizing to the antagonistic duo of Gerald and his awful mood.

"I still think it's awful what she did to you, to say nothing of the dozens and dozens of victims she's claimed…and there's the families of all those poor souls." She put his hand on the towel rack so he'd have his bearings, then turned to leave. "Probably a couple hundred people she's made absolutely miserable, and for what? What the hell is the point of all this carnage?"

"Why does fire consume oxygen?" Gerald shed his underwear, pulled open the glass door, and stepped into the shower. "Honestly, I don't think about it. I don't need to give that piece of shit any more of my headspace than she already takes up, and if I were you, I'd try to think of more pleasant things."

She muttered something he couldn't hear, then raised her voice back up. "Do you want me to wait out here to help you?"

"No, go get breakfast ready and turn on the audio-GPS system. I can use that to find my way to the living room. I turned it off last night but I guess I still need the stupid thing. After breakfast, we'll go straight to the D-K building."

"Yes sir, Mr. Byrne."

The drive to the Dunning-Kruger building was pleasant enough, any bad smells the city had to offer mercifully tamped down by the encroaching cold and rush hour. Streaming through the car stereo was the middle of a long podcast documentary on weather manipulation he'd been trying to finish. Lacking any visual distractions, he found it easy to pay attention to the monotonous host describing oceans seeded with iron phosphate while Gerald theorized what this big meeting could be about. While listening, he quietly pushed around variables related to accepting or rejecting the Guinea-Bissau narcolord's offer; trying to arrange them so they'd give up the perfect decision, like an ancient Roman laying out chicken guts.

All of this was neatly filed away when Ann informed him they'd arrived—even the guessing. Gerald would know what the meeting was about soon enough.

As the elevator took Ann, himself, and the courtesy security guard up to the seventieth floor, Gerald found it necessary to comment.

"Jesus, I don't remember the elevators here being so loud. Have you guys been messing around with them?" The security guard politely told Gerald that nothing had been changed recently.

His other senses were beginning to adapt. He didn't like it.

Slightly embarrassed at having to be led by his assistant, a white cane being simply too much as far as he was concerned, Gerald found it difficult to remember the specifics of the paintings he knew he was passing while they went down the long hallway toward the building's main boardroom. As they reached the two heavy redwood doors and waited for two more security guards to pull them open, it occurred to Gerald that the art might have been shuffled and he'd just spent the past minute trying to remember an environment that was no longer the same as when he last saw it.

Warm sun against his face as he entered the boardroom reminded Gerald of something that had to be the same, the two-story-high glass ceiling his father had insisted on. It was shaped to a point not unlike the prow of a dreadnought, which both Kruger and Dunning had agreed was suitable since the building was in many ways their flagship. During construction, a tragic accident occurred and a large pane of tinted, golden glass fell all the way down to street level.

It splintered on the pavement with such force that several of the shards shot out and embedded themselves in nearby vehicles. Others shattered and sprayed pedestrians with glittering yellow shrapnel that fast turned red. Lawsuits were still being filed. Kruger complained that this was what came of using a construction company you didn't own, while Dunning pointed out it enabled them to shift the blame.

Ann rattled off the names of fourteen individuals seated around both long and one short side of the table. Gerald knew them all reasonably well and he couldn't help being reminded of an interview he'd listened to the other day, a rather intelligent discussion with a home-schooled porn star who was surprising people the world over by being not only a talented performer, but also an engaging columnist and a charming individual that almost anyone would enjoy eating a meal with. Describing the pornographic acting community in the San Fernando Valley, she'd said, "Everybody's constantly fucking everybody and we all love to gossip."

None of them drew attention to his new disability and disfigurement. He secretly loved them for this. As the chatter of the room died down, Gerald willingly surrendered visual recall and focused almost purely on what was being said, as if these masters of the universe were floating adrift in the black void of nothingness preceding the big bang.

"Thank you all for showing up today." Dunning purred. "I appreciate that even thirty minutes out of the schedules of men and women such as yourselves is a lot to ask."

"Let's get right to it then." Kruger clasped his hands. "After twice asking them to check and cross-check their results, a representative from the Grell Institute—a think tank we've all sponsored—has come today to let us know the results of their exhaustive three-year study."

The two men's chairs scraped the floor as they took their seats. A heavy door swung on its hinges as someone entered and—Gerald guessed—stood at the empty end of the table.

"Mossberg, the floor is yours," Dunning said.

When Mossberg spoke, Gerald was pleased to have his guess confirmed.

"I'd like to start by congratulating you all on achieving consensus among yourselves to even consider funding the kind of work I and those beneath me at the Grell Institute have been working on. What I'm about to tell you may smack of moralizing. However, I assure you that moralizing is not my work." Mossberg breathed in with an only-slightly-exaggerated patience. "My work is to provide you with the means to enrich yourselves and the corporate entities you oversee. I do appreciate the off-putting cultural leanings you may attach to words like renewable and sustainable. Please keep in my mind my priorities as I go on to use these words—"

"We really do have less than thirty minutes, Mossberg." Kruger snapped his fingers.

"Mr. Kruger, I apologize. It's difficult to know exactly where to start when you're talking about something as all-encompassing as the viability of broadly defined business practices among almost all of the largest corporate entities in the Western hemisphere. The results of our study?" Another deep breath, causing Gerald to add a few pounds to his idea of what Mossberg looked like. "I could drown you all in numbers, except you have those in the physical report if you fancy reading past the executive summary. Please allow me now to give you a verbal summary of that summary. Huge, dramatic changes need to take place in the way you all run your businesses, the way governments handle their role, and the way the individual in society is taught to think. Really, these changes should have been made decades ago. The current path simply isn't sustainable. More consumers than ever are not only unable to afford to have children, they can't even afford the lifestyle they're being sold."

The rap of a knuckle on the table, Mossberg adding emphasis to his last sentence.

"Meanwhile, the techniques you've all employed to keep them over-stimulated and working against their own interests are yielding lower and lower returns..."

Gerald's mind wandered. Many times he'd been told what he and his contemporaries were doing couldn't go on. Every single time, it did. The conclusion drawn from these sorts of studies was often not only to continue with the same ways but to double down on them, to take even more and give back even less. Say what you will, this had worked well for everyone else in the room except maybe Mossberg and Ann.

It wasn't a secret to anyone at the table that their actions left hundreds of millions without financial security, sense of community, hope for the future, their health, or even their lives in a lot of cases.

Still, they'd likely commission a new study from someone more motivated to provide the results they'd like to hear.

Gerald seriously doubted Mossberg knew more than Dunning when it came to pacifying the public. In the days since receiving Dunning's advice, Gerald had found himself agreeing with it more and more. The more they all just went for it, the more resources were required by those enforcing the law to regulate—or even stop—them. It was also certainly no secret who had more resources to spend.

As for the public at large, there might be the odd riot to vent increasingly inarticulate frustrations, but the Bastille wasn't going to be stormed any time soon. Say what you will of the condition of peasants in revolutionary era France, they shared the bond of a common culture through which they could all relate to each other and they weren't suffering from chronic crisis fatigue. Gerald figured if Marie Antoinette had been able to give her people things like the illusion of choice, twenty-four hour news cycles, and the cult of personal interest above all else; then just maybe she would have been able to keep her head.

Mossberg's voice was rising, causing Gerald to drift back out of the echo chamber in his skull, since the speech sounded like it was winding down.

"Ladies and gentlemen, the fact of the matter is that we've been behaving as if we were in a dream world where there are no lasting consequences to our actions except material wealth. The time has come to wake up."

Letting Mossberg vanish from his imagination even before hearing him storm out of the room, Gerald knew what he preferred to waking up: controlling the dream.

28. The Tide

As Mary put her lunchbox on the windowsill of the junkyard shack, she overheard Carmine muttering something about how he didn't have time to get the coffee today. This was followed by some reasons that wouldn't hold up under any real scrutiny, but she cut in before Vance could cut them down.

"Um, Carmine?" Mary asked. "I'll, uh, go get the coffee this morning if that's alright. I mean, if you don't feel like it, not that you wouldn't do it anyway if you didn't feel like it, but, um, you know what I mean." Before Carmine could answer, Vance stepped into the junkyard shack.

"That'll be three days in a row, chachka, aren't you worried he'll get sick of you?"

Mary's face grew hot. Vance must have chatted with Ahmed when he came by with their coffee the other day.

"Aw, geez, I dunno, I mean," she burbled.

"Go on; pick up the usual stuff for all of us." Vance handed her a twenty dollar bill and slapped her on the back. "Just remember you need to get your work done here as well." When the shack was a few paces behind her, Mary heard Carmine laugh uproariously and Vance joined in. It wasn't hard to correctly guess Carmine had told some dirty joke he'd been holding in while she was around. He seemed to interpret her shyness as prudishness. Mary didn't mind much, but it would've been nice if he included her in those moments.

Mary hurried to the coffee shop. She figured that by taking less time getting to the shop she could afford to spend more time on the walk back, enjoying a leisurely review of fresh images of Ahmed's face or the sound of his voice. One of the old industrial structures along her route had recently been demolished and its dust had spread over the road. This caused little clouds to shoot out when Mary's feet hit the tarmac, each step making it look for an instant as if she'd just popped into reality from some supernatural plane populated by eager looking spirits wearing thick denim and work boots.

Mary felt a burst of endorphins rush outward along her shoulders as she turned a corner to see O'Malley's. She loved the license being with Ahmed gave her to lean hard into feelings she'd often had trouble accessing, let alone experiencing with any intensity. He was a key to somewhere better and she loved him for it. Maybe it was "too soon" by some people's schedules but she loved him, she loved him, she loved him.

Pausing by the front entrance, hiding for a moment so she could catch her breath and slow her heart, Mary looked at the ring on her finger with its Check Engine light. Would he be wearing the ring she made him? Maybe it would be too impractical for work. Maybe he'd put it on a string to wear around his neck. She hadn't seen it on him the last two days but she'd been wearing her ring, hoping he'd notice, hoping he'd think about his. He said he liked the ring she made him. He sounded sincere.

"Oh, come on already," Mary whispered through a smile, then turned and entered the shop. Her breathing was back to normal. Her heart maintained the beat of a marching band.

Once again, Mary found herself at the back of a long line of customers, struggling for a glimpse of Ahmed while planning to let people go ahead if it made sure he served her. After moving up two spots, she got her glimpse, quickly blocked by the shifting shoulders of some gangly, red-haired giant. Something wasn't right. Pushing her head up as high as she could, Mary caught another glimpse of

Ahmed. He saw her, too, looking back through two swollen black eyes.

Ahmed wasn't actually working a till, he'd just come out from the stock room with some baked goods for the counter. Understandably, his interaction with the public was being kept to a minimum today. He had spent a few very tense, strange minutes convincing the manager to even let him work. As he turned to ask for a short break to speak with Mary, she broke from the line and quickly walked up to where she could overhear the answer, "Sure, but I'll have to take it out of your hours for the day."

Ahmed gestured to a table for the pair of them to use. She barely heard him mutter, "Christ, I need a new job," while they took their seats, her face growing darker as she noticed more and more little bruises and cuts on him. Sitting down, he took her hands in his and they stayed like that for nearly a minute. Eventually, it was Ahmed who broke the silence.

"Well, I guess I should tell you why I look like this. We both have to get back to work." He sighed. "So, I didn't have such a great time last night."

He sat there quietly for ten long seconds, Mary staring at him.

"Remember those two guys, reading the newspaper, who saw us eating ice cream? That saw you kiss me?" Ahmed looked away. "I wish you hadn't provoked them like that."

"You wish I hadn't kissed you?"

"No, no, I mean, I just…" Ahmed looked back at her. "I just wish they hadn't ambushed me on my way home from work last night and beat the shit out of me. Sorry. Between that, the emergency room, and spending time at the police station, I'm kinda exhausted."

Mary began stroking his hands, wanting to touch his face yet wary of hurting him.

"The officers I spoke to made me feel like I was the troublemaker, asking me things like 'Did you provoke them?' which kind of blew me away since both cops were black. Shouldn't they have been more sympathetic?" Ahmed was half talking to Mary, half talking to the imaginary audience he seemed to proselytize to from time to time. "I remember this brown cop in the background, doing some paperwork, who kept looking over at me with sympathy in his eyes. I wish I'd been talking to him instead, and I think he felt the same. I'm sure life's been harder for him since this Sears Tower shit, too."

"Are the police going to catch them?" Mary asked, incredulously. "These fucking assholes?"

"Probably not. I don't know. I'm looking at things kind of cynically right now," Ahmed replied, focusing more fully on her again. "Not that they're the real problem. You know one of them had the latest issue of that same shitty free paper? I bet they read all kinds of casual, coded racism in that fucking anal leakage before seeing me come down the street."

"Good God," Mary said. "Somebody should fucking tell reporters at that place what kind of horrible shit they're encouraging."

"They're the ones being encouraged, Mary, if not outright told to say the kinds of things they're saying. It's not even the reporters at the paper who are really the problem, it's the owners of the paper and whoever owns them, I guess."

"Well, something should be done about them, then!" Mary exclaimed. "You're not going to just roll over on this, are you? You quit school because of your beliefs, surely this—"

Ahmed made a gesture with his hand, asking her to keep her voice down as some customers were staring now, taking in Ahmed's injuries.

"I've reported my attackers to the police, and honestly, maybe they will be punished for what they did. I hope they are." Ahmed placed the hand that had gestured for quiet back over Mary's. "But I don't have the resources or the will to dedicate a huge portion of my life to wringing any sense of justice or meaningful change out of monolithic corporate entities and the oligarchs running them. You have to do what can, what you're willing."

"What you can," Mary repeated. "What you're willing."

"Yeah."

"Oh, Ahmed." Mary came close to tearing up. "How could anybody hurt you? Those fuckers, those—your face, your lovely face."

"I know, I know." Ahmed took her right hand and gently drew her fingers along a yellowing bruise bulging across his left cheekbone. She winced, he didn't. "I'll be keeping a careful eye out, and for the next few nights I might get one of my pals to meet me, to walk with me for the last leg of my trip home."

"Okay," Mary meekly replied, still upset anybody would hurt Ahmed. Her Ahmed. He let both her hands go and reached into his pocket, pulling out something that put a shaky smile on her lips.

"Plus," Ahmed began, placing something familiar on his finger. "I'll be wearing this good luck charm somebody nice made me."

"Oh!" Mary exclaimed. "You do like it." Ahmed stood up and she did the same.

"Yeah, I do. Kind of middle school, in a charming way." He smiled. "I've been keeping it in my pocket, I admit, because the thought of wearing it in front of my coworkers made me a little self-conscious. Fuck that and fuck this job. You made me something nice and I'm going to wear it."

Mary put her arms around him, played with a bit of his hair, and then kissed him. It was difficult but, in the moment, she was able to ignore the split running down his lower lip. After, she just held onto him and would have done so for some time if he hadn't interrupted.

"You should be getting back with coffee for everybody at the junkyard, right?" he asked, softly disengaging from her and turning to go behind the counter. "I'll make it up for you and you can pay me back the next time we see each other, okay? That way you can get out of here quicker."

"Thanks, that'd be great," Mary replied, going on to relay the usual order. She quietly watched him as he went through the entire process, meekly nodding when Ahmed checked to make sure she still liked sugar in her coffee or that Vance wanted a large.

"Listen, I gotta wait to see what my schedule is like," he said, handing her a cardboard drinks tray with her cargo. "But as soon as I know, I'll give you a call and we can make some plans, okay? I don't want this crap to put any more of a damper on our fun than it has to." Mary nodded again, trying to blink her eyes dry as she did so.

Whatever extra time Mary might have bought by hurrying to O'Malley's had been spent in conversation with Ahmed, yet still she moved as if in a dream—albeit a distant cousin of the kind she'd been looking forward to. Ahmed's face was at the forefront of her imagination, signifying much more than it had on the way to see him. Worry and frustration formed a marriage of inconvenience for Mary. She wanted to pay for him to get the best medical care in the country, something she couldn't afford with a year's worth of wages from the junkyard. She wanted to protect Ahmed and wasn't sure how. Most of all she didn't want to do anything to jeopardize their brand new relationship, its feathers still wet from having left the shell.

But she couldn't just stand by and do nothing.

More than ever, Mary had to trust her hands to take care of the day's tasks. While they tore down and dismantled car after van after truck, her mind tried to find a solution while still respecting several slowly eroding boundaries.

"Hold it," she muttered to herself, casually knocking a driver's side mirror off with her crowbar.

Hold it, she thought, walking past the corner store near her apartment as she found her way home at the end of the day.

Turning the key on her apartment door, Mary thought about calling her mother before realizing she was in even less of a position to give the necessary specifics and, if she spoke in vagaries, it would be impossible for her mom to give any advice that could possibly help.

Could she do nothing?

Shucking off the day's denim and pulling on some sweat pants, Mary turned around and played a trust exercise game where it was her bed's job to catch her. Lying perfectly still, Mary continued to try to sort out the Technicolor tangle in her skull. Ahmed's bruises, his touch, the light from his bedside lamp, the light through the coffee shop windows, bite marks on her neck, knife marks on her shoulder blades, white fur, leopard print. "Shut Up & Slow Down," the words printed along her belt, began to fall out of the tall woman's mouth over and over like a mantra. Nobody could hear them, not even her.

Mary's thin, white arm reached out across the bed for her phone. Research had to be done.

What lay locked under the bathroom sink wasn't a weapon to be picked up and pointed at someone you wanted to die.

It wasn't a tool.

It was the tide.

29. UNDERTOW

Black lines were carefully reapplied where needed. A hiking backpack, with the support frame still intact, was loaded up. A too-large woman's suit, shoplifted from a second hand store on the other side of town, was buttoned up over two sets of skin. Then a puffy blonde wig and far too much makeup were applied, leaving an exaggeration of a successful female executive. A set of keys were placed by a hand shaking with emotion into the placid, outstretched palm of another. As always, it would take a while to get from zero to sixty and then again to push the needle into the red.

Mary headed over to a stretch of bars where the wealthy sometimes came to pick up partners who could be impressed by the flash of a platinum credit card. Having changed, The Figure stepped out of the woman's washroom of what used to be a student bar, but which was now in the process of converting to something that might attract those platinum pieces of plastic. A few of the clientele, between the wig and the makeup, wondered if they were seeing a drag queen. She didn't notice their looks as she pulled out her phone to summon a cab, using an app that let her punch in the destination as well as the pick-up point. A cost estimate for the journey came up on the screen and, somewhere deep down, Mary winced.

The Figure was trying to do her best with a different set-up than usual. Tonight there were orders. Tonight it was not acceptable to turn back if the pieces didn't fit together well enough.

Blessedly, the driver didn't attempt any small talk as he took The Figure on a direct path to a nightclub in the financial district, dropping her off outside the doors. The real action was inside and several stories up, on a rooftop patio kept active this late in the season by several inefficient gas heaters modeled to resemble palm trees. At street level, there was nobody except a bouncer and a couple of anxious souls trying to convince him to let them in. None of them paid attention to The Figure as she paid the driver and waited for him to pull away, out of sight, before heading across the street.

Mary was deep beneath the surface by now. However, her anger and sadness over Ahmed's injuries occasionally shot up like luminescent jellyfish propelling themselves through black water, causing small ripples in The Figure's steady rise toward a crest where she could come crashing down. Step by step, corner by corner, a circuitous route was taken until heels The Figure wasn't terribly comfortable with were removed outside the shipping entrance for a fifty-five floor column of granite and glass. Without looking up, she knew the various holdings of Trinity Media would still be working overtime to collect and distribute information on the death of one of the building's cousins over in Chicago.

After all, an anonymous source had provided them with some new information regarding the perpetrators. The vicious churn of the twenty-four hour news cycle made it better to risk publishing retractions than to get beat out by one of the other papers, programs, or websites.

Twelve minutes later, The Figure scooped out the brains of a woman in an Avalanche uniform who had only moments before been monitoring camera feeds from all over the building. Normally, she'd already be moving on to the floor of her choosing, but a vague sense of tit-for-tat vis-à-vis fear-mongering had been woven into the night's actions. As much as The Figure could have feelings—had begun to have feelings about anything—she didn't care for this. It felt like window dressing. Reluctantly, she spattered the reddish-pink mass on the end of her crowbar across charcoal carpeting.

Cold light from several screens played over The Figure's leopard-print non-features as she clicked through cameras on every floor, assessing possible threats and choosing between potential destinations. She soon exited the room, leaving the crowbar on the carpet. A skeleton keycard from the dead woman in front of the monitors let The Figure into a reception area on the forty-sixth floor. Nobody was at the front desk just now, the blocky red logo of *The Sentinel* hovering over an empty chair like a nosy relative trying to read the email of whoever might sit there.

Knowing that being able to move quickly was about to become a priority, The Figure silently shucked off the hiking backpack and stood it on the floor behind the desk. Pulling drawstrings, the pack's main compartment opened its mouth and The Figure reached in. First came a pair of work gloves for grip, then a modified butcher knife with a custom sheath made from old denim and car seat leather that could hang on her belt. Finally—

"Don't worry, I'm not going home, I just need the bathroom!" a spindly, spiky-haired young man called over his shoulder as he came into the reception area from the office. Crossing the threshold, he wondered if he'd be required to stay up all night in the office, only to cab home for a change of clothes and a quick shower before stepping right back out the door again. He wondered when he would get to truly rest. In the next instant, a river of gore dyed a white dress shirt that still had folding lines left from when it was originally packaged.

Drawing back her weapon, The Figure observed the young man to see if he needed to be hit again. Instead of dropping, he only staggered back half a foot and hunched his shoulders slightly. Whatever his face had looked like a minute ago, it would never look the same way again.

What The Figure held was a two-foot length of six-inch pipe. On one end, there was ring after ring of lug nuts, soldered on to add weight and bulk. Poking out from between the rings were blades taken from short carving knives that had, in turn, several fishing hooks welded on in all the right places to up the odds of them catching something. The whole thing had been spray-painted matte black, as if for greater contrast with the fluids it would be freeing.

The unpaid intern's forehead, now a flesh and bone bomb crater, leaked down over where his nose had been torn off and across lips that quivered as they struggled to process the last electrical impulses sent by their owner's mind. Unsatisfied and unwilling to see if they'd eventually manage to form a sound to draw others, The Figure swung the mace again, shearing off the front of the boy's skull with the destructive ease and dispassionate attitude of a bulldozer clearing away a new housing development that hadn't taken off.

Reaching out to grab a fistful of bloodied shirt, she controlled his fall to the floor so it would make minimal noise. Dragging the body behind the front desk, The Figure realized there was still a good two or three pounds of him left behind, near the floor where he'd been standing. Her new tool was not conducive to subtlety. Sneaking from cubicle to cubicle, break room to copy room, was plainly not the way to go this evening. However, before work could be seen to properly, there was still one more thing to do.

Reaching into the backpack once again, The Figure pulled out an old bike lock and a decent length of its companion, a skinny chain encased in light blue plastic. Once the combination was pulled from memory, The Figure was able to secure the handles on the two thick glass doors leading from reception into the elevator bay. This was it. The surf was set to pound upon the sand.

Rounding the dividing wall that held up the organization's logo and obscured the rest of the office, The Figure started off at a casual stride with the mace hanging by her thigh as a British constable of old might have carried her truncheon while patrolling a rough neighborhood. Greeted by an open concept office with few dividing walls above waist height, the lay of the land was pretty much what had been seen on the security guard's monitors a few minutes before.

The carefully arranged cubicles were all abandoned, their office supplies and personal nick-knacks lit by an Excel spreadsheet of ceiling light panels left half off as a cost saving measure. At the furthest point was a meeting room with blurred privacy glass where four employees of various ages sat in a semi-circle with laptops, tablets, and take-out trays on the table between them. They were all intently focused, chattering amongst themselves and gesticulating at their screens. A burst of laughter, muffled by the meeting room's closed door, found its way to The Figure's ears.

Nobody was currently in the small kitchen to the right, one of only two other areas with any doors, walls, or privacy glass to keep workers from seeing each other clearly. Along the right, close to the meeting room, were a series of three modest offices for the higher ups. A light was on in the middle one. Thinking of past experiences, The Figure knew the smart thing was to take care of that lone individual before trying to deal with the cluster in the meeting room.

Despite knowledge of the bike chain, there came a fear the boardroom workers might hear the killing in the office and flee. It wasn't The Figure's fear, it wasn't only fear. It was that moment where realizing you're in a dream is the thing that wakes you up, pulling you toward consciousness. Mary was drawn to the surface as if her body had all of a sudden been strapped with several life preservers. No matter how hard she fought this, she came closer and closer until—

"Oh God," pale lips whispered from behind tightly drawn leopard print. "I've killed someone." The wave broke and began to recede, leaving Mary washed up on the coast, all alone.

Terrified of being spotted, Mary turned and began to run before dropping to the ground on all fours. Surely, they wouldn't be able to see her then, right? Except Mary wasn't confident about the paths of sight available between the desks, so she began to weave in an almost random path as she crawled back toward reception. She kept the mace. She put it down. She came back and picked it up again, the uhs and ums of her daily speech finding their way into her movements.

Bumping her hip on the corner, Mary rounded the floor-to-ceiling wall displaying the company logo and crawled behind the desk. The already rising stink of the dead intern hit her nose, causing her to rear up on her knees before falling back on her behind. There he was in front of her, face as visible and clear as the break of dawn.

"I'm…" she whispered. "I'm not supposed to be seeing this."

Eyes closed, hands over her face, Mary tried to figure out what to do. Glimpses of what The Figure did at night had been coming back to her for weeks, but never anything that could be used as a guidebook for how to escape the situation she was in. Compounding this was the way Mary had done everything she could to forget those glimpses, often overpowering them with fond memories of Ahmed, like putting a poster over the crumbling impact crater of a fist driven into drywall.

As she tried to remember the combination for the bike lock, Mary desperately wanted to feel hot tears cloud her vision. Muscles in her face tightened, her lips quivered, her eyes stayed dry; no combination, no catharsis.

"I'm sorry," she mumbled to the body. "I'm sorry, you're probably not a threat to Ahmed. You're probably just trying to do something you care about. Maybe you… maybe you'd even do something good in the world. I have to remember there are people trying to do something good in the world, and it's not always in vain, it's not always—"

Lost in her thoughts, Mary didn't hear the woman coming up from the main office until they spotted each other. Turning, her features polluted by fear, Mary saw a threatening combination of curves, glasses, and confidence walk into her field of vision. Both women burst into an expression of shock, though only one was able to see the other's. Mary pounced on the woman and pushed the mace's handle across her throat.

"Shhh, shhhh, shhh," Mary urged. "You can't tell anyone, you can't tell anybody, you—"

"My name is Anita," she told Mary. "My name is Anita Pearson and I'm not a hostage, not a bargaining chip, I'm a person like you."

This was something Anita half-remembered from a show she'd seen once, something a character had done to make it harder for his captors to write him off as an expendable asset in their bank robbery. Anita wasn't sure if this was actually something people were recommended to do in real life, but it was all her memory would give her at the moment.

She wasn't even sure what *this* was. It certainly wasn't a robbery, and although this strange figure was blocking her view of the intern's head, she saw stains on the carpet and his legs poking out from behind the desk. Anita guessed he wasn't in good health.

This figure, this woman pinning her against the wall with strength borne of fear, was talking to her in a way that reminded Anita of the pleading her younger sisters would pour into her ears whenever she caught them doing something against the rules, begging that she not tell mother.

"Please, please just be quiet and sit on the floor with your back against the side of the desk," Mary pleaded. "Sit on your hands with your back against the side of the desk or I'll hit you."

Anita did as she was told, the intern's feet jutting across the left side of her peripheral vision.

"You know there's no money here, right? I'm not even sure if there's any real money in the entire financial district, it's all electronic. Maybe a few safety deposit boxes, but those aren't—this is the office of a news site you've broken into, you know that, right?"

Mary crouched down behind the desk and tried hard not to look at the intern's body as she began to rifle through the remaining contents of the backpack. There were a few items The Figure would have recognized as her emergency kit. None of these was a pair of handcuffs or gag for a prisoner. There wasn't anything to cut through the bike chain, either. Mary began to have trouble breathing. Hyperventilation. She'd worked her way through that before, but never in this kind of situation.

"Please be quiet. I—I don't want to hurt you." Mary lied. The more truthful statement would have been, "I don't have it in me to hurt you."

Anita had been forced to intimidate several employees and managers of companies her bosses owned, reminding them they may have their little fiefdoms, but she represented the true lords of the land. She was certainly getting a familiar feeling, that the person she was talking to could be easily pushed into doing what Anita wanted her to do.

"Listen, my name is Anita. What's yours?" Only the sound of frantic rummaging through a bag was given in response. "Alright, well, I've got to tell you that security will be here soon enough."

Mary began to sweat, darkening several spaces between her spots.

"Now I don't know what your grievances with this company are, however, I assure you there are better ways of addressing those, ways that won't land you in jail for who knows how long."

"Stop. Speaking," Mary replied. Despite having thoroughly explored the contents of the bag, she checked again.

"Oh, I think I see a security guard at the door now. He's awful curious about that bike lock and he's looking at me for answers. What should I tell him?"

Mary stood up in alarm, saw there was no guard, that Anita was lying. Picking up the mace, she walked around and stood in front of Anita.

"Stop it, I'm serious," she told her.

Anita, with her back to the desk, couldn't help noticing Mary's hands were trembling slightly.

"Why don't you leave? If you leave now, maybe you won't be caught," she suggested. "'Cause if you stay, if you do anything else you aren't supposed to do, then you'll just be making it worse for yourself in the long run and—"

Mary cut off Anita by crouching down and forcing one shaky hand over her mouth. For a moment, they only stared at each other. Mary tried to act tough, wrenching Anita's head to the side as she removed her hand. This put the woman's vision square on the two or three pounds of intern left smeared across the carpet near where The

Figure had first struck him. Boardroom bravado could only do so much. Anita's screams were long and uninhibited, even after Mary clamped both hands over her mouth.

"Stop it, stop it, stop it, stop it, stop it!" Mary repeated over and over in a harsh whisper. She kept repeating herself, the joints in her hands beginning to hurt, and with each repetition, her voice grew more hoarse and quiet.

Finally, mercifully, the undertow pulled Mary down again, down, down, down into soothing blackness where she couldn't be hurt, where she couldn't see or feel anything at all. Fingers were drawn away from Anita's face. Feet coming from the direction of the other journalists could be heard.

"Anita? Are you alright?" one of them called.

Seeing The Figure freeze in front of her, Anita felt like maybe she'd gotten through, like she might be about to get what she wanted. Hearing her coworkers coming, surely the woman would flee as fast as possible.

This was not the case.

30. $$$ $$ $ (C_C) $ $$ $$$

Martha Steiger liked to take a few minutes each day to sit back and appreciate what she had. Sitting upright from staring down at the oversized tablet that doubled as the surface of her desk, she flicked a finger to turn on the rosewood-pattern screen saver and swiped across the bottom right corner to lock it. Now, if she wanted to, Martha could lean on the desk without waking it up.

Rain was gathering in staccato streaks on the window to her left, the only thing to be heard in her private office. A year ago, Martha had tried spending five hours in a sensory deprivation tank, a device that'd been around for decades but had only recently spent time as a fad among micro-managing millionaires and billionaires who were desperate for an edge over their competitors. Some clever tank salesman had managed to infect Martha's social circles with an idea; the clarity brought by laying in body temperature water with no stimuli could help provoke one's mind into producing otherwise unattainable insights.

Some executives tried it, some liked it, most got bored quickly and moved on to other things. Martha had been one of the few who'd thrown herself into the practice and stayed with it, even after the fad was replaced by another. Now she did her best to cut down on stimuli, as best as someone who shared ownership of a corporate empire worth a hair's breadth under a trillion dollars could manage.

She only used the one device, her desk, while at work. The sound system now went largely unused. The walls were bare, devoid of the expensive art her peers would have placed there to passively brag about how sophisticated they could pay to appear.

Her personal staff remained outside in what was a large reception area or a small office, depending on whom you asked. The executives who worked there privately referred to it as "the bridge", both for its sterile, sci-fi spaceship design and the importance their work played in guiding the company.

Martha had had a tank installed in the floor below, with a private shower and changing area just for her. Standing away from the desk, she took a few slow steps to stand by the window and considered her schedule for the day, trying to see if she could shuffle things around for a quick two hours in body temperature water. Something big was hovering on the horizon and Martha wondered if her twin sister felt it, too, wherever she was at that moment. Taking inventory of the blessings in her life felt like the thing to do in the face of this vague, yet compelling, sensation.

Martha only managed to list "Wealth" and "Health" before hearing two gentle knocks on the door. It had to be her personal assistant, Blake. She privately joked about his having the cheekbones and quizzical expression of a catfish, yet that didn't mean Martha lacked genuine affection for someone who she still thought of as a young man, even though he'd crested into his forties not too long ago.

"Come in," she replied, speaking loud enough to be heard on the other side of a sturdy, newly installed security door. It looked the same as any other wood-paneled door, except the way it swung open betrayed the weight of three-inch-thick steel plate and a magnetic locking system Martha could operate from her desk, phone, or a small device on her keychain.

Blake stood in the doorway, as pale a pink fish of a person as ever. It was the man behind him who drew Martha's attention.

"It's alright, Blake, please let Mr. Kruger in, and close the door behind him." Gliding backwards, her assistant got out of Kruger's way and did just that. The less sociable half of Dunning-Kruger was, with some concentration, breathing in a measured fashion.

"Are these walls soundproof?" he asked, not taking one more step forward.

"Of course," Martha replied, keeping her gaze directed toward the window.

The sound of rain softly spattering the window was once again the only noise. Martha, keeping a part of her mind on a game of scheduling Tetris with the victory condition of fitting in some sensory deprivation relaxation, spoke first.

"Would you like to yell at me?"

"Among other things," Kruger replied, flexing the muscles in his right hand. "Stop staring out that window. Sit down."

"You're lucky my sister isn't around to hear you speak to me like that." She remained standing, staring.

"I suppose it was her idea to go against my request for a media blackout on that psychopath?" Kruger asked, knowing roughly what the answer would be. The Steiger sisters had a good-cop-bad-cop routine they liked to pull whenever they weren't in the same room and someone was confronting them; whatever the agitated party was concerned with would always be blamed on the sister who wasn't there.

"Yes, it was, it was." Martha confirmed for Kruger. "But, Derek, you have to understand that I would likely have gone down the same path, although I would have provided you with the courtesy of a twenty-four-hour warning. You know how Angela is." She then turned and took the few steps necessary to stand behind her desk chair, pausing to look expectantly at Kruger. Martha waited for him to take the seat opposite her. He knew he'd be conceding a sliver of authority to her by doing so, however, he'd also look the fool if he refused and remained standing by her doorway. Pondering these sorts of little power plays consistently consumed a percentage of his thought processes.

"Alright." He exhaled, petulantly taking a seat so luxurious most people wouldn't even know where to buy one. Only then did Martha sit in her own, taller version of the same chair. "So…" he continued. "It was Angela's idea to break the blackout. Does Angela plan on somehow reimbursing me for the stock tips I gave you as compensation? The property in Florida? My backing out of the bidding war over the Dallas branch of Autonomous Arms?"

"No, Angela feels we provided adequate return on your investment by keeping a muzzle on the entirety of our news media properties these past eight weeks," Martha explained with exaggerated patience. "Besides which, at this point we couldn't possibly keep one of our people at Trinity Media or the Sentinel from leaking the news. For God's sake, Derek, she murdered six employees as well as two Avalanche security guards. Have you seen the photographs?"

"Yes, and I understand how much more difficult it would be to maintain the blackout. However, I think you could do it if you made the effort," Kruger replied. "I also understand how tempting it would be to scoop all the other news outlets, the more obedient ones who were still keeping their reporters on a leash—at least until you let your dogs off the lawn."

"If you truly understand our position, then what is it that bothers you so? What brought you here to grumble at me in person?" Martha asked. "What?"

"You know what." Kruger snarled.

Three hours earlier and twenty minutes across town from where Kruger and Martha had their late morning conversation, Gerald was just swallowing the last of a red pepper omelet Ann had prepared for him. She swore she wasn't a great cook, even though what she served always tasted great to him. Whether it was the treat of having something made for him in his home by a non-professional or the gradual sharpening of his remaining senses, Gerald wasn't sure.

"So, Ann, what's the first item for today?" he asked, carefully wiping his mouth with a cloth napkin. He didn't feel anything on his lips, but he liked to be extra sure these days.

"Well, there's a series of phone calls between nine am and eleven am. The first is to Juan Pablo so you can see if he's still interested in working with you, the second is to that factory owner in Greenville, and the final call is with the director of Autonomous Arms Dallas branch, to see if it's not too late to get in a bid as a favor to your father."

"That has all the makings of a good morning, I think." Gerald stood up, pleased. "I do hope Juan Pablo has heard a soft no before, that he hasn't run off around town trying to find someone to take my place."

"Your afternoon is more flexible, Mr. Byrne," Ann said, letting him know roughly where she stood in the kitchen. "I think you said you wanted to try and drum up some new business?"

"Yes," Gerald replied, taking his coat from where Ann had been told to make sure it was always hanging. "I've got a file of leads I plan to work through, some of which can be delegated, I'm sure. None of the black collar stuff, though. I'm not yet sure who of the new staff I can trust with that."

"I'll continue to be careful what business I discuss on the office floor," Ann replied, shifting to open the apartment door for Gerald before taking his arm and leading him down the hallway to the elevators. Yesterday, she'd taken his hand in a manner that left them both a little curious about what the other was thinking.

Gerald didn't know what he'd do if his building ever made any major renovations. He wasn't quite at the level where he could afford what realtors referred to as a condo estate, essentially half or even an entire floor of a building that he could customize to suit his needs and wants perfectly. It would take him a good while to learn such a large, new space well enough not to need a white cane or audio GPS guide, but the level of control justified the effort.

However, before he could do that he'd have to put in the work to continue to build his personal fortune. Gerald figured this meant taking Mr. Dunning's advice to go bigger, bolder, and better in every way possible. Stepping out into the lobby, his mind was swirling with possibilities. All of these were shelved when he heard Ann gasp as they exited the building.

"Ann?"

Gerald couldn't hear the next-to-silent flashes from several high-end DSLR cameras which had temporarily blinded Ann, nor could he hear three television cameras and a half a dozen phones filming him. Upon being asked the first question, images of all this popped into his head.

"Excuse me, Mr. Byrne, would you be willing to comment on this woman or women responsible for murdering almost two hundred people working in the city's financial sector?" Unlike his PTSD-induced nightmares about The Figure, Gerald's familiarity with the "surprise press mob" scene from television and film did in fact make it easier to handle in real life. He just smiled and gripped Ann's hand, pulling her in what he hoped was the direction of the car.

"Mr. Byrne, is it true this woman was hired by one of your competitors?"

Ann, having blinked away several lens flares, made Gerald's focus shift to his left elbow as she corrected their course.

"Mr. Byrne, is it true you returned to work less than a month after you received such terrible injuries?"

Shoulders and sleeves of winter jackets seeing their first action of the season brushed against him as they wove among the journalists. Wary a camera might accidentally collide with his head, Gerald placed one hand on his Oliver People's sunglasses.

"Mr. Byrne, how has all this affected your relationship with your clients? With your new employees?"

Ann guided him into the rear passenger-side door of the car. The queries of the mob became slightly muffled, then quieter, and finally were replaced altogether by the sound of the car's engine as they pulled farther and farther away.

"Mr. Byrne?" Ann this time. "I'm sorry but if navigating media like that is going to be part of my job then I'll have to ask for a raise."

"I'll consider it," Gerald replied. No, he wouldn't. There were plenty more where she came from. What Gerald chose to think over as he was driven to the office was the last reporter's question. Almost all of his white-collar clients were sure to get nervous. He'd already had to massage each of them individually, smoothing over the break in continuity as they were suddenly given new liaisons at Byrne Investments. Discovering everyone except Gerald had been "forcibly retired" could send damn near his entire client list running for the hills.

All the more reason to further invest in black-collar possibilities with the likes of Juan Pablo. Drug dealers were used to business partners losing employees to sudden, unexpected bloodshed.

Back in the present, in Steiger's office, Derek Kruger had had enough of Martha and was letting himself out. As he reached the door, Kruger turned his head and asked, "Why have you never been married, Martha?"

"Same reason you've never stayed married, Derek. I like my sluts. They're all I need." Martha teased. "It's a shame I couldn't have had this conversation with Dunning, he's much more charming."

"He's a fat fuck."

"He's a good fuck," Martha chided. "And his hands don't stink of eucalyptus hand sanitizer, you germaphobe."

The disguised security door's hydraulic hinges kept Kruger from slamming it on his way out. Twenty minutes later, as she lay in the soothing darkness of her sensory deprivation tank, Martha grinned. Having just finished counting her blessings, the ability to deny Derek Kruger satisfaction was quietly placed at number eight.

31. refraction.net

James took a deep breath, watched it slowly rise up from his mouth. The first frost of the season tiled crystal flakes in geometric patterns over concrete and grass. Looking across the neighborhood, James saw silhouettes in his apartment window. From a vantage point three blocks over and seven stories up, on the roof of the Emerson mall, he swallowed hard and turned away. An old laptop bag gently bounced on his hip as he pulled open glass doors and stepped inside the shopping center.

A few days ago, James had begun carrying the bag with him every time he left home. Inside was his old tablet, some clothes, his costume, the lead pipe he'd found, basic toiletries, the last of his money, and a few sentimental photographs; toddler James sitting triumphantly on top of a pile of cousins he hadn't seen since, a smiling girl who no longer spoke to him, a woodland sunset that meant nothing to anyone but James. It wasn't much of a go-bag but it did the job, for the short term. Having woken up this morning feeling rested and calm, James had felt distrustful of the sensation and decided to go outside, taking the bag with him.

It was only yesterday he'd started checking his apartment window from the mall as a habit before heading home. James had planned some kind of big Fuck You sign-off to his unpaid internship with the artist. Stepping past the acrid tang of a hair & nail salon, he was pretty sure he wouldn't have time. No, he definitely wouldn't, and it would be a waste if he was caught in the artist's loft essentially telling off a bully.

Letting an escalator bring him down past a large hanging object d'art from the decade before his birth, James reached out and slid dust off its blue aluminum side. He focused on the tactile sensation, the promise of static electricity, trying to block out a rushing, roaring river of thought he desperately wanted to ignore.

"Please," he quietly exhaled. "Just a little while longer."

He'd said goodbye to a dingy little box that had held his body, possessions, dreams, and nightmares for three long years that passed all too quickly. He'd said good-bye to whatever the internship had been. There was at least one more good-bye ahead. James sighed as he reached the ground floor. The window for that farewell was closing. It wouldn't be long before they'd be switching from passive to active tracking of his web and phone activity.

There was a corner where teenagers tended to congregate because it was out of sight of the security cameras and rarely patrolled by mall security. James used his foot to sweep aside candy wrappers, cellophane packaging from any number of products, and muffin crumbs to make a space on the floor to sit down cross-legged. Rapidly tapping and swiping, James was reminded of old rhythm games from his early childhood, where his father would play guitar and sing while he'd sit there in his Oshkosh Bgosh, happily thwapping away at the multicolored drum set. The controllers modeled after musical instruments were faded and cracked, left over from his parents' university days, and they always had put a smile on his face when his dad would reverently pull their worn cardboard box out from under the couch.

Plugging tangled ear buds into the headphone jack, James checked and was thankful to see his father was online. Contacting him via chat, James quickly tapped out, *Is Mom around? Do you have time for a video call?*

Greg Thompson is typing... appeared for a few moments before being replaced by *No. Sure.*

The software played a stylized version of what James knew had been the sound of dial-up modems, something supposed to make users his parents' age nostalgic, and then he was greeted by his father's face.

Familiarity filtered his view of him. To James' eyes, he always looked about ten years younger than he actually was. He was handsome in a down-to-earth way and even though he knew this didn't make anyone a better person, in his case, James couldn't help feeling it did. He knew what few aspects of his own appearance he was willing to accept as attractive generally came from his dad's side of the family. For this, James was grateful, when he could remember to be.

"I need to talk to both of you. Where's Mom?" he asked, receiving a mute reply. Normally, he'd have more patience for what followed, the inevitable fiddling by his father to try and get the software to recognize the microphone as being plugged in, but every second wasted on technical difficulties caused the tension in his arms and shoulders to grow a little tighter. It was bad enough his tablet had so many dead pixels James felt like he was looking at his father through a screen door.

Did his pursuers' look, up close, like the guys he'd seen pull that man out of the expensive rental car that one time while walking home from a barbacking gig in the summer? What kind of non-lethal weapons would they be carrying and how non-lethal would they actually be? Rubber bullets would remove an eye as easily as if they were the real thing. Tasers could fry flesh and induce heart attacks with enough repeated presses of a bright red button. Sonics would drive nearby dogs wild as they ruptured the finer parts of his—

"James? Hello, James? Can you hear me?"

"Yes!" James instinctively brought the tablet a little closer to his face, as if that would help. "Yes, yes I can hear and see you just fine."

"Sorry about that. Your mom is at work. They had some hours for her today."

James tried to remember the last time he'd spoken to his mother. It had been about three weeks ago and they'd mostly discussed the differences between her two book clubs. As last conversations went, it was mundane and unsatisfactory. Unless his mom was sent home early, it seemed that that was the good-bye he'd get.

"Anyway," his father continued. "Have those people at Norquest called you back yet?"

James paused for the second it took him to realize what his father was talking about. Three months ago, he'd applied for a minimum honorarium internship with Norquest, LLC and never head back. However, he'd made the mistake of telling his father about the application as he'd actually had a good feeling about it. Since then, his father asked James about it every other time they spoke, guaranteed. His dad meant well, but all it did was remind him of another missed opportunity that felt like a personal failure.

"Well?"

"Dad," James half-whined. "I told you, you'll be the first to know if I ever hear back from them or anybody else but I won't, so you won't. Please stop asking me about that."

The backdrop moved as his father took his old laptop into the living room. Over his right shoulder was a painting James had done in his teens. Even though the three point perspective wasn't so hot, it was nice to see his best attempt at a watercolor of the park near where he'd grown up. On visits to his parents, he'd always make a point to go there to try and force some profound thought, some clear mission statement to draw a firm line between the time before he'd sat on a swing or teeter-totter and the time after. This brought James a moment's serenity and usually left him galvanized for the challenges ahead.

Now he'd had a firm line drawn for him, with that park placed well behind it. His neighbors were probably being questioned now, not that they'd remember anything of him, unless he'd managed to wake them with some noise projected through the thin walls of his apartment. "Yeah, asshole always slams the door when he goes to the bathroom," didn't feel like such a strong lead for his pursuers to follow.

"Sorry, James. How about Melissa? Have you two talked lately?"

"Dad," James repeated with greater emphasis, then breathed in slowly. "No, we—it's been ten months since the break-up. We sort of tried being friends. It didn't really work out. We don't even talk online anymore."

"Well that's her loss, then. That Norquest company, too." he replied. "This isn't parental myopia speaking, either. You just need someone to give you the right chance and you'll be fine, you'll see."

It always amused James how his father could turn on a dime in his opinion of people, depending on whether or not he thought they were going to provide anything of benefit to his son. Employment. Companionship. Even a simple smile from someone on the other side of a counter, someone paid to give that smile, could sway his dad if it was directed at his boy.

At a time like this, his optimism was hard to bear; over-inflating the importance of his son's accomplishments, glossing over his failures, and seemingly going out of the way not to acknowledge the sheer scope of the obstacles in James' path. It usually made him want to do nothing more than tear himself down in front of his father, to focus on the failures and repeatedly guide his vision to the terrifying sights James saw on his horizon.

Today he didn't feel like doing that to his father. Besides, say he brought him around to his way of thinking, then what? Then what? They stare at each other in silence, having agreed that all efforts are futile? In this, James found a little bit of courage, and decided to spend it on his father.

"Dad!" He interrupted. "I don't have a lot of time to talk. I just wanted to say I miss you and Mom. I really miss you today and I wish I could be there to give you both a hug. That's all, really. That's all."

"Ha, well, we miss you, too. What on Earth has you talking like this? You sound like a soldier going off to war."

"Aw, well," he deflected. "Does there have to be a big reason?"

"No, I guess not. You're so clever, James. Keep your head in a good place and I know things will turn around eventually."

Somewhere else in the cavernous ground floor of the mall, an authoritative voice yelled, "Hey! Stop what you're doing right now!"

James jerked his head in the general direction of the cry, saw some shoplifters being busted. A decent sized group of what looked like recently homeless people had swarmed a grocery store shelf and were now spreading out in the hopes that only one of them might meet the wrong end of the pursuing security guard's nightstick.

"James? What's that? Are you alright?"

"Yeah. Listen, I should go, okay?"

"Okay James, I love you."

"I love you, too. Give Mom a hug for me."

"I will."

And then the brief, never-quite-comfortable moment where they both saw each other's eyes dart to wherever on their respective screens the end-call button was, followed by the re-appearance of the software's logo on a white background, a teal collection of curves vaguely resembling an old telephone and guaranteed not to offend anybody. James told the tablet to shut down, removed the case, and ejected the battery as well, hoping that would keep the device off the web.

Getting up and walking away in a purposefully even manner, James reflected upon how it might not be long before he found himself raiding a supermarket shelf. Even more than when he had left school, ordinary life had just been redefined as a luxury item.

Stepping outside, James decided a park would be a good place to hide for the time being, so he devised a path with several twists and turns through alleys and side streets. The old laptop bag bounced on his hip and he gripped it to stop the clasps from clicking, from providing evenly spaced announcements of his presence.

James supposed he'd soon be wistful for the life he had in that little apartment over the past three years. The truth was, though, the years spent there hadn't made him miss the student life much. He might have had less financial worry during his school years, in the short term, but he'd always had an idea of what was coming. It had been a real challenge for James to work hard at something he'd been told was simultaneously worthless and also the only path to a secure future someone from his background could get. The diploma at the end of the stick had felt like an increasingly expensive lottery ticket he'd spend the rest of his life struggling to pay off, a lottery ticket with long odds that kept getting longer.

Jesus, when had that man in the London Fog coat started walking behind him? James ducked into a greasy chicken joint and pretended to use their washroom for ten minutes. Leaving, the man behind the counter asked him if he thought the only-for-paying-customers sign on the door was just a suggestion. James barely heard him. Scanning the sidewalk and seeing nobody familiar, he resumed his path to the park.

There had been grants, of course, but they almost always went to children from wealthy backgrounds who only needed a little bit extra to be able to get out of school debt free. What he didn't know was that helping close the gap for students whose parents could almost pay the entire tuition up front represented a smarter financial investment. At first, James couldn't believe how the school had to charge such high tuition yet managed to afford nice sushi bars and other high-end amenities. It wasn't until late in his second year that he realized the point of those amenities was to attract those same wealthy students the grant system was more inclined to help out.

Even more confusing was how many of the professors, these dispensers of wisdom meant to save people like James from poverty, were underpaid adjuncts who either lived slightly worse than the students or were older versions of the rich kids at the sushi bars— people who didn't need their meager university income to get by. He desperately didn't want to imitate the former, who largely stayed because they'd devoted their lives so far to getting where they were, and while he'd have liked to be as financially comfortable as the latter, he couldn't relate to them at all.

Early in his third year, it had become more difficult to ignore the student debt he was racking up. Increasingly, it felt like the point of higher education wasn't to give people like him new opportunities. Instead, it was to punish the non-wealthy for being what they were, to provide them with a debt that would keep them in their place. Horrified, it was right before Christmas of that year when James had dropped out like an animal chewing off its foot to escape a bear trap.

He was free from school, but there was a bill for what he'd completed so far.

Plus interest.

Do I now qualify as "a person of interest"? James wondered. Nervously weaving between homeless people selling bootleg Blu-Rays nobody wanted, James once again wished to drop out, this time from society as a whole. Crossing the street to enter the park, he wondered if he could live there. It was a ridiculous idea and he knew that. It provided a moment's relief nonetheless.

Eventually he came across a small clearing encircled with strong young fir trees and a sand pit from which sprouted two plastic blue whales on powerful coils. A strange sight, a tall, pale blue can with a finely detailed nineteenth century ship printed on it, bought him another few moments respite from thinking about the contents of the mail he'd left sitting unopened on his desk for so long. It looked like it had been sitting in the sand for a while, a small miracle given all the homeless people who barely let you finish your drink before taking the container so they could return it for the deposit.

Picking up the can, James could no longer distract himself. However he might die one day, the arrival of those envelopes had been when his life truly reached its conclusion. Staring blankly ahead, the can held limply in his hand, James recalled their contents.

The gist of the legal jargon printed across dull white paper in bold red ink was that his time was up. Officers from the powerful debt collection arm of the Department of Justice had been dispatched to wring from him whatever fiscal worth they could before he'd be sent to a privately run prison owned by whatever corporation would buy his debt for a fraction of its worth. There, he would spend decades working off what he owed by making whatever products they'd train him to make. These days this was, in fact, the most likely way a young American could find work in manufacturing.

James had known he was due for a message like that in one form or another for over a year, and just kept pressing on as if even the possibility of this happening simply didn't exist. Though he couldn't often lie to himself, James could omit with the best of them.

Reflexively, James tried to re-direct his attention to anything, anything at all. This meant dropping the can, pulling out his tablet, replacing the battery, and turning the device on. His left foot sent out little clouds of dry sand as it tapped up and down while James waited for his web browser to wake up.

When it did, all worry about his pursuers was shoved to the side as multiple tabs opened, each with a different social media site or news service. After skimming a review of the latest episode of his favorite TV show, an episode he hadn't actually watched since his normal morning pirating ritual had been disrupted, James came across a headline that brought the outside world back into focus.

Listening to a short, shaky video clip of Gerald Byrne walking from his building's lobby to a parked car, James read every syllable of the adjoining text as if his life depended on it. Finally, The Figure had escaped the gutter mutterings of infohose.com forum threads and other such corners of the Internet. Lo and behold, right at the end of the article, was a new clip just like the ones he'd been watching for weeks.

Hurriedly clicking through content warnings designed to titillate, James began to watch footage taken from a front desk security camera on a floor of the same media company that ran the site providing the video. It started much as others had, with her bold, decisive movements quickly leaving what he thought of as some corporate lackey dead on the floor. Never mind that James would have happily done anything to have had that lackey's role in the company.

Then something curious happened. She seemed to lose her nerve. No longer did she move like a leopard-print skin filled with ocean currents come to life. Instead, she moved like a scared street addict suffering withdrawal symptoms. Since when did she try to hide bodies? He couldn't believe how she actually appeared to be negotiating with the next office worker who walked in on her, though the caveman part of his brain appreciated this woman not being turned into a corpse right away, since he rather enjoyed the shape of her body.

The Figure moved the woman down to the floor, against the front desk, and James recognized her from his miserable attempt at having a fun night out. He couldn't believe it—Anita! She looked almost in control of the situation, perturbed by the vicious implement The Figure held, but keeping it together. God, how he wished he'd had the money for a second drink that night.

Sitting down on one of the springy whales, James stared holes in the screen. A real whale could have sprung up through the sand and he wouldn't have noticed until after it ate him whole.

The Figure was crouched down with both hands over Anita's mouth now, eventually wrenching Anita's head to one side in a childishly bullying move. So far, he'd been unable to hear what they'd been saying to each other. Either the security camera's microphone wasn't that hot, his tablet's crappy speakers had finally died, or the audio had been removed for legal reasons. Still, it was obvious whatever Anita had seen outside the frame had panicked her into screaming with such physical intensity that James' imagination dubbed in the sound for him.

For a moment, this The Figure looked panicked as well, then she stood up stiffly and tilted her head back slightly. Was this some sort of Zen shit, focusing her center or whatever? James didn't know and his question was forgotten as The Figure swiftly picked up her horrible homemade mace and turned it on Anita. She confidently moved on to the two men that came in to see what the fuss was about, fuzzy network censorship blurring the areas of impact. No amount of post-production pixilation could cover up the raging house fire of conflicting emotions this sight sent shooting up through James' body.

The Figure was still doing her thing, but she'd had her first moment of weakness.

Gerald's face came back on the screen, his assistant hurrying him into a car. He was the only financial sector employee to live through one of her assaults and, barring the anomaly of this recent attack against these newspaper employees, he was a perfect example of the type of person she'd been targeting ever since her first appearance.

Surely, she'd see this or some other news item. Surely, she'd return to Byrne Investments to finish the job. A creature like her wasn't one to wait long before acting. Maybe she needed his help or she could help him. Maybe they could help each other.

Looking up the address of Gerald's business, James wrote it down on an old grocery receipt he found in his back pocket. Task done, he walked over to a nearby garbage can and chucked his tablet in so hard he heard the screen crack as it hit the bottom.

As dependent as he'd been on the Internet his entire life, it felt wonderful to say good-bye to that as well. Once again, James committed himself to a short, self-destructive path, this time finding true freedom in the act. Freedom from expectation. Freedom from responsibility. Freedom from caring about his future, about poor Anita, about himself.

Hearing footsteps coming down the path, James weaved through the trees directly opposite. One way or another, his life was over. At least this way it would end on his terms.

32. JAMES

In the hours between tossing away his tablet and nightfall in the financial district, James rode the high peaks of an undulating, emotional sine wave running between his temples. The burdens of his adult life fell away in heavy, sodden layers as he lost himself in the game of hiding from his pursuers. He couldn't believe his success at times, rationalizing that these officers of the Department of Debt were accustomed to quarry paralyzed by despair. Not him, no, he'd been galvanized by it.

The Figure would be there tonight, she would. Perhaps those flamethrower drones didn't clear out every last debt refuge. Maybe she was a member of one so underground it was a genuine secret, not just something the majority of the public were unaware of. Maybe she was a brave leader looking for recruits in a revolution, a societal surgery, and her manifesto was being written in the blood of those who'd held so many people face down in a pool of their own tears.

Whoa. Ha, okay, James had stopped and thought. *Getting a little poetic, aren't we?* As with so many things that smacked of sincerity, James didn't trust poetry or poetic phrasing. It always struck him as something fancy he couldn't afford, a way of obscuring a trap, or both.

Killing time in a library—something he hadn't done since school—James pulled back on the strings of his high flying fantasies about where tonight could lead. Guessing from what he'd read and seen of her thus far, odds were maybe fifty-fifty they'd run into each other tonight and this was being generous.

There was also a curious new development to consider. He'd never known her to speak, something he inferred from Anita's behavior in the soundless video he'd watched earlier. As with every instance of The Figure being spotted, her face was nothing but a longish oval of leopard print. Yet Anita had plainly been reacting to spoken statements, she hadn't just been bargaining for her life. What did that mean? How might it impact him? Was Anita's death the result of a failed…recruitment?

Needing to keep his thoughts simple for a while, tightly packed so there wouldn't be cracks for doubt or other saboteurs to sneak in, James spent most of his bus ride downtown producing detailed drawings in his mind of what she might look like under the mask. He had to be careful not to borrow too heavily from women he'd known. Giving her Sarah the bartender's nose nearly put him on the skids, off down an alley filled with sexual frustration. He quickly erased it in his mind, replacing the nose with a soft, round one borrowed from a pleasant young girl sitting up behind the bus driver.

He got off at the corner of forty-seventh and sixth, two blocks south of his destination. Just prior, he'd settled on a proud, plain set of features for The Figure that Norman Rockwell might have given a farmer's daughter. Well, her lips were a bit fuller and more sensual than Rockwell would have gone for.

He paused to sit on a curved, black metal bench outside a realtor's office. The office's front windows were dotted with advertising for condos that would likely be bought by the exceptionally wealthy so as to rent the units to the fairly wealthy. With these listings looming behind him, James let his thoughts off their leash a bit.

The idea of The Figure leading a secret debt refuge or even a revolution was scaled back by this point. Resting his head in his hands with eyes closed, James figured she might be a loner. It would go a ways to help explain her strange behavior in the middle of her most recent attack. Perhaps loneliness was wearing her down? Did she need someone to lean on?

"For God's—come on, be practical," James muttered, steering his mind away from questions he didn't have the answers to. He gathered The Figure took pains to obscure her costume with easily removed clothing like tear-away track pants, only revealing herself once she was near or even inside a building. James had had no chance to prepare such a shell and his bulkier costume would make a second layer of clothes look noticeably misshapen. Then again, he was already a fugitive. What difference did it make if his face was caught on camera?

Oh man, this is a strange kind of wonderful, James thought as he opened his eyes and stood up. Looking at the sky, at the comforting gray dome of light pollution, he could feel tension leaking down from his shoulders and along his forearms to drip from his fingertips onto the pavement.

It was as dark as the financial district ever got this side of a blackout. Crossing Fifth Avenue, James could feel his heart begin to beat that little bit faster. He almost wanted to cry, he felt so relieved. That night spent barbacking when he'd seen The Figure drive past, a DJ had started playing shortly after. The bass line from his favorite track of the set began to pulse through the back of his mind.

Reaching the broad, shallow concrete steps of the building, James' lower lip trembled and he staggered his pace. His feet moved along the stairs slowly, silently, alternating between pushing himself further with thoughts of encouragement or abuse. Taking the top step brought back his full momentum and he entered the revolving glass doors at a disciplined pace. The artificial twilight of the streets flickered through a nearby tree to brush against against the hard edge of the lobby's meticulously arranged track lighting, which left not a single shadow.

The Avalanche security guard sitting behind a faux marble, wrap-around desk on the left side of the lobby saw James' go-bag and figured him for some intern being dragged in after hours by a merciless middle manager. A little voice in James' head whispered to him that it wasn't too late to go back. He drowned it out with satisfaction at having crossed from the front entrance to the elevator bank without being stopped.

Arriving one floor above Byrne Investments, James found his way to the men's washroom. In he went, feeling ready to knock down anyone he might find. Motion-sensor activated lights flicked on to reveal an empty, freshly cleaned room. Slinging his bag off one shoulder and in between two sinks, James stepped up to the polished bronze counter. Looking into the mirror, he wanted to roar the way he imagined Celtic barbarians had as they came down a hilltop to ambush Roman soldiers.

Not yet, not yet.

The floor was dead quiet, so James felt comfortable behaving as if he were in his own bathroom. At one point in his afternoon's adventure, it had occurred to James his pursuers probably wouldn't look for him in the makeup and perfume section of a large department store. He'd ducked into a slightly more upscale mall before grabbing the bus downtown and found something appropriate. Once there, he thought of the war paint he'd applied in the artist's loft and then again at home.

Every little bit helps, he figured as he began shoplifting several small items. Not giving even one ounce of a fuck at the time, his hands had moved using the kind of swift confidence he associated with The Figure. Removing each little black plastic and clear glass item from the bag, his fingers trembled in a way James identified more with himself.

What's the point of this? You'll be wearing a mask, a voice in his head argued. *Shut up*, he replied. *I don't care.*

Again, a band of silver was drawn from ear to ear, across closed eyes. A pale orange was applied to his fingernails—an approximation of the angular, orange, dotted lines carving through the gray fractals of his costume. Finally, there came the white and black, curved triangles along his cheekbones. Pointless as they might be from the standpoint of protecting his identity, anything that could cause even a moment's extra work or irritation to the Department of Debt was something worth doing.

It did help, the repetition, the ritual. How did she get there? What were her rituals?

What will your mother's reaction be when footage of your first kill leaks to the news? What will your dad's face look like when he hears about his son? the dissenting voice delivered as if from on high, laying a hand to the cheek of his conscience and a fist to the stomach of his ego.

James' hands clamped hard on the counter top as he silently screamed. Shoulders shaking, he smothered the voice with layer upon layer of imagery. Women he couldn't afford to go out with. Home ownership. Raising a child. Security in old age. Being able to buy gifts for friends and loved ones. Comfort that, if he was injured or fell ill, he'd be properly cared for. The ability to see the years ahead as a clear, straight line he was navigating, instead of a series of short, vicious cycles dragging him ever closer to nothingness.

"I don't have any of those things," he let out in a low growl. "So I have this."

Eyes coming back into focus again, he looked at himself in the mirror and marveled at how self-doubt had actually shut up. Even if this were a temporary affair, he was glad for it. A smile of exhausted relief crawled across his painted features. He began to strip, to trade his clothes for the hastily folded costume in his bag. Soon enough he was cocooned in gray fractal patterns, a mathematically generated illusion of disorder, overlaid with the hard, forty-five-degree angles of dotted orange.

"Here I am," he spoke aloud to the mirror, then pulled the hood of the jacket over his head and zippered it up to cover his face. A moment was spent looking from behind the upside-down, silver, reflective plastic triangles in his mask. Then he was off, lead pipe in one hand and go-bag in the other.

"Here I am," he said while opening the doorway to the stairwell.

The clasps on his bag clicked and clacked as he came down the stairs. James welcomed anyone to hear this and come investigate.

Standing around a corner from the glass doors of Byrne Investments front desk area, James paused. This was it, if he hesitated he was doomed. Language kept trying to come together in his thoughts and he kept tearing it down into formless abstractions. James was unaware of the spiritual peace The Figure felt in moments such as these, but if he had been, he would have yearned for something similar.

It took such great effort to keep disassembling the words in his head before he could process them that, instead of quietly lowering it, he nearly let his go-bag fall heavily to the floor. His other hand held the lead pipe in a loose fashion, letting the heavier end hang low like a pendulum at rest. Great arcs of color, tsunamis of light, raised on high and collided behind his eyes.

"Here I am," he said to himself, darting around the corner. No longer was he in his head, James was in his calves and feet, carefully minding how he brought his heels down so freshly polished dress shoes didn't clack loudly on hard floor. Coming up from the left side, he was in his hands. His left reached across to push open one of the two swinging glass doors leading into Byrne Investment's front desk area, his right took a firmer grip on the heavy pipe.

Pivoting into the room, James' mind truly did go quiet, truly did go blank for just a moment, but there was no peace or pleasure in it. In his arrogance, Gerald had decided to cut costs by having a humble secretary at the front desk instead of the awkwardly titled secre-curity guard he'd had before. At the time, he imagined the police would catch someone as loud and audacious as The Figure long before she could possibly end up on his doorstep again. Thus James wasn't greeted by someone with a weapon, an amateur tough guy he could feel justified in striking if only through a convoluted interpretation of "self-defense". He was greeted by someone taking advantage of the after-hours peace by reading a book.

The secretary was a blonde woman with a soft chin, white blouse, and lovely green eyes growing wide at the sight of what stood before her. Not taking those eyes off him, a phone appeared in her hand, the thumb of which hastily dialed 9-1-1.

"Jesus Christ, don't do that." James gave the command in a suggestion's clothing. Taking a step forward to try to intimidate, his was the body language of a police officer approaching a crazed gunman with hopes they'll hand over their weapon.

Her eyes quivered, went a little wider.

Her thumb pressed *Send*.

James gave the woman's blonde hair three red streaks with one panicked application of the tool in his hand.

Just the sound was enough to make him gag with disgust. No amount of even the darkest, realest footage from the Internet had been adequate to prepare him for this. Even seeing The Figure ending lives in her manner hadn't been enough, the supernatural ease with which she committed the act always undercut James' ability to process it as being part of the same world he lived in.

This was a part of his life now. He'd done it. After weeks and weeks of trying to work up the nerve, he'd done it. A strange sliver of triumph slid in around the cloud of guilt gathering in his gut. James stood perfectly still, looking at the woman lying on the floor where she'd fallen from her chair. Her perfect green eyes were still open, still wide, and there was a tremor in her fingers that was already winding down to perfect stillness.

In tandem, James' heart was slowing ever so slightly from the staccato beat it had been maintaining for what felt like an entire month. The roar of blood in his ears dulled just enough for the sound of the glass doors swinging open behind him, of a thumb pulling back a plastic safety, to register.

Avalanche Security had a personnel roster littered with men and women who'd tried their best, yet failed to become police officers. The man readying his Taser to shoot James was among their number, had ended up there because he'd lacked the cautious attitude preferred by the city's police department. Calling for backup had occurred to him when he'd walked in front of the doors to Byrne Investments and witnessed a horrible murder, but why not stop this costumed killer and claim a hefty bonus all for himself?

James turned to see who it was that had come up behind him and the twist of his body caused the guard's Taser darts to sink their teeth into the far left of his hoodie instead of the center. There they found only air behind cloth, the bulky nature of the costume working in his favor. Terrified, James forgot all about the wet, red pipe he carried. The guard cursed and used his other hand to reach for an extendable baton on his hip.

PSST HSST

In the next moment the guard forgot all about his Taser and his baton, pained confusion flashing across his face. A thin wisp of black smoke came up from the back of his head, both his hands rushing there to try to do something. Had it been fire, he would have probably succeeded in putting it out. Instead, he only managed to rub a mixture of battery acid and his own hastily dissolving flesh onto his fingertips.

Now it was the guard who turned and stepped to the side to see who was behind him. The Figure rewarded this action by spraying water and then acid directly in his face. Not having much of each fluid left in the two spray-nozzle Nalgene bottles she held, The Figure hastily emptied them onto the guard. *PSST HSST PSST HSST* they went, coating his mouth and throat. Crumpling to the ground in an agony his mind could barely process, the guard only managed to make a wet, gurgling groan before silently writhing on the floor. He kept touching his wounds, fingertips pulling away strands of flesh like hot taffy.

James watched all this with a mixture of awe and horror. In time, he might have sorted out his feelings and realized that this was not for him, that The Figure was not something he genuinely admired. In this moment, he saw her in two lights, his savior to embrace and a monster to be avoided or killed. He remembered his hopes that they might become partners. He remembered the pipe in his hand.

Satisfied the security guard was no longer an issue, The Figure dropped the two empty Nalgene bottles and shifted her gaze to James. The blank, leopard-print oval stared directly into the reflective silver triangles hiding James' eyes. Something deep within The Figure recognized what she saw before her wasn't prey, but a threat all the same. Cogs within her clockwork mind went *tick, tick, tick*.

"Hi…" James began.

Tick, tick, tick.

"My name is—"

THUNK

The slate gray knife was buried halfway to its hilt in James' forehead, the long blade reaching inside to neatly bisect his brain. His last sight was a blurred, stereoscopic view dominated by the visible length of burnished steel. The Figure stayed in the background, out of focus, as he read the stamped letters near the hilt—*Ellis Knives, Made in the USA*.

James didn't have the chance to reach his own conclusion about The Figure. In the end, she'd made up his mind for him.

*

The Figure stared as the stranger wearing a gray, angular camouflage suit fell to his knees before he toppled onto one side. It was only then she made the connection between the spots of gore on his pipe and the pale woman collapsed behind the desk. She'd been right, he had been a threat. The Figure was far from a philosopher but even she had at least an ounce of curiosity. Crouching down over the man she'd just killed, security guard still writhing a couple of feet behind her, she attempted to see behind the hooded mask.

It wasn't meant to be. Her knife hadn't only cut between the lobes of his brain, it had jammed up the zipper running from waist to crown. The mechanism was jammed by a mixture of the knife and its own broken teeth. The fresh emergence of crimson seeping through the tangle of metal wasn't helping things. After a few frustrated tugs on both the zipper and the knife, The Figure stood back up. This was the only face she'd ever know him by.

Curiosity was replaced by a cold anger when she noticed the secretary's phone. Even the most minimal police presence was more than she wanted to deal with and any response would quickly snowball into an unbeatable swarm of blue once they became aware of her presence. If she went for Gerald—she remembered the name now—it would certainly lead to death or incarceration. His survival was completely unacceptable, but a faint signal from across an ocean reminded her losing access to Ahmed was even worse. For the first time, The Figure wished she had any idea who Ahmed was or why he was important enough to redirect her course.

She knew she had to leave as fast as possible. Deciding to retrace her path back to where she'd first entered the building, a small loading area in the back, she took the stranger's bloody pipe and left the reception area. If she wasn't in the habit of expressing herself non-verbally, The Figure would have felt like yelling at someone. She wouldn't have been the only one.

Despite their preference for private security, the oligarchs of the financial district wanted the best of everything and so they'd bent the right ears for the quickest police response time in the city. This contradiction was playing out in an increasingly tense scene down at ground level, directly in front of the main entrance where James had passed through only twenty minutes before. Detective Huntley was furiously jabbing his index finger into the gym-toned chest of an Avalanche security guard blocking the doorway with his broad frame. Behind the detective was his plainclothes partner and a second squad car with two beat cops stepping out into the periphery of two overlapping testosterone clouds.

"Do I really need to start tossing around phrases like 'obstruction of justice' here or what? Or what?" Huntley continued, punctuating with further spiteful jabs to the security guard's chest.

"Detective," the guard replied with his best take on *Professional Law Enforcement: The Voice.* "Avalanche security has decided that it would be best for the sake of our client's faith in our services if we are to resolve the ongoing situation with the costumed intruder."

"The what? The 'costumed intruder'? Seriously?" Huntley took a step back, whipped around to lock eyes with one of the two beat cops. "They've got that faceless murder-bitch running around in there. Call for backup, everybody in the borough they can spare." The officer nodded, then spoke into his jacket collar. The other beat cop turned to receive his orders. "You get the shotguns and circle around back. Cover any exit points you can find and stay in touch, got it?"

"Excuse me," the security guard interrupted. "This is an Avalanche security operation. Our jurisdiction, not yours."

Huntley turned back to face the guard, pistol in hand, and his partner stepped closer to lend the weight of his physical presence to the first detective's words.

"That law hasn't fucking passed yet, you asshole," Huntley yelled right in the guard's impassive face. "And if the police lobby has any say, it never will. Now get out of my way or I will cuff you and have you up on charges for everything I can think of and then some."

The guard smirked, made a big show of shrugging in resignation, and stepped aside so the two detectives could enter the building. As they charged past him, he switched to an even more patronizing tone, informing the two men, "There's no need to be so agitated. I think you'll find Avalanche has the situation perfectly under control."

Meanwhile, in the rear loading area, one of the guard's compatriots was feeling the full fury of The Figure's frustration. A swollen bruise on her forehead was the least of her injuries. Spread out on oil stained concrete, the guard had had both arms broken in several places by a lead pipe taken from the rapidly cooling, costumed man lying on the floor in Byrne Investments reception area. Completely incapable of defending herself, she could only watch as

The Figure sat on her chest and began to ram the pipe down her throat.

Pipe and blood, her mouth was inundated with the taste of copper as the cruel implement was thrust past her tongue's spirited, ineffectual attempt to block its path. The Figure, shoulder and arm muscles shifting slowly as they went about their work, only became more livid with each passing moment. Not only had she been denied the opportunity to finish her work on Gerald, she had been denied the pleasure—the peace—that came just before doing what she'd been born to do.

She. Needed. That.

As the last ounce of resistance drained from the woman beneath her, The Figure withdrew the pipe like a splatter-house Excalibur and walked toward the exit. Increasingly able to think in terms of the past and the future, The Figure wanted a memento of the strangely dressed young man who'd given her the gift of curiosity. Before she'd wondered about the face behind his mask, she hadn't wondered about much at all.

A desire for vengeance was also new on the scene. Using only the broadest definition of language, she felt more than thought a vow to return as soon as possible, to use the heaviest of hands in letting this Gerald Byrne character know he wasn't getting off lightly. His continued breathing denied her very purpose and this was inexcusable.

The old laptop bag she'd found abandoned in the halls outside Byrne Investments began to make a clacking sound as she sprinted out into the night. Placing a hand on the bag to still its clasps' noisemaking, The Figure remained blissfully unaware of the huge favor Avalanche security had just done for her. Thanks to the delay caused by the conceited guard up on the front steps, the beat cops came around back with their shotguns a full sixty seconds after she was gone.

"Christ," one of them said upon seeing the dead guard's brutalized form. "What's it going to be like if she ever starts using guns?"

33. $$$(?_?)$$$$

A week to the day that Byrne Investments lost another front desk person to less-than-random violence, Gerald was heading off to meet with Juan Pablo. Slouched in the back of the car while Ann drove, he was allowing himself the luxury of a few minutes self-pity. He might not have, but figured Ann's eyes were focused on the road and that his sunglasses helped this moment of weakness. They leaped up an inch, thanks to Ann driving a little too fast over a speed bump, and landed slightly down the bridge of his aquiline nose.

"Careful, Ann, there's no rush."

"S-sorry, Mr. Byrne."

There was that stutter again. Ann had been the first to discover the trio of bodies in reception and ever since then he'd been hearing superfluous letters sneaking into her speech. Gerald had surprised himself by suggesting to Ann she take some time off on mental health grounds.

When she'd answered that she, "couldn't possibly abandon him," he accepted it and moved on. On some level, Gerald was aware that when people said things like that, all you had to do was push back and they'd not only do what they should do, they'd be doing what they really wanted to do in the first place. All he'd have to have said was, "No, no, I insist," and Ann would have gratefully taken off as many days or even weeks, as she needed.

Gerald hated that. He didn't acknowledge or care about how this conflicted with the labyrinth of lies and doubletalk that characterized the work of him and his peers. That was their business. Other people—including employees—shouldn't be coy about what they want if it's so important to them.

Feeling the car take a wide, right turn, Gerald found himself resenting the momentum that pushed him a short distance closer to the rear, passenger-side door. He was even less fond of the recent turn in what a consultant referred to as his ongoing media narrative. When the blackout had first broken, Gerald had been able to hire that consultant to spin the whole thing on an angle of heroism.

See Gerald. See him keep pursuing The American Dream, never letting horrible injuries slow him down. Dream, Gerald, Dream!

But a second attack, combined with the reveal of his having done nothing to increase security since the first, had taken the story out of his hands. The media consultant happily took his money, yet couldn't quite steer the story somewhere beneficial to Byrne Investments. Gerald was now beginning to be known, and not unfairly, for hubris and arrogance in the face of real danger, for being cavalier with the lives of his employees by not providing them with adequate protection.

The employees that fled had to be replaced by the kind of sub-par, desperate souls who'd take work at a company known for having had two incidents of multiple murder on the premises. Those who'd stayed were almost as low on options, generally being the sort with less skill or imagination and therefore less career mobility that might allow them to jump ship. Thus, the quality of Byrne Investment's services had dropped dramatically in a short period, further driving away clients and making it an uphill struggle to attract new ones.

In the past, at moments like these, Gerald would lose himself in the city as it passed by his car window. Denied the option, he found himself ricocheting around the confines of his skull. Normally this was a highly ordered, carefully controlled space. However, each night brought more and more dreams in which he could barely call himself lucid. It was getting too easy to be distracted, to be an unfocused, constantly moving flock of appetites like so many of his peers. There were times when, given the option, Gerald would happily bash in their heads with something pulled from a toolbox.

What, he thought, *would be my costume?*

"We're here, Mr. Byrne."

"Thanks, Ann, I suppose I'll need you with me, though I'd prefer to go in on my own," Gerald replied. "Maybe I should get a seeing-eye dog for occasions like these, but I'd be lucky to find one as loyal as you, huh?"

Ann's "Yes sir" was masked by her exiting the car, closing her door, and opening his. Gerald exhaled a lungful of metallic, conditioned air and traded it for a fresh lungful laced with several odors of the city, all fighting for his attention. The acrid sweetness of gasoline won, setting Gerald to try to figure out which part of town they were in.

"Ann?"

"One of Juan Pablo's m-men is letting us inside, Mr. Byrne. I think he's going to lead us to…wherever his meetings are held. I'll g-guide you through."

Doors opened. Smells changed. Uneven floor tiles. A brief trip up some stairs that felt far too short for them to have gone up a whole floor. More doors. Gerald found the whole experience as pleasurable as his last rash. He resolved only to meet with others in his own office from now on. He also decided that should he have to move Byrne Investments to a new location, he would rebuild it exactly the same as his old one. It could have machine guns hidden behind the kitchen cupboards and an eight-hundred-pound gorilla at the front desk, but every support column had damn well better be the same distance from each other.

Feeling the relief of a nauseated traveler finally stepping out of a hot car, Gerald realized he must be in Juan Pablo's office when Ann let go of his arm. Doing so, she subtly turned him to face a few degrees right of where he'd been "looking", likely so he'd be pointed directly at the man he'd come to speak with.

I was right, Gerald thought. *She is a good deal better than any dog.*

Juan Pablo greeted him, his voicing coming from about ten feet ahead. "You're welcome to take a seat, Mr. Byrne."

"That's alright, Juan, I'm happy to stand after a car ride." A chair scraped along what sounded like concrete, then settled roughly.

"Well," Juan continued. "I assume you won't mind if I take a seat. I've been standing quite a bit lately, running around town to see who else might be interested in partnering with me."

"Partnering? You talked about being a subsidiary."

No sound. Another shrug?

"I did, I did," Juan eventually answered. "A partnership is what I offered the others, but you—you I knew would still want to be on the top of the pile."

"Everybody wants to be on top of the pile, Juan. It's whether or not they can get there that's the thing. You're top of the pile where you come from and I'm top of the pile here." A throat was cleared, whose was it? Definitely a man's.

"Well, you'll excuse me saying so, Mr. Byrne, but I think we both know that isn't exactly true. I met with a man just last night who wields far more power than you do, a Mr. Kruger. Perhaps you've heard of him?"

"Heard of him? We're having dinner not long after you and I finish here. He's known me since I was a boy." Gerald made a show of a grin slipping through, as if he were stifling laughter instead of anger. "He's like a father to me."

"I assume you've come here because you've reconsidered my offer?"

Gerald tilted his head down at what he hoped was the right angle to stare directly in the Columbian's face. "I thought about our years of mutually satisfactory business and reckoned it was the least I could do for you."

Juan Pablo's laughter was hearty and warm, the way you'd want a grandfather to laugh at something you did to amuse him. "What, because I speak English with an accent, you assume I don't keep an eye on the news? I know what kind of trouble you've been having this past week. As the cliché goes, if anybody is doing anyone a favor here—"

"It's me doing one for you. Yes, I might be having trouble lately but I can always find more money. It doesn't sound like you're having much luck finding legitimacy through anyone else in the city."

"Let's not snipe at each other." Juan tutted, chair creaking as he shifted his weight. "That's hardly a good start to a long-term business relationship, is it?"

"No, it isn't." Gerald "looked" away, as if already moving onto the next deal. "You're in, then? We can work out the numbers in my office. Ann, when's my next available window?"

"Th-th-that would b-be three pm tomorrow."

Gerald clapped his hands together, the echo confirming his suspicion that they were in a large room with a tall ceiling. "Great, then I guess I'll see you—"

Juan Pablo slapped his hand on the table…angrily? It was hard for Gerald to tell. "Just a second, Mr. Byrne, I'd like a few hours to think about this. Can I call you in the evening to let you know my final terms?"

It was Gerald's turn to take an extended pause. He thought he'd seized the momentum of the conversation, now he wasn't so sure. "Mmm, alright. I wouldn't call before eight pm or after eleven pm, though."

"Not a problem. That's everything for the moment. One of my men is going to lead you and your assistant out now."

Originally the decision to follow through on Mr. Dunning's suggestion of getting in bed with Juan Pablo's new North American operation had seemed daring. Gerald's cash reserves now perilously low—by a financial mogul's standards—this deal felt more like an alleyway he'd been herded down by circumstance. No, by that creature in the costume. He still didn't want to expend any time, money, or energy trying to do what neither the police nor Avalanche had been able to. Lucky for him, there was one course of action that already came as part of the package with Juan Pablo.

"Just a second. Juan, you mentioned a bodyguard. What exactly would that entail?"

"Oh!" Juan Pablo's voice perked up. "A wise decision, Gerald."

So he gets to call me by my first name now, does he? Gerald thought, working to keep his features inexpressive.

"I'll give it some thought, then choose whomever I think would be most suited for the role. If you prefer, I could make a shortlist. Does that sound alright by you?"

"A shortlist would be fine. Three candidates. I'll be on my way, now."

Back they went through the irritating maze with its smells of damp wood, steps too narrow for Gerald's feet, and a slow ticking sound he wanted to know the story behind. He never would, though. Not getting to learn the root cause of sounds and smells was a much more common part of his life now, one of the trickier things for Gerald to accept.

Back to the tang of gasoline, just outside the entrance and not too many paces from the car. Ann continued to lead them right up to the rear driver's side door, her arm interlocking with his in a way that suggested something curious to Gerald. He wasn't, however, in the habit of listening to suggestions.

The slight impact in his ears from the doors being slammed too hard. A brief pull on his center mass as the car started its journey. The thought of Juan Pablo grinning, probably ear to ear, after he left. Before, even. Maddening. He'd liked the man a lot more when he was just a concept, an idea, an apparition on the other side of the Atlantic who occasionally sent Gerald several million dollars in exchange for an easily rendered service.

Gerald found himself wondering when he'd be done adjusting to his new state. Still he kept noticing little things shifting in him, responding to a sightless existence. At the moment, it was his new, childish desire that all restaurants be at ground level from now on. He used to love dining above street level, even if it was only a single floor. Now the view wasn't his to enjoy, there was just stairs or an elevator ride to have to put up with between leaving the car and sitting at his table.

Ann told him his father had texted her where to meet him. Gerald cut her off before she could tell him, saying he didn't really care since he was going to eat at home. There was still the odd misfire when finding the food on his plate and he wasn't comfortable risking that in public just yet. Ann said she understood. Gerald wondered if she understood she'd be preparing that dinner for him.

"Even with those sunglasses on, I can tell you're not having a great day, are you, son?"

"Mr. Kruger, I'd appreciate it if you didn't refer to me as *son*. Despite our age differences and the respect I show a man of your accomplishments, I still find it a little bit condescending."

His father huffed at this, but Gerald figured he needed to be reminded certain lines had been drawn. They were in public now and Gerald could tell from the level of ambient noise that the place they were in was fairly small and not too populated. Oh, it was probably popular, but if this was where he thought it was then part of the appeal of the restaurant was the wide space between tables and the premium gratuity you had to pay to help justify this luxury to the owners. He was able to pick up bits and pieces of other conversations, so Gerald felt right to be standoffish with his father.

Even though she was well aware of the familial connection, he'd had Ann sit at the bar.

"Alright, Gerald, I can call you Gerald, right?" Kruger continued. "I've respected your desire not to talk about this over email or the phone, and now we're here. What exactly do you plan to do about this woman?"

"What are we, mobsters? I plan to—"

"Gerald, the waiter is here."

Irritated at being interrupted, he let it show in his voice as he informed the waiter he'd just be having a double of Jim Beam, neat. His father ordered something in German, further narrowing down the possibilities of where they could be eating. In his mind, tall red curtains appeared over long, oval windows, then he changed his mind and they were replaced by evenly spaced wooden slats in front of rectangular windows.

"Anyway," he continued. "I plan to let the police sort this out. She can't possibly evade them for much longer, it's not exactly like her crimes have been subtle or few in number. I mean, how many people has she killed in the past two and a half months?"

Noticing the table cloth draping down across his lap, Gerald pinched some of it between thumb and forefinger. Spider silk. That helped, a bit.

"Gerald?"

"What are you going to do, Mr. Kruger?" Gerald replied, putting undue emphasis on the syllables in his father's surname. "What's your big plan then, Derek?"

"First, I'd stop interrupting my f—, my elders, if I were you. Next, I'd shut down my little firm that's bleeding out worse than the poor girl at your front desk did, remove myself from the public eye a while so my reputation could recover, and maybe keep busy in the meanwhile by doing some kind of consulting work for a larger, more established firm. I can think of one that might take you in, if you can get through this dinner without being too rude to me." Kruger paused to thank the waiter as their drinks arrived, took a sip, and continued. "As for myself, I don't really need to do anything. I have a controlling interest in one of the top three security companies in the world and if that damn bill finally passes through congress next month I'll be able to re-brand one arm of Avalanche as private military contractors who'll be able to operate with impunity on the grounds of any Dunning-Kruger building, compound, or facility."

Kruger paused to catch his breath, didn't quite find all of it.

"I'd like to see that little bitch beat back assault rifle rounds with her fucking crowbar or whatever." He exhaled.

Enjoying the brown liquor swirling around his mouth, Gerald was in no rush to reply to all this. He glanced to his left not for the sake of his eyes, but his ears. Turned at that angle he could hear a little bit more of what was being said at a nearby table—some amusingly awkward first date where the man's voice definitely suggested a May-December relationship. After getting a satisfactory payoff in the woman's unenthusiastic reply to a suggestion of going back to the man's penthouse, he swallowed and turned back to his father.

"That's all really...something, Mr. Kruger. I guess you're properly covered for all eventualities and I appreciate the offer, but I've decided I'm going to keep the firm going. I might re-brand if necessary. Meanwhile, I've just lined up a substantial source of black-collar income and a new bodyguard, so I think I'm good for now."

Kruger began to reply, was interrupted by his food arriving. Gerald took the chance to listen closely to the waiter's voice. Turnover wasn't high at places his father patronized, restaurants that actually paid their employees the wages necessary to guarantee pleasant service. He did sound a little bit familiar. Gerald's mood brightened as he narrowed his guesses down to just three establishments.

For another long couple of minutes the sound of his father eating was all the conversation had between them. Gerald figured his father was taking a moment to think over what he'd just been told. He was wrong. Kruger was going to give the same answer no matter how Gerald rebuffed his advice and that answer sat patiently in the back of his mind as he tried to enjoy his food. Kruger had never known what it was to be poor, but it suited his personal mythology to imagine he had, to pretend there was novelty for him to find in a meal whose main ingredients were fast becoming unavailable even to the microscopic remaining middle class, let alone the majority of the population.

"Alright, Gerald, you do whatever you think is best." Kruger let his knife and fork rest on the plate, swallowed heartily. "If you want to be apart, then you're really going to be apart. As of this moment, Avalanche security is breaking its contract to Byrne Investments and will be removing all personnel from not only your floor, but the entire building."

"Dad?"

"Oh, I'm your father now, am I? If I'd known this was the sort of thing it took, I would have taken the tough love approach years ago."

"Dad, you'll have to break contracts with three other companies as well as the owners of the building itself. That's a lot of money you'll have to dole out in…"

Gerald let his sentence trail off. What was he saying? His father easily had enough wealth to lose that business and Avalanche was an international company with an established reputation; one unhappy building in one city wasn't going to ruin them. Kruger knew this and he knew his son knew it, too.

"You'll just have to hire some second-rate outfit like Object, Hachette, or maybe even those clowns at Pyongyang Security. This is assuming you aren't too tapped out, of course. I guess you have those black-collar funds coming in soon enough." Kruger stuffed some more food in his mouth, took pleasure from talking around it. "And that's that. I'm done trying to protect a child who won't even acknowledge his own father in public. My mind's made up and I wouldn't recommend crying to Mother about it, I've spoken with him about all this already."

As ever, Gerald's mother was out of sight and out of mind. Kruger hadn't mixed up his genders mid-sentence, he was sarcastically referring to how in the past Gerald had gone to Dunning for advice or even financial help when Kruger had been reluctant to provide either. For the first time in years, Gerald could feel his will bending backward like a tree in a strong wind. Tired of the way his father was pushing down against him, he twisted the conversation in a different direction.

"When you texted Ann where I was to meet with you this evening, I told her not to tell me."

"I see."

"I'm curious, is this the…Wechsler Brasserie?"

"No."

Maddening.

An hour and a half later, Gerald was finishing the last bites of a stir-fry Ann had been surprisingly decent at preparing for him. He was eating on the east balcony of his condo, trying to let the cool evening breeze carry some of his stress away and down toward the ocean. It wasn't working.

The glass door slid open. "It's Juan Pablo on the phone, Mr. Byrne."

Gerald took his phone from Ann, let her remove the small folding table in front of him with his empty plate on top. Cutlery clinked as she left, and once he heard the glass door slide shut again, Gerald put the phone to his ear.

"Hello, Gerald?"

"Mr. Byrne here."

"Yes, good, excellent. I've given it some thought and I do believe I'd still like us to go into business together. My coke. Your connections and legitimacy. Is this agreeable?"

"Yes, Juan, it is." Gerald let out a long, silent sigh.

"Well, alright then, though I must advise you of one change I would like to suggest."

"And that is?"

"I'm not a stupid man, I know on paper you will have to be CEO or whatever and that I will be beneath that. But in the practical distribution of authority, I think it is important we be equals in this endeavor."

Even this high up, Gerald heard a car's tires screech as it took a turn too hard. He wished Juan Pablo was under it.

"Well…" Gerald trailed off.

"I think it is most important."

Gerald knew this was a suggestion the way he suggested things to

Ann.

"Sure, fine. But I better be getting back what I put into this and I don't want you to ever show up at my main office without an appointment. When you're there, you aren't to bother any of my employees either, got it?"

Juan Pablo knew Gerald would need to make rules like these in order to feel comfortable enough with agreeing to his demand. He quickly acquiesced to Gerald who, after three more minutes of business related small talk, thanked him for his time and hung up. Gerald turned the phone off, let it rest in his lap for a moment. He wanted to kick the balcony's railing in frustration, a brief wave of vertigo held him back.

As carefully as a cartoon character just realizing they'd walked ten feet past the edge of a cliff, he reached back, found smooth brick wall and then edged his way to the sliding glass doors. Taking one step in, he enjoyed the feel of the cool carpet on his feet, sticking up between a couple of his toes. A deep breath, then he called across the condo. Hopefully, Ann wasn't standing right beside him.

"Ann, what time was it when Juan Pablo called?"

"A-about eleven fifteen pm, Mr. Byrne."

That was it. He'd said to call between eight pm and eleven pm, he'd said so, goddammit. Juan and his father and that woman in the costume and his eyes and Ann's stutter…

"Oh, and M-Ms. Steiger c-contacted me while you were on the ph-phone with Juan Pablo," Ann called to him. "Sh-she's retracting her offer f-for you to w-work under her and her s-s-sister. But y-you didn't w-want that anyways, right?"

Gerald needed to dominate something, to possess every inch, every atom and exert his will upon all of it. He stood there, his feet on the carpet, his mind on his problems, thinking. Thinking. Thinking.

Her voice had sounded like it was coming from his study, on the other end of the condo, where he knew she would sometimes rest while he was busy.

"Ann?"

"Y-yes, Mr. Byrne?"

"Come here, please."

A few hours later, Gerald lay in bed calmly listening to the rhythm of Ann's breathing in her sleep. He'd made her take the side with the wet spot, naturally.

It had been a fun way to calm the stutter out of her. Hopefully, it wouldn't be so annoying listening to her speak tomorrow. He'd wanted to make her sleep on the couch, except his desire for distance was briefly outshone by his desire for novelty. Gerald couldn't remember the last time he'd actually let someone spend the night in bed with him. He hoped whatever feelings she had that had allowed such an abrupt shift in their relationship wouldn't affect her work performance.

This was just a challenging period of transition, he told himself, and soon enough he'd have the funds to rebuild bigger and better than ever. He would be bigger and better than ever, better able to focus his mind on problem-solving and kingdom building with one less sense to distract him.

"To what end?" he muttered. Ann remained asleep.

There was a question he wasn't in the habit of asking. *Greater power and wealth*, was the answer, of course. It was his purpose in life, wasn't it? Never mind the body, he was an agile mind that preyed upon—

She's the predator, he thought. *Dismantling small companies, siphoning money from the government and spinning gold from thin air won't keep her from putting a crowbar through your forehead.* Stress shot through his nerves as Gerald was back in his office watching The Figure doing just that.

Gerald didn't reply to this with language, just sheer will. A tenseness in his chest, he saw the image of The Figure bringing cold metal down toward him and pushed back. She slowed down. Lying in bed, the muscles around his eyes bunched together as his empty sockets reflexively focused a gaze that was no longer there.

He couldn't believe it, he couldn't believe it was taking this much energy to control his own mental imagery. The imaginary Figure loomed over Gerald, her dark blue crowbar moving with all the speed of a continent, still attempting to finish its arc toward Gerald. Back in his bedroom, he realized how wound up he was and began a simple breathing exercise.

As he exhaled, a hail of knives flew through the air to carve The Figure up into ten thousand bloody fragments. They looped back around and dived through her again and again. The crowbar didn't just drop to the floor, Gerald willed it to do so.

Right, he thought. *Right. The hell with her and all the other obstacles. I will deal with them. Me*! Feeling gifted with being the distilled essence of the true and righteous might of what is empirically measurable as the best of all there is, Gerald was able to calm down. Tiredness could finally be allowed to take him where it always did.

Losing consciousness, he noticed his breathing began to sync up with Ann's. Irritated, Gerald purposefully held his breath for a few seconds to throw things off. He had one more thought before finally falling asleep.

When the hell are the police going to do their job?

34. WE GOT'ER

The pressure on his stomach of a belt optimistically set one notch smaller than necessary. Cold glass against his smooth palm. Predominantly masculine, barrel-chested chatter with a sprinkling of footsteps and pouring sounds. Detective Huntley opened his eyes to look across the bar from his chosen place, wedged back in the corner furthest from the entrance. Young men, who had undoubtedly helped raise funds for various community projects by appearing in beefcake calendars for cheesecake eating women, were freely drinking with wrinkled, gray-haired compatriots. Several old timers had terrible burn scars visible on their hands or faces, ravaged landscapes warped and reset by searing heat. A few were even missing the odd ear or finger.

Huntley was putting the finishing touches on a light breakfast. Unlike the firemen, his day was just starting. All the same, beer was starting to become tempting.

BUH BUMP BA
BUH BUMP BUMP BUH
BUH BUMP BA

Aggressive bass began to reverberate through the cold Thursday morning, causing circular ripples in Detective Huntley's orange juice as if there was a dinosaur coming his way. Some of the firemen looked outside with irritation. Taking the cup off the edge of the table before it spilled, Huntley took a long sip while he watched his partner give grief to the owners of a car that had just rolled up outside, its stereo demanding everyone's attention at 6:23 am.

Here they were, two accomplished detectives in the Major Case Squad and still his partner felt the need to discipline teenagers as if he was a truancy officer. It made Huntley smile, a rare treat. Guberman was an excellent profiler who had previously worked about as far from the streets as you could get, chasing white-collar crime in the financial sector. Frustrated by the many ways in which the world seemed to conspire to cheat him out of meaningful arrests, he switched to chasing killers. He liked to joke that he was just swapping one set of sociopaths for another. Push him for any more detail than that, though, and he got pretty mad, pretty fast.

Guberman's experience made him a natural choice for the case, which had been giving them such grief over the past ten weeks. Huntley, as his partner, came along for the ride both metaphorically and—on days like today—literally. Huntley had started as a beat cop and spent plenty of time giving grief to inconsiderate youth, leaving him perfectly happy to focus purely on the more significant crimes littering the city. Coming from where he had, Guberman wasn't worn out on petty misdemeanors. He still had the old school one-broken-window attitude and couldn't stand the thought of anything more severe than jaywalking going unpunished.

BUMP BUH BUMP BUMP BA

BUMP BUH BUMP B-B-BU—

"There we go," Huntley said to his juice, watching Guberman reach in and turn off the kids stereo. Now Huntley could faintly hear the rapid tones of a tongue-lashing he'd only been able to lip-read for the past minute. Then it was back to lip-reading as a low, menacing voice was employed for the big finale. Satisfied, Guberman turned away from the kids in their graduation present of a car and walked inside toward Huntley, who hastily handed his empty plate to a server.

"A fireman's bar, eh?"

Detective Guberman set his two-hundred-and-thirty-five pounds, stretched over a six-foot-four skeletal canvas, in the heavily varnished wooden chair opposite Huntley.

"Yeah, I like coming here instead of the usual cop bars. I haven't heard their stories a thousand times before and they haven't heard mine."

"You're not just here for the eye candy?"

"This is what you want to talk about?"

"No." Guberman, barely settled, stood up from his chair. "Of course not."

Huntley followed suit and the two headed out to greet the morning sun.

"Do you ever think any of these guys, when they've been sent to put out a fire at a drug dealer's house or a known sex offender's place or whatever..." Standing on the sidewalk with his hands in his pockets, Guberman let his eyes drift skyward. "Do you think they ever just let that fire burn?"

Huntley shrugged and dropped himself into the driver's side of his metallic-green sedan, his partner showing a bit more grace as he got in the passenger side.

"The hell are we doing out here at this hour?" Guberman asked, letting his first question drop.

"Because we got an anonymous tip that The Figure was spotted passing through this area and you wanted to follow up on that," Huntley replied. "Because that's how stupid this investigation has gotten."

"A neat little nickname to give me, 'this investigation', but I guess it fits." Guberman playfully put out there in an early morning slur, his energy levels already low after chastising the kids with their stereo cranked up. "I have to be honest; I'm getting a little discouraged."

"Ah, come on Arnold, you're just feeling rough from not enough sleep," Huntley said as he leaned in toward Guberman, who looked at him, gave an exaggerated sigh of resignation and let himself be given a quick kiss. Satisfied, Huntley pulled back to his side of the car and continued, "How about we go over the basics again, to help center ourselves? I think the horseshit over at Byrne Investments left us both a little scattered."

Another sigh. "Alright, Danny, alright. While I do that, you can find us somewhere to get a couple of breakfast sandwiches. I just burned a lot of calories trying to instill some civilization in those brats with the expensive rims. I'm guessing you haven't eaten yet?"

Daniel Huntley nodded, stomach acid breaking down his first breakfast, and carefully pulled out from their parking spot in front of an ice cream parlor.

"Okay, we don't know her race or ethnicity and we don't have any prints or DNA." Guberman tapped one long finger on the passenger door side arm rest. "We can guess she's Caucasian due to video evidence from the killing of Sharon Carter, who succeeded in cutting open the killer's costume in several places. However, that really is just a guess since those cuts were so bloody and the video quality wasn't great. She could also be Asian or, if you squint a bit, an exceptionally pale African-American, likely of mixed race, maybe even Puerto-Rican."

"So we don't really know what her skin color is other than she probably isn't the child of two black parents," Huntley said, slowing to stop at an intersection. "And the blood from those wounds wasn't recoverable thanks to the fire she lit. Meanwhile, the full body stocking keeps hair and skin flakes contained."

"Let's go to Bertie's. Their bacon wrap is great."

"Sure thing, good choice." Huntley turned left as the light became green.

"So yeah…" Guberman continued. "Her weapons are all scavenged or welded together from scavenged parts, because the hell if we've had any luck tracing all those crowbars, claw-hammers, and what-have-you to whichever store they came from, let alone whoever made the original purchases. The battery acid strongly suggests someone who has access to a lot of cars, but it's difficult to confirm since there are other places one could gain access to those chemicals."

Huntley brought them down past Emerson Mall's beige bulk and turned right to take them to a convenient parking lot near Bertie's. The sun was just barely starting to make its presence known, casting reddish-yellow light across the hood of the car and bouncing up into his eyes.

"There was something of a loose pattern to the killings. She's always hit a big investment firm or a bank, always at their offices in the financial district. The one time she runs into a regular customer—a disgruntled homeowner—all she does is take the battery from his phone. So obviously she isn't killing willy-nilly. But, aside from her target's industry of choice, there doesn't seem to be much connecting her victims."

Huntley pulled into the parking lot at Bertie's, braking a little abruptly. A grand prize for this being the thousandth time he'd done that, Guberman shot him a look of irritation. Huntley continued from where his partner left off, keeping the subject of his minor infraction from being broached.

"Until she hit that newspaper owned by Trinity Media, *The Sentinel*. Those were media, not financial types. Plus, her behavior seemed a little off around the middle of the attack."

Stepping out of the car, Huntley was once again blinded by the morning sun. He stubbed his toe on the first step leading up to the tall, smeary glass door.

"Agh."

"Good point."

"Don't be a smartass."

"I meant the newspaper attack, not your little grunt there." Guberman teased as he opened the door for Huntley. Sore toe be damned, he walked through with better posture than usual and ordered for the both of them, going against their routine. Guberman rolled his eyes at his partner's embarrassment over such a mundane bit of klutziness.

Waiting for the girl in the striped polo shirt to come back to the counter with their food, they looked around the restaurant. Shift workers. The elderly. A trio of exhausted looking office workers who weren't too high on the totem pole. A couple of construction workers. Typical morning crowd. Typical morning.

Bertie's had been started several years back by what most people of the time would have called a hipster. She'd carefully designed the look of the place from a scrapbook in her head that was filled with clippings from movies, TV shows, song lyrics, and assumptions blended from all three. Over the years, the owner became older, less enamored with her pretensions, and the neighborhood changed as the money moved elsewhere. What started as simulacra of blue-collar establishments from the nineteen-thirties with a customer base of tech workers, young trust funders, and the sort eventually became much more like the real thing.

The girl came back with two brown paper bags. The morning's contemplative silence between the two detectives came to a close as they stepped outside to lean against the trunk of the car and eat their breakfast. Guberman unwrapped his sandwich and bit into it, feeling grease and nutrients being pulled into his system through the surface of his tongue. Huntley pulled out a lighter and that's as far as he got before Guberman exclaimed, "What's that?"

Huntley left the cigarettes in his pocket, put the lighter back there with them. He stuck a straw in his mouth and let it hang there like he was Humphrey Bogart. Guberman grinned, took another hearty bite of his mediocre sandwich.

"Do you think it was something personal that triggered the attack on the newspaper?" Huntley asked around his straw.

"To know if it's something personal, I feel like I'd have to know more about the person."

"And how do you know her now?"

"Honestly, it's frustrating. Even from just the preliminary research on the young man who killed the secretary before this lady killed him, it's not hard to begin to understand what brought him there. It's even pretty clear to me why that arrogant shithead Gerald wouldn't upgrade his security or even accept police protection after the first or second attack…but the woman, the woman…" Guberman trailed off.

"You can't really color in that character sketch you're trying to draw." Huntley offered.

"Yes, thank you, yes." Guberman sighed. "Just an outline."

They both chewed for a while. The street was almost silent. There wasn't a lot of traffic coming through here anymore.

"Do you think that bill is going to get passed?" Guberman asked. "It's finally going up to vote next week."

"If you don't like me swearing, you'd best not get me talkin' about that shit." Huntley replied.

"I don't like you swearing the way telegraphs used STOP. Swearing about a bill that will practically make corporate-owned land a sovereign nation on American soil is reasonably justified, in my assessment." Guberman popped the final piece of his sandwich past his teeth, the last bite nowhere near as satisfying as the first. "Well, corporations of a certain size."

"Honestly, I don't think they'll quite manage to pass it. Something big, or several somethings, would have to happen to make the public okay with it. Gotta say, I have a hard time imagining what that'd be." Huntley sighed, finished his own sandwich. "Doesn't mean the idea doesn't piss me right the fuck off, though."

Huntley made to go back in the car but Guberman shook his head and gestured to stay leaning against the trunk. He was enjoying the peace and quiet.

"Good point there. I mean, Jesus, we practically had to be smothered in dead kids before beefing up our gun laws," Guberman replied. "Even then, we're no Canada or Britain."

"Plus, it just drove the real gun nuts to hoard, stockpile, and generally try to work around the law even harder. Then you've got the fuckin' militia actions in—"

"What's that?"

"Fuck's sake, I just put my hand in my pocket to rest it there! You gotta—"

Guberman grabbed his partner's shoulder, shook it, and pointed him toward the other side of the street. There was a figure, moving with some difficulty, covered head to toe in leopard print. An off-white, fake fur coat increased her profile and one hand was shoved inside the jacket as if she were a truly radical, alternate-universe Napoleon.

Huntley began to bring his index finger up to make a shush gesture but his hand barely rose above his sternum before Guberman's tiredness and frustration blew out of him like back draft in a house fire.

"Freeze right where you are!" Guberman bellowed, his voice echoing up and down the block.

Flummoxed, Huntley brought a hand back over to his shoulder holster so he could join his partner in pointing their service pistols at the most ambitious killer the city had seen in decades.

The figure removed her hand from her jacket. As well trained as they were, both paused a moment longer than they might have when dealing with another criminal. From day one, it had been obvious The Figure didn't use guns, yet here she was holding the kind of revolver that earned the title hand cannon; like everything else with The Figure, it was larger than life and surreal. The gun being such a shock, it wasn't until much later Huntley would remember the fingers holding it were soaked in the owner's blood.

Four shots were fired, two from The Figure and one from each detective. The rear window of their patrol car made a dull thump as a heavy round impacted, failing to penetrate it. Huntley's shot parted the fur along her left shoulder like a truck tearing through a cornfield, drawing no blood. Guberman had more luck, tagging her left shoulder precisely where Huntley had been aiming for in an attempt to disarm, making him feel compensated for her second bullet tunneling through his right bicep.

Nearly dropping her pistol in shock, she turned and fled down the street. Huntley glanced quickly at Guberman, looking at his eyes instead of his injury. They told him what he needed to know and he left his partner behind to nurse the non-fatal wound. Charging after her, he could already hear Guberman calling for backup. Even with the relative emptiness of the neighborhood, a gun battle in broad daylight wasn't something they wanted to go on longer than necessary.

He didn't feel bad about leaving his partner alone any more than Guberman felt badly for letting Huntley chase a dangerous maniac by himself. They'd always known situations like this would happen and had laid down several rules over a series of brunch, dinner, and bedtime conversations during the early weeks of the relationship. No matter what happened, when danger reared its head they would behave as if they were connected only by their badges and not the hearts that beat beneath them. Otherwise, it would be too easy to make emotional decisions that could lose them their quarry or lead to one or both of them getting killed.

Huntley clicked the switch on his gun to activate a tiny camera embedded along the barrel. A stream of wireless data began to mark his movement across the cracked tarmac, something to make life a little more straightforward for later, when he'd have to justify every bullet fired. *If only the criminals used these, it'd be so much simpler*, Huntley thought before adrenaline's full effect kicked in, pushing little asides like that far, far down his list of priorities.

He took a firing stance just before she rounded a corner and did his best impersonation of Guberman's thundering bellow. "Stop where you are or I will shoot to kill!"

She didn't stop. He didn't shoot. It was literally a long shot, her body far away and mostly around the corner by the time he finished his warning. He considered sprinting as hard as he could, but then Huntley noticed the trail of blood she was leaving along the sidewalk and decided to pace himself. He'd heard of guys getting winded at just the wrong moment and paying for it dearly.

Edging up to the corner, his back to the wall, Huntley focused on images of Guberman to level himself out. Gunfights were horrible enough, it didn't help when you were on your own and clear memories of every mutilated body your prey had left in the world weren't helpful either. Huntley had no illusions about the possibility of dying in the field. However, he wanted to at least be able to have an open casket funeral.

She could be right around that corner with her pistol aimed squarely for my center mass, ready to blow away my center ass, he couldn't help thinking. Remembering the well-polished lighter in his pocket along with the forbidden cigarettes, Huntley had the kind of idea that seems sensible in the moment. Keeping the gun ready in his right, he used his left hand to snatch out the lighter and edge it ever so slightly around the corner to try to see what was there.

He couldn't make out a damn thing, but he also didn't get his hand blown off by a waiting lunatic. That would have to be enough. Huntley put the lighter away, squared his grip on the pistol, and took a deep breath. He let it out slowly as he pivoted around the corner, ready to fire, ready to empty out everything he had if that's what it took.

The remote hard drive downloading his pistol's stream wouldn't have any new gunfire to record, it just saw what Huntley saw, a woman in a strange costume sprawled out on the pavement not fifteen feet ahead. She lay face down in front of an empty retail space whose available-for-rent sign had become faded from so many weeks spent in the sun. The large, angry revolver had grown too heavy for a hand struggling to get enough blood to function and had been dropped about five feet behind her. If she was playing possum, it was a hell of a performance.

Huntley quickly put himself between the revolver and the woman, then froze, his pistol still aimed directly at her. Her torso wasn't moving the way it would if she was breathing. He calmed down, holstered his pistol, and cautiously came up alongside her. Standing right by her head, he crouched and was relieved not to have a leopard-printed hand drive a hidden knife deep into his guts. Huntley placed two fingers on her neck, was almost saddened to detect not even the faintest trace of a pulse.

Guberman would have wanted to question her and Huntley would have liked to see his partner gain at least some satisfaction from hearing her answers. Now there were bound to be at least a few more sleepless nights as Guberman tossed and turned, trying to figure out that disconnect, that void they'd been discussing only a minute and a half before. Huntley reached into another pocket and pulled out two surgical gloves. Snapping them over his hands, he knew he should wait for the forensics guys to show up but also knew he wanted to see this woman's face badly enough to ignore protocol.

"Slowly or like a Band-Aid?" he muttered, having already made up his mind. The body was rolled onto its back. Velcro fasteners along the collarbone were ripped off. The hooded mask was pulled up.

"Shit!" Huntley exclaimed. "She's as black as they come."

35. التسجيل الرابع

"Hello, Mary."
"Hello, Ahmed."

They'd greeted each other ten minutes earlier, but it felt good to do it again.

So this was it. Since waking up stiff and inexplicably angry only seven days ago, Mary had felt herself pulled along by an ever increasing inertia toward this moment. Seven days feeling sorely cheated of something she desperately needed, knowing that that and more would come to her wrapped up in a handsome package with soft lips above a strong chin.

"You look nice in a skirt."

"Aw, well, it's just, you know, from a thrift store."

On their first date, they carefully stole looks at each other. Now, they brazenly took as many as they could bear. Mary enjoyed his forearms; he lost himself in the subtle tones of the hair she was growing out.

"This was a good idea."

"Yeah, definitely worth the, uh, effort."

They stood before a two-story-tall window, the city glittering behind them. Bored of coffee shops, bars, and the like, they had decided to meet somewhere with a bit more novelty.

"And I appreciate the trust. Not a lot of girls would want to come out with a guy to somewhere like this, especially after dark."

"Ha…well, I, ha, well…"

Knowing Paris or Las Vegas were out of the question, Ahmed had still felt a burning desire to take Mary on a little adventure. He'd heard friends talk about an abandoned ballroom overlooking the downtown area and the romantic imagery couldn't have appeared in his mind with greater clarity.

"Isn't it nuts that beneath us are thirty floors of luxury hotel?"

"This space is so beautiful, why don't they use it?"

They held hands while gazing around what the post Ahmed had read on cata-x-philes.com, an urban exploration blog, referred to as "The Not-So-Secret Ballroom". It had long been a fixture for young people with camera, flashlights, and a desire to commit mild transgressions before reporting it all back to the Internet.

"Nobody knows. There's some stories online about different owners, legal battles, failed and abandoned renovations. Mostly, I'd just like to know the story behind how the maintenance guys almost never lock the door that gets you in here."

"Ooh, I like all the tall column-things."

"Columns?"

"Yes."

There was a complex history to the building. However, they didn't care to know it anymore than they cared to know all the geological movements that placed the earth beneath it. For their entire lives, the challenge hadn't been finding information, it had been cultivating a sense of genuine mystery through selective, willful ignorance.

"Oh, geez."

"Ha ha ha!"

Walking along the western length of the ballroom their view across that side of the city was blocked by a condo building eighty years the hotel's junior. Directly ahead from where they stood in dappled moonlight was a kitchen with marble counter-tops and track lighting that illuminated a man in a bathrobe rubbing one out to something on his phone. The lights cast shadows down the man's thoroughly engaged body with all the stark anti-flattery of a disposable camera flash. Mary looked to see if Ahmed was grinning before allowing herself to do the same. As the man began to look up, the two of them quickly scooted out of sight, moonlight bringing a glint to eyes peeking from the shadows like a pair of mischievous spirits in a sexually charged fairy tale.

"We might as well just go to our separate apartments." Ahmed chuckled. "I don't think anything else tonight will top that."

"Pfft…ha ha…oh man."

Still grinning and giggling, Mary let Ahmed lead her around to the south side of the ballroom. There was another condo building erected long after the hotel, though this was about a block away, so they didn't feel like they were intruding on anyone. The space between was all ground level parking, allowing them a clear view of the city but for this one perfect, concrete rectangle with its dozens of rows of identical glass rectangles.

"From this distance and with this building, it's like row after row of monitors."

"Ha! I just saw a guy go off frame from one and then appear in another two windows over. It was like he teleported! I mean, I know he must have taken a hallway we can't see, but still, I like the idea."

"Yeah, all those 'screens'. Can I tell you a crazy idea I've been thinking about?"

"Sure." Mary was watching the man, hoping he'd repeat the "trick"'.

"Well, I don't know how much attention you pay to TV and web show ratings, but neither of them ever manage to generate some of the obscene view counts old TV shows used to." Ahmed breathed in. "A show called M.A.S.H. had over one-hundred-and-twenty-six-million viewers for its series finale, a number that's never been beat except by one year's Super Bowl, and odds are you'll never see that many people watching the same episode at the same time of any series ever again."

"I, uh, didn't know you were that into TV." Mary wasn't sure what to make of this, but hey, at least it wasn't something to do with a horrible news item of the moment. Bored with the "teleporter", Mary was now watching a woman in the far right window on the twelfth floor of the building ahead of them. She was playing with a cat that appeared to be cute, though Mary couldn't be sure at this distance.

"I'm not super into it; I just had this idea and did a little research. The reason you'll never see that many people all watching the same show at the same time again is because back then there were maybe a dozen channels in most people's homes and there was no Internet like we have today." Ahmed offered one palm and drew the other away as if a big bang had spawned a universe between them. "Now there's a bajillion TV channels, online video channels, social media sites, and so on and so on. There's so much more competition for people's attention, so now a show with ratings that would have gotten them cancelled back in the day can be celebrated as a breakout hit."

"Okay, I guess that makes sense." The cat moved so it could be seen to be fat, a plus in Mary's book. The bigger and dumber a house pet was, the more she liked it.

"Right. That's entertainment. Now apply the same dynamic to news and the general act of raising awareness of important issues. In no previous era do I think it would be possible for me to be aware of more terrible things, people in need, public debates, and so on than I am now."

Mary turned away from The Fat Cat & Lady Show to look at Ahmed, who was already looking at her. "Sure, but you like to keep on top of what's going on in the world."

"True. But, like, the Internet makes it pretty easy. Even when I'm not trying to, stuff comes to my attention. Friends share shit, related links crop up at the bottom of articles or ads appear around the edges of something I'm watching. I'd say the average person is much more aware of all the big happenings in the world than ever before." Ahmed paused for effect before continuing. "Even someone like you is aware of more than she wants to be, right?"

"Yeah, I suppose." Mary chewed her lip. "I suppose it's fair to say I'm aware of more than I want to be."

"Right!" Ahmed was pleased Mary was following along instead of burying her head in the sand. "Therefore, just as even really popular shows today have far less fans—and therefore far less die-hard fans—than shows from back when there was less choice...so, too, do we now have less people paying attention to any one issue at a time and therefore even less people who commit to trying to help solve a big problem or pressure those in charge to solve it."

Mary thought for a second. She was trying hard not to shut down; she wanted to be able to offer Ahmed the kind of conversation he was seeking.

"So, okay, it's less likely to get enough people consistently working to solve an issue or pressure the guys who should be solving it, since there are, like, so many issues we're made aware of and new ones coming up all the fuckin' time." Mary's fingers interwove, pulled against each other. "Which I guess, um, is also part of how all but those directly affected forget about tragedies in weeks that we used to remember for, like, years."

Ahmed smiled. Mary guessed this meant she'd inferred the right idea and was pleased. Then her mood folded in on itself as she silently kept going with it. Seeing her expression change, Ahmed put his hands on her shoulders, as if he could steady her against the terrible wind blowing through her head.

"Which is awful because it can make it next to impossible for people to feel like they can do a damn thing, and it means the loudest dickholes always get the most attention when they're basically never the people that should be listened to." She continued talking to Ahmed's chest while looking right through it. "So, bull's-eye, this is so much of why I hate talking about this shit because I just feel totally powerless about everything but the socks I wear...and I can't even afford nice socks."

"Hey, hey, come on. It's not a perfect theory. It's not a proven rule of the universe. It's just a way of looking at the world that I was playing with, a way of trying to understand why things are the way they are."

"But it's so cynical and horrible and and and hopeless." Mary moaned. "And, like, what… Do you feel clever for looking at things that way? Does it actually solve anything or just make people feel bad when you point it out to them?"

"I'm sorry. I didn't think of that."

"You should have."

Anxious that he was ruining the evening just as it began, Ahmed guided Mary to the north side of the building with hopes the current conversation could be left behind on the south side, as if it were an unwelcome cloud. On the north side, their view through the series of two-story tall windows was unobstructed for miles and miles. The edge of the city could be seen on the horizon, where the suburbs began to give way to a rural life Mary had left behind when she'd moved out of her mother's home.

Ahmed kissed Mary on the forehead and gave her a cuddle that wasn't reciprocated. He didn't realize just how difficult it was to redirect Mary's mind once the gears started turning at speed. Eyes closed, nuzzling against his chest, she didn't want to say what she felt compelled to say next.

"Ahmed, you quit school for the reasons you did. You have all these opinions and theories about…the world, right?" she said, her voice felt by his chest as much as his ear. "You think it's so important that people stay informed, otherwise they're a kind of…um…delinquent, basically?"

"Oh no, Mary I—"

"No no no." She pulled back to look him in the eyes, careful not to break the circle his arms made around her. "That's how you feel, it's okay. I shouldn't be an exception just because you like me. But I have to ask what…what is it, exactly, about what you do that makes the world a better place for a body?"

"A body?"

"A person, a person…"

"When I quit school, I stopped supporting a university helping to facilitate institutionalized racism with my tuition dollars." Ahmed began to turn his head away, keeping his eyes locked with hers. "I did what I could."

"That's true," Mary admitted. "What have you done since then?"

Ahmed's nostrils flared and his eyebrows tightened. The conversational siege machinery he always employed in these kinds of debates with his friends started to be drawn out of storage. But Mary wasn't one of his old friends from school, he wanted to make more of an effort with her than just reciting a mixture of talking points from his own beliefs and those of others who he thought were worth parroting.

"Well, I keep on top of things. You don't study to work in international law without a voracious appetite for news of world events." He paused to think, to head off a knee-jerk comment, then continued. "I also sign online petitions relating to causes which matter to me and injustices I want to see corrected or avoided." Ahmed knew this wasn't nothing, yet it didn't exactly feel like something. The look on Mary's face showed she had a similar opinion.

"Right, but you seem so passionate about all these things and more than a little judgmental of people who don't feel the same way. And all, all the stuff you know, what's it worth if you don't do anything with it? Aren't you more of a spectator then a, like, participant?"

Ahmed just looked at her, unsure how to answer. Mary could only wait for him to answer for so long, the gears were turning in her head so steadily now. She spoke again.

"Wouldn't it have been better for you to finish school so you could try to change things from the inside, or whatever? And now, couldn't you join any number of charities or other organizations? Couldn't you protest?"

"Protest?" This got Ahmed's mouth moving again. "Mary, even

you have to know what happens to protestors these days. As for charities or human rights organizations and all that? They're all just focused on one thing to the exclusion of—"

"So you choose nothing instead of something!" Mary didn't mean to raise her voice, it happened anyway. "And isn't choosing nothing how, how, how everything got so…" Her lower lip trembled with worry at the intensity she could see growing in Ahmed's smooth features.

"Mary," he said carefully. "I don't mean to sound like a little kid tossing your words back at you here, but don't *you* choose nothing? What, exactly, do you do to try and make the world a better place for…a body?"

"What do I do?"

And with that, despite the company she was keeping, despite the incredible effort she'd expended for weeks on end to keep the different parts of her life separate, a kaleidoscope of crimson spiraled up in her mind, the kind of imagery that would make a veteran war correspondent have to close their eyes.

Was The Figure a completely separate personality from her, a mask she wore, or, worst of all, just a convenient excuse? There had been moments when she colluded with it, where she'd been grateful for it, times where she could recall her actions and so many more where she couldn't, where she didn't want to, where she—

"Mary?"

Coming out of herself after much longer than she realized, Mary saw Ahmed's intensity had changed back from confrontation to concern. Her words ran on from the conversation in her head as if Ahmed had been a part of it.

"It's just I…well…oh, my mom always told me just to figure out if something felt like your purpose…" Parts of Mary's sentences were only being said in her mind, leaving sections of her thoughts to come out as speech like humps of a sea serpent rising above the water. "But that's not really… You've…got to just pick the place where you can do the most…so at least, hopefully…I…oh…"

Her hands failed to complete little gestures, opening and closing; the mouths of animals who'd just swallowed something sharp and painful.

"Mary, what are you talking about?"

"I'm sorry Ahmed, I'm sorry I'm being such a—"

A sound like a wooden plank hitting hard floor echoed throughout the ballroom, interrupting the young couple from wrestling with each other's thoughts. They kept still, waiting in silence, wondering if a hotel employee or maybe some other trespasser was about to disturb them. After what felt like the right length of time, they resumed the conversation with a renewed awareness that they couldn't stay in this bubble of decaying luxury forever.

"I'm the one who's sorry. I don't think I want to have these kinds of conversations with you. I just want us to enjoy each other's company." His words spilled out quickly as he tried to head off further upsetting this woman he felt drawn to. "You're a nice girl and you don't deserve to be distressed like this."

Ahmed drew her back against him and held her there. Once again, Mary spoke into his chest. "I want that, too. Let's get out of here. This place doesn't feel so wonderful anymore."

Stepping around a gigantic chandelier that had been left in the middle of the dance floor, the two of them calmly found their way to the corner exit, which brought them down one flight of stairs and back into the brightly lit corridors of hotel luxury they had come through earlier. Quickly, quietly, they did their best impersonation of People Who Should Be Here and found their way to an elevator with gilded mirrors on its walls and ceiling.

I can't believe I just did that to her, Ahmed thought. *She really likes me, she dressed up as best she could for me, she trusted me to take her somewhere a murderer might lure someone, and I upset the living hell out of her.*

Feeling guilty, only wanting to heal her, to take care of her, to wrap her up in him, Ahmed picked Mary off the ground and placed her against one of the mirrored walls. At five foot ten and about one-hundred-and-fifty pounds, Mary knew it took some strength to move her around like taking a porcelain doll off a shelf. Her eyes went wide with a mix of excitement and wonder as he looked at her for one long moment before pressing tightly against her, kissing and comforting as best he was able.

An altogether more pleasing kaleidoscope of images played across the interior of the elevator, Mary occasionally opening her eyes to watch.

Eventually they hit the ground floor, slowly disentangled themselves, and weaved through the busy lobby with sheepish looks on their faces. Stepping out into the night air, they paused to look at each other for the first time since they'd been in the elevator. Ahmed spoke first.

"Okay, that was kind of…"

"Yeah, I mean, I liked that last part, but…"

"What's something kind of chilled out we could do?"

Twenty minutes later, they were sitting in an adjacent neighborhood where the buildings were lower and so were the average annual incomes of their inhabitants. This was where many of the workers from the financial district lived, the servers, the cleaners, the interns, the drivers, the security guards and so many more of those that supported the people who preyed upon them, or people like them.

Sitting on the sidewalk opposite a restaurant patio they weren't sure if they could afford to drink at, Mary and Ahmed took long sips from plastic bottles of convenience-store orange juice they'd spiked using a tiny bottle of vodka purchased along the way.

"I really am sorry for my little freak-out back at the ballroom."

"Oh, Mary, it's okay. You don't—"

"No, no, let me finish. I just wanted to say that it's precisely because—even when I try to bury my head in the sand—there's this never-ending bunch of terrible things in the world that leave me feeling distracted and doomed, that…" Mary thought carefully. "I don't like talking about all those things with you for a few reasons, but the biggest is because when you're near I can focus. I can really, really focus and feel good about myself, even about the world. Talking about those, uh, subjects…breaks that. When it's just you and me…" Mary reached over and stroked his hair. "It really is just you and just me, you know?"

She felt relieved by telling him all this. It had taken a little while, yet she was perfectly comfortable around him now. The conversation at the ballroom felt like a resolution to her, like they'd never have to talk about that sort of thing ever again. With him, there was a future to be excited, not frightened, by.

A future with no need for The Figure.

"I'm touched you'd share that with me," Ahmed replied. "And even if I don't want to go there again, I'm glad we were able to have the conversation we had. It felt very real, when so many of those kinds of conversations that I have with others strike me as nothing but some jerks—myself included—only talking to fill the silence."

Mary had mostly found the experience stressful, but was glad that at least Ahmed got something out of it. A couple across the street clinked glasses, drawing her attention to them for a moment.

"I feel like I could share anything with you, Ahmed. I want to."

The couple on the patio were grinning contentedly, legs touching under the table and tongues perfectly still. They didn't seem to need to speak.

Mary continued. "I know I've been a bit much at times and this is only our fourth date." She put her ghetto Screwdriver on the ground, pulling close beside Ahmed and draping his arm around her. "I really want to share something with you, right now, even if maybe magazine and Internet articles have decided it's the kind of thing that should wait for date seven-point-three or whatever. Okay?"

She closed her eyes, in case of an undesirable answer. Ahmed rested his head on top of hers and listened to the sounds of the street. The patio laughter. The last of the fall leaves blowing along cracked concrete. Cars accelerating on a fresh green light. The gentle breathing noises of this warm, soft creature leaning against him.

"Go ahead, Mary. I'll listen."

She kept her eyes closed.

"I haven't been able to stop thinking about being in bed with you that time." Mary paused as her face grew hot. "I mean, yeah, it was nice for all the reasons people usually get into bed with each other but, uh, you remember that clarity you mentioned? The clarity being near death brings?"

Curious, Ahmed wanted to take over the conversation, to begin asking questions and extrapolating from their answers. It was with some restraint he simply replied, "Yes, I remember."

Her right hand pawed across his chest, feeling the texture of the V-neck T-shirt she was enjoying the smell of. "I've only ever felt that around death...until I was there in bed with you. I felt it then, or at least something very close to it. I felt like I was at the heart of a warm sun, burning so brightly I couldn't see anything at all, anything but you." Her voice became softer still. "It's all I ever want to feel, it's all I ever want."

A flutter came to life in Ahmed's chest, its vibrations bringing down the tower of questions for and about Mary, which had been building inside him for some time, including the one about why she may have just implied a great familiarity with death. Nobody had ever attributed such a powerful sensation to him as she had just now; nobody had ever expressed such a need for him. Ahmed was glad he was already sitting down because there was flattery and there was flattery, and then there was this.

"Mary, I don't think anyone's ever said anything so sweet, so special to me."

Until now, Mary had rarely found confidence anywhere except in anger. With Ahmed, she had just begun to take it from a healthier place.

"You'll never guess what I have in my freezer."

A moment's silence. Ahmed wasn't one to fill the air with a long, "Uhmmmm."

"Oh geez, Rocky Road?"

"Yup. We should go to my place and eat some. Don't you think?"

They finished their drinks on the bus there, the vodka-infused orange juice bringing so many of the best sensations up and down their heads, arms, torsos, and toes. After all the heavy conversation of the night so far, an unspoken agreement was made to simply enjoy each other's presence for a while. As Mary watched the city go by, fantasizing about all the good times they could have at this place or that, Ahmed thought about what it was that drew him to Mary.

Maybe it's old fashioned, he thought. *But I feel like I should have a clearer idea before we...* Then his thoughts were hijacked by images of what came after that ... .

Mary mistook his sigh for one of contentment, when Ahmed was sighing with the relief he felt at relaxing enough to let the analytical part of his mind take a break for the night. He made no effort to return to his attempt at fleshing out why he wanted Mary. He just did and, for now, that was enough.

They got off at a stop by the convenience store where Mary got her ramen noodles.

"You know it's a classy joint when all the signs are in black marker on construction paper."

"I know, right?" she replied, happy to break the silence now that they were back on foot and so close to her home. Not bothering to explain, Mary looked back over her shoulder to see if the homeless person's abandoned donation cap was still on the corner. It was.

"Just a second."

Mary let go of Ahmed's hand, fished out a nickel, made a wish, and then tossed it in. She figured the tiny miracle of the hat's still being on the same corner after all these weeks made it special enough, for her purposes, to be a wishing well.

"Okay, I'm good."

Ahmed let her take his hand and lead him down the street.

Nervousness over showing him her home was doing battle with a stronger feeling and losing. Mary sped up the pace so they were almost power walking toward her building. Still, some fealty had to be paid to apartment self-consciousness.

"I know everybody always, uh, apologizes for their place," she said. "But, like, I play for keeps with that shit. Messy floor. Tiny. Not much of a bathroom."

"But it's all yours, right? That's cool."

Recalling several award-winning lonely nights in a long running series, Mary just shrugged. Reaching the T junction in front of her building, she gripped Ahmed's hand tightly when he tried to cross the empty street.

"Don't worry," he responded. "There's nobody coming."

"I nearly got hit here once, when I was distracted and thought I was in the clear."

"Oh! Fair enough."

Satisfied, Mary then pulled him across the street to the lobby doors. Waving a gray plastic key fob in the general area of the door handle like a witch who'd lost all but the tip of her wand, Mary heard the lock unlatch with such volume it may as well have been a starter pistol.

Ahmed unknowingly mirrored Mary when she'd first come to his apartment, wearing wide eyes and a quiet mouth as he filed away every little detail he could. What made him most curious was the light, pastel green of Mary's walls. He could have sworn there was an interesting fact he'd read about that color but he couldn't remember. Then, having removed his shoes, he stepped in a pile of denim.

"Oh, sorry." Mary blushed as she bent down to pick up her work clothes. "When I get home from work, I always feel so gross. I just shed everything on to the floor like some kind of, uh, snake or something."

Mary went over to her closet, opened it only just as much as necessary to shove her work clothes into a hamper, then closed it before Ahmed could see any of the old shirts she was embarrassed by.

As she did this, Ahmed had a bold thought. He imagined himself being more like James Bond for a moment, pointing out how if Mary wanted to shed her clothes right now then that'd be fine by him. He opened his mouth, nervousness closed it again. He'd lost track of how many times he'd fancied a sentence as being charming, only to put a girl off.

Mary walked up to him and played with her hair for just a moment before exclaiming, "Oh, hey! Here's the coffee table I made."

Ignoring the bed, which dominated one side of the apartment, the pair of them took all of two steps to stand by her old couch, dying television, and the convenient excuse not to address the so-horny-it's-almost-cross-eyed elephant in the room. Under normal circumstances, Ahmed would have genuinely been interested in the cleverly welded coffee table made of crankshafts. As it was, he struggled to think of anything to say. "It's pretty heavy looking."

He'd been working so hard at appearing interested in the table that Ahmed hadn't noticed Mary slipping behind him. She went to plug her phone into a little set of speakers on the kitchen counter that roughly divided the apartment in two. Music by the band his friend had gotten them in to see on their second date began to wash over them both. It was one of the group's more melodic tracks; more importantly, it was one he'd emailed her first thing on the morning after that night spent sitting close together in those comfortable brown couches by the bar. Delighted, he turned around to face her.

"Oh! I wondered if you'd gotten those songs I sent you."

"I did! I did. I just don't always feel as if I have the right vocabulary to really talk about music without sounding like an idiot," Mary confessed, gripping the counter as she leaned against it, if only to give her hands something to do.

Ahmed coyly took the three steps needed to be directly in front of her, eking them out to almost five. "Aw, Mary, you shouldn't feel like there's some special club you have to be in just to talk about something you like. Honestly, I used to be the same way about—"

Ahmed interrupted himself by kissing Mary, speaking in a low, conversational tone right up until their lips met, causing her to chuckle into his mouth. He'd stopped caring about what he'd been saying from practically the first syllable, a few brain cells given the grunt work of continuing his sentence while every other part of him focused on more captivating goals. Belt buckles clicked together and hands began to ramble over exciting terrain.

The song playing in the background featured a man and a woman taking turns singing to each other. The call and return of the lyrics mercifully articulated so many of the broad, deep feelings filling Mary and Ahmed's veins, circulating at a greater and greater speed with each beat of their hearts. Mary was surprised at her own naiveté when Ahmed began to explore beneath her recently purchased skirt.

Oh! she thought. *Of course, that's something a skirt allows.* Her blush was produced by embarrassment before an audience composed only of herself, but the reason for her flush cheeks soon changed. She felt snapped out of a dream as Ahmed ceased slowly tugging at her underwear, disentangled himself, and took a step back.

"Wait, wait. I just realized the perfect way to do this." As with so many young men before him, he was trying to burn off nervousness with a game.

Confused and curious, Mary looked at him with a face he could only interpret as *And that is?*

Ahmed took her hand and they stepped back over to the door, then turned to face toward the bed area, as if they had only just now come into the apartment. Mary had trusted him to take her to an abandoned ballroom; she figured she could trust him with whatever the hell this was. It was just a shame the break in what they'd been doing allowed her own nervousness to sneak back into her system. Ahmed, having long ago realized it was a good idea to pay close attention to Mary's mood, saw something of this in her and hurried into what he was increasingly unsure had been a good idea.

"I was thinking we could get undressed, Mary-style."

Mary paused for a second, then realized what he meant and laughed. "Okay," she replied. "But let's do it for each other, alright? Quickly as possible."

Making a game out of things helped them not think too hard about what they did as they hastily undressed each other and dropped clothing into two piles around their feet. Anything slower and one or both of them might have lost their nerve or made too big a deal out of something. This suited them, like running and diving into the deep end of the pool.

After Ahmed realized Mary's bra clasped in the front, they stood still and took each other in. Mary smiled, breathed in deeply. She leaped on him so he had no choice but to carry her, staggering over so they could fall onto the bed as one, leaving the two piles of their clothing to keep each other company by the door. Using just their eyes, Ahmed asked a question and Mary answered with an emphatic *Yes.*

A starburst of relief pulsed out from the base of her skull as Mary achieved a degree of focus others could seek for decades in monasteries and on mountaintops. For a moment, there was pleasure and then, better still, there was nothing.

It was too brief. It always was.

"Mary, are you on your period?"

"No, why?"

"Look."

Mary didn't have to look. Not having any solution other than what they'd just begun doing, she'd chosen not to think about it at all. Besides, weren't guys supposed to like this? Wasn't this supposed to be flattering?

Ahmed recoiled, sitting back on his heels, just staring. Mary was still coming up from a blissful haze, unsure what the big deal was. It hadn't hurt, at least not so far.

He breathed in sharply, let it out through his nose, and released absolutely none of the tension that had just snapped into him. She couldn't believe how suddenly things had turned.

"I'm sorry, Mary, I don't want this responsibility."

He got up and stepped into the washroom to clean himself off at the sink. Mary didn't want to move, vainly hoping if she remained on display then maybe he'd change his mind and return to her.

"Ahmed, what do you mean 'responsibility'? You're not responsible for anything." She had to strain to hear his reply over the tap gushing.

"I don't know what you think about me, I grew up in America, okay? America. I don't want or expect any virgins after I die and I'm not obsessed with meeting one in the here and now. I grew up in this very city, God damn it, and while my parents and I respect the culture of my great-grandparents they're just...I just..."

"What...what are you talking about?"

"I don't know!" He ran a hand through his hair, turned to stand in the bathroom doorway. "I just...this is one thing too much for me. I think I've been very patient, but man, oh, man. First, there was the three-am phone call after we'd only been on one date, one date! You never did tell me what the matter was that night, anymore than you explained those cuts all over your chest and shoulders." He ran his other hand through his hair. "To say nothing of how careful I have to be not to trip over certain subjects that make you wilt like a fern under a blowtorch. And I know it wasn't your fault those assholes beat me up, it wasn't your fault, but still, but still..."

Something Ahmed's eyes had picked up on when he entered the washroom finally clicked. "Mary, why on Earth is there a padlock on the cupboard under your bathroom sink? What do you keep in there?"

Mary silently stared at him through sad eyes, unable to answer.

Ahmed gave up, walked over to his pile of clothes and began getting dressed in a manner so hurried, it actually slowed him down by being uncoordinated.

Mary could feel something slipping out of her grasp.

"Anyway," he continued. "I'm sorry but I just don't think I can be the person you do this with. Things with you are intense enough as is and, trust me, they'd only get more so if I became the man who took your virginity."

Mary could tell there was a story behind Ahmed's attitude, probably involving some girl he knew before her. She couldn't bear to ask. A lead blanket of inevitability had settled over her and she wasn't strong enough to slip out from under. She just lay there, propped up on her elbows, as Ahmed decided for her how she'd react to something he saw as yet-to-be when it had pretty much happened already.

"Plus, we haven't even known each other that long. I mean, I like you. I get excited when I think about you, sometimes."

Mary just stared at him. His pants were back on. The timer was counting down.

"But then there are other times I think about you and, um...."

Since when does he pause or say "um"? Mary thought. The socks were on now.

"I'm sorry, it should be with someone who's able to love you back, really, truly love you at the time it happens."

The belt.

"It should be poetry, not just some quick tumble. You, you need poetry."

It felt as if Ahmed was taking away her ability to move her limbs, as well as her agency. His tone implied he meant well.

The shirt was on. A final check for keys or change on the floor, in case they'd come out of his pockets in the rush to get undressed only a few minutes earlier.

Why wouldn't he look at her? All she could do was look at him. He thought he was doing what was best. His hand was on the door handle.

"Ahmed."

"Mary."

"You have no idea what kind of decision you're making for me."

"I can't get pulled into a discussion about this. I finally got a new job. I start tomorrow evening, I need to get home to rest up or—"

"Shut up."

"Listen, I'm so—"

"Shut up!"

The door closed. Mary's eyes did the same.

Every second passed meant Ahmed was another step further away from her apartment. She wouldn't chase after him, figuring you don't chase after a bullet that's just bored through your flesh. This moment lined up with every unhappy moment in Mary's memory like glass lenses in a powerful telescope, amplifying and magnifying her worst assumptions as she looked at her world, her life.

Mary got up on unsteady feet and turned off the speakers, the music now as unpleasantly stained as the sheets. Eyes closed again, Mary could feel herself being carried away along waves she no longer wished to swim against. There was nothing for her on land and rescue was not an option.

Minutes later a young woman's body sat upright in bed, nude but for the skin tight, leopard-print covering that ended just along the line where neck gave way to collarbone.

The inverse of a hooded falcon.

At the core of her body, a drum slowly began to beat.

36. HAND IN HAND

Gravel ground under heel as The Figure flitted between fences. A rising wind buffeted boarded-up windows. The odd car could be heard in the distance, the only other sound of human activity in a mostly empty industrial estate between the junkyard and a more populous neighborhood that supported O'Malley's coffee house. The Figure couldn't tell you Mary's favorite color or the name of the boy with whom she had her first kiss. Points of overlap were easier to access, such as the location of an abandoned machinist's workshop where Mary had been more complicit in The Figure's activities than she would ever admit.

Neither of them knew what was going on with the owners of this cube of concrete and metal siding. Whoever they were, they cared enough about the property to leave the electricity running and to install a security camera, albeit an easily evaded one, above both front and back entrances. On the other hand, Mary had clipped off the original padlock on the back entrance and replaced it with a different one over seven weeks ago and there was still no sign of them noticing. The Figure knew she needed a key and could deduce where it was kept underneath the bathroom sink, back at the apartment. This knowledge was treasure The Figure had found while sneaking down corridors of Mary's knowledge left unmonitored since the latter so willingly became absent.

Pushing open the heavy wooden door, The Figure saw a complete absence of tools and froze. A metal worktable sat in the middle, bolted to the floor, and there were a few hanging lamps; little else remained. Shutting the door behind her, she did something that had only become an option recently—she thought through the situation. Obviously the owner of the building had removed all of their own tools, but where were the tools Mary had used to craft weapons like the mace?

The Figure had begun to become greater than the sum of Mary's fears. Mary's attempt to direct her actions had caused a cascade of past and future to spill into The Figure's consciousness when before she had only ever existed in an isolated series of murderous, reactionary instants, a flipbook with huge chunks torn out. The Figure had just begun to be aware of anything beyond the most recent moment, peeling back pieces of the present to expose the past as if tearing from the top of a dense stack of event posters moldering on the side of a telephone pole.

Running fingertips over wall brackets previous intruders had exposed as they sought out copper wiring to re-sell, she tried to read psychic Braille created by the indentations of Mary's time in this space. Standing out from discarded discs of sandpaper was a slip of white rectangle, its blue ink having not quite faded to illegibility. Picking up the receipt, The Figure felt a tremor in her forearm.

No.

She felt Mary's tremor in her forearm.

Mary as she'd stood at a hardware store unable to return a portable power grinder because the receipt had been left behind, unable to replicate a routine she'd established, and panicking. Everything used in creating The Figure's more terrifying implements had been purchased from different hardware stores, carefully used once and then returned for a full refund. The power grinder had taken a different path, eventually being slipped into the trunk of a sky blue mini just before it was put through the crusher at the junkyard.

That junkyard was somewhere else The Figure could feel isolated points of familiarity, pinholes through a broad sheet of black canvas. She didn't know the stretches of the yard between those points, but she'd had enough practice improvising her way through unfamiliar offices not to feel worried. Unconcerned about anyone hearing the noise, she began to pound the palm of one hand against the metal work table in time with the beat in her chest.

The noise didn't drive Mary out of hiding, didn't bring her close enough to the surface so The Figure could frog-march her to the nearest hardware store and back to make simple machinery for mining thick veins of blissful peace from the soft surfaces beneath suits and satin shirts.

Just how complicit was Mary in the dozens of deaths the financial distract had seen these past eight or nine weeks? Why wouldn't she help now? Ceasing her pounding of the table, The Figure tried to think, to look inward once again for answers. Further chips of knowledge began to fall from the walls erected between Mary and The Figure. Picking one up, The Figure learned Mary's crankshaft table and her ring had been made with the same tools. She learned this was important to Mary, that her making the harmless objects helped her deny the harmful ones.

Wait.

Hadn't Mary made two rings? Who had the second one been for?

The wall around this information was all but impenetrable. A name, Ahmed, burned so brightly its outline was clearly visible from the other side, while facts like his appearance or why he warranted such protection from The Figure's eyes eluded her. Hands that felt like Mary's kept moving to prevent The Figure from learning anything about him. Maybe Mary wasn't as dead to the world as she wanted The Figure to believe. Sensing opportunity, she tried to grab at this presence to pull her up, not quite succeeding.

Fine.

There wasn't really time to make anything too impressive anyway. Another, quicker method of filling her bag of tools would have to be found. She ran her hand over her face, palm still stinging. Where could she go? How could she draw Mary out and force her to handle any verbal communication? Even if she was being dragged along like a rag doll, Mary had to know on some level she was going hand in hand with The Figure toward An Ending.

Leaving the back door ajar, padlock hanging free, she left without any care for the camera. Wind flowed over her body, helping to clear her head and focus her brand new thoughts. The Figure could now think beyond striking the next finance criminal in her immediate view and, more than that, she had begun to do something for the very first time.

She'd begun to plan for the future.

37. Last Call at the Junkyard

Carmine pulled out the day's sandwich and took a hearty bite.

"Oh, God, do I know what I'm doing with these things or do I know what I'm doing with these things?" he muttered through carefully cut meats, vegetables, and a sauce he'd spent hours perfecting. It had been hell collecting just the right ingredients on the weekend, mostly due to his girlfriend's complaining about the cost, but each bite justified every moment he'd spent fending her off while rifling through stall after stall at the community garden market.

Leaning back against an old mini-van he'd been taking apart for most of the morning, Carmine enjoyed the cold snap through his Halloween-themed sweater. It had been about this time of year when he and his girlfriend had first met, so the shift in temperature always brought him back to that moment when they'd spotted each other across the dance floor at his younger brother's wedding. This combined with the excellent sandwich to put him in a great mood, even if he'd had to cover for Mary today.

Heck, she had a point about the cost of fresh ingredients, he thought. *It's not like I totally disagreed, what with swiping that beef and bacon sausage from the new butcher when he wasn't looking. Texas asshole wants to charge that much more than the European butcher he replaced, he can expect to lose a little off the shelf.*

Carmine clutched onto his sandwich tightly as two plainclothes detectives showed up in front of him. Vance was with them, looking almost forlorn, which was itself rather strange. The larger of the detectives spoke.

"Hello, Carmine. I'm Detective Guberman and my partner here is Detective Huntley. Can we have a moment of your time, please?"

Carmine swallowed.

"Yeah." He put the sandwich down in the driver's seat of the van. "No problem."

And so they briefly quizzed him about Mary, of all people. If he knew where she was today. If he'd ever noticed anything strange about her. Had she ever expressed any grievances with those who work in the financial sector? They wouldn't say why they were looking for her, only that it was urgent. After ten minutes of Carmine doing his best, while not being able to tell them anything of substance, the smaller detective sighed.

"Well, thank you for your time." Huntley's words rolled out of the side of his mouth. "Please be sure to let us know if you remember anything significant or if you come into contact with Mary."

Guberman gave Huntley a short, dirty look for his lackadaisical manner, then pulled a business card out of his jacket and handed it to the younger junkyard worker. Carmine, unable to see the fresh bandage on Guberman's bicep, wondered why the detective's arm moved so stiffly. They nodded as they said good-bye and Vance led the policemen over to the front gate. Carmine reached back into the mini-van and secured his sandwich. Four more bites and Vance had returned.

"You lock the front gate?" Carmine asked, realizing nobody was watching it.

Vance just looked at him like he was an idiot, which Carmine took to mean *Yes*.

The older man had fetched himself some water from the shack's dirty taps before coming over. He took a long sip of the suspect liquid, decided he could deal with the taste, and then took a seat on the hood of a red Corvette directly across from Carmine. Even though they'd been reinforced, the knees of Vance's overalls were wearing thin and a beige coating of dirt provided a unifying texture for the various oil stains. Some of the dirt even seemed to have found its way into the folds of his face, adding ten years.

"So, I guess we know where Mary's been today."

"Oh, yeah? We do? Where's that then?" Vance asked.

"Robbing rich people or hiding out with her cash or some shit. S'why they asked if she had a vendetta against bankers, right?"

Vance squinted and rubbed his forehead.

"You ever notice how little Mary reported finding in the trunks of the vehicles she worked on? Or do you remember how not once but twice she had vehicles with batteries that had leaked all their acid before we got'em?"

"Uhm, yeah?"

Carmine waited for Vance to connect the dots for him, as he so often did. His boss couldn't be bothered, he didn't seem to have the energy, despite having been a dynamo when they'd come in at the start of the day. Whatever conversation had gone on between Vance and the detectives before they'd come to see Carmine, it had drained him something fierce.

"Okay, do you also remember how you didn't get why I hired Mary?"

"Yeah, Vance, I do. I agree she grew into the job nicely, but at the time she'd done nothing except intern at fuckin' McDonalds and before that she'd stacked shelves somewhere, right?"

"Something like that, yeah. She told me she left for the city hoping to find some opportunity, and then there she was probably having to sneak food from her internship just to stay alive, barely making rent. I'm no doctor, but no way was she getting enough of the right vitamins in her."

Carmine though for a moment. "So, you were taking pity on Mary?"

"I was, yeah. Somebody fucking should have," Vance answered. "You didn't talk to her as much as I did, so you probably don't appreciate how alone she is. Maybe if more people paid attention to her, tried to help her, maybe if everyone just took a little more care of each other…"

Vance's overalls had voluminous pants pockets on each side that he usually kept stuffed with rags and smaller tools. Setting aside his plastic cup of water, he reached into both and pulled out two beers. The green bottles had an old wooden life raft printed in orange and white on their sides.

"I brought these this morning, thinking I could surprise her with them at the end of the day, a treat for her to enjoy with that kid from the coffee shop." He sighed. "I don't expect we'll be seeing her again."

He stood up and handed one to Carmine, who couldn't help feeling a little sad, if only because his employer did. Putting the last of the sandwich down, he took an opener from his keychain and popped open the two bottles. Dark green glass clinked and they each took a swig.

"Good luck, Mary," Vance offered to the horizon. "I'm sorry I couldn't do more for you."

38. Eu não sou o que você deve fazer o seu inimigo

A slick, pearly white, four wheel-drive Audi sports car swung out of the parking garage of what used to be the office for a tanker refueling station. It would take Moriba about thirty minutes to drive over to forty-seventy and fourth from Juan Pablo's temporary set-up by the docklands. With nobody else in the car, he could run his favorite playlist through the stereo, largely made up of American and British pop music from ten years ago. The sun was shining. He was immaculate.

At the first red light he hit, Moriba paused to admire his clothing. He'd learned a lot from the Congolese Sapeurs he'd lived with before coming to Guinea-Bissau. This subculture of African dandies defied an atmosphere of perpetual poverty by sacrificing everything to be able to afford custom-tailored suits in one, two, or even three bold colors. It had been an incredible breath of fresh air when he'd stumbled into Brazzaville at the age of thirteen, having fled LURD and MODEL forces breaking up the blood diamond party in Liberia.

He wore a burgundy red dress shirt beneath a light mustard yellow coat. Pants matched the coat, except at the bottom where they were rolled up to reveal a white that neatly mirrored the ascot tied loosely around his neck. Herringbone, circular framed glasses did nothing for his eyesight and everything for how people saw him.

It was certainly a step up from the clothing of his early youth. Like many a child soldier forcibly recruited by a deranged warlord, he'd been assigned a cast-off American T-shirt for his uniform. Soon, he was wildly firing an AK-47, to burn off the excess energy of the cocaine he'd be given before battle as much as kill their enemies. His ad-hoc battalion had worn Titanic T-shirts and they had learned to fear the sight of anyone wearing Tupac Shakur on their chest.

Middle school children in American TV care so much about clothing as a way to identify groups, Moriba thought, not for the first time. *Let them try growing up the way I did, middle school might not seem so bad.*

The Liberian warlords all had strange names, General Titanic DiCaprio having been Moriba's commander. What the grown men wore into battle was often stranger still. Various reasons were given, usually having to do with mysticism and protection from bullets, for tearing through villages while wearing wigs and wedding dresses, stolen U.N. Helmets and blue body paint, or even nothing at all. Looking back as a grown man in his mid-thirties, Moriba knew it all came down to one thing—fear, hiding and provoking it.

The cigar in his mouth burned brightly as he inhaled, then blew smoke against the windshield. Before he'd turned ten, Moriba had had to keep it together in the face of machete wielding men in what he'd only recently learned were Hulk Hogan masks. He'd assassinated one warlord who kept a semi-domesticated hyena on the end of a long rope that was always in hand, and lived to tell the tale. They probably still spoke of how, after having been captured, he escaped being ritually sacrificed by Joshua Blahyi. That sacrifice would have involved his ribs being cracked outward and his heart consumed raw, something he had been abundantly aware of while being kept under guard.

So no, he wasn't terribly intimidated by the bright yellow Hummer filled with gangsters giving him stink eye, which had just rolled up alongside. Word was starting to get out about Juan Pablo's operation and the local competition wasn't pleased. Oversized sports jerseys. Metal teeth coverings. Chains. Garish.

He'd been fortunate to find refuge amongst the dapper men of

Brazzaville. He'd greatly benefited from his time there, but his years as a child soldier had put more than cocaine in his veins. When South Sudan was birthed, he packed up his best suits and went there to begin a new life as a mercenary. Earning his pay in conflicts from Somalia to Algeria over the following years, Moriba eventually was drawn to fight in the latest civil war of Guinea-Bissau.

After the war, the government was like a sick vagrant, unable to bat away an insect resting on its eye. There was almost no police force or military, to say nothing of health care, education, or anything else to bind a society together. It wasn't long before Juan Pablo and his fellow Colombians started taking advantage of the relative lawlessness to create a nexus for shipping cocaine up from South America, then through to Europe and the Middle East.

Juan Pablo, having heard tales of Moriba and his men, hired them for the inevitable conflicts when other Colombian drug lords saw the potential in Guinea-Bissau. They'd worked under him ever since.

One well-polished shoe pressed down on the accelerator, taking him off and away from these men that bored him so. A serendipitous moment occurred as his favorite lyric from his favorite song came over the speakers at the most satisfying point of leaning into a turn. He began to sing along in his unique voice, a pidgin of Portuguese, Creole, and Monrovian English accents.

Five more minutes passed and he was stepping out of the car onto the sidewalk at forty-seventh and fourth. Taking his Union Jack umbrella and a crocodile skin suitcase, Moriba began his way up the steps to report for his first day as Gerald Byrne's bodyguard.

39. LIGHTS OUT

*B**ING*
Burnished bronze elevator doors opened to reveal two slim men in Brooks Brothers latest. Each looking down at their phones, the pair stepped out in unison to enter the small reception area of Byrne Investments. Despite it being a large firm, the two Germans hired to design the forty-second floor offices took an approach of quality over quantity. Small rooms containing expertly chosen decorations, luxurious carpeting, and carefully placed lighting that had a way of flattering your features, no matter which angle you were facing, filled the floor.

The reception area fit the aesthetic perfectly. Two Wassily chairs still bearing their production run numbers in stark white against black, #006 and #007, were set at forty-five degree angles to a white marble coffee table bearing the Byrne Investments logo along its surface in Yves Klein Blue.

Not that the two businessmen were interested in any of this. The one on the right was reading an article on the *Economist* website about the end of the long tail in streaming video while the other was seeing what *Gawker* had to say about an errant dick pic of Sen. John Turgid that had found fame on the Internet earlier that morning. He sniffed at the all-too-obvious headline as the receptionist, Ahmed, buzzed them through the frosted glass doors that opened into the rest of

Byrne Investments.

Neither man interacted with Ahmed in the slightest, but he was okay with that. Ahmed was brand new to this role, an odd mix of secretary and security guard his company had only recently begun offering to higher-end clients, competing with Avalanche Security's own version of the service. The idea of two roles for one paycheck greatly appealed to the CEO of Byrne Investments, so here he was in front of a brand new tablet with a stun gun on one hip and a phone on the other.

Pushing back the fringe of a haircut he wasn't sure about, Ahmed sighed while contemplating going home tonight to the results of a relationship decision he was only marginally more confident in. He'd ended things with her just last night and today she wasn't answering any of his texts or emails. His phone was still filled with her old texts and emails, messages that had seemed interesting to him at first.

BA-DEE-DEEP

A text from her. Was he was still as excited as she was about their relationship moving to the next level? That had been just after the third date, when they'd started referring to themselves as "we", as a couple. On an almost daily basis, Ahmed's phone had the habit of barfing back up old texts from days or even months ago, which he considered seriously irritating behavior. Even as a ghost, the text made him feel anxious about them acting committed too quickly. Somewhat ironically, one of the reasons Ahmed was becoming more certain about ending the relationship had to do with how she so often made him realize he was playing to negative stereotypes about men. He didn't like that.

Shit. Daydreaming about the problem of the text meant using up valuable reply composition time. Maybe an emoji? No, too juvenile and open to interpretation. A nice, safe "Yeah!" would work but then he'd come home tonight to see her stuff in his bedroom and it would only get harder to admit he'd not so much liked the idea of her moving in as the idea of a girl liking him enough to want to do so.

"Yes," he'd said to that feeling. "Yes, I like that you are into me that much," would have been the truly honest thing to say to her. He'd even been dishonest with himself, fantasizing about grand gestures like a trip to Paris as if they were something he wanted when what he truly wanted was the adulation they'd inspire.

Christ. That was at least four minutes of daydreaming about an old problem and still she hadn't replied to the text he'd sent just a few minutes before those businessmen came in.

BA-DEE-DEEP

Crap. Ahmed didn't log the employees returning from dinner into the system, he was so distracted by the ghost text. Now he was getting more texts that looked like they were from Mary but—

BING

"Hey, remember when doing your job was a thing?"

Ahmed looked up from his phone into the expensively landscaped teeth of Gerald Byrne himself, CEO and top man at the office. Holding his arm was the assistant whose name Ahmed didn't know yet. She must have whispered to Gerald that he had been looking at his phone. Ahmed wasn't sure how to reply and he felt sheepish for not noticing the elevator. Luckily for him, Gerald didn't need anyone else to talk in order to get satisfaction from a conversation.

"It's like…" Gerald thought out loud. "Ever since this whole shitty century got rolling, it's all been about terrorism or random shootings. Like, was there a memo sent out to the crazies? Attention madmen! From now on, it's all just one big explosion of violence. Don't create a nice narrative with spaced out, individual killings. Don't establish a theme, don't build a pattern. Just get a gun, a blank look on your face, and then show up to kill as many people as you can for as vague a reason as possible."

Gerald added to this little bit of performance by adjusting his ivory cufflinks while approximating a thoughtful expression.

"I know how it sounds, but I'm just being honest about how news is only entertainment."

As with most things that Gerald tried to put out there as slightly edgy or profound, it was as dull and uninspired as the look in Ahmad's eyes when he stared up at a man who was very much his master.

BA-DEE-DEEP

BA-DEE-DEEP

BA-DEE-DEEP

"Huh, sounds like you've got someone who really wants your attention there!"

Ahmed nodded in reply, then felt stupid as he remembered his new boss was blind. A quick glance revealed three seemingly innocent questions from concerned friends about how he was feeling after the breakup, none of them questions he wanted to answer.

"It's alright, go ahead and answer whomever it is. I know it's against the rules, but really…" Gerald made an exaggerated look around the tiny lobby. "It's not like we've got a crowd here and you're hardly going to miss someone coming in."

Gerald finished the sarcastic performance by raising his sunglasses a little, then making a grotesque, conspiratorial wink as if he'd given Ahmed permission to flip off one of the wealthy investors they were bringing in over the next week to try and seduce. As Gerald put his sunglasses back in place, a sterling silver bracelet on his left wrist gleamed from underneath the cuff, before Aiden Patent Oxfords by Salvatore Ferragamo carried the young CEO briskly past Ahmed and into the office. His assistant followed, being led by him when normally, due to his resistance to using a cane, it was the other way around.

As this happened, a whiff of some expensive cologne Ahmed couldn't name or afford wafted off Gerald and caught the young secre-curity guard—a terrible job title but the one Hachette Security Solutions had given him—right up each nostril. It was actually kind of nice, making Ahmed feel like he'd just had his nose in a glass holding some properly warmed, well-distilled brandy, like his father used to drink.

BA-DEE-DEEP

BING

Anxious about whether the text was another ghost or a fresh reply, Ahmed chose to look at his phone instead of the elevator door. He'd managed to read, *I think we need to talk*, and was going to start a reply before being interrupted by the impact of an eight-pound sledgehammer colliding with his temple.

The young man was instantly catapulted out of his chair and onto the carpet. His survival instinct took a similarly swift path, going straight past fight, past flight, and arriving at a state not unlike that of an airline pilot who just discovered that none of the controls were working anymore.

Horrified to still be alive, Ahmed was unable to properly process the soft thump of the sledgehammer dropping to the floor.

An ankle swathed in leopard-print tights crossed his flickering, unfocused vision before merciful unconsciousness swept over Ahmed as his own stun gun was set to maximum, then jammed into the recently exposed portion of his frontal lobe.

The last, lingering wafts of Gerald's cologne were gently swept away by sickly sweet smoke.

*

Frost. Sunflowers. Twilight.

Snowsuit. Little Mary. Years ago.

Mary's mother watched from the kitchen window, her drying of the dishes growing softer and more caring as she began to wish she was holding her daughter. It wasn't time to interfere yet, she could see Mary was learning something; she just wasn't sure about the subject of the lesson.

On the other side of what seemed like miles of deep snow, across the backyard, Mary craned her neck to look up at the heads of the sunflowers surrounding her. The tips of their stems were bent down, staring right back. The wind was dying and so were they.

Mary had planted every one of them back in the spring, her stubby fingers poking holes in warm earth for each seed. Once they sprouted, she would check each day to see how they'd grown. Sometimes her mother would point out how Mary had grown a little bit, too.

She didn't understand why it had to end. She couldn't fathom that next spring the cycle could begin again with new seeds and new flowers. Even if she could, they wouldn't be these flowers. Mary had spent enough time playing in the backyard and admiring them that each one had gained simple personalities inferred from their height, facing, placement, and leaves.

One of the outermost sunflowers made a sharp series of cracking noises as its midsection weakened. It ceased to support anything above, bending in the middle less like the mighty green oak of Mary's imagination, more like a rubber hose no longer kept firm by running water. The flower's upper body began to topple before resting at an angle against one of its fellows. Mary gasped, fearing a domino effect, then silently willed encouragement at the flowers to support their sicklier companion.

The idea that her thoughts and feelings could directly affect the world was held to be true and known to be false at the same time. This discord upset her even more. Hadn't she loved them enough? Had she loved them incorrectly? What did she have to do? What was expected of her?

Nose and eyes wet, Mary made up her mind. Reaching toward the tallest, the strongest, her favorite, she began to hold the one she'd always known to be the big brother of the sunflowers, the one she'd always been greeted by when looking out of her bedroom window first thing in the morning.

It wasn't her fault.

She didn't know this would finish it off.

*

Chest heaving, The Figure paused over the dead secre-curity guard to catch her breath. Running at full steam while swinging a sledgehammer had been no mean feat with the load of equipment she was carrying. Turning off the stun gun, she stuck it in her belt before slowly lowering the large duffel bag from her back to the floor. The sound of everything inside settling against each other didn't carry far.

The Figure extended each finger on her left hand while running through a mental checklist. She hadn't needed much in the way of preparation before, hadn't even been able to process things like a mental checklist. Ever since her eyes began to open in the apartment during the wee hours of the morning, The Figure had felt a fragility spreading within her alongside the steadily increasing beat of a drum only she could hear. The further this momentum built, the more each wave of ecstasy threatened to shake her apart.

First, she searched for a key on the guard's body to lock the twin doors letting people into Byrne Investments from the elevator bays. Looking through frosted glass for any sign of threatening silhouettes, The Figure made sure the doors were closed properly. After turning the key on the locks, a length of heavy chain was pulled from the old laptop bag still hanging on her shoulder. Grimy with oil stains, the chain had strength enough to be used for towing the largest vehicles a junkyard could ever need to process.

After wrapping the chain around and through the handles of the lobby doors, The Figure further secured them by sticking a U-shaped bike lock through the two large links on each end. Both the keys for the door and the key for the bike lock were placed under the tongue of the dead secre-curity guard, a pair of secrets he'd never share.

A quick listen to see if any office workers were coming to the lobby satisfied The Figure that everybody was still at their desks. It was after six pm; those who left for home had mostly separated themselves from the ones who were working late.

And the beat grew louder.

And the beat grew faster.

And The Figure zipped open the large duffel bag to reveal a two-foot-long gray cylinder. Bits of dirt and small scraps of duct tape shook off as it was removed. Six turns of the cap allowed something shiny, black, and insect-like to push its way out, eager to get to work.

*

Around noon of the same day, while Vance and Carmine had their first sips of the beer intended as a gift for Mary, The Figure had used Mary's key to unlock the junkyard gate and slip in. Over on the northeast corner of the yard there was an ancient 1990 Ford Taurus station wagon Vance insisted they never scrap. "In case someone wants to buy the parts."

The Figure knew the signs of having buried something in the junkyard wouldn't take long to arouse the curiosity of either Carmine or Vance. However, nobody on God's green earth was ever going to purchase parts for a 1990 Ford Taurus station wagon. Thus, not long after Ahmed's impromptu visit with some coffee, Mary had hidden the cylinder along the rear axle of the vehicle. She'd done this more out of a hoarding instinct than with any real thoughts for using it in the future, an instinct brought out by the rareness of the find.

With both men in the same spot, distracted and drinking, it wasn't hard for The Figure to sneak from car to truck to bus to pile of scrap as she found her way to the cylinder, secured it, and worked her way back out of the junkyard. There hadn't been purpose enough for such an extreme tool before, not until Mary and The Figure had sat among blood stained sheets, completely unable to reconcile two facts.

Ahmed wouldn't love Mary back.

Gerald Byrne was still alive.

Though to The Figure these were read as:

"Ahmed ....

Gerald Byrne is still alive."

Both statements being true at the same time was unbearable. One of these had to change and Mary hadn't the faintest idea how to make Ahmed reconsider. That he wouldn't love her back had quickly set in her mind as a fundamental rule of the universe, like entropy.

Not allowed to know anything about Ahmed, only that he'd somehow distressed Mary, The Figure set about righting the wrong it could see clearly.

It was already the middle of the afternoon and there wasn't much time. Earlier, after taking the cylinder from the junkyard, The Figure went back to Mary's apartment only to spot two police detectives entering it. Like dragging a reluctant toddler along the floor toward a dentist's chair, The Figure had finally managed to sit Mary in the pilot's chair when they stepped into the gaudy spectacle of a knives-and-gun show.

Hundreds of meters of musty, reddish-brown carpeting lay unrolled across concrete aisles. The convention center's gymnasium-height ceiling was ringed with diffused spotlights giving shine to the balding scalps of the male dealers. Their folding tables chastely covered with dark blue cloths, each booth had bullets, blades, and boasts about both. *Cuts through triple-weave Kevlar!*, *The rifle that pacified Athens!*, *Gun Control Is Not About Guns*, and so forth boldly stated on signs with graphic design resembling porno DVD covers and eliciting a similar excitement from their intended viewers.

The Figure could get by with the odd index card on the rare occasions when words were needed while she went about her work, but they were never anything more than blunt demands for whatever passwords, keycards, or victim locations she required. Financial transactions needed too many words for this to be practical and The Figure could never speak out loud. Even now, with a crude capacity for feeling and thinking, she wasn't a complex enough creature.

Despite Mary's efforts to bury her head in the sand, The Figure was aware of how strengthened gun control laws had combined with increased public awareness of government and corporate surveillance to form a potent cocktail certain individuals were all too keen to drink. Private militias and weapon stockpiling had soared to levels never seen before once it became an established fact that no, your emails were not private, your phone calls were indeed monitored, and every piece of information you put out into the world was being hoarded in gigantic server farms that were this generation's grand project much like the Space Race, World War II, or The Hoover Dam.

Both The Figure and Mary found it distasteful to deal with these people, but the former played puppeteer as the latter found a booth manned by men exploiting the traditional lag time between the invention of new ways for people to hurt each other and the legislation of laws to rein them in. As with any group made up almost entirely of men, they were more than happy to help out a young woman who seemed like she might be in line with their way of thinking.

What little savings Mary had managed to squirrel away was quickly spent on a few key items "for home defense" or as "something purely for display in the living room or den". Maxing out her credit took care of the rest.

Afterward, stepping back into daylight, Mary was all too relieved to be pushed back down into the deep black void. Though she knew it would never be enough for anything she truly wanted, it still saddened her to see the last of her money spent, and made her even more accepting of The Figure taking full and indefinite use of her body. As for what it was spent on, she chose not to think about that in the final moments before going under, when her hand limply dropped several fliers the men had given her onto the threshold of the exit.

*

With the automated tripod fully deployed in a corner where it could see all across the small lobby, The Figure pulled out a black case from the duffel bag, entered the password, and opened it to see something she normally would never use. Like the head of a black beetle with a silver tube for a mouth, the automatic shotgun looked little like anything Mary's grandparents would have called a gun. Over a hundred rounds had been neatly loaded into its ammunition magazines, a pair of bulging metal pods screwed onto the sides. A sliding plate on top of the tripod secured it by neatly screwing into the weapon's wide, flat underbelly.

Both tiny golden rectangles—each continually sending a signal to the tripod that repeated *FRIEND. DON'T SHOOT. FRIEND. DON'T SHOOT*—had been super-glued to the inside of The Figure's belt before she came to Byrne Investments. This was not the kind of thing about which one took unnecessary chances. She watched the smart tripod and its new head carefully as she activated the entire apparatus.

The Figure admired her reflection in the shiny black head of the turret. It only had one mind and one purpose, for which it was perfectly suited. The creature looking out from behind a smooth, leopard-print face could only aspire to its purity and focus.

This would be her backup in case the police arrived too soon. This would be her Cerberus guarding the gates to a hell of her making.

Behind the reception desk was a floor-to-ceiling, eight-foot wide partition with one doorway-sized opening on each side. Before passing through, old laptop bag slung across her shoulders so it wouldn't be so easy to drop, The Figure reached into the duffel for one more item: a length of thick lead pipe still bearing dark black blood stains from when a young man she'd unwittingly captivated had used it on the last person to work the front desk here.

Peeking down the hallway, The Figure was grateful Gerald Byrne didn't subscribe to the open office philosophy. There were a couple of communal areas, such as the break room or a meeting room, but the majority of Byrne Investments small roster of on-site employees enjoyed private offices. This was a place to wow visiting clients as well as shuffle around sums of money that would bring Croesus to tears, not to get an air miles card when you open a new checking account. Gerald didn't think anybody he'd want to do business with would be impressed by sitting in front of a desk situated among a field filled with the same.

She remembered Gerald's office was at the far end, right on the corner of the building, and there was no avoiding having to pass by a dozen of the more modest little offices in order to get there. Pausing to think, The Figure was surprised at the lack of any further security guards. She was unaware of the current disagreeable state of affairs between Derek Kruger and his son, as well as the fact that the young man she'd killed at the front desk had been arranged through a temp agency purely as a stop-gap measure until a contract could be negotiated with a different security provider than Avalanche.

Black gloves, with small metal plates sewn into the backs and knuckles, were removed from the laptop bag and pulled on. Spaces between the beats began to close tighter and tighter. The pipe twitched impatiently in her hand, a few pale blonde hairs still stuck to one end. The realization stealth might not be necessary, that she could abandon all restraint, brought the beat of the drum inside her to such a volume it rattled the windows of her eyes.

These people who worked for him, who helped shape the world to his will, they were difficult to ignore. Best to shear the beast of some of its limbs, even the vestigial ones, so it can do less harm. Best to clear them out again, lest they multiply to even greater numbers than before.

A tall, plain man in a white-collared, blue dress shirt stepped out of the nearest office and noticed The Figure from the corner of his eye. As she drew her arm back, the spaces between the beats of the drum closed entirely. Now there was just a hum in heart and head, growing louder still. Time slowed down, then sped up. She did not hear his final word.

Spoken.
Her heart.
Oh! Her heart!
Never mind her heart.
Never mind his head.
Oh! His head!
His head.

Broken.

Falling to his knees, the man wasn't as quick to die as she expected. Normally she'd pace herself, instead The Figure huffed and puffed as she brought the pipe up and down, over and over. The wet, pulpy, crunching, smacking sounds stood out against the office's soundscape like a streak of hot pink spilled across a plain of dark gray. The next worker to peer out of her office and into the hallway screamed.

Slowly at first, reluctant to believe something like this was happening to them, a dozen or so employees all began to seek escape. Knowing what waited in the lobby, The Figure stood over her kill patiently, ignoring one small woman who passed within arm's reach, as they all charged toward the exit she wasn't blocking. The Figure closed her eyes in anticipation of a sound she only guessed at, having never experienced the fire of an automatic shotgun outside of stories on screens.

Expecting thunder, she was surprised to hear something much more sedate.

Mary had been in too much of a stupor to pay attention to the specifics of what she was buying earlier in the afternoon. The men in their mesh back hats and pop culture approximations of military camouflage had sold her the deluxe model of an automatic shotgun, which came with integral sound suppressors.

The first two office workers to enter the lobby were flung back into those immediately behind them, a bouquet of red holes opening up in their bodies. The thump of their landing was joined by a sharp, mechanical exhalation of air and something akin to the earliest credit card machines being raked back and forth. The copy/fax machine sitting thirty feet away made far more noise as it continued on with the business of copying, collating, and stapling several documents related to a cash grab lawsuit against the city police over their handling of The Figure's previous visit.

The third row of office workers, those standing behind the ones knocked to the ground by the freshly shot front row, stood in shock as they tried to process what had happened. That was all it took for the machine to adjust, then fire again. Exhalation. *SNICK SNACK.* Another of the workers now lay on the ground with shells cheaper than butter having rifled through flesh, stuck themselves in bone.

Two were lying prone, underneath the bodies of the first to be shot, terrified to move and attract the semi-intelligent drone's attention. The remaining six, four men and two women, turned around to see The Figure had maneuvered herself behind them. Theo and Calvin, the two larger men, did some quick math. They looked at each and silently agreed they'd been working on the same equation, then yelled a litany of curses as they came at her.

The Figure was reminded of why she had always operated the way she had. Moving without hesitation, picking off her targets one or two at a time, making as little noise as possible, she'd been able to work her way through truly astonishing numbers while hardly ever encountering any resistance she couldn't handle. It had taken a prewarned, large, and confident individual like Sharon Carter to give her any grief; and even that woman had met her end pinned against glass by her desk, aflame with broken arms flung wide like a phoenix who knows it isn't coming back this time. Amazed her growing endorphin rush had yet to hit the high-water mark, The Figure eagerly stood directly in sight of a half dozen people whom she had made it abundantly clear she was here to kill.

Weekend warriors both, Calvin got lucky by hastily grabbing a binder containing hundreds of sheets of paper detailing Byrne Investments' convincing the elderly of the wisdom in taking what were essentially payday loans against their pensions, thus defeating the purpose of saving for tomorrow. This thick wedge of dishonesty took the brunt of The Figure's pipe as Theo ducked low and drove his shoulder into her stomach. Calvin let the binder fall from his grasp so he could get both hands around the wrist beneath the pipe.

Her free hand swung hard, driving steel reinforced knuckles into Theo's cheekbone. Adrenaline and anger borne of fear kept him from giving up entirely as bone splintered beneath his skin. His partner came up and took The Figure's other wrist before she could get in a second punch.

The more timid men, Barry and Jerome, saw the success of their larger coworkers and rushed in to help them wrestle her to the ground. Each man holding a furiously struggling limb, they succeeded in pinning her to the carpet. One of the women, Elena, pulled out her phone to call a police department that had already dispatched several cars the moment they'd received a call Ann, hiding in Gerald's office, had made the second she'd heard the first scream. It might have ended there.

Except.

The pair of workers laying still under the bodies of those who'd entered the lobby before them decided to try and slowly slide out, away from the opening the drone was monitoring. Hiding beneath the dead was an old trick on foreign battlefields, so old that military contractors had integrated it into the tripod's software. They barely moved an inch before it exhaled once again, a mechanical sigh followed almost immediately by their own last breaths.

Calvin, his cheek already swollen, noticed this and began shouting abuse at The Figure at the top of his lungs. The other three men holding her down caught on soon after. With six of their colleagues having been processed by a machine into a modest pile of corpses not ten feet behind them, Theo, Barry, and Jerome were far less inspired to intervene when Calvin changed his approach.

Planting one foot on her forearm, the large man began to bring his other heel down on The Figure's wrist again and again. She refused to drop the pipe, no matter how long he continued to punish her. Their blood up and confidence stirred by someone else having already made the same decision, the other three men began to completely obscure The Figure with a flurry of vicious kicks and punches she couldn't do much to defend herself from. Barry and Jerome were amazed at how therapeutic they found the activity.

The other woman, Astrid, eyed the scrum as if looking for an opening where she could get her own licks in. Elena sat down on the floor, horrified by every aspect of a terrible situation that had taken barely five minutes to erupt. Just before it had started, she'd been drawing up ideas for her wedding invites; a small reward for having made excellent progress at her assigned task of finding loopholes in what few laws still protected citizens who attempted to protest on corporate property. A half-finished Post-it doodle sat on her desk, cupids flying circles above a cruise ship, as she struggled to breathe.

*

"She feels totally overwhelmed," Mary's mother explained to the doctor. "I don't understand how a twelve-year-old girl can be having these kinds of...anxiety attacks? I guess we'll call them that. All I had to worry about at her age were boys and keeping my grades up."

"Well, school and boys can be very stressful," the doctor replied. "Vomiting isn't an ideal reaction, but there are certainly worse things that could happen." She was only a general practitioner, doing her best for a concerned parent who couldn't afford a psychiatrist or counselor.

Sitting in the hallway, Mary did her best to pretend the discussion in the doctor's office wasn't happening, that she was at the local medical clinic for something routine like being weighed and having her height measured. She was already tall for a girl her age, taller than the cartoon rhinoceros stapled to the wall directly ahead of her. *Five-foot-seven* rested on the tip of his horn, taller animals following to the left and shorter ones to the right.

Mary's pants legs ended just above her ankles, something she knew was a result of her having to make clothing last that much longer, so her mother could keep a tighter budget. Looking down the hallway at a nurse wrestling with an old blood-pressure machine that didn't want to fit through a doorway, she couldn't help wondering if the clinic had similar problems. Almost everything in Mary's world seemed like this, pieces not wanting to fit, not exactly the right size or shape due to some kind of deficiency.

Head in her hands, she began to wonder about aged potholes in the street, the empty stores in the mall where her mother would take her close to Christmas, the concerned tongue-clicking noise her gym teacher would make when muttering about how some of her classmates "should be bigger at their age". Sometimes he'd offer those kids vegetables he'd grown at home.

She wouldn't be able to articulate it for years to come but, sitting there on a worn, fuzzy orange chair, Mary couldn't help feeling like there were some malevolent entities responsible for all these little lacks in the world. There had to be. She couldn't accept what she was so often told by those older than her, that this was "just the way it is".

This inability to accept things the way they were had recently begun to collide with a growing concern over what Mary saw around her. The sparks struck by this had birthed a short circuit in her head, in her chest, causing her to do things where…

Well…

She'd do the kinds of things that made her mother try to wring therapy out of a woman in a white coat whose expertise lay with rashes and sprains.

*

Down came Calvin's foot, further bruising a wrist The Figure no longer was able to feel. Taking another punch from one of the others, she couldn't tell if the lead pipe had stayed in her hand or not. Her body writhed in a vain attempt to avoid their blows, doing little to reduce the impact of a third fist burying itself deep under her ribcage. As still another fist was drawn back to ready the next strike, Theo accidentally put his elbow into Calvin's freshly fractured cheekbone.

The injured man howled and stumbled back, taking his weight off her arm. Distracted by this, Theo discovered—along with The Figure—that she had indeed kept hold of the pipe. She cleaned out the front row seats of his gums instead of striking his brow as she'd intended, but it did the trick in getting him to let go of the arm she could still feel.

Snatching the stun gun from her belt, she quickly set to electrocuting and bludgeoning Barry and Jerome into releasing their grips on her lower body. Knowing if even one of the men got back on an even keel it could be the end of her, The Figure clumsily kicked herself back along the carpet before using her elbows to push back up onto her feet. There was a distinct wobble as she became upright again. Pain could be ignored to a point. Damage to bone and muscle would hinder her regardless of what was felt.

Elena, who'd been considering coming over to get in a few kicks of her own, yelled at the men to get their act together. They didn't get the chance.

For the first time since laying eyes on her, the four men heard The Figure make a sound. Grunting with pain and exertion, she flailed and fought with all her strength, alternating between striking whichever man was still in the best shape. In this way, she kept herself from being piled upon again, bouncing the men's increasingly battered bodies off the walls of the narrow corridor as well as each other. A few more punches found their way to her midsection and shoulders, growing weaker and weaker until finally stopping entirely.

Eventually, The Figure was back on the ground again, entangled among those who could no longer pose a threat to her. The lead pipe slid from her hand along a palm slicked with purple, red, and black. The stun gun made a plastic clicking sound as, empty of all its charges, she kept it pressed against Calvin's blackened neck.

Elena lost her nerve. Fetching Astrid up from where she sat on the carpet, they took refuge in the nearest private office. Desperately needing a moment's rest, The Figure just watched them as the latch on the office's door rather assertively alerted anyone still able to listen that it was being secured.

Lying peacefully amongst the four dead men, The Figure shifted her gaze to the first pile of bodies over by the lobby opening. The drone was up on her by one kill. Neither of them had a thought to spare for the lives these people had led outside of their crass financial manipulations, it simply wasn't in their programming.

Suddenly, The Figure began to twist within the tangle of bodies. She sat upright, chest heaving, foul air beginning to pass her teeth. The words NOT and YET blinking on and off in her mind like an applause sign dictating orders to a live television audience. Failing to control her internal organs through sheer willpower, The Figure grabbed the nearest of her former attackers and turned him so his mouth fell open, facing the ceiling. She frantically pulled at Velcro and lifted her hood up to just beneath her nose, as if she were a superhero about to kiss a swooning love interest.

A few short coughs went into the mouth of Calvin's corpse, followed by the contents of The Figure's battered stomach.

*

Mary leaned over the porcelain and, deciding it was finally safe to do so, began to wipe her mouth with some toilet paper. Seventeen years old and what her mother called anxiety attacks hadn't become any less frequent. Standing up, she began to take inventory of her body, staying in the stall for fear someone might see her and offer their own opinions. Maybe something had changed since looking only a couple of minutes before vomiting.

She'd reached her full adult height of five foot ten, on the tall side for a woman. Her figure had filled out a bit, more muscular than she sometimes wanted, but it wasn't like she'd grown a third arm. Not that a lack of major flaws ever stopped an insecure mind from conjuring a few out of the ether. Surely several split ends were to be found among the hairs in her wide streak of golden brown that fell down to just above the band of her bra from the Salvation Army. A stomach kept perfectly flat by adolescent metabolism must be a little chubby, right? An unforgivable crime if it was, right?

Hopefully, he'd be too distracted by the minefield of freckles spread across her face to notice her big stupid lips. Maybe if she kept her mannish arms crossed it'd help obscure her annoying tits that hung several horrifying millimeters lower than was ideal. It'd taken a while to save up for them, but Mary figured it was worth the investment to buy her new pair of boot-cut jeans for the wider hem at the bottom of the legs. This helped to partially conceal what she considered to be clown feet, especially when wearing the red Converse sneakers her mom had innocently bought her.

Stepping out of the girls' washroom, Mary completely failed to notice any of the admiring glances she was given by some of the boys in the hall; it never occurred to her they might look. That day, there was only one person in the world who could distract Mary from her many concerns. He had a strong cleft chin, always wore these great red shirts, and answered to the name of Christopher, not Chris. Most importantly, he knew Mary was alive and even responded kindly when she made her best attempts at conversation with him.

What had sent Mary to the washroom with blurry vision and an over-stimulated stomach was nervousness over her plan to ask him out at the end of next period, which was English class. Taking her seat directly behind him, she remembered her breath and grabbed some gum to chew with a closed mouth. Sticky with sweetness, her lips parted unevenly when the teacher called upon the pair of them to read a scene from *Macbeth*, with him as the titular character and her as Lady Macbeth.

Mary would have preferred *Romeo & Juliet*, of course, but her mother had long drilled into her the idea of making peace with what you got in the world. Like any good seventeen year old, she rebelled against the idea except when it suited her. Right now, she needed the calm it could bring.

After class, while everyone shuffled back out into the hallway to get their bags before heading home, Mary attempted to put her plan into motion. As she'd imagined dozens of times in the past few days, Christopher went to his locker three down from hers. She quietly followed behind him, not sure if he noticed. He began a well-practiced ritual of unlocking his locker, grabbing what he needed, and slamming it shut. Mary stood waiting, planning to say at least one of the carefully prepared sentences she hoped would lead to their becoming a couple.

Christopher spun around, backpack still hanging in hand. "Oh, hey, Mary. What's up?"

Surprising both of them, Mary hugged Christopher and pressed him back against his locker, making the term 'crush' a bit more literal than usual. Two inches taller than her beau-to-be, Mary fought off fears of intimidating him as she enjoyed the feel and the smell of this boy she'd wanted to touch for so long. The moment was eventually punctured by woohoos and pleas from fellow students for the pair of them to get a room, dialogue that would be cut in her future recollections of this triumph.

Pulling back, she looked at Christopher with focused, expectant eyes. A little stunned at first, he smiled and said, "That was nice." Three minutes later and Mary had arranged what would be the first of many dates they'd share together. Then they both remembered the dire, end-of-the-school-day imperative and charged off for their respective buses.

Within ten minutes of relaying the good news to her mother, they were turning the kitchen into a familial warzone, not for the first or last time. As ever, Mary had been excited about something and her mother had tried to temper this, angering her daughter with a speed that always managed to surprise them both. After they spent a few minutes filling in the blank spaces of a form argument, her mother held up her hands in surrender.

"Oh, Mary." She sighed. "I'm sorry. I must seem like such a downer all the time, huh?" She reached over and stroked her daughter's hair, untangling knots as she did so. "I'm not walking around full of hate and bitterness; I wouldn't want you to be that way either." She continued, "You have to understand that when I was your age I was told a great many things which later felt like so many lies, lies about what life could give me if I only did this and that.

When I say maybe University isn't the best idea or you shouldn't expect life to be so much better in a big city, I'm only trying to protect you, as parents do."

"As for men, it's true...I chose not to have one be a part of our little family. A child is all I really wanted. It was my choice to make just as it's your choice, your perfectly natural choice, to want to pursue a boy. Just don't assume he'll be the answer to all your problems, my darling. It's not the way to go."

They leaned against the counters and were quiet for a moment, Mary trying to read the thoughts behind her mother's expression of careful consideration.

"Men can be wonderful, Mary, it's true. I knew a few pretty decent guys before I decided to put that part of my life up on a shelf." Her mother's gaze shifted from some vague point on the linoleum to meet Mary's eyes. "But some men, Mary, some men are the greatest single danger a woman can ever encounter."

*

Moriba had watched the whole thing, curious as to how it would play out. He was Gerald's bodyguard, not the whole company's, so he was satisfied to stand attentively by the young CEO's office door while The Figure struggled against those she'd sought to slaughter effortlessly. Now she was wiping vomit from her lips with a dead man's expensive tie. He figured it might be time to step in. Waiting for the enemy to catch their breath and come to you wasn't the strategy he'd been taught as a young child ravaging the Liberian countryside, his adult superiors constantly driving him forward.

Locking Gerald's door, Moriba assessed the young woman's costume and condition. Even with all the blood spattering her short, white fur coat he had to admit she had more style than any of the local gangbangers he'd encountered. This being his first day, Moriba hadn't yet been fully briefed on this woman so he only knew what was in the papers—not much—and that she was responsible for blinding Gerald. He didn't think intimidation would work on someone who had just done what he'd seen her do, but it was always worth a try.

Maintaining eye contact as best as he could with an oval of leopard print, he opened his crocodile-skin suitcase and laid it on the floor at his feet. Crouched down, still staring at her, he made a show of how calm he was while removing his mustard-yellow jacket to fully reveal his burgundy shirt in all its bespoke glory. As he folded the jacket and placed it underneath some other objects in the suitcase, Moriba was glad for his shirt being on the darker side today—it would hide the sweat he had begun to feel once the bodies had started to literally pile up ahead of him.

This is natural, he thought, reminding himself, *The body feels fear no matter what you do. The question is, do you?*

Moriba didn't have to think hard about what he would remove from the suitcase. Ready and loaded, wrapped in a navy blue silk handkerchief, lay a custom item he'd purchased from a Spaniard not long before coming to the U.S. with Juan Pablo. The Spaniard claimed it was a one-of-a-kind item, a point that Moriba couldn't argue even with his lengthy firearms experience, and exactly the kind of grotesque that seemed suitable for the occasion.

The revolver had a nickel-plated frame, blued steel cylinder and barrels, as well as checkered hard-rubber grips that were still crisp. All these details had appealed to Moriba, sealing a deal that had begun with his noticing what made the pistol truly unique—its three barrels. The cylinder was designed with six clusters of three chambers and the appropriate amount of firing pins allowed this monstrosity to do exactly what it promised, to fire three rounds at roughly the same point with a single pull of its heavy trigger.

As he lovingly unwrapped this weapon and checked its load, The Figure pulled her hood back down from her nose before standing up from her latest victims, their limbs sliding off her from where they'd made last-ditch attempts at self-preservation. Taking the old laptop bag from her shoulder, she withdrew one last item that had been purchased earlier in the day. Recently oiled and prepped to look good on display, the collapsible machete made no sound at all as its four sections unrolled from the hilt and locked into place. In his peripheral vision, it appeared to Moriba as if The Figure's left arm had extended a long, silvery claw.

Gun at his hip, Moriba stood and placed his feet in a gunfighter's stance. His instincts bellowed at him to shoot first, shoot again, and then ask someone else questions about what this woman's deal was. Instead, he let his finger rest against the trigger, then he did his best impersonation of the U.N. soldiers he remembered killing so many of in days past.

"Please put down your weapon. If you fail to comply, I will not hesitate to shoot."

Except he did hesitate. Gerald had been supposed to legitimize his status as a Corporate Personnel High-Threat Response Guardian through a company called Avalanche. Today Gerald said that was no longer a possibility, that some other solution would have to be figured out. He was fairly certain you could shoot a person as an act of personal defense in America, yet wondered how his weapon and immigrant status, both undocumented, might complicate matters. The last thing Moriba wanted was to end up spending time as an illegal immigrant in an American holding facility.

The Figure mistook this hesitation for intimidation, ducked, and charged right at him.

Moriba raised his gun and fired, knowing the recoil would throw off his aim enough that he'd be lucky to steady himself and shoot again before she was upon him. He provided The Figure with the kind of thunderous, exaggerated gunfire noise she'd expected from the drone. Going for the heart, his bullets went a little left and took a strip of flesh from her side as two of the three rounds skidded along the curve of a rib. All three sent a small cloud of white and red fake fur out in a narrow cone, sprinkling the dead men behind her like the final spices on a freshly cooked meal.

Though the gun's weight kept Moriba's hand from being jerked too far from where it started, his estimate had been correct. By the time he almost had all three barrels pointed at her again, The Figure's machete was raised high and about to be buried between his eyes. He'd seen the bite of enough such blades to know he had only one thing he could raise in his defense that would keep him alive.

Freshly sharpened steel struck the length of the revolver's barrels and scraped down, across Moriba's knuckles. The machete went further still, taking a shallow length of meat from his forearm, a new cousin for the fresh wound beneath her right breast. Dropping the gun, he drove his forehead directly into hers as hard as he was able.

This was more than The Figure could ignore. Lightly concussed, her head snapped back and barely returned to position before Moriba struck his broad forehead against her brow a second time. Disoriented, she could do nothing as he began wrestling the machete from her hand, broken designer glasses sliding off his face to the floor. Sensing the vague outline of an opportunity in this latest development, The Figure put her entire shoulder into the motion as she stiffened the first two fingers of her numb hand and drove them into a freshly exposed eye.

*

Mary blinked sharply, pushing away tears. They'd only begun to fall as she finished reading an email letting her know she hadn't been approved for a scholarship which would have made attending University feasible. With her middling grades, she'd known her odds hadn't been good, but it still stung to know in an era when those with Master's Degrees struggled to find work that could sustain a life worth living, she'd be entering adulthood with so much less.

There were loans, of course, yet one warning Mary had chosen not to ignore from her mother was the one about how banks would always happily give her enough rope to hang herself. The never-ending payments on her mother's own student loans, which led to so many more sacrifices while Mary was growing up, had made this warning very effective.

A year after she first hugged Christopher, Mary gave up on higher education and decided to ramp up something she'd been toying with in the back of her mind for over a month; a plan which had snuck into her thoughts like Santa Claus, that jolly home invader, leaving colorful surprises for her to open up.

A quick couple of texts and Christopher agreed to meet at The Perfect Place, an exact midpoint between their two homes, made perfect by the many times they'd spent there. Her mother smiled when Mary hopped on her bike and said she was going to hang out with a friend. She knew her deeply introverted daughter could only mean one person.

Going off the cracked pavement onto a worn dirt path, the judder of her bike's suspension did nothing to interrupt the way Mary's chest began to raise and fall. Tall, wild grass stroked along her legs as she rode in the late August heat. Right before leaving the house, she'd put on the one summer dress in her closet. Sewn from a childhood bed sheet, the silhouette of her body stood out beneath thin blue cloth decorated with a pattern of faded cartoon sea creatures. It was as close as she could get to the outfit she imagined herself wearing, part of a watercolor tableau Mary hoped would become real, would commemorate a major turning point in her life.

Seeing across the field, past the tree where she planned to stop, Mary spotted him; the boy who'd been so patient with her when their hands wandered waistward. The boy who'd understood when she found it difficult to be at large parties for too long. The boy who'd said, "I love you, too."

"I love you, too," she silently mouthed, wiping her earlier tears away with the back of one hand. Cool breezes wandered easily through this open field with its one tree, this one tree, their one tree, caressing every inch of skin the two of them ever exposed. Mary believed in a beauty and there he was, dismounting his pale beige bicycle under the leaves whose shade they had so often enjoyed. He smiled, waving, and she did the same as she pulled up in front of him.

They hugged, Christopher having gotten in the habit of bracing himself for Mary's enthusiasm. Not wanting him to see the wetness beneath her eyes, not wanting anything except to do her best to occupy the same space as her guy, she dazzled him with an array of kisses anyone would be lucky to receive. When the demands of oxygen forced her to pause, Mary had practically put little hearts in each of his eyes.

"Wow, it's nice to see you, too!" He chuckled.

"Christopher, I'm ready."

Christopher went quiet, still smiling. As Mary looked at him lovingly, she began to slowly lower herself further and further. Misreading the situation, Christopher began to lower himself to meet her amongst the grass where they had first kissed.

"No no," Mary corrected. "You stay standing up."

A cacophony of cheers went off in his head as Mary, and her mouth, moved below his belt buckle. Christopher was delighted to discover, or so he thought, that his dad's old saying about how "if you tell your friends at work a lie often enough, it becomes true" was the real deal. Mary paused to glance back up at him, breaking into a wide smile at the goofy, pleased look on his face.

"Christopher Jacob Lee," she began. "Will you do me the honor of taking my hand in marriage?"

It was then he realized Mary had only gone down on the one knee. An incredibly quick reshuffling of his thoughts began. Large swathes of higher-thinking brain cells that had been happily powering down—no need seen for them in the next few minutes—furiously shuddered and juddered as they attempted to power back up again.

"W-what?" he managed.

"Well, I was thinking, I was thinking about the future." Mary's words tumbled out. "I was thinking about how long it takes people to find someone, how some people even, like my mom, just give up somewhere along the way and I was thinking that you and I were lucky. We should seize the opportunity to leave high school with a partner, a real partner in life, so we can do more than love each other—we can help each other, protect each other, save each other from all the terrible shit in the world."

Christopher stared back at her, stunned. His lips moved slightly, making no sound.

"I was thinking…" she continued. "That maybe we could come home to each other at the end of the day, that maybe we could be two halves of something better, something strong enough to—"

"Mary!" he interrupted. "Has anyone ever told you you're pretty intense?"

"Uh…"

"Mary, I meant it when I said I loved you, but I'm not ready for marriage." Christopher got down on one knee, looking her dead on. "We're only eighteen, for God's sake."

"Well, yeah, but um…" Mary stumbled, already having trouble looking him in the eyes. "Maybe we could try anyways?"

"Mary, I told you, I'm going to school on the other side of the country."

"But, instead of living in residence, wouldn't you rather come home after class to me in a little apartment?" she asked. "W-wouldn't that be nice?"

Christopher went to kiss her on the lips, took the cheek he was presented with instead. He began to pour sickly sweet disappointment into her ear; she wasn't listening.

She'd thought if a man she loved, loved her back, if she didn't have to be alone, then maybe she could cope. Now Mary didn't know what to think. Incomplete ideas and images were rapidly birthed and burst. Most had to do with her worries over what came next in her life. A noticeable minority had to do with how she might be less "intense", how she might "fix" herself. One kept repeating, a mish mash of conflicted feelings amid the realization that the same person who was hurting her was still talking, still trying to comfort her.

Putting a hand over his mouth to stop him, Mary pulled them both down into the long grass and they lay there holding each other under the tree one last time. After over an hour of silence and subtle, incomplete movements, they stood and took to their bikes. Christopher apologized.

"I'm sorry, Mary, I'm sorry I'm not the guy who'll take your hand."

*

Had he not had room to jerk his head back, Moriba would have lost his eye. As it stood, he was blinded and a great deal more viscous material than anyone could want to lose was yanked back on The Figure's fingertips when he pulled them out. Spending most of his life on battlefields filled with maniacs, he had learned to keep a lid on his fear. Anger was another matter entirely. Self-control feeling as distant as the day he might see in both eyes again, Moriba shouted directly in The Figure's face.

"This?" He shook the numb left hand, with its freshly moistened fingers. "This is mine now, you hear? It's mine now!" Using his bulk to pin her right shoulder to the wall opposite Gerald's office door, Moriba's scarred and manicured hands stretched out The Figure's left with practiced ease.

She hadn't the strength or the leverage for her free hand to do much to his unguarded kidneys, even with the reinforced gloves. Too dizzy to risk returning the head-butts he'd given her earlier, The Figure craned her neck as best she could in an attempt to bite his face through her mask. The tricep driven beneath her chin made this impossible. Shaking under his grip, The Figure winced as she swung her hips toward him and drove a knee at his groin. Anticipating this, he shifted his thigh so her last, best shot thudded against tensed muscle.

She had to stop him. She had to. She had—

Pivoting on one foot like a seasoned dancer, Moriba brought the blade down with such force it buried itself in the wall, passing through The Figure as easily as if she were a troublesome spirit haunting the halls of Byrne Investments. As her left hand ceased to be part of her body, she was able to wrench herself away from her torturer, spinning as she fell

down

scarlet trailing behind her

down

lights flaring in her vision

down

almost joining Mary in the void

down

stopping short

to bounce as she hit the floor, landing not more than two inches from where nickel plate and blue steel boldly stood out against the carpet's design.

With no firearms experience, The Figure wasn't a good shot; with three barrels at point blank range, she didn't have to be. Moriba still clutched her severed palm like it might grant him his greatest desires, the first at this point being that he'd be able to swing the machete faster than she could pull the trigger.

Three dum-dum rounds, their flat heads mushrooming upon impact. Upon exiting through his back, they expanded to create a tremendous, triple-pointed gap; a recreation in ruined flesh of the metal chambers they'd called home less than a second ago. Driven into the wall behind him with incredible force, the Liberian bounced back and dropped across The Figure where she'd fallen.

Releasing the gun, The Figure knew she had little time before bleeding out. With her one hand, she carefully loosened the knot on the bodyguard's white ascot, knowing if she went too far and undid it then she could never remake the knot. Soon she was able to slide it up over his head, slip it past her raw stump, and pull the silk as tight as she could.

Looking up from beneath a well-dressed corpse, The Figure saw no further obstacles between her and Gerald's office. Sliding out from under, she regained the pistol and stood before Gerald's door with feet planted firmly on a stretch of carpet freshly dyed red. Her body's last reserves of endorphins flooded through every vein, a familiar high she'd chased over and over in this building and others like it, temporarily obliterating discomfort and distraction.

The Figure worshipped no god, yet something very much like religious fervor caused her to shudder in delirious ecstasy, the hum of the universe vibrating through every one of her atoms.

It compelled her to open her mouth and

*

Scream.

Yes, that's what she'd just done, Mary confirmed. Standing before her television she felt as if she'd lost time, probably a few seconds. Startled, she settled back down on the couch she didn't remember standing up from. Something told her it was normal to be upset by such an odd experience. Something else left her feeling a calmness she had never known.

Strange and seductive, it was a sensation she wanted to cling to. Mary sat perfectly still, eyes closed, only hearing the sounds of the neighborhood she'd moved into not so long ago. Eventually, the feeling dissipated and was replaced by a powerful curiosity. What had brought the scream? The calm?

Checking her phone, Mary saw several hours had passed since last she remembered. What had she been doing?

The news. She'd been watching the news, a habit she'd been trying ever so hard to kick. Mary didn't know why, but she rarely forgot anything terrible she learned about. Without knowing even the friend of a friend of anyone involved, Mary could call up from the past fifteen years every school shooting, every squashed protest, every environmental or natural disaster, every homegrown war crime, every unpunished war criminal, every unpunished finance criminal, every article about how things were always getting worse and any positive developments came at a terrible price.

So why couldn't she remember what it was that had been on the screen right before she lost time?

It wasn't a mystery as to why she felt so grateful for her memory gap. The accumulated weight of her archive of daily horrors had been building for so long. After high school there came a long stretch of stacking shelves in a gigantic warehouse filled with a seemingly chaotic body of products whose placement only made sense to a computer program Mary had nothing to do with. She was far more familiar with the hidden corners where she could go to weather another panic attack without anyone seeing her, corners that grew more important with each passing day.

This was precisely the kind of attack she'd worried might strike before or even during her job interview scheduled for the following afternoon. Having no experience with junkyards or cars in general, Mary hoped her desperation would be chalked up to enthusiasm. What little she'd saved while continuing to live with her mother for two years was dwindling fast and the thought of going home again felt like admitting her life was already over.

This didn't bother her now. The desire to figure out the trigger for her loss of time and whatever she'd done during those hours began to weaken further still as Mary realized she was no longer worried about the job interview. She actually felt some distance between her and the walls that always felt like they were closing in on her, a space to breathe. There was something else, too.

Someone was there for her.

Not her well-meaning, impotent mother, who forever tried to lower Mary's expectations, drowning them beneath a gray soup of disillusion. Someone bright, colorful, and strong. Someone actively fighting, pushing back on her behalf. Someone that could scare *them*, could hurt *them*, could eat away at *their* world. A vent, an outlet for the incredible pressures Mary felt pushing against and building up inside her for so many years.

The psychic erosion of what her advocate did on her behalf would eventually damage the barrier allowing Mary blissful ignorance, would eventually damage Mary herself. But before these consequences of diminishing returns became the lion's share of what came from The Figure's actions, Mary led the most confidant, serene few weeks of her life she'd ever known.

Sitting on the couch, almost three months before she would be mutilated in the halls of Byrne Investments, Mary chose to accept her lost hours and all that came with them. Into the calm blue ocean she dove, not caring what monsters might swim beneath the surface.

In her birth, her new protector had taken a burden of knowledge from Mary, the knowledge of what was on her television screen just moments before. It had been a news magazine show. They'd been trying to illustrate how trickle-down economics, once again in vogue, only caused the costs—never the benefits—of capitalism to trickle down from "job creators" onto everyone else. Having had his stock portfolio recently ravaged by Byrne Investments' manipulations, it was no coincidence the journalist behind the piece chose to put up a large photograph of Gerald Byrne, using him as a prime example of the kind of investment banker whose callous actions exacerbated poverty, environmental decay, the decline of public education and more; the kind who not only go unpunished, they are lavishly rewarded by others and themselves.

Gerald's actually being guilty of these things meant little to the journalist.

The idea of Gerald and people like him meant a great deal to Mary's freshly born guardian, who imprinted on him like a patricidal baby bird. Her first act in protecting Mary would be to wipe the image of him from her mind. Then she would scour his kind from the world, marking him as the first bipedal problem in need of figuring out, a problem to be forgotten as soon as it was solved. She didn't want to think of Gerald, of any of them, one more second than necessary.

*

Firing with her back braced against the opposite wall, The Figure pulled the trigger again and again as she blew open Gerald's office door. The recoil bruised her wrist, but it didn't worry her; there was only a little bit of work left to be done.

The handle blown to pieces, it took the barest of nudges with her foot for what was left hanging in the doorframe to swing back. The Figure stepped forward into the room like a grandstanding General, confident the locals had been pacified by his men.

A stained silk ascot hung from around her bloody stump. Her fake fur coat was more red than white. Tattered black electrical tape still held several slits in her leopard print skin closed. A fresh slit showed pink tinged rib between blackly bruised flesh. In her remaining hand was a gun dreamed up by a bored teenage boy. She was quite the sight for a blind man.

Standing behind his desk was Gerald Byrne. He'd eclipsed other white-collar black hats of comparable or even greater danger to the world by having twice escaped her punishment, giving him a totemic quality The Figure found impossible to ignore. He'd become the platonic ideal of her prey, like something out of the Australian dreamtime by way of Gordon Gecko. This creature standing before her was exactly what she'd been created to remove from the world, to make it a safer place for Mary.

The Figure paused to assess her terrible wounds. Protecting Mary, hadn't that been the point of this?

"Ohhhh, G-g-god!"

Some woman was lying on the floor, evidently caught by one of the dozen or so bullets that had come into the room ahead of The Figure, her advance guard marching in after the trumpet of her scream. Clutching at her side, she saw The Figure and even appeared to be battling a powerful stutter, desperate to say something.

"Ann? Where is she? Is she near me?"

His voice. The Figure had heard him briefly speak on television; in person, the experience was truly something else again. It was such a warm and friendly sound for someone who so often delivered such cold, uncaring words; frequently convincing others to do things going directly against their needs. If hypothermia had a voice, it would be a perfect imitation of Gerald Byrne's.

"Ann? Are you alright?" he said, checking on the status of a useful possession.

Had she herself been blind, The Figure would have used the sound of his voice to guide her aim. In the past, The Figure had stayed away from guns since their noise had a way of alerting others, especially police. As time progressed, The Figure found satisfaction in killing by hand, a pleasant ancillary benefit of fulfilling her purpose. This time, this time satisfaction was mandatory.

"G-g-g-gerald watch out! S-s-s-she still has a gun!"

Gerald wasn't perturbed by this. He stood perfectly still, aware that even if he ducked behind his desk it would only be a moment's effort for her to find and shoot him. Deciding bullets were too easy for him, The Figure flipped the heavy gun around in her hand so the handle was poised for pistol-whipping; except the gun kept going as it tumbled from her grasp to land on the floor. Dizzy and weak from blood loss, The Figure followed.

"That sounded encouraging. Ann? Care to fill me in?"

The Figure wasn't sure what was more painful, her injuries or being forced to listen to Ann stutter her way through an explanation of the scene.

"I can't believe you've forced me to use this." Gerald could have been chastising Ann, the woman who'd shot her, or both of them. He extended a slim, white cane and navigated his way over to The Figure. She strained for the gun but the weight of the reinforced glove and the weapon itself slowed her down when she finally began to lay fingers upon it. Much to his delight, Gerald was able to find the gun and kick it across the room before it could be turned on him. "Right then, you and me, let's have a little chat."

He crouched down, having to fend off The Figure's feeble, shaking fingers as they sought to find what they could behind his empty sockets. With one hand, he held her at bay, the immovable object to her far-less-than-unstoppable force. An alphabet of blood types were smeared across his shirt collar, neck and chin.

"Adorable."

The Figure, still vainly trying to force her fingers up and into somewhere they could do some good, began to feel a comedown proportionate to the high she'd surfed in on. A simple creature, more of a persona than a person, she had few feelings outside of her unrelenting drive. Now she felt a guilt—guilt for failing her charge.

"I never will know quite what you look like, and with most people I honestly wouldn't care." Gerald's bracelet slid right up against his wrist as he used his free hand to search for the bottom of The Figure's hood. Engaged in his task, he didn't bother to complete the couplet with an explanation for why he wanted to learn more of her appearance. Gerald's fingers dragged the silver links of his bracelet through wet, wet fur as they explored the shocked and awed landscape beneath them. Finally, they found appropriate purchase.

"There we go."

As the hood drew back, The Figure did what she could to send an apology across what used to be an oceanic divide between her and Mary. When the hood was completely removed, blank eyes stared at the ceiling for one long moment as The Figure finally burst and vanished like a dish soap bubble after all the water had drained from the sink.

"Hmm, not quite what I'd imagined, which is nice."

Mary awoke to Gerald's hand mapping her face for him, methodically feeling her flesh like a vampire squid. She found herself coming into new information as well, the entirety of The Figure's history rushing into her, every base thought and action. Whether or not she wanted to, Mary was finally seeing her own big picture.

"Oh…" she muttered with dry lips. "I…"

The drum and the hum of The Figure's essence escaped into the world as the heavy thumping of a police battering ram was heard. Mary knew the chain would hold, that they'd eventually have to try something else. For now, it was only her, Gerald, and this poor woman who'd been caught in the crossfire.

"I'll never really know what you look like, will I? Now I just have this fuzzy three-dimensional model. Fuck, I really was better off before."

Mary looked up at him, feeling the echo of a command to try again at scraping the inside of his skull with her fingernails. It didn't matter to her anymore. With such a precarious hold on life, her perspective had shifted too far to see the value in that.

"Yes, ha, well, to say I was better off before you is a hell of an understatement," he continued, his carefully modulated tone beginning to slip.

"Oh! Ahmed!" she cried. "I'm, I, Ahmed…"

"Shut up!" Gerald shouted, determined to force her attention upon him. "Who gave you permission to speak?"

She asked herself a question she only now remembered asking just moments before screaming all those weeks ago. How could she make it right?

"You've taken so much from me, set me so far back. Christ, do you have any idea how long it'll take me to rebuild my firm? My fortune? My reputation?"

"My hand?" Mary held up the silk ascot, sighed, and began to feel her teeth chatter. "I—what did I do? What did I accomplish?" All the ums, ers, superfluous likes, and so on fled from Mary's language, unable to sustain themselves on her deep insecurities, her attempts to correct herself deemed too intense, too much trouble.

"What did I tell you? Shut up!" Gerald repeated. "I'm in charge here, don't you understand? I don't want you to make a sound. I just want you to be quietly dealt with in the appropriate manner and you will be, you will be."

Glass shattered down the hall as a policeman tried a different tack. The sound startled Ann, who cried out a question unheard by Gerald and Mary.

"You hear that? They're coming to clean you up, you weak and terrible stain, they're coming to clean you up."

Finding courage in her frustration and pain, Ann repeated herself. "W-w-why? Why have you been d-doing this?"

"Huh?" Mary snorted. "What do you want, a neatly written letter of intent? Maybe I could email—I could fax it to you! I could cc everybody else at the office, while I'm at it. Make sure everybody is in the loop, make sure they all have the chance to 'add value' to the conversation." Mary rolled her eyes back and swallowed hard.

"I'm scared, okay?" She slapped her remaining hand against Gerald's chest. "That's my manifesto! I'm scared!"

"I'll pay some doctors to make sure you live." Gerald couldn't care less what Ann or Mary had to say, and continued speaking over the two women. "I'll pay some lawyers to make sure you spend the rest of your life in the worst corner of the foulest jail—preferably run by one of my father's companies—and I'll never think about you again."

A now familiar *SNICK SNACK* was heard from down the hall. Next came aggravated cries from the police as one of their number discovered the drone the hard way, having tried to reach around broken glass and do something about the chain securing the entrance to reception.

"You'll know nothing but misery, trapped in a place you can't escape. That's what's left for you." Gerald spat. "Do you hear me?"

Mary chuckled, sighed again, and looked back up at the ceiling. No, she didn't hear him. Her hand went limp against Gerald's chest as even the energy to acknowledge his presence become more than she cared to give. A demolition charge was used to blow apart the heavy chain and what was left of the reception area doors. Ann screamed.

"You hear that?" Gerald shrieked. "You! They're coming for you! No escape!"

Gerald would later sue the police department, seeking compensation for the loss of data on all Byrne Investment hard drives within the radius of the electromagnetic pulse grenade that had just now been tossed into the reception area to deal with Mary's drone tripod. A small bang preceded a brief, terrible buzzing sound as several of the lights in Byrne Investments went off.

"Whatever I did, it's done now," Mary mused, barely audible. "I hope you all enjoyed it."

Gerald shook as he loomed over her. Mary's own trembling began to subside, a welcome warmth washing through her, making her feel as if she were being bathed in all her fondest memories, their current pushing her down a river leading somewhere better.

Ann screamed again as the police, wary of further automated surprises, tossed a second, cautionary pulse grenade not far from Gerald's office door. The bang. The buzzing.

And then
all
the
lights
went
out.

*

Mary fell on her behind in the snow, dead sunflower leaves all around her. Wearing hastily thrown on winter clothing, her mother came out and stepped through knee-deep snow toward her little girl. Scooping the crying bundle up in her arms, she covered her daughter's cold, wet face in kisses before whispering in her ear, warming Mary with her breath.

"Shhhh, shhhh," she cooed. "It's time go inside now, my darling."

Together they began to head back toward the pale, yellow light of the kitchen, of their home.

"It's time to go inside now."

Epilogue

Gerald breathed in the expensive, carefully chosen scents emanating from several candles burning away at the edges of the room. Face down on the massage table, fifty floors above the city streets, he could understand why Mr. Dunning had recommended this luxury spa.

Gerald truly felt it was a shame such a great man was no longer among the living.

In the month since heavily armored police stormed into his private office to find him trying to cry tears of frustration over the limp form of some nobody called Mary, a change had come about. More and more people were imitating that terrible woman.

Ann had described Mary's face to him, something Gerald decided was a fire-able offense.

One of the imitators had rammed Dunning's vintage Lamborghini Urus SUV with a garbage truck, sending the mogul through concrete barriers and off the edge of the city's tallest bridge to fall into the river. It was assumed Dunning tried to escape while underwater, drowned, and then was carried off into the ocean. His body had yet to be found.

This was the most high profile attack and it, along with the violent deaths of several of his peers, heralded his father's worst nightmare. Mary had become a martyr, inspiring others to continue her work.

Had the driver of the truck yelled, "Slow down and shut up!" as he collided with the SUV?

Whether or not Gerald wanted to admit it, Mary had managed to alter a fundamental law of his universe. Now "the money" no longer protected him and his kind, as Derek Kruger had so often preached. It put them in danger.

Relaxed as he was, Gerald's thoughts were far away from all this. He was contemplating spending some of his new drug revenue on a much-needed vacation, when Biyu the masseuse paused for a moment to get some tools she needed for the task at hand.

A blue steel claw hammer and a skin-tight, leopard-print hood.

THE END

ABOUT THE AUTHOR

Oliver Brackenbury grew up around the corner from a five-story deep nuclear fallout shelter, as you do. This may explain why his first story was about the world exploding so humanity could learn the value of saving their allowance. A writer and filmmaker in Toronto, Canada, he continues to explore the dark corners of action, horror, comedy, and other adventures with a satirical wit befitting his history.

If you enjoyed reading this, I would be grateful if you would support my work by posting a review where you purchased this book. I read every review personally so I can get your feedback and make my writing even better.

Thank you again for your support!
Oliver Brackenbury

Oliver Brackenbury is ON the "INTERNET"
Moonbase Alpha: http://www.oliverbrackenbury.com
He's very chatty on Twitter: https://twitter.com/obrackenbury
Get updates on his new books or films, original fiction, and more in his bi-monthly newsletter: http://tinyletter.com/oliverbrackenbury

You can also find him in all these lovely places. Say "Hello!" and he's bound to reply.
http://www.goodreads.com/user/show/6615400 oliverbrackenbury
https://www.facebook.com/brackenbooks/
http://www.youtube.com/user/Geigerdog
http://instagram.com/obracken
http://igotopinions.com/
http://about.me/oliverbrackenbury

ACKNOWLEDGMENTS

Special thanks to Jacqueline Hoffman for editing my very first draft, Michelle MacAleese for holding my hand through my first submission letter, Alan Aumont for letting me crawl all over his junkyard with blood pouring out of my ear, and Tom Lewis for "Titanic DiCaprio".

Not to forget my lovely readers: Lindsay Denise, Christina Manuge, Peter McKracken, Shawn MacLean, Mirana Novielli, and Gavin O'Hearn. All good people!

Oh and I *guess* my parents are pretty decent folk, as well as the many friends, acquaintances, and anyone else who's patiently listened to me talk about this story while I've built it up from a bunch of swirling ideas to the final product you now hold in your hands.